Sharmila's Book

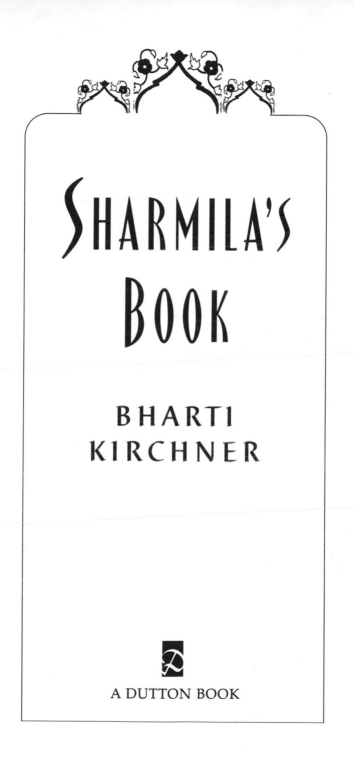

SHARMILA'S BOOK

BHARTI KIRCHNER

A DUTTON BOOK

DUTTON
Published by the Penguin Group
Penguin Putnam Inc., 375 Hudson Street, New York, New York 10014, U.S.A.
Penguin Books Ltd, 27 Wrights Lane, London W8 5TZ, England
Penguin Books Australia Ltd, Ringwood, Victoria, Australia
Penguin Books Canada Ltd, 10 Alcorn Avenue, Toronto, Ontario, Canada M4V 3B2
Penguin Books (N.Z.) Ltd, 182–190 Wairau Road, Auckland 10, New Zealand

Penguin Books Ltd, Registered Offices:
Harmondsworth, Middlesex, England

First published by Dutton, a member of Penguin Putnam Inc.

First Printing, April, 1999
10 9 8 7 6 5 4 3 2 1

 REGISTERED TRADEMARK—MARCA REGISTRADA

Library of Congress Cataloging-in-Publication Data:

Kirchner, Bharti.
    Sharmila's book / Bharti Kirchner.
        p.   cm.
    ISBN 0-525-94368-4
    1. East Indian Americans—Fiction.   I. Title.
PS3561.I6835S47   1999
813'.54—dc21   98-41801
                                                CIP

FIC

KIRCHNER
B

Printed in the United States of America
Set in Palatino and Ringworld
Designed by Eve L. Kirch

PUBLISHER'S NOTE
This is a work of fiction. Names, characters, places, and incidents either are the products of the author's imagination or are used fictitiously, and any resemblance to actual persons, living or dead, events, or locales is entirely coincidental.

This book is printed on acid-free paper. ∞

For Kachi, Niveditamami, and Tinni,
who always make homecoming a joy for me,
and for Tom

Acknowledgments

I am indebted to a number of people for their help and encouragement in writing this novel.

My deep gratitude to my editor, Rosemary Ahern, for a wonderful collaboration. Your interest and help have made this effort worthwhile. It's always a pleasure to work with my agents Jane Dystel and Miriam Goderich. Thank you both for your guidance. I feel fortunate to have such a strong publishing team.

To my husband, Tom Kirchner, for all the help and patience and for enduring yet another book. You of all people know what it takes.

With much affection to Nancy Pearl and to our once lively monthly group—Marci Sillman, Sheila Bender, Migael Scherer, Christie Killen, Christine Widman, and Kip Rosenthal.

Once again to Seattle Writers' Association, particularly the following members for their enthusiastic support: Dick Gibbons, Barbara Galvin, Leon Billig, Diane Ste. Marie, Art Mickel, Romola Robb Allrud, Ann Devine, Alle Hall, and Barbara Craven.

With warmth to Savithri Machiraju, Prasenjit Ranjan Gupta, Amy Laly, and our delightful e-mail group. Your comments and suggestions have been invaluable.

To Pamela Harlow and Susan Wells for answering my art questions and for the lovely time spent in doing so.

I feel fortunate that you have touched my life.

I STILL can't believe I agreed to an arranged marriage. I, Sharmila Sen, a thoroughly modern, thirty-two-year-old Chicago-style woman. I wear a power suit by day and teach aerobics evenings in skin-tight Lycra that my sari-clad mother says are both shameful in the eyes of the gods. Oh, my looks are Indian, all right. You know, big eyes, full mouth, shoulder-length black hair, and a slender body. But to someone like me, a second-generation American who speaks broken Hindi with a Midwestern accent, India is pretty much a mystery. I'm almost the last person I'd expect to marry an up-and-coming young executive in New Delhi, ten thousand miles from Chicago's Lake Shore Drive.

At Indira Gandhi International Airport, I shuffle robot-like in a line inching toward a distant immigration officer. It's seven-thirty in the morning New Delhi time, an ungodly hour by my internal clock. I took this flight only at the insistence of my mother, so I'd arrive in time to meet my betrothed at an hour declared auspicious by her astrologer. He recommended that my first encounter with my future husband take place at a time when the planets are in proper alignment to ensure good fortune in our life together. I've never believed in astrology, and to this day it is beyond me why Mother would consult him about the best day to start a journey, move to a new house, or schedule an important meeting, let alone when to meet one's future husband. But I remind myself that she was raised in an environment where the position of the stars and planets determined important matters such as when to plant the rice, whom the king should marry, or when to declare a war. So I say to myself, If it'll make her happy, what do I care?

Just ahead of me in the line is an Indian man in an Eddie Bauer jacket—an expatriate from the Minnesota address on his luggage tag. He grins as he babbles to the immigration officer about how ecstatic he is to be setting his feet on his native soil once again. I envy him. Will this feel like a homecoming for me? Suddenly I'm plagued with doubts. I am here nine weeks before my wedding, to get acquainted with my future husband and make the transition to life in a new city. It all seemed like an adventure back in Chicago, but now I must confront the consequences of my choice—and all the changes it will bring. I chew the inside of my lip nervously.

The immigration officer raises his head from my passport and says, "Ah, an American." The starched white shirt, well-pressed fir green trousers, and an impassive face lend him an air of official dignity. "How long do you plan to stay here?"

My reply corresponds to the length of my visa. "Six months."

But I know I'll stay here indefinitely. Because of his many business interests abroad, my future husband Raj has expressed a desire to split his time between here and the States. For me that's ideal. I'll polish my Hindi, study Indian art, and try my hand as a graphic artist, all the while learning my parents' tradition. At the same time, I'll have plenty of opportunity to visit my family and friends in Chicago, to keep up on things in the States, and to retreat to my cabin in the California Sierras whenever I want. How could I lose?

With an authoritative flourish, the officer stamps and signs my passport, then slides it back to me.

The walk to baggage claim takes forever. Eyes bleary, I finally arrive at the luggage carousel, aware of a musty smell. Flickering fluorescent tubes cast waltzing shadows on lime green stucco walls. A soldier in khaki saunters by, carrying a rifle that looks like it was made a hundred years ago.

Ours wasn't the only jumbo jet to land. Hundreds of other

passengers, all as exhausted, irritable, and filled with anticipation, crowd the baggage claim area and jostle for position around the carousel. Almost immediately, an argument breaks out in some Indian language that is strangely familiar yet incomprehensible. I fling my purse over my shoulder and stand on tiptoe, searching for my luggage, fearing every moment that I'll be hit by someone's trunk. Time slows to a crawl, and the wait seems interminable. I see a suitcase that looks like mine and reach to grab it, only to have an elderly Indian man with an accusing look in his eyes snatch it out of my hand. I mumble an apology, then spy my three suitcases lurching along the conveyor belt. I heave them onto a luggage cart and take my place in a ragtag line forming in front of the customs counters.

The customs officer, a man with blurry eyeglasses and a stony expression, orders the Indian woman ahead of me to open all her suitcases. I hear him saying, "Ten watches! Four cameras! Three alarm clocks!"

"Coming home after five years, sir," she says, opening her palm to expose a crumpled hundred-dollar bill. "All those nephews, nieces, and cousins, you know . . ."

Without appearing to look down, the officer relieves her of the money. "Very well." He waves her through.

Ah, a case of greasing palms, of baksheesh giving.

I'm still trying to formulate a suitable excuse for the amount of luggage I'm carrying when my turn comes. Another customs officer has taken the post, this time a bearded young man, jovial and not bad-looking. He moves his gaze up and down my body, finally directing it at my luggage. "Any *Playgirl* magazine?"

His crude remark causes me to stiffen. He snickers at my discomfort and waves me through. I gather up my luggage, along with my poise and what's left of my sense of humor. I've traveled to Mexico and Europe on vacation, but this trip is already becoming more difficult. My parents would have accompanied me, but Dad couldn't leave his practice until just before the wedding, and my excited mother has already spent a good two months here attending to the wedding details. She returned to Chicago a week ago for some last-minute shopping, leaving her cousin Mistoo, who lives in Delhi, to handle the remaining formalities.

My next destination is the passenger reception area, filled

with screeching sounds of rolling luggage carts. People are milling about searching for loved ones in the crowd. More than one head of hair smells of coconut oil. My eyes look for Raj. I know I won't have any trouble spotting my prospective groom. I've committed his photograph to memory. His voice will be familiar from our many phone conversations.

I flip to the second time zone of my watch: Chicago time. It's still evening there. The lights will be on in my parents' condominium. Mother is probably standing in front of the fireplace, looking up at the clock above it, kept permanently set to Indian standard time. It's now striking eight-thirty a.m. If her astrologer's prediction is correct, this very minute on this very Wednesday, November 20, is the most auspicious moment for me to lay eyes on my future husband.

My watch says eight thirty-one. I know I've set it a few minutes ahead, but can't remember how much. Did I somehow miss the most important moment of my life?

Butterflies do a fox trot in my stomach and all along my extremities. Retrieving a compact mirror from my purse, I study my face: jaws tensed, lips parched, temples tight from stage fright. I force my facial muscles to relax, draw the lipstick across my mouth, and dust a little powder on my nose. Then, with a few strokes of my comb, I smooth my shoulder-length hair. Finally I check my clothes. The long, straight print skirt was a good choice—the fabric looks fresh even after twenty-one hours of flying. Yes, I'm as ready for Raj as I can be under the circumstances.

As I fumble through my purse, my fingers brush against a soft blue aerogramme: Raj's letter. The edges are frayed from many readings. I open the letter and the neat handwriting bespeaks an organized mind. Fine pen, blue ink, ample blank space between the lines.

> Dear Sharmila,
>
> I still remember the day my mother handed me your photograph. I couldn't toss the picture aside as another "tall, fair, and educated" bride my mother had picked for me. There you were in front of the Chicago Art Institute. A lovely face, a brilliant smile, eyes that held a dream. As I looked and looked at it, the picture seemed to come alive. It was as

though you walked toward me and stood so close that I could touch a wisp of your hair. At that moment I knew my bachelorhood was over.

I'm not a philosopher. I can't discuss fate, destiny, or coincidence with you. I'm a businessman with but a few poems in my heart. I just know you're someone I shouldn't let go.

Day by day, minute by minute, I await your arrival. My mother is taking care of the practical arrangements for the wedding, but I've entrusted myself with the courtesy of meeting you at the airport. In my own humble way, with all the affection in my heart, I'll welcome you to New Delhi, to my home and to our new life.

Yours,

Raj

I fold the letter and put it back in my purse.

A man steps forward, a pole-mounted placard in hand. The bold English letters, carefully constructed in black, say: SHARMILA SEN.

"Are you . . . ?" he asks in a hushed, deferential tone.

I nod a gentle yes, but a violent quaking has started inside. If this is Raj, he's several inches shorter than the hunk in the family video that was sent. He has a pleasant bearing, is dressed simply in white slacks and shirt and a V-necked navy sweater, and appears to be in his mid-thirties. Absent are the waves in the hair, the prominent jawbone, the bushy eyebrows that framed the face in the photo.

Have I been deceived? I decide quickly that I'll not embarrass him, or me. I force a bright smile.

The man joins his palms together at his chest in salutation. "I'm Prem, your driver." The soft voice, the quivering lips, and the rounded shoulders convey a hint of apology.

I thank all my mother's gods silently that this is not Raj. "I'm pleased to meet you, Prem."

"Raj-babu will be here shortly. He had to make a phone call. It is possible he will have to fly to Mumbai on business today—an unexpected situation."

My prince charming will yet be here. In the meantime I'm just happy to be met. Automatically I proffer a friendly hand in greeting. Prem looks away uncomfortably.

Of course. I withdraw my hand and edge back a pace. In my

disoriented state I'd forgotten that in India a woman doesn't greet a man by shaking hands. Not knowing what to do with my rejected hand, I stroke an earring and wait for the awkward moment to pass.

A tall figure emerges from a clutch of people, a suitcase in one hand, a bouquet of vibrant pink roses bound by a matching silk scarf in the other. He approaches me with a self-assured stride, a light aroma of cologne about him. This is definitely Raj. I'd have recognized him anywhere. Suddenly I'm face to face with the stranger who has dominated my thoughts, worries, and dreams for the past several months. I pull myself up straighter, and my body tingles. I forget that we're standing in a busy passageway and focus all my attention on my flesh-and-blood fiancé. He regards me with a delighted expression, his commanding dark eyes pulling me in.

"Sharmila . . ." Raj sets his suitcase down. "I'm sorry I'm late." He offers me the bouquet. I glance at its delicate beauty, inhale the faint rose fragrance, and smile with genuine appreciation. "Oh, Raj, how lovely. Pink roses are my favorite." I notice the visible relief in his eyes as he realizes that I am not angry over his tardy arrival. Then to fill the silence, "I was just getting acquainted with . . ." The chauffeur's name escapes me.

"Oh, you mean Prem."

Both of us turn to look. Prem has moved off to a discreet distance. He's screened by a huddle of people, and only the top of his head is visible. I'm glad for the privacy. I smile at Raj.

Abruptly he grabs my elbow, pulls me roughly to one side, his face taut with alarm. Quickly I glance over my shoulder and spot a huge pile of luggage rolling at me at great speed.

"*Sambhalo!*" Raj yells. Watch it.

The young porter pushing the iron trolley jumps to the command and swerves his load barely in time to avoid hitting me.

We move back and away from all the comings and goings, and find ourselves next to a wall lined with textile art and travel posters. From the tea stall that just opened a few feet away comes the brisk, pungent aroma of steeping tea leaves. I take a deep breath and gaze at Raj in relief. He radiates an aura of vitality and intelligence.

"You can't go through a day in Delhi without one major collision." Raj grumbles in annoyance, though his eyes twinkle.

"Well, I've just fulfilled my quota."

Raj's face breaks into a boyish grin, then quickly becomes grave. He shifts his weight. "My mother wanted very much to come to the airport to welcome you, Sharmila, but she has come down with a bad cold."

It's just as well that his mother didn't come. I'm enjoying having Raj all to myself. He's attentive and caring, but not overly so. I can see how easy it'll be to fall under his spell.

Raj's eyes never stray from mine as he continues, "I've put Prem in charge of taking you home and escorting you around town until you adjust to the rhythm of life here. He and I have been friends for years, and I trust him. He'll be available whenever you need him. You'll find him a superb guide and a pleasant companion."

We've only just met. And now to be separated again? I'd imagined he would at least take the day off. How can he treat me like this? The next moment I realize that this is perfectly acceptable in Indian society. My father goes on business trips leaving my mother behind without a second thought. No doubt the hectic preparation for this journey, coupled with the jet lag, is making me over sensitive. A hot bath and a soft bed is what I really need. Everything else can wait. "Prem told me you're flying somewhere on business. Where are you off to?"

"My boss is sending me to Mumbai. We have an office there."

"For the day?"

"Actually, for the next several days. I'd much prefer to be home. In fact, I'm extremely disappointed. But our business there has picked up considerably of late. We have an opportunity to close a really important deal." A gloom deepens his eyes. "Can you forgive me, Sharmila?"

"Yes . . . of course." I break eye contact.

Oh, yes, I'm disappointed, even a bit angry. My gaze falls on a framed travel poster behind Raj's head. A Hindu temple, a mosque, and a Buddhist pagoda juxtaposed, examples of Delhi's architectural treasures. After all, this "modern" capital of thirteen million people dates back to 1000 B.C when it was called Indraprasthra, the abode of god Indra. I convince myself there'll be plenty here to occupy me while Raj is away.

"I can't tell you how happy I am to see you here." There's a tinge of yearning in Raj's voice. "These last three months have seemed terribly long. At least now you'll have my family to rely on."

Staying with one's future in-laws is not a common Indian custom. Though social changes are taking place, many families still consider it improper for unmarried people to live together. I'd have moved in with my mother's cousin Mistoo, but she lives in tight quarters with her invalid mother and two brothers. Raj's mother suggested that since the Khosla apartment had plenty of space and servants, I'd be able to adjust to my new way of life in pleasant surroundings and get to know my future husband better before the wedding. We never had one of those family-arranged meetings that normally precede a conventional marriage. The only other alternative would have been taking a room in a hotel by myself, but that would have gone against tradition. "*Chee, chee,*" Delhi society matrons would whisper. Shame, shame. "That Sen girl stuck in a hotel. How can her relatives be so inhospitable?"

My mother, after considerable thought, had consented. So now I tell Raj, "I'll probably spend the next two or three days getting over jet lag and getting acquainted with everyone in the family."

"I'm so happy to hear that." Raj looks at me with wonder. "But, remember, Sharmila, just be yourself. I don't expect you to behave like an Indian woman. I've lived in the States, I know how different things are over there."

I find a hint of comfort in the deep, resonant voice, his obvious empathy, and in the protective way he leans toward me. I reply with an appreciative smile.

An internal alarm seems to go off. Raj looks at his watch with a start. "Oh, I barely have time to go to the domestic airport and catch the flight. You'll be okay?"

"Don't worry. I'll be just fine."

"You are very considerate, Sharmila." Raj spins around. "Take good care of her, Prem."

Prem has materialized and is standing a few feet behind Raj. It's apparent he's anticipated his employer's wishes.

Raj's wistful eyes hold mine a long second. "I'll return to you in a few days, Sharmila."

"Thanks for the flowers," I murmur, clutching the bouquet to my chest as if to keep a part of him with me. I watch him disappear into the milling crowd, eyes pinned to the back of his charcoal sports coat, taking note of his slim neck, his powerful walk. His abrupt departure leaves me with an empty feeling, and once again the doubts collect. How did I get into an arranged marriage? I've traveled more than ten thousand miles to put my fate into the hands of a stranger. I suppose the seeds of my current situation were sown many years ago.

M Y teen years were angry years. Mother refused to allow me to date. In traditional Indian families unsupervised contact between single boys and girls was out of the question.

I was born in Chicago, though, and in America hormones trump tradition. I'd often sneak out of the house to movies, ball games, and for the occasional steamy necking session in the back seat of a car. But I was always back home by ten.

After graduating from college with honors, I took a position as a graphic artist at Carson's department store. My salary allowed me to rent my own apartment. Finally I could look forward to a career, hobbies, and men. Yes, men. They were everywhere, and I found mine in professional arts organizations, singles bars, upscale supermarkets, all over.

My boyfriends came from all cultures and walks of life. In the seven years following my graduation, I drifted into and out of relationships—some casual, some serious, but all ending up unsatisfactorily. I refused to jump into bed on the first date, and my girlfriends always lectured me that my standards were too high. I liked to think I was particular.

Inevitably some of my dates were Indian Americans. Nitya was shy and socially awkward, lacking in confidence and I understood why. His parents supervised and controlled his social activities and constantly hounded him about his studies. I faced the same pressures at home except I didn't succumb to them. I found it easier to relate to native-born Americans like Al from Moline, Illinois, who called himself a "meat-and-potatoes" man. Al approached women with abandon and distanced himself equally as well. Sports and beer and sex composed the complete list of his interests.

I knew love must hold something more and tried not to be discouraged. And sure enough, three years ago I met a man, brilliant, fascinating, and irreverent. He surprised me—he could actually locate India on a map. Not only that, he knew more about the history and politics of the country than I did. Our initial attraction burgeoned into love, then into mutual vows of commitment. We started living together and even talked about marriage, but things quickly soured. It took me a long time to acknowledge that we were essentially incompatible—that we'd never make each other happy. That was my longest relationship—fourteen months, six days.

And so, nine years out of college, I found myself single, as lonely as a bruised fruit culled out of a supermarket display. Everywhere I went I saw cozy couples—at the stores, in the movies, strolling hand in hand in the street. My art career had flourished to the point that I went out on my own working freelance with a full roster of clients. My aerobics classes were packed. I still went to movies on Thursday nights with my old college pals and gave dinner parties once a month. But I didn't have what would make all of this meaningful to me—that one special man. My biological clock was ticking too loudly for me to ignore through long days—and longer nights. Stability and children dominated my thoughts, along with a numbing fear that I'd be alone the rest of my life. The nesting impulse was so strong that on one lonely Saturday evening I found myself browsing the personal ads.

Wanted: Tall, Skinny Latte
Temp Position Available
Naughty girl?

With a derisive snicker, I read on. Lonely though I may be, I am not yet desperate enough to answer to the description of

"Tall, Skinny, Latte." Then, toward the bottom of the page, a genteel one caught my attention.

> Cultured Indian engineer in his thirties seeks
> artistic and beautiful modern bride. Caste no bar.

Should I answer it? I hesitated. No, no more thinking about this, I decided.

I tossed the newspaper in my garbage can and picked up *Gora* by Tagore. This early twentieth-century Bengali novel is one of my favorites. Mother had given me the book as a graduation present, and I'd read it many times since. The story is that of an orphaned English boy named Gora, which means white in Bengali, who is raised by a Hindu woman who takes him into her family. Her name Anandamoi means joy, and her features are so fine they seem "hand carved by the gods." That liberated Hindu woman, who travels everywhere with her husband, maintains a happy household and though a Brahmin, raises a Christian child as her own, always fascinated me. And to think she manages all of that within the confines of a conventional Indian marriage.

I closed the book. My mind flashed on my mother, who also flourished within an arranged marriage. By the age of thirty-one, she was settled in a foreign country with a husband who was well suited to her, and was raising a child. I began to wonder if there wasn't something to the traditional Indian way of matchmaking, after all.

About a month later I was having lunch with Mom. I recall the sun peeking through her kitchen window and an aroma of cloves, cinnamon, and cardamom in the air. She emerged from the kitchen in a purple-bordered white sari with a platter of my favorite *murgir jhol*—that's chicken in a thin spicy sauce. Her hair is still mostly black with a few white streaks in the front. Her face is so finely chiseled that my father frequently compares hers with Goddess Durga's. Mom was going on and on about a niece in Calcutta, married a year—arranged, of course—who had recently given birth to a boy. She waved the baby pictures under my nose.

"What was it like, Mom, to have a marriage arranged for you?" I asked.

"Better than discos and computer dating, I can tell you that, *beti.*"

That stung. A bit more cautiously, I probed further. "Didn't you have doubts?"

"Who doesn't have doubts about marriage?" Mother said the word marriage tenderly, as though it was a fragile, precious object. "I was only twenty-three then. But, Sharmila, I'd been taught that a proper marriage, one arranged by your parents, is blessed by Lord Ganesh and Lord Krishna. And I knew both our families were behind us one hundred percent."

I'd heard those lines ten years before and laughed. Now they didn't sound so ridiculous. "Were you ever in love when you were growing up?"

"Oh, I had a crush on a boy." Mother hiked the scarf end of her sari higher on her left shoulder, a subtle move that I learned long ago signified her discomfort. "Quite a dashing boy, as I remember. He was rich, played tennis, attended the best schools. We admired each other from afar. But I knew nothing would come of it." She stirred her curd a little longer than usual. "I never told anyone. I was born in India. Love was just not a subject open for discussion."

"But I was born in America, Mom. Everybody here believes romantic love lasts. Didn't you ever worry that once you agreed to an arranged marriage, you'd lose any chance of finding true love?"

"I understood that love develops after marriage. It grows strongly, steadily, sending forth deep roots. Such a love does not evaporate like mist."

A nice sentiment, but I wasn't ready to buy it. "By coming to a marriage this way, doesn't a man respect his wife less? Wouldn't he think of her as something he bought, kind of? You know, because of the dowry?"

"You've seen how your father treats me."

I had to admit Mother had a point. At home my father was what is known as a Bengali *babu*, relaxed, genial, a dignified gentleman, who avoided making trivial decisions about day-to-day life. These he left to Mother, whom he treated as a more or less equal partner. Indeed, in all my years at home, I'd never heard him raise his voice to her.

"With love and respect," I tell mom. "But he must have gone into the marriage willingly."

"No man ever marries willingly, Sharmila. He does it out of desperate attraction, for money, or to keep a family obligation. Money gets spent. Attraction fades." Then, scrutinizing my face, she added, "This American way hasn't worked for you, has it?"

I couldn't deny the truth of Mom's observation, but it hurt. I found myself staring at the paisley tablecloth. "Still, I don't know if I could ever marry a total stranger."

"Stranger?" Mother rolled her eyes skyward. "You'll feel close to the one the stars have picked for you in an instant. Your father and I did."

Mother and Father have never been wildly in love. But then, they aren't wild about anything. I struggled to suppress a laugh.

"You're my daughter," Mother blurted out. "I know when you're unhappy, *beti*. It breaks my heart to see you so miserable. And you've been very much in your dad's mind, too."

That explained the concern I'd detected in Dad's voice when he called me the other day out of the blue and talked offhandedly about his work. I didn't realize at the time that it was actually me he was worried about.

"Lately I've had trouble sleeping. I lie awake in bed for hours, worrying, What will happen to my little girl? With so many eligible boys in India, why is she single at age thirty-two?"

I was on the verge of tears as I pushed my half-full plate away.

Mother hunched over the table, her six bangles ringing. "Would you mind if I searched for you, Sharmila? Would you agree? Just for your poor mother's sake?" There were dark circles under her eyes. "Mind you, you can say no anytime and I'll stop."

In a tiny voice, I said okay.

Flush with victory and a sense of mission, she dug into her food with a new gusto.

I watched my mother with a newfound respect for her perceptiveness. I'd always admired what I call her "immigrant energy." She had so many abilities—this unflappable woman who was always willing to do a bit extra, to exploit any opportunity that came her way.

I should have known Mother would move quickly. The following Thursday, she called as usual and mentioned, "I've been checking candidates. A dozen so far."

"You found that many so quickly?"

"Why not? You wouldn't believe the number of Indian matrimonial websites, Sharmila. Your father has helped me surf the Net. And of course, my relatives in Delhi are more than willing to help. Still, the harvest could be better. Mrs. Tripathy's son visits her once a year for three days only. That's very short when you consider he lives in Bangkok, which is not a terribly long flight from Calcutta. I don't want him for a son-in-law. And Dr. Gupta's son manages a small taxicab company. Imagine, a doctor's son managing a small business! He won't do."

I was at once impressed with Mother's choosiness and a little nervous with her use of technology I didn't even know she was aware of. Principally though, I felt relieved that her scheme wasn't working. I told her about the boring blind date I had the night before and hung up. There was no more mention of matchmaking until I dropped by two weeks later.

Mother served me a tall glass of fresh pomegranate juice, saying proudly she had found some exceptionally high-quality fruit in Devon Street and bought them for me. I inhaled the fruity aroma, took a long, appreciative sip of the tartly sweet beverage, and began talking about a film I'd seen the previous night. Mother loved to hear about movies, but she seldom went herself.

At a point where I was describing the hero stranded in an elevator with a gun-toting woman villain, Mother interrupted, her eyes rounding as though in a great discovery, "I've found the groom."

Like a clap of thunder in a Chicago summer storm, the words shook me. I set my juice glass down. "The who?"

Mother wrapped the *pallu* of her yellow crepe sari around her chest, a dead giveaway she was excited. "Prithvi Raj Khosla. They call him Raj."

I tried not to show it, but the name was a delicious mouthful. Not to mention the meaning of the word "Raj." The king. The one in power.

"Raj has an MBA from Columbia University. He's with an up-and-coming electronics firm in Delhi, quite well off, and his family is wealthy too. He's only three years older than you, a widower. There are no children."

At thirty-five, the man was too young to have lost a wife, I thought. Perhaps at this very minute he was enduring a similar talk from his mother. I felt a wave of sympathy for my potential intended, a desire to comfort him.

"And that's not all. He likes that physical fitness of yours, and he is a connoisseur of the arts and Indian literature. So you see, you'll begin your life together with many interests in common. Isn't that what you've always wanted, my dear?"

Too sudden, this well-planned ambush. I grabbed the table and tried to formulate a diplomatic refusal, but all I could do was sit in mute silence. Quickly, Mother thrust a photo into my hand. Sari swishing, "Made in India" Bata Company sandals flapping, she strode out of the room, leaving me to stare open-mouthed after her. My defenses had been breached even before I'd had a chance to erect them.

In a daze I examined the three-by-five black-and-white photograph. A face with well-proportioned features, topped by lush, wavy black hair that rose above a high forehead. The eyes conveyed warmth and a depth of character, while the upturned curve of the full lips hinted at sensuality and playfulness. Had I met him here in Chicago, I'd have dated him in a minute, no encouragement from Mother needed. I was still bent over the photo when she reappeared, a video of this hero in hand, a triumphant smile spreading over her features.

Later that day, Dad dropped by my apartment on the pretext of borrowing a novel. He mentioned in passing receiving an e-mail from a colleague. "It's been over ten years, but the family remembers the Khosla boy," he said. "They met him in New York when they were new there and trying to get situated. He was a graduate student. He helped them a lot. Where to shop for Indian groceries, how to take the subway, how to be safe. He even baby-sat for them once."

Alone at last, I watched the home video, which featured Raj at a house party. Clad in a Western suit, he moved among friends and relatives easily. I rewound it several times. A few days later, an audiocassette arrived in which Raj's mother narrated the family background. Each polished sentence started with "We Khoslas" or "My son Raj." His voice energetic, if a little self-satisfied, Raj added a few words about himself. That particular Sunday he was going to spend rereading Tagore's *The Home and the World*, attending a cricket match, and stopping by the reception of a renowned artist at the National Museum. He seemed to enjoy a full life.

For the next six months, international long-distance calls flew back and forth between our mothers. And so it happened that I was introduced traditional Indian-style to Raj, former college cricket star and scion of an illustrious Delhi family. He shared my passion for workouts and Indian art. Like myself, he was an avid reader of Bengali literature: the works of Tagore, Bankim Chandra, and Ashapurna Debi. More and more, I was coming around to the idea of an arranged marriage.

Still, I had occasional spasms of doubts—that is, until Raj called from New Delhi one morning. I'd just showered and was padding about my apartment in a threadbare old bathrobe, with a towel wrapped around my hair.

"Hello, Sharmila. This is Raj." The voice was so eager and ingratiating that I held my breath and kept listening. "Our mothers have done enough talking. It's time we got to know each other a little better. After all, it's our future."

His "our" indicated we'd formed a bond already, a secret alliance against motherly conspiracies. I wrapped the bathrobe tighter around me. "Raj! So good to be able to talk at last." Then my mind went blank.

I heard him say, "I wish we could talk face to face."

Suddenly I felt like jumping onto a flying carpet.

We chatted about this and that, nothing serious, just listening to each other's voice, the nuances and pauses like two predestined mates who'd never talked before, but who recognized they had much to share.

Just before hanging up, Raj said confidently, "Sharmila, I want you to be my wife."

Like icy pellets of hail in a spring downpour, the sudden dramatic words struck me and I heard myself shakily reply, "I'll think about it very seriously." The receiver almost slipped out of my hand.

Before work that morning I had two extra cups of coffee, both so hot they burned my tongue. And for the rest of the day I was giddy, laughing unnecessarily, my feet barely touching the ground.

A week later, at a family dinner, I gave my parents permission to set the wedding date. As if this happened every day, my father calmly raised his glass of lassi in a toast, then, meal unfinished, hurried off to call his friend in New York. Mother mumbled how happy she was, extended her arms toward me in an embrace, and broke into tears. I was in shock. I couldn't believe I had done it.

How quickly the news spread via the communications network that extended from Chicago to New Delhi. Within a day a congratulatory message came to my father via e-mail from a college friend with a profusion of praise about the Khoslas, seconded by express mail from my mother's cousin Mistoo.

Then came a letter from Raj, the one I carried with me in my purse when I came to India. The last of my doubts began to crumble at the prospect that I'd be by the side of a man who was not only strong and influential, but more loving and considerate than any man I've ever dated. I gave notice to my landlord and sold or gave away my furniture, but put my favorite artwork, books, and CDs in storage.

My friends were shocked by my decision. "You're doing what?" said one. "You haven't even met him. You don't know what you're getting into."

Now standing at the passenger reception area of Delhi airport, I think to myself that maybe I should have listened to her warning. Here I am all alone in a strange land, thousands of miles and several oceans away from home. The man I've come here to marry has just left. My only possessions are my bags, my wits, a bouquet of roses, and a blurry, dreamy image of him.

3

"MAY I take you home now?" Prem's voice jerks me back to reality. "Mrs. Khosla is waiting," he says softly and deferentially, adding to my irritation.

Remembering my aerobics training, I inhale, shake out my arms unobtrusively, and tap a foot on the floor. That gets my blood circulating. I snap out of my funk.

Aware that he has offended me, Prem stoops to pick up my luggage—three heavy, bulky bags, the lightest of which weighs twenty five pounds. Mother has sent gifts for our relatives, right down to the tenth cousin. Prem lifts the heaviest one easily, scoops out the second with two fingers of his right hand, and struggles to get hold of the third with the remaining free fingers. Finally succeeding, he heads for the exit, calling out over his shoulder, "Follow me, please."

Though not a large man, Prem handles the load effortlessly. Even a macho weight lifter would be impressed. I conclude that size is no indication of strength in India. Still, I catch up and try to take the lighter bag from his hand.

"Oh, no, madam, please. You must not . . ."

Reluctantly I let go of the bag and fall in behind him, carrying my purse and flowers, a trifle ashamed of my behavior. As a fit and independent young woman, I've long resisted the notion that women should defer to male chivalry when it comes to physical tasks. Now, as I follow Prem, I'm surprised to find myself enjoying the feeling of being pampered.

Despite his clumsy burden, Prem maneuvers adroitly through the crowd, looking back every now and then to make sure he hasn't lost me. After a long corridor we finally emerge into a haze of yellowish-brown smog. A parking lot packed with cars stretches before us. We zigzag past rows of taxicabs waiting to pick up the new arrivals as they stream through the exits. At that moment a cold breeze knifes through my clothing. Mother did warn me about late November cold spells. The temperature is probably around forty-five degrees, and the wind chill makes it near freezing. I envy the shawl-shrouded laborers squatting around a smoldering wood fire in one corner of the lot, heating tea water. Prem stows my luggage in the trunk of a gleaming blue Mercedes, opens the rear door for me, and, after I'm settled in, hands me a gray wool blanket.

"Please, for your lap, madam. It is cold this morning."

Madam. Must be a common form of respectful address here. No one has ever called me that before.

Prem turns and stops by the front door, folds his hands, touches them to his forehead, offering a prayer to the morning sun. The sunrises seen from my vacation cabin in the California Sierras flash through my mind—flaming reds and golds fanning out in a firmament of melted sapphire. It has never occurred to me to salute such a spectacle. A custom I make a note to adopt.

Prem climbs in on the driver's side, informs me that the ride will take about forty minutes. He solemnly offers a large bottle of Pepsi over the seat. "You must be thirsty after the long flight."

Pepsi so early in the morning? It's totally ridiculous, yet I sense his eagerness to please. "Thanks," I say gently. "Not right now. Maybe later."

"Mrs. Khosla's cook is making breakfast for you." The voice is high-pitched; the language flows in a lilting rhythm. "He was already working in the kitchen when I left this morning. They're all delighted you're coming."

It dawns on me that the chauffeur must have got up early and traveled a great distance to meet me at the airport. A major inconvenience, surely, and I regret my earlier sharpness. As he out of economic necessity. Still, the fraternity between a chauffeur and his social superior raises questions in my mind. "Raj mentioned you were good friends. But you call him *babu*."

"It's a way of showing respect. When I first met him, he was richer and older, and I liked to tease him. Now it's quite appropriate given our situations. I work for his mother. A respectful form of address is required. But still, Raj-babu is my friend." Prem glances back. "He has always been my hero . . ."

His remaining words are drowned out by a police truck roaring by. I'm struck by the logo on the side reading: Delhi Police— With you, for you always. We're threading through heavy traffic, and Prem concentrates on his driving. I lean back, still clutching the rose bouquet to my chest. The tips of the soft blossoms give off a faintly sweet smell; they touch my chin with a foamy lightness. A feeling of lassitude washes over me. My resentment at Raj's desertion begins to fade.

I ask Prem, "Did you major in economics like Raj?"

"No. I studied tourism in Delhi University with special emphasis on history and culture. I couldn't afford to go to one of the top colleges like Raj-babu, but it was a good program. While I was finishing my B.A., he went to America for his MBA. He worked there for a while. When he came back, he took an executive position with a company. I worked for a travel agency."

"Raj said you're a good tour guide."

"My clients seemed to think so. I loved the work, but my boss and I didn't get along. I lost my job and couldn't get another one right away." Prem pauses before speaking again. "Fortunately, Mrs. Khosla took me in. I was supposed to work just for a few months, but she extended it. Now she wants me to show you around. Shopping, cinema, restaurants. Just tell me where you want to go. You see, Raj-*babu* works long hours."

So I won't be seeing as much of Raj as I'd expected. I'd had visions of our getting to know each other: the two of us looking up at the fluted tower of the Qutb Minar; dining on chicken korma at the venerable Karim's restaurant; watching the moon rise over the timeless Jamuna River. How silly and hopeless these were.

I begin to have second thoughts about the wedding and consider telling Prem to turn the car around so I can take the next flight home.

But I've come too far, both emotionally and physically, not to

turns the ignition key, I ask what I believe to be a polite (
among Indians: "Do you have a family?"

"Oh, yes." The ride is quiet and smooth, and his voice
easily. "I live with my mother, a younger brother, and a
My older sister got married three weeks ago and went
with her in-laws. She didn't know them very well, but
making the adjustments necessary."

I lean back against the beige leather seat, and remind m
of the joys and difficulties of living with relatives. Nearly ha
our extended family has emigrated to England, Canada, or
States over the years. We've held many family reunions. Au
uncles, and cousins would stay with us the entire summ
Mother would place bunk beds in my room for my lit
nephews and nieces. Our living room would become the cent
of a tornado of conversation and laughter—and then there wa
the food. But my American side needed private time. Every few
hours I retreated to my room for music, drawing and peace
Then inevitably Mother would tap at the closed door. "What are
you doing all by yourself, Sharmila? Your grandmother wants
you to comb her hair."

Or, "Cousin Tinni won't touch her food until you join her."

Or, "Nephew Manik needs a hug before his nap."

I hear her voice now and picture my room's black door with
a shiny brass knob.

"We're in South Delhi," Prem says at last.

I check my watch. It's nine-thirty. Sunlight is breaking
through a suffocating haze that hangs over the city like a gossamer curtain, but I'm pleasantly surprised by the lush greenery
on either side of the street. There's some truth, after all, to the
billboards proclaiming "Clean and Green Delhi" that go by
every mile or so. Below the advertisements of Nathu's Sweets,
Tanoon Computers, and the *Hindustan Standard* newspaper on a
lamppost, I see one for Maha Electronics, Raj's company.

I ask Prem, "How long have you worked for the Khoslas?"

"About two and a half years. Mostly part-time."

"Do you know Raj well?"

"I've known him for many years, madam." Prem throws a
glance over his shoulder. "Since college. He's only two years older."

It's obvious from Prem's speech, mannerisms, and social
graces that he's college-educated. Most likely he's taken this job

give this a chance. I say to Prem, "You can show me Delhi. I've started to read about its history, and I'm fascinated."

"History's my true love." Excited for the first time, he smiles, his hands strong on the steering wheel. "Is this your first trip to Delhi?"

"I was here when I was ten years old. All we did was visit our relatives. I didn't see much."

"Do you speak any Hindi, madam?"

"I understand it better than I speak it."

"The Khoslas all speak very good English."

That's a relief. I roll my window down for fresh air, and immediately smells of the street hit me in waves: delicate incense, pungent mustard oil, acrid diesel exhaust. Silver notes of temple bells rise above the traffic noise. Delhi is unlike any city in the States. Here the streets are an extension of living space, shared with friends, merchants, and strangers. As we approach an intersection, I notice a band of men—all dressed in white shirts and pants—standing about, chatting, and leisurely sipping tea from tiny glasses. The word *loitering* has quite a different connotation here.

Prem turns on to a wider street lined with mansions and well-tended gardens. "When you have rested, I will show you all the famous sights. And some special spots only a few locals know. Even Mrs. Khosla was delighted when I took her to a bangles market she'd never been to."

"So you drive her too?"

"I did, especially this past year. You see, many wealthy families wanted their daughters to marry Raj-babu, and Mrs. Khosla met with them all. She must have screened a hundred potential matches. She narrowed them down to a list of ten or so for Raj-babu to consider. Out of them all he picked you." Prem falls silent, as though to give emphasis to his next thought. "You're artistic, you're active, and you're from America, a combination of qualities the other candidates lacked. Also, you reminded him of his first wife, Roopa. You know, he was heartbroken when she died."

"Oh . . ."

I've heard very little about Raj's first marriage, and I haven't bothered to inquire, assuming it was a union of obligation and that she was the typical dutiful wife. I'd expected to be Raj's first true love. Now I realize such isn't the case. He loved her deeply and maybe still does. On top of all the other challenges and adjustments, am I going to have to compete with a dead wife? The fact that I resemble her gives me a chill.

Prem continues, "Also, he liked reading the excerpt from your diary that your mother so thoughtfully sent along with the videotape."

"My diary?"

"Yes. Raj-babu's car broke down last week, and he asked me to drive him to his office. Usually he's talkative, but that day he sat quietly in the back with a letter. Finally I asked him if anything was the matter. He just shook his head and said he was going over some papers sent from Chicago. Later he showed me your sketch. The skeleton of a tree, two birds sharing a branch, and your words under it: 'Brittle branches fall, new buds blossom, birds cluster.' Raj-babu took it as a sign that he should stop grieving—as if unknowingly you'd written a personal message to him."

How could my mother betray me in this way? Inwardly I am seething, biting my lip, fidgeting in the seat. My diary sketchbook is where I record my thoughts and feelings, and draw objects and images that catch my fancy. It's my private world, where I can be completely honest. Now it has been opened to a stranger. I'd made that entry in my sketchbook after I'd broken up with a boyfriend. It was a message to myself—not Raj or anyone else. Cheeks inflamed, I bolt upright in my seat, feeling as lonely as those fallen branches. I could strangle my mother. It was a mistake to ask her to house-sit when I went on vacation. It had given her an opportunity to go through my personal effects, eventually locating an old diary, copying a page, and mailing it to Raj. What nerve. I know exactly how she'd respond if I confronted her with this outrage. Sweetly she'd utter: But why would you keep secrets from your husband, dear? Truly, why do you have secrets at all?

"Your handwriting is beautiful," Prem says. "Like pearls on a string."

The chauffeur read my diary too? In embarrassment I look out the window. Really, I don't want to hear any more.

"And every line you draw expresses deep feelings."

Has he no idea what I'm going through right now? I look

bleakly out the window. There's a sign pasted above a booth: Internet, E-mail, Video Phones, Fax, Local and International Phone Calls. Stop, I want to yell. I want to halt this assault on my senses and emotions.

Before I can speak, we turn onto a main road and skid to an abrupt halt, stopped by a procession marching past. My anger fades as I stare out the window and am caught up by the sight of the men, women, and children marching. One dark and emaciated man, clad in a dhoti, casts hesitant glances all around, as if he doubts his right to be on the street. His feet are caked with dust, his sandals tattered. The woman beside him is dressed in a worn sari of faded yellows, purples, and blues. Glass bangles are her only ornament. The young girl holding her hand has faded white flowers tucked into her plait. Two huge banners flutter in the breeze in the middle of the procession. One reads DALIT SAMRAJ in black, and another reads BURN THE POLICE! in red. A chant erupts from a thousand throats. I turn to find Prem's eyes are intent on the unfolding scene. He seems remote, inaccessible.

Swallowing, I ask, "What's this march about?"

"It's a protest." Prem continues to stare out the window. "Yesterday the police shot and killed some innocent people in a slum."

"Criminals?"

"Perhaps." Prem blinks, interlaces his fingers, then in a barely audible voice asks me, "How much do you know about our caste system?"

I'd always taken it for granted that my family is upper caste. Knowing the subject to be a sensitive one, I attempt a neutral reply. "I was born into a Hindu family."

"Even though India is eighty percent Hindu, we are a divided people. It's not religion that divides us, but rather the caste system. When I was a little boy, my mother explained it to me once while picnicking on a seashore. 'You see all those seashells, Prem? If you put most of them in four big piles and call them priests, warriors, traders, and laborers, then you've got the four recognized castes and, along with that the hierarchy of the caste system in that order. And as for all those others scattered about? They're the casteless ones, the untouchables. They can only get the filthiest jobs and have no position in society. How foolish,' my mother cried. 'For when a wave rolls up onto the shore, it will wash them all away, and they'll all become a part of the great ocean again.' "

I am touched by Prem's mother's explanation, but wondering what it has to do with the procession. My question was a simple one. Is the answer really so complex?

"I know all that stuff," I retort impatiently. "In Chicago nobody cares about caste. Our Indian community is split along language lines. Bengalis have their own association. Gujaratis celebrate their *garba*. South Indians are building a temple. My parents' generation might have worried about castes, but to Indian Americans my age, it doesn't make a—"

"It makes a difference here."

"I keep up with the news," I reply, not willing to be dismissed as ignorant of Indian affairs. "I've read in the *Hindustan Times* and *India Today* that the Indian government has done away with the caste system. The untouchables—"

"Dalits," Prem interrupts, correcting me. "The oppressed."

"All right," I say impatiently. "Don't the Dalits have strict quotas in jobs and education? Haven't many of them won political elections? And what about the fact that the tenth president, K. R. Narayanan, was a Dalit?"

"All that's true." Prem's words are rapid, his face tight. "Yet yesterday the police raided a Dalit slum and beat up people because one of them had bathed in a Hindu *ghat*. When the Dalits fought back, the police opened fire. Seven people died . . ." Prem trails off, clearly anguished by the tragedy. He regains his composure and continues, "But Dalits have decided not to take it anymore."

My gaze turns back to the procession, to an open truck loaded with bundles draped in white, scattered with pink and yellow flower petals. A somber quiet descends on me. The pain of the mourners touches me deep inside. I offer silent sympathy; wishing I could be with them instead of being in this fancy car. Gently I ask, "So the whole community is marching then?"

"Not quite, madam. I should be marching too."

In stunned silence I shrink back against the seat. I've never met a Dalit before. In a flash of revelation it dawns on me that when I marry Raj, I am also making a commitment to embrace what has nurtured him, to learn the distilled wisdom of thousands of years. Only a couple of hours in India and already I feel the weight of her long painful history. I visualize Mother India before me—a benign figure whose weary, all-seeing eyes radiate compassion. She beckons me to come sit at her feet. What do I know of life? Of love? Of suffering? When I look out the window, my former existence seems shallow and vain.

The goddess disappears, leaving me with a sense that she'll draw me out, imbue me with earnest intensity, wash me in tears of joy and pain, and reshape me to her timeless ways.

The procession is thinning out, and Prem starts the engine. A gust of wind blows a wisp of hair into my eye. The cold leather of the car seat makes me shudder. It's as though I'm someone who doesn't know how to swim, but is already in deep water.

4

S HARMILA, come in." A melodic feminine voice greets me as I
approach the second-floor landing of a swank apartment
building. "Please come in. I'm so happy you have arrived
safely."

Palms joined, Mrs. Khosla glides toward me. Time and family
responsibilities have buttressed her figure, but it's easy to see
that this aristocratic woman was a ravishing beauty thirty
pounds ago. A fine hand-woven cotton sari, white with a thin
blue border, drapes her ample body in graceful folds and long
sweeps. The tip of her nose is pink from the cold Raj mentioned.
Yet I sense a barely contained energy, the same as I saw in her
son.

Trying not to blink, I hold her gaze and realize that I'm in the
presence of a dominant personality. I feel drab. My printed skirt
and black velvet jacket, chosen so carefully for this initial encounter, seem tacky. With hands together, bowing deferentially, I
begin, "Mrs. Khosla . . ."

She tilts her head back, for I am taller than she by at least five
inches. She nods, as if to say, At least you're tall enough for my
son. I hope that's a sign of approval. "I'm so sorry I couldn't
come to the airport," she says. "This cold has been a terrible burden to me."

Indian custom dictates a woman guest be escorted by a female member of the family. I'm forced now to consider if she's really that sick. Why didn't Raj's sister come? Should I feel slighted? What I do feel is confused and awkward.

Just then Prem comes up the stairs with my luggage. He arranges the bags neatly and shuffles his feet to get our attention.

Mrs. Khosla gazes over my shoulder. "This is all of her luggage?" With a note of derision she says, "I pack a trunk and two suitcases just to go to Agra."

She turns to Prem with a broad smile and unleashes a torrent of Hindi at him. I assume it's the small talk of two people with a warm, close bond. They banter back and forth as if I were not even there.

Finally Mrs. Khosla reverts to English. "You'll be returning later, won't you, Prem, to show Sharmila around our city?"

"Yes, Madam. I'll be back this afternoon."

A small protest forms: Shouldn't she consult me about my wishes first? Before I can speak, though, Prem bids her good-bye and hurries down the steps. His departure leaves me even more drained. I realize that I'm utterly unprepared to deal with a future mother-in-law.

Mrs. Khosla turns to me with a set smile. "Please come with me, Sharmila." She walks ahead, each firm step owning the ground it touches. "It's really quite a large flat."

She's not exaggerating. The apartment occupies the entire second floor of a two-story house and has a private entrance. Doors open on either side of the long hallway; I count at least eight. The textured walls are freshly painted a pale yellow. The tiled floor gleams, still damp from a recent mopping. We take an immediate right and enter a commodious living room with a square seating area. Mrs. Khosla motions me to a red-brocaded sofa. She herself takes a seat in an armchair. Between us is an exquisite coffee table of rosewood inlaid with ivory. Just this one piece of her furniture would set me back at least two paychecks.

This coveted address in the Defence Colony of South Delhi will be home, shared with Raj, his mother, and his sister, possibly for many years to come. In India it's customary for grown children to live with their parents even after marriage. Someday I'll have children of my own and they'll grow up here.

Sunlight floods in through gaps in the chintz curtains and paints the floor with slanted strips of glowing gold. A door to my left opens onto a balcony, permitting the fragrance of the garden below to waft in. The whole effect is warm, cheery, and expansive.

The Khoslas own this property, the price of which must be astronomical. But then, they haven't had to worry about money for a long time. I remember my mother mentioning that Mr. Khosla once owned a mansion that his widow sold for a fortune after his death. She still maintains a small home in the mountain resort town of Darjeeling, where the family goes to escape the summer heat.

Now Mrs. Khosla asks me how my flight was, a polite question of a proper hostess. "It was mostly pleasant but dreadfully long," I reply.

"And the food they serve is terrible," she commiserates. "You see, I used to fly to New York often with my husband on business trips."

For a moment Mrs. Khosla's eyes become distant, then quickly she snaps back. She has an inner reserve that can withstand the loss of a spouse, Delhi traffic, or a miserable cold with equanimity, of that I'm sure.

"The next few weeks I want you to relax, Sharmila. I'm not inviting any relatives or friends. So, you'll have plenty of time to rest, shop, and sightsee."

"That's very thoughtful of you. I think I'm going to like living here, but I appreciate the time to get acclimated."

"You won't have any problem with the language, I assure you. I had English tutors for both Raj and Neelu from the time they were five. They studied in English medium schools exclusively. Most of our help speak some English as well. You'll find, no matter where you go in Delhi, someone speaks English."

That's a relief, since I barely speak my parents' two languages: Hindi and Bengali.

"If you have money, Delhi is a most wonderful place to live," Mrs. Khosla continues breezily. "Servants will take care of all your needs. Without them this city simply would not run. All we have to do is get up in the morning and decide the program for the day. It makes life quite easy." Her expression darkens. "That's not the case with marriage, which is a big responsibility.

You lose most of the freedom that you take for granted as an un-married woman." She lets out a sigh. "You learn to take the good with the bad."

I attempt to make light of the situation. "I realize things are different here, Mrs. Khosla, but my mother has trained me. She's an ideal partner to my father. They have a happy marriage."

I wait for a few words of commendation, but hear instead, "You must be exhausted. I'm sure you'd like to get settled and freshen up a bit." At my nod Mrs. Khosla rises from her chair in one abrupt motion. "I'll have our cook Mohan show you to your room. He apprenticed at the Maurya Sheraton Hotel for several years before coming to us. The Maurya has some of the finest food in the city. We feel most fortunate to have acquired his services. I haven't had to go into the kitchen since he came. He even learned a good bit of English while he was there. It's a most pleasant change from the illiterate cook my parents used to have. Mohan!"

I expect a stocky middle-aged man, but the figure who appears at the door is young and slender. He glides in and folds his hands, his eyes wide open with curiosity and respect. I'm captivated by his smile, which has the brightness of sunshine reflected on marble.

"Welcome to India, to Delhi, and to our home, memsahib. *Namaste*. I'm so very happy you've arrived safely."

His tongue dances around the *v* sound, making it a *w*, and a *w* into a *v*. Even though his English pronunciation isn't perfect, his words of welcome convey sincerity. I hope this gregarious cook will see me as a new palate to please.

"Do be careful with her luggage, Mohan."

Mohan almost jumps at Mrs. Khosla's command, hoists my suitcases and proceeds toward the door.

While I pick up my purse, Mrs. Khosla continues in a whisper, "I suspect he's excited about your arrival. Normally he's very capable, but this morning he dropped a basket of eggs on the kitchen floor and made a horrible mess."

I suppress a smile and follow Mohan, more sure than ever that I'll like him.

My room is large and airy, though the sandy shade of the walls lends a gloom. A massive mahogany bed with carved bed-posts occupies more than half the space. It's just right for someone who loves to spread out on her bed the way I do. A still-life painting, blue iris in a crystal vase, hangs on one wall. Someday I will change that. There's an armoire with a full-length mirror. Across from it a half-open door reveals a closet. Just ahead, beneath a tall window, is a writing desk. A bottle of Bislery water and some stationery are set on it. I visualize all the letters I'll be writing there, and a lump of homesickness catches in my chest.

Mohan sets my luggage down next to the closet and turns to me. "Any dish you want, memsahib, just ask me. I can make them all. Chinese, Thai, Continental. You see, I've cooked for Europeans, Australians, and Americans. The British, of course, don't like any spices. The Australians—I had a most difficult time with their pronunciation. The Americans were the nicest. One kind American lady used to joke that my french fries had legs because they sold out so quickly. Every morning she called down from her room to reserve a double order. She gave me a good baksheesh when she left."

"Please, no french fries for me." I cringe in feigned terror, then burst out with a laugh. "I love Indian food. Just serve me what you serve everyone else in the family."

"You like our food?" he exclaims like this is terrific news. "I will be sure to make many special dishes for you, memsahib. There is so much variety in Indian cooking. Most foreigners ask only for tandoori chicken. As you understand, there's much more."

A thought bursts into my head. "Will you give me lessons?"

"With great pleasure." Mohan beams, then turns to leave. At the door, eyes wistful, he hesitates. "I hear America is a beautiful country. Maybe someday I'll be going for a visit. Are there any discos in Chicago? I've watched *Saturday Night Fever* twenty-seven times." Seeing my surprised reaction, he continues, "Twenty-seven! That's how old I am."

"Yes, Chicago has lots of discos," I reply, suddenly realizing that despite a recent disco revival I haven't been near one. I'm not quite with it.

"I love to dance." Mohan whispers like I'm a trusted friend. "It's difficult for me to save money because I spend it all discoing."

His eyes flash, as though given the slightest pretext he'll twirl around the floor. Just then Mrs. Khosla's voice booms out from down the hallway. "Mohan! You're still standing there? For goodness' sake, show her how to use the shower, then leave her to get settled in. And be sure to make a couple of extra parathas. Neelu will be up soon."

The smile vanishes from my erstwhile Travolta's face as he hurriedly leads me on a tour of the bathroom, then hurries off to the kitchen.

I stand under a forceful hot shower and think about Mohan. The prospect of learning Indian cooking from a man of his expertise and enthusiasm is exciting. Of course, I know the basics like dahl and raita, but I'm completely out of my league when it comes to kormas, kebabs, or parathas. I could have learned it all when I was still living at home, but then I was into tennis, volleyball, art projects, and boys, not necessarily in that order. Recently I'd begun taking cooking lessons from an elderly Indian woman who lived in my apartment building in Chicago. She was one of those grim-faced, old-country grandmothers who crack a smile once every full moon—and is a sorcerer in front of the stove. I wanted to learn everything in a couple of months and told her so. She was grinding mustard seeds with a mortar and pestle. Her voice rose above the sound, stone on stone, as she replied, "It's going to take a little longer, Sharmila. You know, our cooking traditions are a few thousand years old."

I was still floundering somewhere around year one when I left for India.

I finish my shower. The running water has washed away the stiffness from my muscles and has put my mind somewhat at rest. Leisurely and with care I dress, choosing a silk *salwar* suit in a coral color. The velvety tunic reaches to my knees; the loose pants gather at the ankles, helping to keep the morning chill out. I wrap a matching gossamer scarf, what they call *odni* in Hindi, around my throat in a quick whimsical motion. Feeling ready at last to face my new family, I head to the living room.

Mrs. Khosla doesn't even notice my entrance. Seated on a sofa, feet flat on the floor, she's flipping through the pages of a lifestyle magazine. Her head is framed by a modernistic glass bookcase lined with Russian classics and statuettes of Hindu gods. Above it is an acrylic painting of an ocean under a violent stormy sky. Blues and blacks in bold strokes. Elemental and terrifying.

Mrs. Khosla glances up. "That one is a treasured family heir-loom." Like a pedagogue she directs my attention to another painting on the opposite wall, a Mughal miniature in a ma-hogany frame, smaller but no doubt more valuable. "It was a gift from my father when I got married."

I step forward to inspect the intricate watercolor. A maiden wearing a parakeet green sari and exquisite jewelry blushes through a diaphanous veil as she stands before her suitor. He's regal in his mid-thigh length *achkan* of embroidered ivory silk, a white turban wound around his head. Her doe eyes downcast, she can only see his shadow. With an enigmatic smile spread on her lips, she's waiting for him to make the first move. I believe the almond blossoms scattered at her feet are symbolic of her chastity.

What a contrast to my encounter with Raj. Dressed in smart American clothes, I looked him straight in the eye. Still, a bond with this Mughal princess begins to form in my mind. We're both betrothed to a stranger—arranged marriages was a long-established custom even in the sixteenth century. The same fear and anticipation grow within us. We have the same trust that our parents, in their wisdom and experience, have made a good match. The same faith that the gods will look favorably upon our union.

Mrs. Khosla asks, "Did Raj meet you at the airport?"

"Yes, but we didn't have much time together."

"They can't seem to manage without him." Mrs. Khosla speaks of her son as though he's a treasure that she's reluctant to loan. "They shuttle him to Mumbai and Bangalore all the time." Then, almost as an afterthought, "But I'm certain that after the wedding he'll cut down on travel and work less hours . . ."

I don't know if it's jet lag, the brevity of Raj's airport appear-ance, or Mrs. Khosla's overblown adulation, but I feel on edge. I definitely need to have a talk with my mother about this situa-tion.

"May I use the phone, Mrs. Khosla? I should let my mother know I've arrived safely."

"Why, yes, of course." Mrs. Khosla points at the phone table. "She's worrying about you, I'm sure." She adds before leaving the room, "Do give her my respects, will you?"

I dial my parents' number. The connection comes easily.

Roused from a deep sleep, my mother recognizes my voice and is instantly awake.

"Child, are you in Delhi?"

"Yes, Mom, I'm here. I can't talk right now. I'm calling to find out if you'll be home later. And don't worry, I'm okay. I'm just fine."

"What is it, *beti*?"

Looking around and seeing that I'm alone, I whisper on the receiver, "I feel uneasy about this so far. Mrs. Khosla didn't come to the airport. Raj did, but he left for Mumbai on business right away. Now I hear he travels constantly."

"Forget about that old custom of coming to the airport," my mother says. "The traffic in Delhi is so bad that you don't go out of the house if you don't have to. As for Raj, your father left me in India for three months when he first moved to the States. I was pregnant with you then. I stayed with my in-laws and made the best of it. You have to be flexible. And it's probably just as well that Raj isn't around for a couple of days. Wouldn't you like to get used to the daily routine there without having to impress a man at every step, right off the bat?"

My mother would have made a great attorney. "Mom, what about the page from my diary you sent to Raj? I'm pissed. How could you? Don't you understand how private my journal is?"

"I don't regret it," Mother interrupts me. "It's not as if I exposed any of your warts. Raj told me he felt it helped him understand you better. He'll love you all the more for it, you'll see."

Looking at the matter from a different perspective, I have to admit Mother has a point, though there's still a little black spot in my feelings toward her.

"Listen, Sharmila dear, you ought to get some rest. You sound crabby, and I don't blame you one bit. A long flight, strange surroundings, and all those new people. That's a cupful. We can talk later. Before you hang up, could I have a word with Mrs. Khosla? If there are any real problems, we'll straighten them out."

"Bye, Mom."

With a heavy heart I set the receiver down. As I poke my head out the living room door, I spy Mrs. Khosla coming down the hallway. She gives me her usual practiced smile, but when I tell her that my mother's waiting to speak to her, the face becomes animated.

While Mrs. Khosla chats on the phone, I wander over to the window, feigning interest in a tree with jade green leaves. All the while I keep an ear tuned to their conversation. Warm greetings. Lots of *achcha, achcha*. Very well, very well. The two mothers surely have become good friends. They're taking my situation so matter-of-factly. I slump into a chair in a corner.

My gaze falls on the Mughal painting, and for a moment I wonder if it was given as dowry from Mrs. Khosla's father. Having discovered my mother's deception earlier this morning, I wonder if my father could have paid a dowry behind my back. I make a mental note to check on this.

I remember being fascinated by my mother's dowry box when I was seven. Made of teakwood, it was a foot square and eight inches high with hammered brass hinges. I remember the click as Mother turned a small, recessed wooden lever and it popped open, exposing an empty interior. So where was the dowry? Noting my surprise, she explained that when she brought the box with her as a bride, it was crammed with rupee notes equal in value to her father's yearly income. After protracted negotiations, Dad's family finally agreed to the amount. To cement their acceptance, my grandfather had given Dad's family two hectares of land, generating resentment among his own sons. Heartbroken, my grandfather died within months of his daughter's wedding. As my mother looked down at her dowry box, her voice caught and she turned away in tears. The remainder of the day I was sad and angry at having seen my mother cry.

So a dowry is one aspect of a traditional Indian wedding I'm determined to avoid at all costs. To me it's synonymous with humiliation. Why should a man demand money or goods to marry a woman? Why should a woman permit money to measure her worth, especially when the money goes entirely to her husband's family, without a *paise* for her? I made that clear to my parents when I agreed to marry Raj. Now I wonder if Dad, despite his promise, is staying on Mrs. Khosla's good side by giving her a dowry. And Mom, though she may not have forgotten her old tears, will go along with the custom as well.

My thoughts are interrupted by the sound of the receiver hanging up. Having finished the call, Mrs. Khosla, satisfaction evident on her face, asks, "Would you like some breakfast, Sharmila? You must be hungry."

Politeness must be in the family genes. Forcing cheer into my voice, I answer, "I'd love some."

"Champa!" Mrs. Khosla's voice rises in a hint of authority.

A slender young woman edges through the door and stands by the wall looking down at the floor. She has enormous Picasso-like eyes and appears to be about twenty. Though her sari is coarse brown cloth, there is a grace and dignity about her that subtly alter the mood in the room. There is no ignoring her presence. One long braid of black hair, tightly woven and glistening from a recent application of coconut oil, hangs down her back.

"Sharmila, this is our maid, Champa. She's been with us now for three years." Mrs. Khosla turns to Champa and speaks in rapid Hindi. I gather that she's emphasizing I've just arrived from America, exhausted, and in need of extra attention.

Silent and stiff, Champa, bowing with closed palms, greets me. I get the impression that her thoughts bypass her tongue and express themselves through subtle body language.

Trying to follow my mother's teachings, I acknowledge Champa with a glance and a nod. In response the maid briefly raises her head. I see her eyes—a bit wild and not exactly friendly. Not a surprise, after all, I'm the outsider. She'll get used to me first as Raj's wife, then in time as a person in my own right.

"Is everything ready for breakfast, Champa?" Mrs. Khosla's voice sounds as mellow as melting butter, considerably less harsh than when she was addressing Mohan. Immediately Champa heads out the door with long, purposeful strides. "I'll be along to help you," Mrs. Khosla calls after her.

"Neelu! Neelu!" Mrs. Khosla's summons rings down the corridor. No response. "My daughter is probably not awake yet. She's nineteen. All she thinks about is fashion, film stars, and Zee TV. She probably read Filmfare by candlelight till past midnight."

"No need to wake Neelu," I say softly. "I'll meet her later."

I get the impression that this woman holds her family together with two classic tactics—the carrot of love and the stick of discipline. Will I ever be able to relax around her?

"Do you take tea or coffee with your breakfast?"

I know that fine coffee is grown in South Indian highlands, and now I'm delighted to learn that my favorite drink is consumed in the North also. "A cup of coffee would really hit the spot."

"I'll make it myself. I have excellent coffee from the Nilgiri Hills. As many times as I have tried to teach Champa to make it, she has never done it right. I'm the only one in the family who drinks coffee. And now you."

"We seem to have a common ground."

Mrs. Khosla either entirely misses my pun or chooses to ignore it. With a gracious gesture of her hand, she guides me to the dining room, then excuses herself. I sit alone at a huge oval table covered with white linen and take in the room: the lemon yellow walls, the large open window, the beige-painted cabinet on the opposite wall holding cutlery and fine china.

Champa walks into the room bearing a tray and sets each food platter on the table with an audible thunk. Not too loud—but clearly she's sending me a message. I sit calmly, pretending to ignore her subtle provocation, and watch her leave. The thick braid of hair down her back waves back and forth like a snake. I pick up my glass and gulp some water down. It leaves a metallic aftertaste in my mouth that causes me to wonder if it is really bottled water or something less savory. It definitely wouldn't do to get sick on my first day in Delhi.

My neck and shoulders are so tense they seem detached from the rest of my body. I do a neck roll, rotating my head in a circular motion. That seems to do the trick, for I'm soon ravenously hungry. A spicy-sweet aroma edged with a hint of chili focuses my attention to the dishes before me. Triangular parathas glistening with ghee, omelet squares flecked with cilantro, crusty chunks of deep brown roasted potatoes speckled with a retinue of spices, as well as yellow papaya and white guava wedges. I wish I could draw this first feast in my sketchbook and preserve it for posterity.

Then I notice Champa standing at the edge of my peripheral vision. She's there until Mrs. Khosla comes around the corner. When I turn to actually look, Champa's gone.

With steady hands Mrs. Khosla pours me a steaming cup of coffee, places it before me without a sound, and pours a second cup for herself. Head up, back straight, the impeccable hostess waits for me to take a sip before reaching for her own cup. I'll probably never acquire her easy elegance.

Drinking the full-bodied coffee suffuses me with a feeling of calm. "At home I set up my coffee maker the night before," I tell

Mrs. Khosla. "It's one of those modern programmable types that makes my life a lot easier. But the coffee doesn't taste like this."

Mrs. Khosla glides past the compliment with no change in her expression. "Raj is the same," she says. "He has to have his bed tea the moment he opens his eyes."

That's nice. I didn't associate bed tea with Raj, the executive. This leisurely custom is a civilized way of waking oneself up and getting into the proper frame of mind for the day ahead. At a specified hour in the morning, a servant carrying a tea tray gently knocks on the bedroom door. He brings the tray inside, sets it down on a table, then departs. The tray is laid with a lacy cloth, a teapot full of steaming tea, a cup, a spoon and possibly a fresh flower of the season.

Seeing my interest, Mrs. Khosla elaborates. "Raj wakes around six and shouts for Champa. He spends at least an hour on his tea."

An hour for bed tea?

"Then later I hear him singing in the shower," Mrs. Khosla continues. "After he gets dressed, he sits down to have breakfast with me. He says, 'Ma-ji, if I start the day with you, it goes better.' "

Ma-ji, revered mother, is how Raj addresses his mother. Although I am aware that the suffix "ji" is used to convey respect to one's elders, I have seldom had the occasion to use it in the egalitarian environment of America. I hope I don't insult someone here by neglecting to use it.

Mrs. Khosla seems unusually close to her son. It is to be expected of a widow, but I'll need to watch this carefully. It might be the source of future problems for me.

The window curtains flutter as a young woman in a mandarin-collar *kameez* and matching trousers breezes into the room. The deep blue color accentuates her fair skin, while a sheer scarf thrown over her neck frames her face in a pattern of flower petals. When she sees me, she comes to a halt.

Mrs. Khosla's face breaks into an adoring smile. Eyes softly focusing on the girl, she announces proudly, "This is my daughter, Neelu."

"Sharmila . . . I didn't realize you were here already." The girl recovers from her surprise, comes over, and takes my hand. With her full black eyes, fine cheekbones, and beguiling smile, she resembles Raj.

"You mustn't call her by her first name, Neelu," Mrs. Khosla admonishes. "She's *bhabiji*, elder sister-in-law."

"But, Ma," Neelu retorts, her voice bearing a touch of rebellion, "Americans call each other by their first names regardless of age or blood connection. They don't go in for any of this 'respected elder sister' business."

Creases appear in Mrs. Khosla's forehead. She stands up. "This isn't America, dear. Here we respect our elders." Then, as quickly, her expression reverts to a pleasant smile. "Why don't you two get acquainted? It's time to give Mohan instructions for the day's shopping."

Mrs. Khosla spins and heads for the door, the *pallu* of her sari slicing the air. In her upturned chin, haughty gait, and heavy steps, I detect stern disapproval of Neelu's behavior.

Neelu sighs, rolls her eyes and flops into a chair. "So, what do I call you? Sharmila or *bhabiji*?"

I am about to laugh, but see Champa lurking in the hallway. "Sharmila is just fine. I've never been much for formality."

"Why aren't you eating, Sharmila?"

The maid's presence is still bothering me. "I'll finish the coffee first. Back home I salute the morning with Starbucks coffee, the way you salute the sun here."

Neelu bursts into a laughter that ripples through her entire body. Her pendulum-like earrings swing in concert. Then with a sudden seriousness she asks, "You don't mind if I eat?"

"No, not really, go ahead."

Neelu rolls up her right sleeve and with nimble fingers tears off a portion of a paratha. She scoops up a chunk of potato and pops the little sandwich into her rosebud mouth. A few bites later she comments, "Paratha has always been my favorite breakfast bread." She attacks an omelet square with another piece of paratha before continuing. "I went to a convent school. My teachers were Australian nuns. Once I was fined five rupees in class for saying, 'I had paratha for breakfast,' when we were supposed to say 'Only tea and toast.' " She imitates a child's singsong rhyme, then falls apart in an uncontrollable fit of laughter.

Neelu's openness allows me to relax. I dig into the paratha myself and savor the flaky layers. Before long I find myself trying the potatoes, omelets, and papayas as well.

Neelu picks up a guava spear and examines it idly. "How unromantic. Raj-bhai really shouldn't have taken off for Mumbai. What should be more important? But no, it's business as usual with him. He's even begun to act like a manager at home. 'Prem, do this.' 'Ma-ji, do that.' 'Neelu, don't forget to bring me . . .' I finally had to remind him I'm not a part of his staff. It was rude of him to have Prem handle your arrival."

Do I detect sibling rivalry? I smile to myself and continue eating. The piece of papaya spurts sweet juice in my mouth.

"I wonder if he's nervous because you're an American," Neelu says. "He had a serious romance once in the States, but in the end it fell apart. He was hurt."

A chunk of potato on its way to my mouth hangs in midair, then is detoured to the plate. Neelu has my undivided attention. Yet she begins to pepper me with questions about the States in the high, curious voice of youth, delighted at the prospect of debriefing a genuine American. "Wasn't Chicago the city where Swami Vivekananda began his States visit?" she asks. "Is it true you can buy all things Indian on Devon Street? Does the winter really last five months? Are the summers as hot as in Delhi?"

While I answer Neelu's questions, Champa walks in with an empty tray, a sudden shadow of the late morning sun. With long, languid motions she starts to remove the empty plates. She's obviously well trained. Absorbed with Neelu, I don't notice until after the maid has left that she has taken away my coffee cup, still half full and warm.

5

I<small>T'S</small> afternoon on my first day in Delhi, and I find myself alone for the first time. Neelu's attending classes at her college, Mrs. Khosla's in her room still nursing that cold, and the maid is nowhere to be seen, for which I'm thankful. It's a good time to drag a cane chair out onto the balcony and curl up with the newspaper. My eyes rest for a moment on the foliage in the clay pots lining the edge of the balcony, and my mood brightens.

I could have taken a nap, as Mrs. Khosla suggested, but I'm forcing myself to adjust to local time. Attired in black jeans, a flannel shirt in geranium red, and my usual gold necklace, I'm comfortable enough physically. But the disorienting impact of all I have experienced in the brief seven hours since I got off the plane reminds me that this is an alien land.

God, I wish Mother were here. Her jewelry tinkling, she'd lean over toward me and rearrange a stray hair on my forehead. "Be patient, Sharmila," she'd say. "What's your hurry? Things will work out if you just give them time."

The temperature has risen noticeably, and the noise from the street below makes a nap out of the question. I hear tires squealing and horns trumpeting and a vendor calling, "Ice cream! Ice cream!" The man's tone implies one would be a fool to miss such a luscious opportunity. I'm tempted to grab my purse and run downstairs, but my body won't budge.

Above my head, a crow circles, a black shadow against blazing blue. I reflect on what it must be like to fly. I conclude it's the same sensation I experienced when I met Raj. A rush, a feeling of lightness—followed by the realization that it's a long way to the ground.

I sit back in the chair and pick up the *Hindustan Times,* but in my bleary state the goings-on in this capital city are only an abstraction. The parliament debates what percentage of seats to reserve for women. Soldiers prowl the bazaars searching for another bomb planted by a terrorist group. An anonymous frustrated, underpaid office worker is quoted as saying, "Pay peanuts, get monkeys." All together not much different from the news of any big-city newspaper in the States.

Dropping the paper, I rise and rest my hand on the balcony rail. I look out onto my new family's emerald green courtyard, symmetrical in the classical Mughal tradition, enclosed by a high stone wall. In a far corner the gardener, a thin, dark man, is working. His long, sinewy arms swing in a practiced economical pattern. With a stainless steel can in one hand he walks along a row of flower bushes, pausing to remove an insect from a leaf with a flick of his fingers or a moth with a gentle wave. The man is immersed in the only activity of any consequence in his universe. An atmosphere of placidity, arising from a total attention to his task, blankets him.

The serenity and connectedness must be contagious, for within moments I feel at ease enough to fetch my diary sketchbook and several pencils. Sketching is faster than writing and allows me to picture my subject more clearly. I like to do one sketch per page, often using them later for a painting. I pick up a charcoal pencil and scribble on the top of a blank page:

From the balcony

The pencil darts across the page, limning in the greenery, the gardener, even insects, the light sky beyond acting as the backdrop. With a sigh of satisfaction, I sign off:

Like a moth bumping against a wall

My Asian art teacher in a calligraphy class in Chicago omitted the customary signature at the bottom of a scroll. He preferred instead to record the word image that reflected his state of mind. The technique seemed so right to me that I've used it in my private journal ever since.

As I close the book, my stomach begins to feel slightly queasy. Nerves? The water? Am I in for a bout of "Delhi belly"? I'm reminded of another hapless traveler's experience from a tale Dad told.

Once a Mongol prince led his armies into India over the Khyber Pass. He cut a path across the north and was victorious in every battle until he reached Delhi. There he was overcome with a severe intestinal ailment. His physicians, unable to find a cure, advised him to leave.

"This is a cursed land," the prince muttered from his bed, "unfit for civilized men."

He dragged his banner and his army to the west. He'd barely reached the city limits when the inhabitants streamed out of their houses and danced in the streets, singing their thanks to the gods, joking that their best weapon wasn't a sword but a glass of water.

I thought Dad's story was funny at the time. How ironic it would be if I, too, was defeated by a glass of water.

I gather up the newspaper and my sketchbook and head back toward my room. As I pass through the hallway, I hear a gentle knock on the front door. When I answer it, I find Prem all decked out in a fresh pair of white trousers, a short-sleeve brown-checked shirt, and the same polite smile he wore when he met me at the airport.

"Mrs. Khosla suggested earlier that I check with you, madam." Prem's voice is proper, formal and devoid of warmth, as though he's addressing one of higher station. "To see if you'd like to sightsee this afternoon."

Just as I'm about to tell Prem that I don't feel like a tour, Champa materializes, a saried figure at the edge of my vision, with a cleaning rag dangling in one hand. The moment I turn to look, she vanishes like some trick of the eye.

"Would you wait here a minute?" I ask Prem, pointing at the living room. "I'll get my purse."

"I'll be downstairs. Come when you are ready."

Back in my room, I run a brush through my hair and put on some lipstick, but decide not to change. Young Indian women in big cities wear both pants and dresses, I'm told, and jeans are considered high fashion.

Prem opens the Mercedes door and takes a step back to give me room. I read respect as well as duty in the barely discernible bow from the waist. As I slide into the backseat, I glance at him, but he avoids eye contact.

Within moments we're pulling out of the gravel driveway onto a side street. "Did you have a pleasant morning, madam?" he asks.

My stomach rumbles, but I reply with more enthusiasm than I feel, "Oh, yes, very nice, very nice indeed."

Prem turns left onto the main road, swarming with the traffic I've been hearing all morning. Something in his manner tells me that despite the noise, he's still listening and I feel bursting to talk. "Everyone's friendly and kind, but I don't completely understand how things work here."

Prem nods. "Here, madam, when a woman takes her husband's name, she gets all that goes with it."

"Marry the man, marry the whole family?"

"Quite right, madam. Family's everything to us. It gives us strength and security. But it can also oppress."

In my present queasy state, I find the word "oppress" distressing. On top of that, a lumbering diesel bus beside us belches a cloud of noxious exhaust in through my open window.

"Prem," I croak. "Please stop the car right now. I'm going to be sick."

Almost as if he has anticipated my situation, Prem hands me a tissue packet over the seat. I tighten my throat and, holding a tissue to my mouth, slide over to the door. Prem swings the car around the corner and comes to a stop. I yank the door open and stumble across the sidewalk toward a tall tree with a huge trunk, its base surrounded by a bed of sand. I bend over on its far side.

In a minute I wipe my lips and suck in a gulp of air. Thank God this is a quiet block. There's little going on, and the adjacent lot is vacant. I walk back toward the car with a sour taste in my mouth.

Prem stands there, holding the car door open for me. His eyes and voice both convey a genuine concern. "Are you all right, madam?"

"Yes, much better." I lean against the car, eyes shut, and tilt my face toward the comforting rays of the sun. "Thanks." Then leaning forward, I open my eyes. "And thanks for finding just the right spot."

With a dismissive gesture of his hand Prem motions me to get in. "As I said, madam, I know the city well."

I detect a twinkle in his eyes. I start to laugh, then catch myself. Though he manages to keep a straight face, it's clear that the ice has been broken.

Prem offers me a bottle of water, which I gratefully accept. My stomach now at ease, I settle back into the seat fervently hoping that I won't be a bother.

"Those are ashok trees." Prem points toward a row of slender trees with triangular tops and elongated droopy leaves lining the roadside. "You see a lot of them in the city. They're very popular because they're evergreen. Legend has it that ashok trees were planted back when Delhi was named Indraprastha."

Just beyond, I see an even prettier tree with feathery light leaves. Its long, curving branches fan out like a net thrown into the sky hoping to catch a bird, possibly the greenbeater that's flying about the top. "And that tree?"

"Gulmohar. In the spring it produces beautiful orange-gold flowers, the color of the sky at sunrise. In summer it's shady."

I ask Prem which trees provide the most shelter from the summer sun, and he answers, "Mango trees. When I was six, we lived in the village of Parampur. I must have spent half my time in a mango orchard. My mother would leave me there and go wash clothes by a pond. Farmers working in nearby fields would chant as they planted rice." Though I can only see Prem's finely chiseled profile from the back, his pleasure in the memory is obvious. "I'd play in the shade," Prem continues. "The grass would be soft under my feet, the breeze like a blanket. In season, I'd get ripe fruit as a bonus. I'd hear the rustling of leaves as the fruit fell, like someone saying 'Sh-h-h.' I learned to tell a mango by its color. The deep orange ones with red streaks are the sweetest." He glances back. "You know, not even once did a fruit fall on my head. My mother told me trees love little children and would never harm them."

Prem falls silent, as though embarrassed from having spoken at such length. His story brings back memories of my own childhood in Chicago. My relatives would bring me children's books from India, and I devoured the vividly illustrated tales of kings and queens, Brahmins and battles. But those had been only stories in a book. Prem's recollection makes me wish that I could have been a child in his village and experienced what he described. Much as I've hiked in my adult years, I never felt that trees loved me, that grass welcomed me, that a warm breeze was my comforter. And I've never listened to a farmer's planting song.

We continue to drive. A little farther on, we come to an affluent shopping area.

"This is Khan Market," Prem says, "where the diplomats shop. It's the closest market to the Khosla residence."

I look out at a boutique, bakery, charcuterie, a garden with benches and a waterfall, even a Chinese carry-out.

"Would you like to stop here, madam?" Prem asks. Then seeing me hesitating, he adds, "Or shall I take you home?"

The last thing I want is to face Mrs. Khosla or the maid with a still unsettled stomach. The next to the last thing I want is to flounder around in a bustling shopping mall. "No. I'm enjoying the tour. If you don't mind, will you drive some more?"

Prem nods a yes. He heads down a street of pastel houses with well-kept lawns edged with red sandstone dust. Soon the scenery changes. The sidewalks give way to hard-packed dirt; the streets have open manholes. Laborers, caked head to feet in dust, walk by. The buildings are older. Walls shorn of paint are marred by graffiti or advertisements. Even a fire hydrant has been plastered with the picture of a busty actress in a movie poster. A billboard says, "Every saint has a past, every sinner a future."

Alongside the road I see a huge green plot with a copse of trees, like in Prem's story. "Oh, look, Prem. Can we stop here? I need some fresh air."

He hesitates, then finally agrees, "All right. I'll let you off, then find parking." He pulls over, helps me get out of the car, and drives away.

Despite the presence of litter and weeds, the ground feels warm and solid through my shoes. I hear children at the far end, their shrieks interspersed with shrill scolding voices of their mothers and raucous cries of crows and magpies overhead. One barefoot boy, his face unwashed, runs past me, chased by another. Up ahead there are swings and slides and trees used to play hide-and-seek.

I meander along, following a dirt path toward a grove of trees, idly noticing a piece of orange cloth caught in some brambles, all covered with a yellow film of dust. Two mothers pass by me, staring in my direction and chattering, but not acknowledging me with a nod or a smile. Still, the gentle breeze caresses my cheeks, raising my spirits.

A broad-leafed tree with a huge trunk and an embroidery of branches compels me to take out my sketchpad from my purse. Art is a way of seeing, my very first art teacher taught me. Right now I'm seeing a shimmering green canopy with topaz sunlight peeking through it, perfect for a silhouette sketch. I've barely taken my eyes off the tree when I hear a long, low whistle. Startled, I look toward the sound. Three young men are lounging under the shade of another tree nearby, leering at me. Ignoring them, I continue to examine my tree. One boy yells something in Hindi that strikes me as obscene.

I don't understand the words, but there's no mistaking the message. Does it have to do with my Western manners? My clothes? Because I'm alone? I stare back at them with a narrowed gaze. One of them meets my stare, smirks, and scratches his belly. Another hums a ditty in Hindi, no doubt picked up from some sleazy video.

I stand my ground stubbornly, but I'm breaking out in a sweat. The belly scratcher slowly approaches me. A bolt of fear dashes through my head: he'll grab me, rob me, rape me. They'll find my body in the woods here days later. My mouth is opening to scream, but there is no sound. I can't breathe. I'm so dizzy I'm about to collapse.

All of a sudden the song trails off. The belly scratcher retreats a step. The eye contact is broken.

"I'm right behind you, madam."

I turn to see Prem slowing to a walk. He's slightly out of breath. His eyes, holding concern, are fixed on me. So he saw this incident from a distance and ran to get here. Taking long, deep breaths, I rush toward him. I am drawn to his reassuring presence.

Edging closer, Prem suggests, "I think it's best to leave."

As we hurry back toward the road, I say sardonically, "That was interesting."

"Those are layabouts." The apology in Prem's voice tells me he's embarrassed at the behavior of those boys. "Park Romeos, we call them. They've probably come from a village and picked up bad manners. They can't find a job. So they go to cheap cinemas and harass women. Women in pants, young women alone are especially attractive to them."

My pleasant walk has been cut short and, worse yet, my freedom to move about as I please denied. With clenched fists and a burning face I say, "Prem, I do what I please and go where I please. And it's none of their business what I wear."

Prem keeps pace with me. We're about the same height; our strides match. "In India, madam, freedom takes a different form. You can express your opinion about any subject, worship as you please, hold any political belief. But you don't go wandering around a bad neighborhood, even two kilometers from your own home. Especially if you're a woman."

What a valuable insight I've received on my very first day in this new country. I ask, "Is this type of an incident common here, then?"

"Yes. Certainly in Delhi. Please be careful, madam."

I take a few more deep breaths to relax, but I'm still disconcerted. We've come to a street corner where a musician sitting cross-legged on the sidewalk plays a bamboo flute. His shirt is worn, his skin leathery, but the face is serene with a hint of intensity lurking beneath the surface. A parakeet hops around the rim of a bowl, a half-shell coconut, he has put beside him. We stop to listen to the music, partially drowned out by the noise of passing cars. Still, the melody, the rhythm, the note of contemplation, soothe away the memory of the incident in the park. The sound seems to tell me: Don't take life too seriously; for in the end all is illusion.

Then as I relax, Raj's face flashes into my mind. I've been too wrapped up in myself to think much about him. Where is he and what is he doing? In a way, I'm glad he isn't here. Insulted or not, I have received a crash course on the realities of Indian life which might not have occurred if he were around to shield me. I silently thank him for Prem, who's turned out to be a terrific companion.

Eyes downcast, Prem listens to the music. Sensing my attention has turned to him, he instantly emerges from his reverie. "Are you ready to go?"

The sun is lower in the sky as we walk back toward the car. The street is partially shaded by buildings, more suitable for walking. "That flute player seems so resigned," I tell Prem. "My parents are a lot like that. I sort of sense where it comes from, but to understand it fully, I guess I'll have to know India better."

"I fancy myself a student of India." Prem smiles brilliantly. "But the more I learn, the more mystified I become."

"I guess there's no hope for me, then."

Prem turns to me, his eyes softly lit, and laughs. "But you're an artist, madam. I notice how you look at everything. It's as though your eyes are new and they see beneath the layers. You go straight to the heart—" He cuts himself off and falls silent.

No doubt Prem is possessed of a keen intellect. It's difficult for me to think about him as my social inferior and that his primary duty is to chauffeur me about. He's a friendly soul, my peer in every respect, and I'm delighted to have his company.

We turn off the shady street into another lane still glaring with the afternoon sun. Light bouncing off the shop windows blinds me, while my clothes stick to me like some sea creature with tentacles. I try not to fidget, but the idea of sipping something cool in the shade grows on me like an obsession.

"Would you like some ice cream?" Prem asks. "I know of a place in Connaught where you can refresh yourself."

I flash back on the ice cream vendor beyond the Khosla balcony. "Splendid. I was just thinking the same thing."

Back at the car, Prem rolls down the windows and drapes a towel over the backseat for me. He makes the fifteen-minute drive pleasant by pointing out various landmarks: India Gate, the Parliament, All India Institute of Medical Science and its population clock. We park the car, take a pedestrian underpass, and emerge in the colonnaded arcade of a multistory building fronting the Connaught Circus. My attention is drawn to a clutter of posters haphazardly plastered on one wall: Indira Gandhi exhorting the masses; Michael Jackson, arms akimbo; women workers picking tea leaves at a plantation.

Prem points a few feet ahead, just past a Lee Jeans sign.

"That's Nirula's ice cream parlor. They have a new flavor every month."

"When I was a kid, I used to say fever of the month."

Prem laughs in a genuine and open way. Seemingly he never fails to enjoy the pleasure of each transitory moment, and that endears him to me.

The shop is clean and modern with stand-up counters in the middle and tables by the window. A cross-section of Delhi waits in a long line to the ice cream case. Women decked out in silks, golds, and semiprecious stones; men in suits and dhotis; a bemused Western woman in a long paisley dress, carrying the mandatory Culture Shock travel guide; an alert but atypically camera-less Japanese man in a baseball hat; and of course, many children.

"Just tell me what you want," Prem says, "and I'll order it."

"If you don't mind, I'd like to see what flavors they have."

"Of course," Prem replies. But I can tell from his expression that memsahibs don't usually stand in line.

The line shuffles towards the counter at a pace slow by my Western clock, but no one seems to mind. I take the opportunity to survey the room. An icon of Lord Ganesh hangs on one wall. I've been told businessmen seek blessing from their beloved Hindu elephant deity for their endeavors. I think of Raj. Each Indian has his favorite god, and I wonder which one he prefers.

The clerk's inquiry, "What would you like, madam?" snaps me back. I haven't even begun to consider my options. Hurriedly I look down at the showcase. Next to usual Western flavors like vanilla and chocolate are such local favorites as mango and pistachio, all available with a full complement of toppings. Off to one side is a large container of kulfi. Mother used to make the Indian style ice cream. She'd simmer milk over a low flame until it finally thickened to the consistency of condensed milk and developed a nutty flavor. Sometimes she'd let me stir it. "Always a clockwise motion, Sharmila." Then, as I stood in greedy anticipation, she'd calmly blended in sugar, nuts, and saffron before freezing the mixture. Each waiting minute was exquisite torture. Later as a teenager, I tried to reject everything else Indian, but kulfi always made the cut. Today would be no exception. I say to the clerk proudly, "Kulfi, please."

"Not strawberry?"

The clerk must think I couldn't possibly like kulfi. My eyes follow his to a sign behind the counter proclaiming THIS MONTH'S SPECIAL. The small lettering below spells out politely:

Strawberry, especially for our NRI guests

He's taken me for another Non-Resident Indian who has lost appreciation for her homeland. I'm insulted. Angrily I look up at the clerk, but he's already turned away from me.

"Vanilla for me," Prem calls out, as if in his choice he's trying to make up for my blunder.

Taste-wise it seems, I'm going East while he's heading West. We both hand some rupee notes to the clerk, who plucks the money from Prem's outstretched hand and says with a knowing smile, "Whoever raises his hand higher has the honor of paying."

I thank Prem. He mumbles something about it being on Mrs. Khosla's account. We sit down at a window table. Next to us, the table is occupied by a mother and her two small children. The shy, dark-eyed girl squirms a bit when I smile at them; the boy studies me with a frank curiosity. I lean back in my chair and lick my kulfi, which is nestled in a crispy home-baked cone, savoring the smooth, creamy taste, absorbing the coolness. This is almost as tasty as Mom's.

My mind drifts, and I become lost again in an album of memories. Her large wistful eyes fixed on me, Mom asking how it tastes. Dad scolding me for eating too much sugar as he reaches for his second helping. Mom laughing, so delighted to see us gobbling down her concoction that she's forgotten to serve herself.

This afternoon at Nirula's I'm quite content to sit with Prem, dreaming about Mom and Dad and kulfi while Delhi street life goes by. From my window I can view the raised circular park at the center of Connaught Circus. Two shoeshine boys hustling, a man napping under a tree, several long-stemmed yellow iris nodding to the breeze. Sound of drumbeats, bold and throbbing, shake the air.

I search for the source. A swarm of tall female dancers undulate past the window, swaying to the compelling rhythm. Clad in garishly colored saris and shiny silver arm bracelets, with garlands of hibiscus flowers braided into their hair buns, they weave their way closer, feet stomping, their belled anklets jingling in concert with the drum. Their features are coarse, not at all feminine. One dancer shakes a tambourine; several others join together in singing a lusty tune. Though I'm entranced by this spectacle, a part of me knows something is odd in the way these performers flash their teeth, look lasciviously into people's eyes, and gyrate their hips. I've never known Indian women to behave in such a shameless manner, even in Hindi movies. A crowd gathers in a circle around them. Clapping and cheering, they urge the dancers on, occasionally tossing coins into the wicker baskets placed on the sidewalk, their laughter and ribald comments reflecting both embarrassment and good-natured humor.

I turn to my guide Prem and notice that his face is grave. "Those dancers are *hijras,* eunuchs," he says, his eyes heavy with compassion. "There are no women in the group. Only men dressed as women."

I break out into a laugh, thinking that here in India I must expect the unexpected. "Fooled me."

Prem goes on to say that *hijras* make a living by showing up unannounced at festive occasions—children's birth celebrations, weddings, and anniversaries—where they sing and dance lewdly until paid to leave.

Finishing my kulfi, I ask, "But why outside an ice cream parlor?"

Prem chuckles "Since family planning started, there aren't as many birth celebrations. These people have to make a living."

Sighing, I turn and notice two half-eaten ice cream cones on the next table. The woman and her two children have left quietly. I ask, "Why did the family leave?"

"Oh, there are rumors about *hijras* that frighten mothers of little boys—but don't believe them."

By now the dancers have moved on, the music has faded, and the crowd has melted away. Prem finishes the last of his ice cream. "I'll go get the car," he announces.

On the drive home, Prem begins again. "*Hijras* had their best period in the sixteenth century when they guarded the harem of our Mughal kings. Because they were made eunuchs, they could be trusted around the emperor's women."

For me it's dusty history, but Prem speaks as though it all happened yesterday and he was present. To me he seems both ancient and modern, very much a part of an eternal circle. Being
raised in America, I've always thought of myself as a product of
the twentieth century. Now I realize I've negated parts of myself
where my ancestors dwell.

Prem pulls up at the pinkish red Khosla residence. "The first
day in Delhi is a test," he says.

"Did I pass?"

"With honors, madam."

I thank him and climb out of the car, anticipating the further
tests that will come. No doubt, it'll take me weeks, maybe even
months, to adapt myself to Delhi, to be fully vested here. That is
why these exchanges with Prem, brief, personal, and good-
hearted, are so satisfying.

MORNING light filters in through the window curtains of the Khosla living room, where I sit and relax. My feet are encased in comfortable satin slippers, and the shawl spread over my lap, a thin blue-gray Kashmiri wool, feels soft as cloud cover. Steam from a gold-bordered coffee cup curls up to tickle my forehead. It's a time to reflect on what's happened so far. In three days in India, I've watched the vivid life of Delhi as it swirls around me, wanting to join in but rebuffed and confused when I try.

So this early morning I find particular comfort in my solitude with a cup of coffee. As I take a sip, the rich, earthy taste and tangy bouquet make me wonder whether the secret is in the roasting or the brewing. So far I haven't seen the kitchen. Typical of Hindu households, it's tucked away at the back, pretty much the domain of the cook. I'm not yet family and to set foot in such a private part of the apartment would not be right.

I open my diary sketchbook and with a few pencil strokes draw the shawl, the slippers, and the steaming cup. I jot down a passing thought:

Savoring a familiar pleasure in this far-off land

There, as best as I can, I've captured the moment. I close the book, set it down on the coffee table, and pick up the *Hindustan Times*. On the front page is a story about an Indian women's group attempting to climb Annapurna in the Himalayas. Go for it, ladies, I think, feeling a sense of camaraderie.

I look up at the flip-flop sound of sandals. Neelu rushes through the door, her dark eyes aglow, her reddish-orange *kurta* imparting a blush to her honey-gold skin. "Raj-*bhai* is coming home," she exclaims. "He called last night after you'd gone to bed."

I tingle at the news but try to sound calm. "I missed his call?"

"He's taking you to dinner."

Our first date. A surge of excitement makes me stand, then is followed by an undertow of disappointment. Why didn't someone wake me up? Why didn't Raj call back and ask me to dinner himself? A telegram, even a scribbled message on a piece of paper, would have made me feel special to him.

The next moment I tell myself: Consider Indian social ways, Sharmila. He assumed you'd go. Don't be too quick to judge.

Neelu asks, "Can you guess where he's taking you?"

"McDonald's," I answer with a straight face. "For some Masala McFries."

"No, silly." Neelu giggles. "Dum Pukht, in the Maurya Sheraton Hotel. The place is absolutely beautiful. 'Dum' cooking. Great chow."

I've heard of "dum," literally, "breathed in," a famous cuisine in which ingredients are slowly cooked in a vessel whose lid is sealed with pastry dough to ensure none of the fragrant vapor escapes. Originally a poor man's method of cooking, it was brought to the royal court because of its fine flavor. The method hasn't shown up in the States as yet. Now finally I'll taste it. Just the two of us, in a classy restaurant. Raj is more thoughtful than I would have believed.

"The hotel's not far from the airport," Neelu says. "Raj-bhai'll take a taxi directly there instead of coming all the way home. Prem will pick you up around seven and drop you off. We dine rather late here, as you know."

Again my heart sinks. Raj has made all the arrangements without asking me. It's as though I'm a playing piece on a board.

Head cocked to one side, Neelu asks conspiratorially, "What will you wear?"

"My long black dress," I say without thinking. "I wear it to
the opera and weddings back home."

"Raj-*bhai* likes short skirts or saris."

"My beige silk sari, then. I bought it in Chicago just before
coming here."

Neelu frowns. "Black, gray, and beige tones are drab. Delhi
has too much dust and soot. You need bright, assertive colors."

I think about my limited wardrobe, but there's nothing even
close. In Chicago bright, flashy clothing isn't the norm. Here I'm
trapped in a world of dazzling fabrics and shining gems, an entirely different fashion standard. "Nothing I have will be right,"
I say sadly.

The words are barely out of my mouth when Mrs. Khosla bustles in, the *pallu* of her sari trailing behind her like a silk banner
in a breeze. She says, "I have a surprise for you, Sharmila."

Her voice is still nasal from the cold, but the words carry an
unmistakable note of authority. I glance at a grinning Neelu and
realize her questions may have been to set me up.

"Because this is a special occasion," Mrs. Khosla says, "I'm
going to buy you a sari."

"Oh, no, Mrs. Khosla, you mustn't . . ."

"Of course, I must, child. It's the custom. This nasty flu has
kept me from shopping, but I've arranged with M. L. and Sons
to send over a selection of saris. I've been buying from them for
years. You go through the pile and choose one you like." She
turns to Neelu. "I had Mohan put them in your room, *beti*."

Beti, dear girl. My mother used to call me *beti* also.

"Oh, and if you don't like any of them, Sharmila, they'd be
happy to deliver more. Delhi is the clothing capital of India, you
know. There will be plenty of saris to suit you."

Back home, the last thing I wanted to wear was a sari. During
Indian festivals in Chicago, I had no choice but to drape one of
my mother's slippery silks around me. Sooner or later, the sari
would slide off and drag on the ground, leaving me clutching for
it while I tripped over the long petticoat underneath. It was awkward and claustrophobic for me, but not for my mother or her
friends.

Over the years I have come to learn that a sari means more to
an Indian woman than just a way to cover her body. It's a work
of art, a treasured possession, almost a language through which

she communicates. She veils her face with a corner of her sari when she blushes, tugs the folds on her shoulder when feeling demure, lets her *pallu* spread out like a fan when in a flirtatious mood. Indian women compare saris, talk endlessly about the color, fabric, and design as though the garb were a vehicle of friendship. This gift may be Mrs. Khosla's way of letting me into her family's female circle.

"Thank you so much," I say, struggling to be brave. "It's a wonderful gift."

"And, oh, they've sent some ready-made dresses, too," Mrs. Khosla says reassuringly at the door. "The styles here are different from what you're used to. But with minor alterations they'll probably fit."

"Come, Sharmila." Excited, Neelu grabs my arm. "Let's try them on."

Neelu's room is bright and cheery, with a large window facing east. On the bed lies a huge bundle of clothing, wrapped in white paper and bound by a cord. Next to it is a nightstand arrayed with a stack of movie magazines, candles, and a box of Choco-Swiss truffles. Neelu is much neater than I was as a girl. "You have a nice room, Neelu."

She turns to the family photos on top of a mahogany dresser topped by a large mirror and points at a brocade-framed picture that has turned sepia with age. "My grandparents," she says.

I can barely discern the benevolent expression on their faces. Next to them stands a snapshot of Mr. and Mrs. Khosla with a much younger Neelu between them. No one is smiling and the camera angle isn't flattering, but the picture evokes the sentimental feeling that comes only with the passage of years.

Neelu points at a portrait of Raj. A confident boy looks straight into the lens. "Oh, look, that's Raj-*bhai* when he was little."

My eyes gravitate to a wood-framed picture of a grown Raj and a woman in front of an American campus building.

"That's him at Columbia University," Neelu says, "with his old girlfriend Helen Trillen. He called her Helen of Troy—he'd always been fascinated by that historical figure. The whole campus called her Helen of Troy."

The woman occupies a larger part of the photo with Raj relegated to a spot in the background. In my mind Helen's a 3B—big, beautiful, and bossy.

"Raj-bhai was in a bit over his head and got hurt," Neelu goes on. "Later Ma told me she hadn't approved of their relationship. She was glad when he came home alone."

The Khoslas had made no mention of Helen of Troy during the marriage negotiations. She wasn't part of the background on Raj. A surge of jealousy swells within me. But then, who hasn't had a romance in college? Come to think of it, we didn't discuss my romances, either.

"Raj-bhai still gets an occasional letter from Helen of Troy."

He does? I make a quick calculation. Raj has been back in India nearly six years, and so they've been separated for a long time. Still, why does this bit of information bother me?

Neelu catches herself. "I'm sorry, Sharmila. I didn't mean to let out family secrets. Ma says I have a big mouth."

I want to pump Neelu even more. "Big mouth means a big smile," I offer encouragingly.

"I can't seem to help it, Sharmila. Secrets pile up inside me like laundry until I can't stand them any longer and just have to get them out."

"Don't apologize, Neelu. There's so much I want to know about this family. I hope you won't feel you have to hide things from me."

"Not at all. I already consider you a Khosla. We can—we will have a lot of fun together, Sharmila. You can tell me all about the States. And I can tell you a lot more about our family."

For the first time I feel I have an ally. Maybe even a little sister.

My gaze moves on to a silver-framed studio photo in color, an eight by ten of Raj and another woman, their shoulders touching. Raj fairly glows, and so does his companion, in a moss green Kanjivaram silk and bunned hair. Though she isn't a classic beauty—her nose is prominent, her mouth a little too wide—her picture conveys a refinement, an inner strength, a loving disposition. I suspect she's someone to whom a man might come home early. Before I can catch myself, I reach out and pick up the photograph.

"That's Raj and Roopa after their wedding."

Even their names go together. My attention is so focused on the handsome couple that I barely notice that Neelu's cheery voice has become choked.

"I liked Roopa very much. She was like an older sister. And Ma liked her, too. She'd known her for a number of years before Raj married her." Neelu pauses, uncertain whether to continue. "Hope you don't mind my talking about her."

"Not at all" I study Roopa's face. There's intelligence in those lively eyes, even though her slightly lowered chin indicates humility. "I'd like to know more about her."

"She had a Ph.D. in economics, but you'd never know. She was so modest. And she could keep Raj under control. He's always been loose with money. Spend, spend, spend all the time. After they were married, he stopped shopping. Now that she's gone, he's gone back to his old habits, when he should be clearing up my father's debts."

I raise my eyebrows. Family finances is a delicate subject, worthy of grave attention, and Neelu's revelation concerns me. But another matter is even more important. I ask, "What happened to Roopa?"

A brief silence is followed by a voice in a downturn curve. "She died, in an accident." Neelu's eyes scan my face for a reaction for a mere second.

I'd heard that Raj was widowed and sympathized with his situation, but hadn't given the subject much thought. Now with his dead wife's picture in my hand, I ask myself: How likely is that? She looks healthy, happy, and too much in love to die. And why hadn't anyone told me about this earlier? I turn a questioning gaze at Neelu, but am met by mountain-like silence.

A moment later Neelu looks up, takes the photo from my hand, and puts it back on the dresser. With a long sigh, she turns to the bundle on the bed. It's clear that the subject of Roopa is closed. A chill runs through me. Why all the mystery surrounding her death? I must ask my relatives, but I'll have to be circumspect to avoid arousing suspicion. I'll have to seek a less direct path of inquiry into the subject.

Neelu unties the knot and begins to separate the saris. The colors alone seem to make the room brighter, larger, and more elegant. I try to push Roopa out of my mind as I lower myself onto the edge of the bed and let my eyes feast on the fabrics spread before me.

"What do you think, Sharmila?"

"I'm dazzled. I'm more used to seeing such shades on a painter's palette."

"We Indians adore color. I even wrote an essay on the subject for a class homework assignment. Let me see if I can remember . . ." Neelu recites, " 'Our love of color goes all the way back to the times when the earth was an emerald valley, the sky a blue bowl, the ocean a cobalt carpet.' "

"Words a painter might use," I observe quietly, then bend to inspect a field of bright pinks, greens, oranges, and blues along with mixed shades I can't name, many embroidered with gold or silver thread. The hues are so vivid they seem like a thousand rainbows, the fabrics so smooth that I could go on stroking them forever, the designs so intricate that they set my head spinning.

"Let's see how this one looks on you." Neelu's voice pulls me back to the real world. She holds a high-voltage yellow sari under my chin, then takes a pace back to examine the effect. "This is perfect for your skin tone."

I contemplate my reflection in the mirror with elation. Running my fingers across the fabric, I find it to be cool and soothing to my skin. I realize a sari is a perfect garb here in sensuous India. My original discomfort at wearing one vanishes. "Mmmm."

"Here's the matching *choli*." Neelu hands me a coordinated sleeveless blouse, similar to a halter top, to be worn underneath the sari. "Would you like to see some dresses now? In case you're more comfortable in them?"

"No, no," I protest. "This is perfect."

"I know my brother," Neelu says mischievously. "He'll like it. May I do your makeup?"

"I hardly ever use makeup, only lipstick."

"That's fine for what you're wearing"—she eyes my jeans and blouse—"but a sari needs more. Besides, the restaurant walls are white, and the waiters wear beige uniforms. With no makeup you'll blend into the background. A little foundation on your skin, a little *kajal* around your eyes, a dab of rouge on your cheeks will be just beautiful."

The Khoslas have certainly moved me around on this matter. I come to the conclusion that it's best to submit. "I put myself in your hands, Neelu."

"Let's start around five. That'll give us plenty of time."

I head back to my room and stretch out on the bed with Tagore's *Gitanjali*. The poetic images of waves, canoes, and seashells lull me into a dreamy mood. Soon I slip into a fantasy world. The sixteenth century, the golden era of Mughal emperors. I am a princess, strolling through a formal garden, the hem of my lavish *salwar* gathering up beads of morning dew as it brushes the new grass. My prince is waiting just across a pond of lily pads, his face hidden in shadow.

I wake up from my trance. The image of Roopa materializes and pecks at my consciousness like a lost lonely bird.

A T a few minutes before five I step into Neelu's room, ready for a makeup session but unsure about surrendering control over my appearance. My face is scrubbed clean and my hair is up. I've done my own hair since the time I was twelve. Not even my mother was allowed to touch it.

Neelu has changed into a sari of alternating blue and green threads. The marriage of the two hues produces an opulent shade that shimmers in the afternoon light. She looks older, more professional as she says, "Sit here, Sharmila." Her eyes twinkling, she moves to a side table covered with a vast assortment of toiletries, including Nivea cream, Pond's Talcum Powder, and Biotique Nail Colors. She fusses over the collection and tells me, "I love working with makeup."

Stifling my apprehension, I settle myself on a stool before the mirror, hearing the flute-like song of a bird through the window. Neelu applies foundation on my face, dusts it with a power puff, and brushes peach across my cheeks in a teardrop shape, accentuating my cheekbones. I watch the girl's reflection. She works with a relaxed, economical motion, frequently stepping back to survey the result, an artist before her canvas. My resistance begins to dissolve.

"You definitely have an artistic sense, Neelu. Are you interested in art?"

"Not exactly. My secret wish is to be a makeup artist."

"Why is it a secret?"

"Because of Ma. She says it's a low-class job. She wants me to be a doctor or an engineer, or go into business like my brother. At the very least, she wants me to get a Ph.D. in mathematics and teach college."

"Come to think of it, that's what my mother used to tell me. I didn't listen, of course. I studied art."

Busy lining my lower eyelids with kohl, Neelu asks, "So, what did you do in Chicago?"

"I did advertising artwork for a department store. It's not as much money as a doctor or an engineer merits, but I still made a good living doing what I love to do. In the evening I teach aerobics for fun and to stay in shape."

"Raj told me you go to California often."

"Since I work freelance, I like to take time off whenever I finish a big project. I go to my cabin just outside Bishop, a small town in the Sierra foothills. In the morning when I wake up and look out of my bedroom window, all I can see are mountains and pine trees and birds. Right now the peaks are topped with snow. My windows are glazed with ice. Sunlight burns on them."

"Are there people?"

"About four thousand residents."

"Quite a contrast to Delhi."

"If I have my way, Raj and I will spend a month there every year, hiking, fishing and boating, and communing with nature."

"I wish I could be like you, Sharmila."

"I hope your mother won't think I'm ruining you."

"Things have changed here, too." Neelu draws coral lipstick across my lips. "Vocational training is becoming popular as an alternative to going to college. Several of my high school friends have gone that route. One of them is taking a filmmaking course. Another is studying hotel management. But our parents resist hard, especially my mother. I wish she could understand our generation." A deep sigh. "Already I like having you in the family, Sharmila. You're someone I can really talk to without worrying about being scolded."

Warmed by Neelu's compliment, I survey my decorated self in the mirror. My eyes, always my best feature, have been emphasized. Gone is the small but annoying scar on my left cheek. My lips are richly colored and full.

Champa slips in, bearing glasses of a frothy white beverage I recognize as lassi. It looks refreshing, but I'm suspicious of any food or drink Champa prepares for me. She gave me impure water the day I arrived, and I was sick from it. She glances at Neelu but ignores me. Setting the tray down, she walks off, leaving me wondering again why she's still so hostile. Neelu explains that this particular rendition of lassi, a blend of yogurt, ice, and flavorings of toasted black mustard seeds, is our cook Mohan's specialty. I trust him and so empty the glass.

Before long, Neelu's expert hands are wrapping the blazing yellow sari around me. She fixes it in place on my left shoulder using a gold brooch glittering with rubies. "This will keep the pleated train in the back in place. You won't have to worry about your *pallu* falling all over the table." Then stepping away from the mirror, she says, "Now it's time for a demonstration. Walk slowly like this." She glides smoothly toward me.

I notice Neelu is moving mostly from the knees down in small steps adapted to the tightly wrapped sari. The message: Forget power walking. I imitate her low-to-the-ground shuffle and, after a few missteps, begin to get the hang of sari walking. My movements aren't as constricted as I thought they would be. But neither can I be in any hurry, I realize. "I hope I won't be chased by a mad bull."

Soon I'm pacing smoothly about the room. The sari is enfolding me lightly but securely, almost like a tailored suit. The silk fabric clings to my body, rewarding every motion with a gentle caress. For the first time in my life I feel at one with my clothing.

"We aren't quite finished yet." Neelu opens a tiny plastic box theatrically. "I have to find a matching *bindi*. You know about *bindis*, don't you?"

Of course, I'm familiar with the *bindi*, the dot of color that decorates the forehead of Indian women. Originally it was a red smudge of vermilion, called *sindoor*, worn only by married women. Now *bindi* comes in a variety of colors, shapes, and designs, and has become fashionable among unmarried women as well. To Neelu I say, "There must be a whole little *bindi* industry out there somewhere."

Neelu laughs, tells me how her best friend jazzes up her *bindi* with tiny, artificial gems, then holds up one with a miniature clover leaf pattern in teal blue, the exact color of my sari border. Centering it between my eyebrows, she says, "Perfect, don't you think?"

I nod in admiration of her handiwork.

"On your wedding day, Sharmila, you'll have red and white *bindi* painted all around your eyes."

This makeup lesson, especially the *bindi* part, has turned out to be fun. "I never paid much attention to my forehead before, Neelu. Now it seems it has been bare."

"Your neck is bare, too." Mrs. Khosla's voice shatters the warm, intimate mood. She comes closer and assesses me with a critic's eye.

"How do you like her makeup, Ma?"

"Very nice, Neelu. That yellow is lovely on Sharmila." Mrs. Khosla turns to leave. "I'll be back in a minute."

Within a few minutes, she returns with a steel jewelry case. She lifts a finely tooled choker and dangles it before me. "What do you think of this one?"

I survey the ornament in awe. Wide as a shirt collar, its delicate design curves in gold lotus blossoms with clusters of tiny sapphires at the center. I tell her, "It's magnificent."

Before I can finish, Mrs. Khosla has slipped it around my neck, obscuring the thin gold necklace, a treasured gift from my parents. She checks me up and down. I think I detect the barest hint of satisfaction on her face, a look reserved for those rare occasions when an offspring lives up to her exacting standards. But it's gone so fast I can't be sure. In its place is the armor she has worn since I arrived here: serene, dignified, and impenetrable.

Neelu says, "That necklace really completes the picture, Ma."

Mrs. Khosla turns. "I'm going to go rest now and leave you two to finish your preparations."

"Thank you so much for this beautiful sari, Mrs. Khosla," I say, rising. "And for letting me borrow this gorgeous necklace. Very kind of you."

"You must not mention it."

I notice Mrs. Khosla cringing a bit. How could I not remember that Indians, especially the older generation, show gratitude by sentiment, rarely by explicit words of thanks? My gushing must have overwhelmed her.

I hear her saying at the door, "Enjoy yourself tonight, Sharmila."

"This necklace was especially commissioned for Ma when she was young," Neelu whispers. "The jeweler inscribed her name on the back."

I feel the weight, both in gold and in memory, and inspect the ornament's reflection in the mirror. Is it my imagination or is my skin glowing with the luster of the piece?

"Last but not least." Neelu pulls a drawer open and picks up a perfume bottle. "*Attar.* For an occasion like this you have to wear a scent. Ma says in the old days, there used to be a scent for every season, every mood, and every personality type. For you I've chosen a clear, floral smell."

I sniff. The scent, reminiscent of jasmine, is perfect with my outfit. This girl is a full-fledged makeup consultant. "Already you know me, Neelu."

She dabs the perfume on my wrists and temples while I gaze at my reflection. Sure enough, the mirror shows a woman much more gracious, stylish, and less apprehensive. Yet there's something faintly disquieting in the face before me. Suddenly it dawns on me. My God, I look like Roopa. I notice Neelu, too, is staring at the finished result with uneasiness.

As soon as she catches my eye in the mirror, she breaks the trance by saying, "It's almost time. Have fun, Sharmila, then hurry back and tell me all about it."

WAITING for Prem to pick me up, I pace the Kashimiri living room rug, tracing the swirling designs on the background of maroon. What will I say to Raj at dinner? How will I act? Maybe I'm better off winging it. Again I contemplate the painting of the Mughal princess hanging on the west wall—feminine and romantic with a touch of vulnerability. When I turn back, Prem is at the door.

I see a brief flash of wonder in my friend's eyes and his smile. The next moment he slips into his usual deferential *namaste.* Bent slightly forward from the waist, he motions with one hand toward the staircase, and I follow him down the pink sandstone stairs like some sort of princess. How softly Prem walks, I notice, for such a solid man. He ushers me into the car without a look in my direction.

Before long we're on the main road, each of us deep in our private thoughts. I'm wishing Prem wasn't quite so distant on the cusp of what promises to be a significant evening for me. During our time together, I've had the feeling that he's cognizant of the difficult situation I am in and is ready to help. He must simply be distracted by the urgency of the traffic. The buses are so loaded with passengers, they tip to one side. An oncoming taxi swerves into our lane without warning to avoid a cyclist. I grip the door handle, white-knuckled and rigid with fear. Prem veers away at the last possible moment. Relieved, I break into a laugh. "That was close."

Prem nods but doesn't respond further, giving me the notion that he must concentrate on his driving. Feeling abandoned, I stare out the window. We're in a neighborhood of mansions with a smug, exclusive look. Evening is settling in. Enormous trees cast intimidating shadows. We turn into the driveway of an imposing white building surrounded by lavishly landscaped grounds. A sign says MAURYA SHERATON HOTEL.

We pull up to the covered entrance, and Prem comes around, lips set firmly in a straight line. He opens the car door and mumbles a few words, wishing me a pleasant dinner. I'm very happy to escape his cold formality. My eyes rest for a moment on a circular flower patch blooming with golden mums and red salvias.

I go up the walk toward the entrance. The heavy, intricately carved lobby door and its gleaming brass handle seem to belong in a museum gallery. A uniformed doorman bows from the waist and opens the door. His eyes are expressionless, looking past me as if I were invisible.

Even in the States I wouldn't feel comfortable entering a restaurant this grand when unescorted. Following a sign, I pass through the lobby, its high, vaulted ceiling making me feel small, and down a side arcade of fancy jewelry shops. The walk is long, and I worry about the front pleats of my sari coming unfolded any minute. At the end of the arcade I descend a wide, curving staircase to the Dum Pukht restaurant.

At the threshold I pause and take a few breaths. Vivacious faces, daring aromas, and audible murmurs of appreciation all announce this as a place for serious dining. It must be pricey as well. The tables are occupied by svelte bodies draped in fine silks, arms and necks adorned with glimmering gold. Neelu was right in advising me to wear brightly colored clothing. The room is pale, the walls creamy white and smooth and hung with pale gray-gold tapestries.

A craggy-faced maître d' in a beige uniform greets me with an easy manner. His "Good evening, madam" has many coats of polish with a small grain of suspicion tucked away beneath. "Are you joining a party?"

"Yes, Raj Khosla's . . ."

"But of course." The tone is pleasant and warm now. "This way, please." Stepping daintily in my flaming sari, I follow him across the room. A few eyes fall on me. Excitement bunches in my throat at the thought that the evening is finally beginning. As we approach a secluded table by the wall, a man stands up in a single joyful motion. He's immaculate in a navy suit and white shirt, his high cheekbones highlighted by the muted light. A faint aroma of cologne emanates from him. "Sharmila!"

I extend a hand eagerly. "Raj!"

He takes my hand and squeezes it affectionately. A hint of fatigue in the corners of his eyes makes him seem more vulnerable and appealing. His intense gaze subdues the surrounding chatter, erases the presence of the waiter, and reduces my oxygen supply.

"Please, Sharmila, have a seat."

Too stiffly I lower myself into a brocaded and gilded chair, snagging the tablecloth with my hand and tipping over his glass, which rolls back and forth. A few drops of clear liquid spill on the starched beige tablecloth, leaving a shimmer of bubbles. Fortunately, the glass was almost empty.

Great start, Sharmila. I feel myself redden as I reach for a napkin. "I'm awfully sorry."

"Please, not to worry." Raj raises his chin slightly, a subtle yet imperious motion that brings a waiter hurrying over to dab the tablecloth dry. The man disappears, only to reappear a moment later bearing a brown beer bottle and a frosted silver mug on a tray. Raj touches the beer, ascertains it is properly chilled, gives his approval—*"Theek hai"*—and the waiter pours. The effervescent froth gives off a soothing fizzy sound.

The waiter turns to me and asks if I'd like something to drink. Seeing an Indian woman in the next table nursing a cocktail, I order a beer. I settle back in my chair carefully, resolved to keep my hands and feet clear of the table for the rest of the night.

"Beautiful sari, a perfect choice." Raj regards me with a connoisseur's eye above maroon dahlias that overflow a vase in the middle of the table. Just as I am glowing from the compliment, his face darkens a bit. Did he notice my resemblance to Roopa? He catches himself, blinks, and says, "Less than a week here and already somehow you've changed."

"A gift from Ma-ji." The word "Ma-ji" rolls from my lips, surprising me with its spontaneity.

Raj smiles—a warm, knowing smile. "She thinks of every-thing." Then leaning forward, in a barely audible tone above the buzz of conversation, he asks, "Did you miss me?"

The intimacy in his voice catches me off guard. My eyes must have given me away. "Yes, oh yes. Glad you weren't away any longer than this," I can't help blurting out. Then I gain a little more control: "It's so good to have you back."

"Did you manage to see the sights?"

"I've seen quite a bit, actually."

"How do you like Delhi?"

I'm thinking: the city's overpopulated, the traffic's impossi-ble, the air unbreathable; I was sick the very day I arrived. "It's quite a place," I hear myself saying in a strange voice. "While I can't exactly say I like everything, it definitely has its good points."

"I can imagine how chaotic India must seem to an outsider. Our streets are mobbed, and some people will tell you Delhi is rude. But step inside a house in any neighborhood and you'll find it clean, well kept, and peaceful. A sanctuary." The shine in Raj's eyes is testimony to the pride and love he feels for his city. "When I came back from the States, I had a hard time getting ad-justed myself. The noise and congestion drove me crazy. I almost caught a plane back to New York. Now I'm glad I didn't. Once I was situated, things worked out much better for me here. Pollu-tion and all, I love Delhi."

Raj picks up the menu with long, slender fingers. Oh, how I'd like to play with them. "Once you've lived here for a while and meet some people, you'll see what an interesting place it is," he says. "Writers, artists, filmmakers from all over India buzz around Delhi. This is where things happen."

I take a sip of my beer, pop a flake of crispy papad into my mouth, and turn my attention to the menu. Hand-written in ele-gant blue letters on a beige silk cloth, it's a minor work of art in itself. The long list of exotic dishes with unfamiliar names in-trigues me. My mother never prepared delicacies like these at home.

"Don't expect Mughlai food here," Raj says. "This restaurant specializes in *dum* cooking. Have you heard about it?"

"Only by name."

"Ah well, you see, it originated in the royal kitchens of Lucknow. You might call it a low-tech version of pressure cooking. The recipes have been handed down through generations of chefs. I've tried all the items on the menu. I used to be a regular here."

"It would take me at least a year to try it all." I gaze up to find a "Do Not Disturb" sign over Raj's face for the second time. I wonder what I've done wrong.

It occurs to me that Raj must have dined here with Roopa, perhaps at this very table. Roopa in a moss green Kanjivaram sari, as I remember from her picture, her hair gathered in a bun. Roopa snatched from Raj in the sunny days of their love. I can't help but wonder why Raj invited me here.

My imagination is getting out of hand. Better to concentrate on the menu. I decide to play it safe and order my favorite vegetable—the old, reliable potato. "Is the *alu-dum* good?" I ask.

"The cook here does everything well *except* the potato," Raj says with a disarming wink.

Suddenly I reach a decision about the evening. I close my menu and say "Would you mind ordering for me? I think I'll eat a lot better if you do."

Raj smiles in approval, signals the waiter, and speaks to him at length in Hindi. I love to listen to the sounds of this language, sixteen vowels and thirty-six consonants—guttural, resonant, and exuberant, blending in a vibrant staccato rhythm that calls into play every expression of the lips and tongue. The waiter passes me a glance from time to time. His meaning is clear: another foreigner with scant knowledge of this haute cuisine. You just wait, I think defiantly. I'll be an expert sooner than you think.

Raj takes a swallow of his beer and chuckles. "Hope you've managed to catch up on your sleep in my absence. When I'm in the house, there isn't much peace and quiet. Ma-ji says the party starts the minute I come in the door. She can hear my voice from one end of the flat to the other. You'll see. I'll be around the next few days."

"You mean you're leaving again?"

"Unfortunately, yes, but not for long. On Wednesday I'm making a quick trip to Bangalore, an air dash, my boss calls it." Raj leans forward, lowers his voice, and mentions the name of a highly confidential Singapore client with whom he intends to finalize a major contract. "But here's my promise, Sharmila." His dark eyes catch mine and hold them captive. "I'll take an entire month off after our wedding. We'll go to South India. That's the best part of our country to visit in the winter."

"Oh, Raj, how fun. Do you know I've always wanted to go there? My maternal great-grandfather was posted in South India for a few years. My grandmother told me about a small village where her family had a vacation home. Coconut palm trees and rice paddies all around. She used to wander around the village barefoot. People were kind to her. They welcomed her to their homes and gave fruits and candy. She told me in that village she knew the spirit of India."

"It's true, Sharmila, the southern states are more purely Indian. Historically, the invaders came from the north and the west. They took the north and exhausted themselves before they got to the south. So the north became a hodgepodge of influences, but the south retains its original character."

"Grandmother used to say that everywhere you looked was green, the temples reached the sky, and the golden beaches went on forever."

"And fish this large." Eyes dancing, Raj spreads his arms wide. I picture myself enfolded in those solid, powerful arms as a background drone of a sitar reaches my ears. "There's a place called Kodaikanal I especially want to take you to. It's a lovely resort tucked away in a mountain valley, famous for a gorgeous waterfall called Silver Cascade Falls. The air is so clean, I can't breathe enough of it. I like to watch the white, foamy water tumbling down over the rocks. You can't hear anything, not even your own thoughts, just the water. That'll be the first stop on our honeymoon," he says matter-of-factly. That word, "honeymoon," gives me goose bumps. "After that, we can visit your grandmother's village."

As Raj continues to chat about South India, however, my surge of excitement is deflated by a nagging worry. I see he's trying hard to please me, but an element seems to be missing. I wonder how much of his heart was buried with his first wife's ashes. I may get only leftover time, attention, and affection, never the whole person. When this initial attraction wears off, will there be enough to sustain us in the years ahead? Will we end up in a marriage perfect in outward appearances, but insipid, maybe even dead, inside?

My concerns dissolve in a cloud of fragrant aromas as two waiters arrive with our food. They set their gigantic tray on a stand and serve our meal on fine blue-rimmed china. I direct my attention to the banquet before me.

"That's harra kebab, made with spinach and paneer." Raj points at an appetizing-looking greenish patty perched atop a flaky flat bread. "It's a specialty. And that pretty yellow sauce is made with arhar dahl, an expensive legume. That mutton korma in the bowl has been simmered for hours with a cook's special blend of spices. A most secret blend."

My eyes travel to the glistening white pyramid of rice flecked with black cardamoms, almond halves, and plump golden raisins, steaming with a nutty scent. Raj remarks, "The rice is the finest aged basmati from Dehra Dun in the Himalayan foothills."

Since I grew up in an Indian household, rice has been a staple of my diet. That's what I take first. After a few bites I conclude that I've never tasted rice as fragrant and delicate as this. All I can manage in response to Raj's expectant look is, "Mmmm."

"I wanted to bring you here to celebrate," Raj says over a spoonful of rice. "I know how hard it must have been for you to accept an arranged marriage. The notion would be unthinkable for most Americans, even for a second-generation Indian like yourself. Your mother wrote to us that you needed persuading, which I find quite understandable. Can I ask you what finally made up your mind?"

I put the fork down and sip from my beer, gathering my thoughts. "Your picture showed a handsome face and kind eyes, and your handwriting showed strength of character. The sentiments in your letter expressed your need for me, and I thought, I could love this man."

I catch a fleeting glimpse of vulnerability in Raj's eyes before he lowers them. After a moment he looks up at me with shining eyes, "You don't know how happy that makes me feel, Sharmila. I'm very lucky. You have real character yourself." His eyes take in my whole face as he reaches across the table and touches my hand. "You know, we can have the best of both worlds. I understand the values you were raised with—I've lived in the States. You're independent, but you see value in our ways as well. You're doing your best to adapt here. It was brave of you, first even considering me from a distance and then agreeing to an arranged marriage. You must have had your own unique way of arriving at the final decision."

"My mother has lived in the States for thirty-two years. She still believes that an arranged marriage works out in the long run. She impressed on me that when two families decide jointly, there's a greater chance of the union lasting. The couple can count on a tremendous amount of support from both sides. Also, you're more likely to accept each other's shortcomings. You think, the wise elders have arranged this, the astrologers have been consulted, and the stars agree. So it must be right. I was born in Chicago, so it took me a long time to realize that Mother had a point." My laugh is actually a pause I need. "I kept going over the pros and cons in my mind, but still couldn't come to a conclusion. Then I went to spend a week at my hideaway in the Sierras to give myself plenty of time to think things over."

"How lovely to have such an option," Raj says.

"It was in the town of Bishop in California that the idea began to make sense to me. I was sitting on the bank of a pond one afternoon. A flock of geese came to the shore. One of them opened its beak and complained. The others gathered around, puffed their wings, listened. Then all became quiet. It was like the answer hung in the air and they simply tuned in to it. A few minutes later, they waddled back to the pond and floated away as a unit, in perfect symmetry. You know, I sat there listening to the wind, the trees, the water. I was just being receptive, not struggling for an answer. Then I felt a sense of harmony. I realized that being one of a supportive group was better than always trying to go it alone. I knew there would be sacrifices to be made. I'd have to give up some of my freedom. But I must have touched the tail of truth's coat. I knew what to do."

Raj's face is smooth and serious. "Oh, that I could express myself as beautifully. In business I look at each situation in concrete terms, as you might guess—profit and loss." He laughs, more to relieve tension, I guess, than from amusement. "Ma-ji and our relatives have been pestering me to get married. I refused candidate after candidate for one reason or another. When the proposal from your mother came, I wasn't so analytical. Perhaps intuition drew me to it. You see, Sharmila, this is a huge step for me, too, but I was able to make up my mind fairly quickly. I surprised everyone in the family."

He's implying bigger forces are at work here, that a cosmic current has pulled us together. I take a breath and busy myself with the meal, particularly the inviting white cauliflower florets cooked with red tomato bits, raising my head every now and then to glance at Raj. There is sensuality in the way he spears a piece of mutton with his fork.

"*Bilkul* perfect," Raj says, nodding. He chews leisurely, with delight, as though making a personal acquaintance with the subtle tastes. This earthy quality of my fiancé is as delicious to me as the taste of the food.

Minutes after we finish, the waiter appears and sets two silver bowls on the table. I inhale the rich smell of thickened milk and look up at Raj.

"I bet you've never had chhenar payesh," he says. "It's their best dessert, a Bengali classic that takes hours to prepare. Even in Bengal they don't make it anymore."

I gaze down at the bowl. Tiny dumplings made of homemade farmer's cheese float in a base of velvety cream sauce, speckled with green pistachio slivers. I lift a spoonful to my mouth and am overwhelmed by a rush of delight. Raj doesn't touch his. He seems to take pleasure at just watching my lips plump up by the taste.

"I have something else in mind that I want to talk about. . . ." His dark eyes have a late evening softness. "I know I am gone a lot. But I want you to know I think of you constantly. And I have a surprise. . . . Sharmila, I'm buying a bungalow just for us."

"A bungalow?"

"In Chanakypuri, in the Nehru Park area. Wouldn't you rather have your own home? Just the two of us. We'd be able to exercise in the park."

I pick up my water glass and sip, delighted by this good news. I had expected to live with my mother-in-law for the next few years. This means we'll have a home done according to our tastes, a domain where we'll feel free, days organized the way we want. Our love for each other will grow and fill the space, not the dutiful, constricted arranged-marriage kind, but one shaped by our personal standards.

Then too, the idea of making love with my husband one room away from my mother-in-law has been decidedly unappealing. Raj has cleverly figured that having our own bungalow is the best of all situations. Adjusting to my new life here will be much easier.

"Oh, Raj, what a wonderful surprise. I'm so happy. Tell me more about it."

He is eager to do so. "The bungalow has three bedrooms, a veranda, a balcony, and a servant's cottage. There are two huge trees on the grounds—a tamarind and a *jamun*. If you take the stairs to the rooftop, you are able to touch the tamarind branches. And you'll love the black *jamun* fruits that come during the monsoon season. There are also rose bushes, a marigold bed, and a kitchen garden."

Raj sounds so sure about this venture that I begin to wonder if there's not a catch somewhere. I hear Neelu's words: Raj spends, spends, spends. Will this latest acquisition put him in debt? "The bungalow must cost a fortune," I attempt a little awkwardly. "I hear Bombay has some of the highest real estate prices in the world. Delhi can't be too far behind."

"Why else do I work?" Raj says, brushing off the objection, "if not so my family could be comfortable?"

"What about Ma-ji?"

"I still have to convince her." Raj's voice, for the first time, is edged with a faint uncertainty. I'm sure he realizes the formidable obstacle his mother represents. "But that won't be difficult. Trust me, Sharmila. More and more children are leaving home and finding their own housing after they get married."

"When do I get to see the place?"

"It won't be long. As soon as the workers finish remodelling the bathrooms. I'm having them done in Western style."

I begin to speak but stop myself. It would be nice to be consulted on room colors and a few other details. But now that I'm beginning to get to know Raj, I'm not surprised. He automatically assumes that I will be pleased with whatever he chooses.

The waiter returns with a small plate of fennel seeds. Raj nods in thanks and launches into an explanation of the digestive and breath-freshening properties of the spice.

An intense anise flavor explodes on my palate. I chew in a relaxed manner while Raj settles the bill. I'm not as drowsy as I'd expect to be after such a sumptuous repast. In fact, I'm keen and alert.

Raj has orchestrated the evening beautifully, entertaining me in a pleasantly elegant yet low-key manner. We're more comfortable with each other, though he's allowed me only a glimpse of a complex personality. It's frustrating to one accustomed to American openness, where in a date or two, you learn about a person's entire past and present. With Raj, however, it's going to be different, for although he exudes charm and accessibility, there is territory beneath the surface where no trespassing is allowed. In any other circumstances, getting a full profile of this man would be an artistic challenge. With the wedding date approaching, it's an urgent necessity.

Raj consults his watch. "It's almost ten. You're great company, Sharmila. I didn't even notice." Sneaking a look at the door, he adds, "I'm sure Prem has had his dinner by now. He was supposed to have been back at nine. He's probably waiting outside."

As I rise, I check the condition of my sari. What a wonder! The *pallu* and the pleats have remained in place, smooth and unwrinkled. The only wrinkle, I conclude after the dinner, is in my mind.

Minutes later, Raj and I slide in the backseat like a royal pair from India's days of monarchy. We sit apart a respectable distance, though once we're on our way, Raj moves closer. He exchanges pleasantries in Hindi with Prem. Raj's Hindi has the rhythm of drums, evoking a tension born of natural passion. By this time Delhi's main streets are deserted except for wandering packs of dogs and an occasional night watchman. The temperature has dropped a few degrees. Now and then I catch a sight of a silver disc of moon through the gaps between the buildings and the network of trees. When the desultory conversation between the two men trails off and the night closes in around us, I find Raj claiming my hand. I surrender willingly. Our palms mold smoothly together like two pieces of satin. Is this a sign we've grown closer in the last three hours?

I wish the drive were longer. Too soon we arrive in the Defence Colony, in front of the iron gate of the Khosla apartment building. Prem eases the Mercedes up to the curb. Raj jumps out before Prem has a chance to hold the door open for me. He whispers conspiratorially with Prem for a minute while I wait on the sidewalk. Though the two men have different stations in life, their camaraderie is evident.

The dark, heavy grilled iron gate invites me in tonight with an offer of comfort and protection. With Raj behind me, I climb the stairs to the second-floor landing. At my door, I look up at Raj and wish him good night. He leans forward and kisses me on the cheek. His lips are light, but they outline themselves clearly, indelibly, on my skin. I glow from a momentary brush with fire.

"Good night, Sharmila. Sweet dreams." Raj's voice is throaty, suggestive. I hear it in my mind as I open my door to go in. His room is at the far end.

I don't want him to go away. Our eyes cling until the last possible moment.

A FTER dinner with Raj, I fall into a deep slumber filled with a dream of South India: forested hills, lush valleys, and a hazy waterfall. Foamy water cascades and buffets the rocks in a frenzy—and in the midst of this picture I see Mitch Epstein. He's standing on a glistening rock on the other side of the waterfall, bending forward from the waist, calling to me. He seems frantic.

"I can't hear you."

This time he screams so loudly that his pale complexion becomes florid. Still I can't hear him over the insistent roar of the water. At last he sits down, buries his face in his hands, and begins to cry. I'm seized with an overwhelming urge to vault the torrent and wipe away his tears. Then I realize the face isn't Mitch's; it belongs to another man, one strangely familiar. I struggle to call his name. Just as it comes to the tip of my tongue, I wake up with a shudder. It's still dark outside.

I suppose it's not surprising that Mitch has popped into a dream at this time. After all, I nearly married him. I can't believe that I came so close. What a disaster that would have been. As I lie in my bed in the Khosla apartment, comparing the Sharmila of yesterday with Sharmila of today, I like to think that now I am wiser, less susceptible to romantic illusions. But I have always had a weakness for dark-eyed, intelligent men, and Mitch certainly possessed both of those characteristics. I can still remember the night we met four years ago at a cozy little joint in Chicago's near north side aptly named the Bliss Café.

Across the street in Lincoln Park, visible even in the fading light, lilac trees were in full bloom. Only recently I'd captured their violet radiance in watercolor as part of my annual celebration of the coming of spring after a long bitter Chicago winter. The Bliss Café, which featured a winning combination of good food and drink, great atmosphere and lots of eligible singles, was fairly busy that evening, the din of conversation growing in volume as more people drifted in. I was sitting at a tiny table facing the door across from my friend Liz. She was my best friend, had been since our high school days. As teenagers we used to hang out together, studying, watching favorite television shows, going to burger joints, and double dating when we finally discovered guys.

Liz was gazing dreamily at the six-foot-tall cowboy type on the stage as he crooned about sunless days, desolate nights, and empty dreams. I glanced up from my wineglass just as a lone man came through the door. He was neither tall nor handsome, yet somehow attractive. His lustrous black hair, bushy eyebrows, and intense dark eyes formed a vivid contrast to his ivory complexion. Of course, I credited my lingering stare to idle curiosity on a long, slow Saturday night.

Liz noticed him as he passed, whispered that she recognized him from a Greenpeace meeting, and called out to him. All throughout the exchange of pleasantries with Liz and the eventual introduction, the newcomer kept eying me. When Liz asked him to join us, Mitch, with another look at me, said he'd love to. In the few seconds of silence that it took him to seat himself, I noticed a flash of resentment in Liz's eyes. I had no idea then how that'd affect our friendship in the future.

With Mitch's arrival the mood of quiet desolation vanished. Words streamed out of his mouth in a torrent. He seemed to be knowledgeable in every subject—terra-cotta pottery, mutual funds, mathematics, even potato pests. When he plunged into a discussion about the subject of population density in India, a "beautiful, enchanted" place he had never even visited, he did a calculation in his head to illustrate a point. He divided the estimated population, a billion, by the number of states, twenty-six, and came up with an average density.

His interest in India was so flattering that I chose not to question the accuracy of his figures. By this time the bar had become much noisier, but he made himself heard above the twang of cowboy guitars, the clinking of glasses, and the crunch of nacho chips around us.

Suddenly I realized Liz was missing. Looking around, I caught a glimpse of her familiar stocky figure on the other side of the room, slow-dancing with the singer while the jukebox filled the air with "Strangers in the Night." That was one of Liz's favorites. Her full face seemed shinier, rounder. I flashed her a smile of approval. She didn't get up and dance often, especially with strangers.

When I turned, Mitch's fierce eyes were staring at me, giving me the distinct impression that they could bore into me. I half expected him to deliver a pseudo psychoanalysis of my character. Instead he commented, "You look so Indian."

"Well, as it happens, I am Indian."

Mitch's eyes swept over my body, lighter than a feather, not at all offensive. "Indian women are beautiful. I know, I know, it's a cliché, but it's true. I can't understand why Indians bribe the groom's family to marry off their lovely daughters. Paying to get her a husband? That's ludicrous. Do you know there are societies where a man's family has to pay, not the woman's?"

"For instance," I said, "the Kikuya and Torkhana tribes of Kenya." I was seized by an urge to let Mitch know that the woman he was lavishing with such admiring glances was also intelligent and informed. "There, it's the groom's family who pays for the bride. But I don't believe anyone—man or woman—should have to pay a dowry."

Face solemn, faint mockery ringing in his voice, Mitch asked, "Could alimony be considered reverse dowry?" Then with an impish smirk, he added, "Pay to get in, pay to get out?"

His wry humor and far-ranging conversation were working their charm on me. Other Chicago men I'd dated could talk about little more than their jobs, the miserable weather, and city politics. I began to regard my new acquaintance with increased interest. By the time we parted that night, he'd asked for my phone number. I remember the flicker of mild anger that showed in Liz's eyes as I exchanged my business card for the torn piece of napkin on which Mitch scribbled his number. Our fingers nudged each other briefly.

Our first real date was also at the Bliss Café—his idea, of course. On our second date we went to a Hindi movie screened for the Indian community at an artsy theater on the west side—my idea this time. The tragicomic story starred the typical sweet young heroine who breaks into a song in a high-pitched falsetto voice and executes a series of frantic twirls every few minutes with an aerobic frenzy that includes push-ups. Just watching her was exhausting. Mitch and I held hands during the show. Afterward, we ended up at the good old Bliss Café, where an uncharacteristically subdued Mitch sat fidgeting with the chili shaker. I'd suggested the movie as an attempt to involve him in Indian culture, so I asked him how he liked the show.

The normally loquacious Mitch could barely summon a feeble "Okay . . ."

"If you ask me, there wasn't all that much to the story, but I still got something out of it. It was wonderful to see India even if it was only on the screen. I'd like to visit there someday."

"Actually, I've never been outside Chicago," Mitch said. "I've always thought, why go anywhere else? Everyone comes here sooner or later. But this movie has got me thinking. After seeing it, I think I've changed my mind." Had I not been in that early dazzled stage of a new romance, I probably would have realized that India was merely an intellectual exercise for Mitch. "You know, you look a little bit like the star in the movie," he said.

"This is the second time you've brought up the subject. It's like reminding a sunflower it's yellow. I am Indian, Mitch."

"No, you're not. And you're American only because you happened to be born here. No, Sharmila, you're in a category all your own. Just like me. Except I'm even more alienated here than you are." Another red flag—if only I had paid attention to those initial signs of Mitch's deep-seated neuroses.

That night he brought me back to my apartment and at the door drew me to him for a long, moist kiss. The next thing I knew my blouse was unbuttoned and my body was extending him an invitation to go further. In a panic I realized we were at a crucial juncture. With an effort of will I pulled myself away and bade him good night in a heavy, breathy voice. Later, alone in my bed, I argued with myself that though Mitch was the most fascinating man I'd come across in a long time, and there was good chemistry between us, I had to stay cool. After our near miss at the door, I was more than a little afraid of my own desire and where it might lead me. With good reason, as it turned out.

Sure enough, on our next date we got no farther than the kitchen floor, where we ended up making love. It was like watching a bud lose its tightness as it opened to light second by second, with the ultimate reward of a full, heavy blossom dancing before the eye. Next morning over coffee and brioche, Mitch suggested in the form of a question that perhaps we should try living together. I hid my shock and tried to make light of the question, even though the deep, sexy looks he was giving me made me want to go along.

We left the question open, but in the following weeks Mitch began spending all his free time in my apartment. We seldom went to another Indian film or the Bliss Café now that we'd discovered each other's bodies. I took to naming our subsequent lovemaking episodes: Gentle Dream, The Collision, Marathon Run, and finally World-Class Event.

Mitch proposed moving in again, on this occasion with a single red chrysanthemum called a Gypsy, a bottle of wine, a theatrical bow, and the words, "My gypsy soul serenades you."

Over the next hour, I learned more about mums than I ever wanted to know. That they came in all colors except blue, that the blossoms stay fresh for weeks because of the thick cushioning of the petals, and that there was even an edible variety. The talk, the wine, and the flower made the evening luminous. This time I agreed, and so, despite my misgivings, Mitch moved in.

Only a few days passed before Mitch's idiosyncrasies eroded the bond that had formed between us. Whether it was parental overemphasis on education or a natural predisposition, I never learned, but Mitch was a creature of his mind. He didn't like to bicycle or work out as I did, nor would he walk if he could avoid it. Even eating and sleeping held no attraction for him. Sex was the only physical activity he enjoyed. His restless, inquiring mind sucked up most of his energy. I, on the other hand, had been physically active all my life. Mother had enrolled me in a ballet class when I was five, answering my father's protests with "She was born to move," and I had been on the move ever since.

On Saturday mornings when I'd put on my leg warmers to teach a class at my health club, Mitch would say, "Those silly socks won't keep your muscles warm. Come back to bed. I'll keep you warm." And I'd be torn between following my natural inclination and satisfying Mitch's needs. It quickly grew oppressive.

Even during sex Mitch needed mental stimulation as a part of foreplay. I made up all sorts of games to arouse him. Once I even recited fragments of an ancient Indian love poem translated into English. When Mitch asked, "Could you repeat that in the original Sanskrit?" I burst out laughing. To my dismay, he became nettled, got up, and spent the evening listening to Beethoven. For me, lovemaking was never the same after that.

Well after the fact, in a coffee shop where one ceiling light or another was always burned out and where the windows were smudged with a dingy, brownish film, I told my mother that Mitch had moved in.

"Living with a man you're not married to?" Mother asked. "Don't you know how people talk? Especially in our community?"

"Don't you worry about what women in your tea circle will say," I advised her. "I can tell you a few things about their kids."

"Never mind." Mom tilted her mug and, hiding a part of her face, drained the last of her coffee. "I don't need to know." Mumbling something about a manicure appointment, she stood up and hurried out the door without another word.

Later that day, Dad called. "What did you say his profession was?" he asked with more than a hint of disapproval in his voice. "He teaches adult education classes in the evening? I guess that's the best you can expect from someone with only a B.A from Loyola."

Dad was clearly worried that Mitch wouldn't be able to contribute his share toward our living expenses. "That's his moonlighting job, Dad. During the day he delivers flowers." I remembered how just the night before Mitch had called me Sharmillia, to rhyme with camellia.

"Fabulous," Dad said. "A floral engineer!"

"Dad, he really is brilliant. You should talk with him sometime," I implored, even though I knew my traditional father would never give Mitch a chance. I was painfully aware that irrespective of the fact that I despised my parents' prejudices, their approval remained very important to me.

Then one afternoon Mother showed up unannounced while Mitch was out.

"So, the floor is his closet?" she asked.

How I wished I had been given warning that our household would be up for inspection. Mitch had yet to hang up his clothes or wash the dishes. His stock answer to my complaints about the mess was that he lived in a world of ideas and couldn't be bothered with middle-class standards of tidiness. No wonder he'd changed residence eleven times in the past year. He did, however, change the water in the flower vase every day and trim the stalk ends.

"Your diet seems to have changed, daughter." Mother had just opened the pantry door. "You never used to eat cookies."

"Those aren't mine, Mom. I don't touch the stuff. Mitch bought them. He doesn't gain an ounce. He burns it all thinking." I remembered how the night before I'd prepared Indian-style red lentil soup that was pink, creamy, and silky on the palate. When I proudly served a bowlful to Mitch, he sniffed distastefully. Too spicy. Too many strange smells. Too Indian. He stood up and headed over to the cupboard for his cookies.

My mother reminded me that if you can't eat together, you can't live together.

At that instant I heard the metal-on-metal scrape of the key in the lock. Mitch walked in, clutching a bouquet of orchids. When I introduced him to Mother, he presented her with the purple flowers. Mother brightened. She loved purple. It was as if Mitch could figure out instinctively how to please a woman. For the next hour she sat on the living room sofa with him and chatted while I straightened the apartment.

Later when Mother called me, her voice was grave. "I can see why you find him attractive, dear. He charms you with his talk and flowers—those flowers are all free, in case you haven't noticed. But when I look inside him, all I see is depression. He's a loser. He's sucking away your life energy."

"But, Mom, he has a tender side. How many men know as much about flowers?"

But I had to admit to myself that Mother was right. I was feeling edgy these days. Why hadn't Mitch's true nature been clear to me earlier?

"You could do better, much better, Sharmila," was my

mother's final shot. "In our community we have many fine, young eligible men, like Amar, Jagjit, and Prakash."

"Prakash is definitely bright, charming, and good-looking, but he's a flirt, Mom. I could never trust him. The other two are geeks. I grew up with them. They mostly hang out with each other. They have to. And Amar tried to rape a woman on a date."

"What are you talking about, Sharmila?"

"It's true. I heard it from Prakash's sister."

I heard a gasp of shock. "Don't listen to gossip. There are rumors about everybody."

The line went dead. That night, I decided that Mitch and I should discuss our parents and their influence on our joint life. I knew he loved to come up with general solutions to universal problems, so I disguised my goal by giving my question a theoretical spin.

"How about applying your analytical talents to a real-life problem, Mitch?"

"Sure, shoot. We'll grind the grain of the topic into a fine flour and blow away the chaff. But first, some real music." He turned off the sitar and the tabla music on the CD player and put on a particularly irritating Bach fugue. "Aahhh!"

I looked at him inquiringly, and my spirits fell as it finally sank in that he didn't appreciate evening ragas.

"Come on, Sharmila, you don't constantly have to prove you're Indian."

I decided not to argue with his implication that I was merely playing at being Indian, but I was deeply annoyed. I am Indian in my flesh, blood, and bones. I have always considered my ties to India sacred. But perhaps for the first time, I was realizing how important it was for those close to me to respect my Indian identity.

We sat in the kitchen, elbows resting on the dining table, heads together. Mitch marked three columns on a yellow pad of paper—us, my parents, and his mother. First, we tried to find as much common ground as possible to reassure me that all would work out. Mitch even resorted to a Venn diagram, speculating that the problem, "the irritation quotient," might be amenable to solution using the Set Theory. We enjoyed a tension-breaking laugh, but in the end nothing was resolved. The evening was another intellectual exercise for Mitch and an exercise in frustration for me.

In the months that followed, I became estranged from my parents, visiting only rarely. The problem was partly their unwillingness to accept Mitch, partly their discomfort at their unwed daughter living with a man. January came and went, and I missed our traditional celebration of goddess Saraswati, patroness of learning. As far back as I could remember, Mother and I would fast that day until the worship ceremony was over. We'd break our fast by placing flowers at the feet of the statue of the goddess and sharing *prasad* together—fruits and sweetmeats that had been offered to the goddess and blessed by her. This year the joyful day approached, but Mother's hand-written invitation invoking the blessing of the goddess with a traditional prayer never arrived.

Mitch realized I was very upset. That night he came home carrying an armful of lilies and peonies. The bouquet was so huge that he had to turn it sideways to get through the door.

As I arranged the flowers in a vase, their sweet fragrance making me dreamy, Mitch asked offhandedly, "Will you marry me?" almost as if he was anticipating rejection. "Wherever I go with you, Sharmillia, I'll find paradise."

His proposal seemed to come from far away, caught up as I was by the delicate floral pattern in pink and white, the curvature of the stems, the soft touch of the petals. A wave of melancholy washed over me. "But paradise is right here, Mitch."

The stunned look on Mitch's face fixed that instant in my memory forever.

Without realizing it, I'd turned him down.

Face frozen in a mask, he spun on his heel and disappeared into the bedroom, slamming the door behind him. I stood motionless, gazing sadly after him, for a moment turning my attention back to the comforting beauty of the flowers. In the past few months I'd become increasingly certain that marriage was no longer an option. I needed a stable life with goals and hope for the future, whereas he existed in a state of constant alienation, living only for the joys of mental acrobatics, acting as if the concerns of daily life were beneath him. But worst of all, he could accept me only as an American, choosing to ignore the essence of my being.

Ours wasn't a stormy relationship, and it didn't end with an argument. Just a few squalls and a lot of cold, moody gray drizzle. One night we were sitting at the kitchen table, our heads down, when in my mind I contrasted the bubbly, high-energy days of our first meeting with my current downbeat mood. "There's a gulf between us I can't seem to bridge, Mitch. And you haven't been much help."

Head bowed, he remained silent.

The next day when I returned from work, I saw that Mitch had put his suitcases by the apartment entrance. With a barely audible good-bye he slipped through the door. At the bottom of the stairwell, he raised his eyes up to me, a haunted, aimless look, and then he was gone.

My hurt, anger, and depression turned inward and festered. I shriveled like a leaf before the approach of winter. I went through my daily routine, but derived no joy from it. Even though I slacked off on my aerobics routine, I lost nine pounds in two months. After work I'd sit in a living room chair the entire evening and stare sightlessly out the window. Although I knew in my heart both Mitch and I were at fault, I began to develop a suspicion of men in general, but even that was of little comfort. One afternoon my mother came over with a basket of mangoes, litchies, and jackfruit. After setting it down on the kitchen table, she drew me to her and whispered softly, "We still love you very much, Sharmila. Be brave, child. In time you will forget." Those consoling words meant more to me than the gift of fruit.

The next day I returned to my gut-busting, sweat-inducing aerobics class and felt cleansed, all in one piece again. Eventually I regained my peripheral vision, so to speak, to the point where I noticed men again. And to my amazement, I experienced a sense of relief. However, my approach to dating became much more cautious. Once, at a professional artists' get-together, I sensed I was being watched from a distance. When I looked up and found myself gazing at a pair of sensitive green eyes, all I could do was nod before turning back to resume my conversation. An impenetrable layer of reserve had formed, born of my breakup with Mitch. At parties I pursued a strict policy of "nonalignment," never spending too much time with any one man to encourage serious pursuit. I concluded that from now on I would need to become thoroughly acquainted with a man over a long period of time before I allowed any real intimacy to develop.

Also during this period I had the disturbing thought that I'd probably never meet a Westerner who would understand my nature completely. Though I'd grown up in America, I was as much a stranger there as any immigrant.

Three months passed. Then one day when Mitch called and said, "Let's have coffee," I was curious, I'll admit, and so agreed to see him.

We met at our old haunt, the Bliss Café, and caught up on what was going on in each other's lives. We laughed over old private jokes, and if we did sigh, we did so silently to hide our embarrassment. We established what I called an "occasional friendship." Coffee together at the same place on the first Saturday morning of every month. That went on for three months. Then came a time when Mitch didn't show up, didn't even call. It was annoying, but only mildly so. I decided to remember him for his nimble, inquiring mind, his tenderness and magnetism, rather than the negative factors that drove me away.

One Saturday night about a year later, I bumped into him at a movie. He was wearing a blonde on his arm, one with clear skin, an anorexic body, and a thin, whiny voice. He threw frequent loving glances at her as we talked. Mitch looked different, more fit than before, with a glow in his eyes, as if a new love had purified him. She was a vegan, not consuming any animal products, not even honey, he told me later on the phone, and announced he had turned vegetarian himself. He concluded by explaining the importance of organic soybean cultivation as a solution to the world's protein shortage, and that was the last I heard from him.

Now, thousands of miles from Chicago, I find myself comparing Mitch and Raj as I lie cozily under silky sheets, my head cradled on a hand-embroidered pillow, my mind in a dreamy trance somewhere between sleep and wakefulness. With Mitch it was rush in and burn. I experience a slight chill when I realize that here I am, rushing in again. Surely I'm not making the same mistake all over again, am I?

My reverie is punctured by a voice calling out sleepily, "Champa!" It's Raj, ordering his morning bed tea. There's a special lilt to his voice, doubtless inherited from his grandfather who was a well-known Delhi poet.

I hear the rustle of a sari and footsteps in the hallway. I picture

Champa taking Raj his tea and realize my own throat is parched. I'd love a cup of that myself, though I can't quite bring myself to ask the maid. She unnerves me with her disapproving glances and quick, dismissive gestures. I've already concluded that a minimum of contact is probably best for both parties.

In any case, just the sound of Raj's voice is enough to cause all thoughts of Mitch to evaporate. Not only does Raj excite me more, he's solid and stable and shares my culture. Indeed, he is helping me learn more about it. There is no question of his accepting the Sharmila that I am. Yes, I say to myself, Raj will make a fine husband. I have not made a mistake.

R AJ and Mrs. Khosla are seated at the table, heads close together like co-conspirators when I step into the dining room
for breakfast. A translucent golden light is flooding through the
open window, enhancing Raj's bright presence in the room.

"Good morning." Raj looks up at me with sparkling eyes. His
freshly shaven face glows with vitality.

"Come, sit down, Sharmila." Mrs. Khosla gives a careful smile
and waves me to the chair opposite Raj. Her bracelets tinkle with
her fluid motion. "So you two had a good dinner at Dum
Pukht?" The tone indicates she already knows the answer.

"Oh, yes, it was a lovely place, and the food was great." In
truth, I barely remember the food and the decor. The two of us
alone together, our acceptance of each other, made the evening
for me.

Raj butters a piece of toast with neat, precise strokes and
slides the plate toward his mother with a tender look. "Ma-ji
doesn't do much cooking anymore." Turning his smile on me, he
adds, "But she's still the best cook around."

It's obvious that despite his frequent absences Raj is very close
to his family.

"When Raj was young, he liked whatever I cooked," Mrs.
Khosla says, "even when my korma sauce was lumpy because I

didn't chop the onions finely enough. I was always uneasy when we'd go to the house of Mr. and Mrs. Dev. They were our neighbors, and Mrs. Dev was an expert cook. On one occasion she served ten courses, every single one done perfectly. I was most envious of her mutton korma. The sauce was velvety and so well blended I couldn't tell which spices she used. On the way home, my husband was silent as usual. He never paid much attention to food. But Raj told me—he was only ten then—'Ma-ji, I don't like Mrs. Dev's korma. It's too smooth and bland. Yours tastes much better.' So from then on I cooked according to my heart and Raj's taste."

They laugh together at the shared memory, enriched by recounting of the childhood incident over many years. Raj picks up his classic white teacup. I decide to join him and reach for the teapot with an eager hand.

I delight in the initial sensation of milky sweetness, though it is all too soon replaced by a slightly bitter aftertaste. I set aside my tea and devote myself to a soft-boiled egg. While cracking the shell with a spoon, I recall a breakfast long ago at which my mother gave me one of her insights into men. "Watch how he talks to his mother, how he looks at her, what he does for her. That's what you'll get someday."

If she was right, my future looks pretty rosy.

Neelu skips into the room, twirling the end of a chiffon scarf. Still standing, she picks up an orange segment from a platter on the table.

"What are your favorite colors, Sharmila?" Mrs. Khosla asks. "The manager of Ferns 'n' Petals is coming over this morning to finalize the floral arrangements."

Still lost in my dreamy space, I half hear the question. "Floral arrangements?"

"For the reception the day after the wedding."

The words send a happy shiver down my spine. My wedding is a reality, and it'll be an elaborate affair. I can picture the pageantry my parents have been planning, starting with a *shamiana*, the colorful canopy held up by four posts, each one signifying one of the Vedas, or pillars of knowledge. Blue and red lightbulbs hanging from a coil going all the way around the top. *Shehnai* music playing both happy and sad tunes. The tantalizing smells of a wedding feast mounting in the air. Cars choking the side streets. The sound of honking horns filling the air, more a sign of merriment than impatience. There will be saris, *kurtas*, flashing jewels, smiles and embraces. In the excitement that wells up within me, I make a note to myself to call my aunt Mistoo and make sure arrangements on my family's side are going well. Indian custom dictates that the bride not do any work. But it's still my wedding. I'm at the center of it all and that's a heady feeling.

In the meantime, Mrs. Khosla's question is hanging in the air. "Oh, I like all colors."

"She likes pinks, reds, and yellows the best, Ma-ji," Raj interjects.

"How do you know?" I ask, puzzled.

"He did research," Neelu says, eyes shining from mischief. "He asked your relatives."

"Up so early?" Raj's voice is gentle, teasing.

Neelu says, "I heard you laughing and I had to find out what it was all about."

A butterfly floats in through the window. I sit transfixed as it flutters about the room on iridescent black and yellow wings and circles closer and closer to my face . . . I am its chosen flower.

Neelu comes up behind me and taps me on the shoulder. "You know what they say about a butterfly in a room?"

"What?"

"Romance is in the air."

I find myself blushing. I steal a look at Raj and catch a trace of a smile. Is his heart racing like mine?

"We've rented a large hall for the party I'm giving," Mrs. Khosla, oblivious to this exchange, announces. "I was fortunate to get the best caterer in town. You know Harilal Catering, don't you, Raj?"

He nods with enthusiasm. Turning to me, he says, "My whole office will be coming and many of my college friends. There'll be close to a thousand people. Not many caterers could handle such a crowd."

"Are you getting Colonel's kebabs, Ma?" Neelu asks. "His are the best."

"Of course."

Now seated, Neelu contentedly nibbles on a piece of apple. Mrs. Khosla picks up her toast with a bejeweled hand, and I turn back to the remains of my egg. Though my eyes are not on Raj, I sense his strong, dominating and reassuring presence. The uncertainty that has plagued me for months vanishes in a wave of euphoria. At this radiant moment I'm convinced our love is blossoming.

A faint rustle punctures the moment. Champa in a pale blue sari strewn with white flowers glides in with a tray. She looks at no one and is ignored by all, yet her presence has subtly altered the atmosphere, a cloud stalking the sun. Mrs. Khosla makes circles in her cup with a teaspoon. Neelu asks Raj if we can all see a movie tomorrow. Raj says there's hardly anything worth seeing and that he plans to take me out for a stroll in Buddha Jayanti Park instead. While brother and sister quibble about which Delhi park is the most beautiful, I finish my breakfast. Raj glances at his watch and sits up with a jolt. His face neutral, controlled and immobile as a terra-cotta statue as he rises without even a glance in my direction.

"I'd better be off. I have a ten o'clock meeting," he mumbles, then starts for the door. At the last moment he turns. "See you this evening, Sharmila. I'll be home around six."

I excuse his abruptness and, keeping my expression agreeable, reply in what I hope is a reasonable tone of voice. "See you then."

But the doorway is already empty.

Later that day a florist, a caterer, and a reception planner stop by. The details: Vivaldi roses for the table, a bird of paradise arrangement slightly above eye level near the entrance, orchids on the wall along with tropical foliage to match my outfit in mauve and moss green. Mrs. Khosla also discusses furniture and linen, how many vegetarian and nonvegetarian guests will be attending the reception, and how much champagne to order.

I'm surprised to hear that champagne is being served. My mother and her relatives wouldn't consider serving alcohol during an auspicious ceremony such as a wedding. Mrs. Khosla seems to notice my reaction. "Alcohol at weddings is not unusual these days. Things have changed since your parents left. Everything you have in the States, we have here," she concludes smugly.

Before I know it, the day is over. When Raj and Neelu aren't around, the apartment somehow feels cold, empty. I consider calling my mother, but she won't be up yet.

Back in my room, I open my sketchpad and draw the clay planter full of delicate pink bleeding hearts the florist had brought for me. Elegant, curved stems on which the delicate flowers hang in clusters. I sign off with:

And they speak for my heart

11

THIS morning, I'm determined to call my mother. It's nine in the morning here, nighttime in Chicago. When I dial her number, all I get is her usual cheery voice in the answering machine. So I content myself with leaving a short message reassuring her that all is going well along with the request to call me back. As I speak into the phone, I can picture my parents' Lake Shore Drive condominium. The living room looking out on the waters of Lake Michigan is now softly lit. In a far corner of the room, behind an ornate teakwood partition, is Mother's private temple. Here she sits cross-legged on a thick carpet before a brass figurine of the Goddess Durga standing on a low dais. Eyes closed, face composed, Mother chants a mantra in a low, rhythmic voice. Damp curls are plastered to her head—her black tresses are always wet when she prays, whether from religious fervor or because she has just bathed to purify herself, I've never been quite sure. She has probably maintained this position for the past hour, and interrupting her devotion to go answer the phone is out of the question. I'll just have to wait until after she's finished with her *puja* to get a call back.

In the meantime I wander into the living room. Stretched out in an armchair, Raj is engrossed in the *Frontline* magazine.

"Could you stand some company?" I ask as he raises his eyes.

"Oh, Sharmila, good morning. I was just thinking about you."
Raj hesitates a moment. "I'm going to the temple shortly. I
thought you'd like to come with me."

He amazes me. I'd never expected this worldly businessman
to have a religious side, especially given the tendency of modern
Hindus, the Westernized ones in particular, to downplay this aspect of their culture.

"I'd love to."

"Have you been to a Hindu temple before?"

"Oh, yes, when I was growing up in Chicago. The ceremonies
were beautiful. I really loved them. But most of my friends
weren't Indian and my Indian friends weren't religious, so I
stopped going to the temple after a while. But my mother is de-
vout."

"To be honest, I'm not terribly religious either. But on my days
off I stop by the temple. Keeping in touch with my grandfather's
tradition, I suppose. Much of his religion was the Hindu philosophy of live-and-let-live, and I admired him for that. I don't put
much emphasis on rituals, but in the temple you'll have to follow a few. They'll probably be new to you. But they're really
very simple. Just do as I do, and you'll be fine."

We're at the door when Mrs. Khosla comes bustling up behind us. "So you're taking her to the temple, Raj?" It's obvious
she knows her son's routine. She gives me a cursory once-over.
"Make sure you're not wearing any leather articles, dear. Animal
products are strictly forbidden inside a temple."

I finger the leather belt of my skirt.

"It's okay, Ma-ji," Raj intercedes. "They're not that particular
anymore."

"As you wish." Mrs. Khosla whirls away. The keys tied to the
pallu of her sari jingle harshly.

My face burning in embarrassment, I mumble an excuse and
hurry to my room. I exchange my leather belt for one of cloth.

The traffic is a vortex of vehicles careening in all directions,
and the air vibrates with the noise, but Raj is imperturbable. His
hands are strong and steady on the steering wheel. Only after
he's driven for a few minutes does the tension in my neck and
shoulders begin to fade. The little run-in I had with his mother
has proven that he already feels protective of me. I'm drawn
even closer to him.

As we turn onto a wide street named Baba Kharak Singh Marg, Raj points out a long row of modern shops, strung together much like a shopping mall, with each store displaying a huge sign overhead. Those are handicraft emporiums, run by the government of different states, Raj informs me. "You'll find everything from wooden chests and carpets to saris and jewelry."

"I'm not much of a shopper," I tell Raj. I am, however, amused to discover the same triumphant glee in the faces of the shoppers that one finds in any mall in the States. Consumerism has arrived here. And now I'm curious as to how it fits in with religion.

"The temple is over there." Raj indicates the other side of the street, then maneuvers the car into a parking space next to a Ford Escort. He comes around to open my door.

"Worship first, shop later," I say as I climb out. "Is that the idea?"

"You're catching on." Raj laughs freely, and I enjoy the light moment with him.

We take a pedestrian underpass and emerge on the other side of the street onto a flagstone sidewalk framed by stately trees. Set well back from the street are several temples with conical steeples. The tallest one is an unblemished white structure that towers over a row of stalls.

"That's Monkey Temple, *Hanuman Mandir*." Raj points up at the soaring steeple. "Look."

The roof is alive with monkeys, at least a dozen, staring at the pedestrians, vaulting across a seemingly impossible gap to a tree in the courtyard and scrambling down to beg for food from the worshipers. Off to one side, two baby monkeys fight over a large piece of white coconut flesh.

"They probably stole it from Kumar Fruit Mart over there," Raj says. "They're experts."

This is not mere sightseeing; I'm sharing Raj's world. "I love watching animals at play," I remark delightedly. "They make me feel so human and at the same time not so different from them. My apartment in Chicago was only a five-minute walk from Lincoln Park Zoo, so I spent a lot of time there." Noticing a monkey hang upside down just above the temple entrance, I ask, "Do they ever jump on people's shoulders?"

"They pulled Neelu's braid once. She was ten years old then. She accused me. To this day she thinks I did it."

From the sidewalk I watch the crowd. At least fifty people are standing in line at the entrance to the Monkey Temple, many old and bent with age. Each solemn-faced devotee drops a few coins into the hand of a vendor at the adjacent flower stall next to the entrance and picks up a brilliant orange marigold garland. Holding it up to his chest, he shuffles through the temple entrance.

"See the temple over there?" Raj indicates an older edifice on the left, whose pastel shade has turned ashen by a coat of soot. Already his feet are turning. "That's where we're going."

He doesn't notice the disappointment on my face, I would have liked to wear a marigold garland.

After taking off our shoes, we pass through a gate. Statues of deities, each in a separate alcove in a large courtyard, stand watching benevolently as we enter. Few worshipers, here and there, move about. The silence is broken only by the faint tinkle of a bell. Raj heads directly to a small chamber housing a gilded icon of Ganesh on a raised platform. A small oil lamp, a *diya*, imparts a soft, ruddy glow to the god's elephant head, casting flitting shadows over the curved walls. A heady scent of incense and fresh flowers waft from a bronze tray on the ground. Raj's eyes lose all expression as he sinks to his knees. He stretches out to his full length on the marble floor, polished smooth by devotees, and presses his forehead to the ground, his hands closing above his head. He lies there relaxed, motionless, and tranquil. I realize with a small shock that deep within him there's a Hindu soul untouched by Western education and business dealings. He's humble and insignificant in the presence of his gods, and that's all the identity he needs at the moment.

His tranquillity affects me. The ritual prayer seems familiar, inviting. Or is it that my own ancestors have passed down to me a Hindu essence I was never aware of? I kneel and touch my forehead to the floor.

In the silence time stands frozen. Sometime later, a minute or an hour, I hear the ringing of a bell. Raj emerges from his trance-like state. We rise in unison. He moves forward a step, cups his palms around the glowing *diya*, then lifts them to his face. As he steps back, I move forward to capture the warmth of the flame with my hands and absorb its purity through my skin.

*   *   *

A priest in a saffron tunic emerges from a side entrance and blesses us by placing marigold petals on our palms and a dot of sandalwood on our foreheads, all the while reciting a hypnotic Sanskrit verse in a monotone. This little ceremony binds us together as a couple and draws me more deeply into the spirit around Raj.

As we emerge from the cool recesses of the temple into the sunlight, Raj says, "In his final days my grandfather spent hours at that temple." He smiles. "But I'm not yet that evolved, or old. Still, it's a way of honoring his memory. And I find that coming here to worship gives me moments of peace."

"I'm really glad. Thank you for letting me come with you."

But I wonder why a regular temple visit is so essential to Raj. Perhaps he is seeking relief from grief, pressures of business, or something less obvious. I wish he would let me know so I could comfort him.

"That's the Modern Bazaar." Raj points at a nondescript building. The voice is lighter, the manner bright and cheery. Gone is his mood of introspection. "You can get anything from fresh jackfruit to thousand island dressing there," he says. "But if you want to experience the real India, Sharmila, you need to visit an old-fashioned bazaar."

He turns off the main road and weaves a way through narrow side streets. We finally park in an alley and are soon immersed in a throng of shoppers browsing in a long row of makeshift stalls displaying vegetables and canned goods, clothing and cheap appliances. The midday heat is stifling in the confined area. Vendors clamor for our attention. "Come here, miss. I've the best sari for you."

"Hello, brother, where are you going? Why can't you spare a minute and take a look at these fine Arrow shirts?"

"You don't want a cabbage today? Perhaps this cauliflower. It's the height of the season."

"What are you looking for, madam?"

I don't know if the last question is meant to be profound, but Raj represses a smile. The aisle is so narrow that our arms are touching. I'm catching the warmth of his skin.

A woman, covered head to toe in a black, tent-like *burkha*, is going through a stack of tablecloths. Her eyes are visible only through a latticework in her robe, and she speaks to the merchant in monosyllables. Any other time I'd have been fascinated by the scene. But not today. I'm too entranced by Raj, who's brushing aside a fly buzzing around his head.

We walk among barrels of spices and come to a large table covered with translucent pickle jars. The crowd is thinner here. Perhaps the pungent smells keep the shoppers away; perhaps it's because the shopkeeper is dozing.

Raj pauses and asks, "Do you like pickles?"

"Oh, yes. I love pickles, the spicier the better. During the summer heat in Chicago, when I lose my appetite, about the only thing I can eat is a dinner of plain rice, yogurt, and pickles."

Raj's face brightens as though I've paid him a compliment. "I knew it. You're a true Indian at heart."

"To be perfectly honest, I've been pretty worried about that since I got here. When you're a second-generation American, you're always a little unsure about your parents' culture."

"Don't worry." Raj leans closer and lowers his voice confidentially. "I like you fine just the way you are. You're one-third Indian, one-third American, and one-third I can't put my finger on, but it's absolutely intriguing."

While I bask in the warmth of his regard, he picks up a porcelain bottle, sniffs it, and studies the label. "I picked up the habit from my grandfather," he says. "He had to have at least one pickle with every meal. In those days pickles were made at home. Two of my aunts were expert at making them. Pickle artists, he called them. Now most women don't take the time, so we buy them. I prefer South Indian pickles. My favorite brand comes from Hyderabad, where there are a number of good pickle manufacturers."

I thought I knew all about pickles, but it's obvious I'm in the presence of a connoisseur. "What's this chocolate-red one?" I ask.

"Ah, that's tamarind. Sensuously smooth, but dangerously tart. And this pickled carrot is so mellow, it'll make your tongue sing with joy." Raj holds another fat glass jar, checks the reddish-orange content flecked with white slivers up to the light, and inspects it. He turns to me with feigned solemnity. "This is garlic. Some people say you should only share it with a member of the opposite sex you're interested in."

I see the mischievous twinkle in his eye and burst out laughing. Who'd ever have believed shopping for pickles could be so much fun?

Raj gathers up several jars. "This lemon pickle is for me. And I dare not go home without ginger pickle for Ma-ji and chili pickle for Neelu. How about you?"

"I'll go for the garlic." My mood buoyant, I add, "Promise you'll eat it with me?"

"It's a promise I'll have no trouble keeping."

I think of slipping the bottle into Mohan's hand at home tonight with instructions for serving at tomorrow's lunch. Neelu and Mrs. Khosla are usually absent at that meal, so Raj and I will be alone.

As we leave the bazaar, I fondly glance back over my shoulder at the market. The place will be forever imprinted with our footsteps, our laughter, the looks we've exchanged. My time in Delhi is already filling with happy memories.

Still, a doubt assails me. Raj didn't just start being charming after I arrived. Has he been good company to all the women he has been involved with? Has he been involved with many women?

Later that night, I retire to my room with heavy eyelids. Still, I'm unwilling to let the day close without a few well-chosen strokes in my sketchbook. My time with Raj had the gaiety of a musical comedy: cheerful high voices, one song fading into another, arms reaching high. In this mellow mood I take up a pencil and produce a swift sketch of the temple with the two baby monkeys fighting over a piece of coconut, with all the details that my mind has recorded. I dress up the margin with a drawing of a jar of garlic pickle.

Signing off simply, "I crave," I close the book with a languorous sigh.

The lunch the next day is all it promised to be. Raj and I are sitting at the dining table, close in conversation, when Mohan delivers an elaborate meal. We interrupt our discussion of the plans for the day and turn our attention to the feast before us. I break off a piece of a freshly made roti, dip it into a satiny smooth rogan josh, and pop it into my mouth. I follow that with a spoonful of chunky, home-style yogurt and a nibble of the newly purchased garlic pickle. My mouth burns with the fiery sensation of chili, then is soothed by the earthy pungency of garlic. I turn to Raj.

Mrs. Khosla calls from the doorway. "Your mother's on the phone, Sharmila."

I excuse myself reluctantly and rush to the phone in the living room.

"Sharmila, my dear, how are you?"

"Everything is going great, Mom. I'm sorry I woke you up that first night. I think the jet lag made me overreact."

"I've tried calling you several times." Mother's voice is a blend of contentment and loss. "You're either out somewhere or sleeping."

"You told me a thousand times India's a different world, but I didn't believe it until I got here. I feel like I've turned upside down. India is so intense, Mom."

"I know, child. Mrs. Khosla tells me everything."

That explains why Mother hasn't called even more often. My mistrust of Mrs. Khosla and her sorority with Mother unsettles me.

"I'm so relieved the arrangement is working out," Mother says. "Now, do you see how well your parents understand you? You're content. We've found the perfect match. Your happiness is what we live for."

"I'm optimistic, Mom, and so excited. But I do miss you and Dad terribly."

"We miss you, too, *beti*. Don't worry. We'll be there in five weeks. Your dad will arrive a few days before I do. He plans to spend time with an old classmate of his in Delhi, while I make a stopover in Tokyo to visit an aunt. She's quite old. I may never have a chance to visit her again. While I think of it, could you pick up your father from the airport?"

"Sure." I jot down the date, time, and the flight number. "I have to go now, Mom. As soon as we finish lunch, Raj and I are going out. We'll have a view of the Jamuna River and the egrets—if there are any—from a bridge, then take a stroll in Buddha Jayanti Park."

"Oh, then I shouldn't keep you any longer. The Jamuna is most sacred. It used to be just breathing the air there elevated your soul." Her voice changes as she remembers something.

"But now it's polluted, so don't stay there too long. By the way, your old friend Mitch left a message."

"Mitch?"

"I never liked him, but I'll see what he has to say. You have put the past behind you, haven't you, *beti?*"

"Yes, of course. I don't know why he called you, but I'm sure it's nothing for you to worry about. We're just friends."

I place the receiver in its cradle gently, as if it carries Mother's blessings, and step back to the dining room with a quiet confidence, wondering what Mitch wants.

A N hour later, Raj and I are strolling in Buddha Jayanti Park, a secluded expanse of gently rolling terrain in a landscape of trees and shrubs interlaced with footpaths. We encounter only an occasional pedestrian—a couple, an old man, a boy. As we round a bend in the path, we come upon a small pond and beside it a group of women.

"They're building a bridge." Raj indicates an islet on which a statue of the Buddha sits in serene repose under a covered pavilion.

The laborers in sari chatter back and forth as they pass bricks to each other. We pause for a moment and stand gazing at the Buddha in respectful silence, then wend our way through a vast grassy meadow past a pair of lovers walking hand in hand, a family seated on a blanket around a picnic, and a kite flyer teasing his rig under a breeze. On the horizon, I notice uneasily, there are lowering purplish-black clouds.

"This is Palas." Raj points at a tree whose leaves spread out like a fan. "In spring it blooms into bright orange flowers, called the flame of the forest. Both myna and leafbirds come for the nectar."

The quiet spot underneath the tree will be just perfect for us, I decide. As I spread our blanket, Raj sits down, stretches out his legs and, leaning back on his elbows, fiddles with the cap of a bottle of Campa-Cola. Sitting cross-legged, I comment, "This is a lovely park."

"Yes, it's my favorite and I know all the parks," Raj says. "When I was still a child, Nana—that's what I called my grandfather—took me to all of them."

"What was it like when you were growing up?"

Raj stares into the distance. "What do you want to know?"

"I want to be there, at all significant times of your life, Raj."

He lies on his back with hands behind his head and gazes up at the sky. "I was always Nana's favorite," he finally begins. "I think everybody knew that."

Sensing the beginning of a long story, I recline on the blanket, my head in one hand.

"To me, Nana was a giant. He was tall and dignified, always dressed in spotless white. Deep-set eyes. He didn't smile much—he'd seen too many of life's miseries. But he had a most kind heart.

"Nana worked as an upper-division clerk for the railway. His job was to answer letters of complaint about train delays, lost combs, and cold tea, what have you. To maintain his sense of humor, not to mention sanity, he wrote poems during his breaks. He was really a poet at heart. He could speak both Hindi and Urdu. He wrote fluently and beautifully in both languages.

"At home he was a dedicated family man. He ruled our household, though it was a benign dictatorship. Ours was an extended family with brothers, sisters, uncles, aunts, children, and grandchildren—all together some thirty people in a sprawling middle-class home. Nana made the major decisions, such as which girl should get married when and the best profession for a boy. He also managed to keep track of a thousand little details. He'd want to know the price of rice, whether the best mangoes had hit the market yet, or where you could get freshly ground flour. The only times he slipped out of his role as the head of the household was when a *mushaira* took place. Do you know what a *mushaira* is, Sharmila?"

Raj must be oblivious to the sky, which is now filled with disturbing blue-black clouds. "A what?" I ask as a violent gust of wind rips through the tree branches above us.

Raj explains that *mushaira* is an ancient form of poetic dialogue that usually takes place in an auditorium. In *mushaira* poets on stage play a game of couplets. One team spontaneously composes a couplet, and the opposing team replies with one beginning with the last letter of the first team's couplet. In the beginning of the game, a candle is lit and given to the first poet to recite. He in turn passes it to the next. The overall effect of the flickering candle, the hand gestures, and the rhythmic cadence of the recital can be quite magical, even otherworldly.

"I was eight years old," Raj goes on, "when Grandfather took me to my first *mushaira*. With several hundred people attending, every poet did his best to win the loudest applause. I was practically holding my breath when Nana's turn came. As he began his chant, his voice seemed charged with a power. There was passion in his delivery and lots of sentiment—that wasn't how he normally spoke. He had an unlimited supply of rhymes that carried the audience. When he finished, the crowd burst into the loudest applause. 'Please, more.' They persuaded him to continue.

"I never found out how it ended. At some point, lulled by the musical voice, I fell fast asleep.

"The next morning I noticed how tired Nana looked. His eyes were dull and sunken even further in their sockets. But he seemed charged with a tiger's energy as he hummed a prayer tune and made his morning rounds.

"Some years later in school, a teacher asked me to read a poem I'd written for an assignment. I stood up and tried to imitate Nana at the *mushaira*. My classmates found my performance hilarious. The teacher thought I was being intentionally disrespectful and gave me a failing mark for my effort. You might say that ended my career as a poet," Raj comments with a wistful smile.

"Yes, Nana made sure I saw his Delhi—the alleys, the bazaars, the temples, the parks he loved so much. He shopped for provisions in poorer sections of town. 'Money doubles in poor people's hands,' he always said. 'They make it last longer. So why not give it to them?'

"When I was fifteen, Nana died in his sleep. My mother gave me the news as soon I got up that day. I ran to his room, crying, 'Nana, Nana, come back,' but when I saw his calm expression, I became quiet. I didn't want to disturb his peace."

Raj sips his cola absentmindedly. After a short period of comfortable silence, he seems to draw new energy from within. "My father was extraordinary, too, but in a different way. I called him Papa. He moved more easily in the world of money and goods. Neither poetry nor poverty made much of an impression on him. Soon after college he took a position with a textile company. He rose up the ladder and eventually became the chief executive. The timing was fortuitous because at about the same time the West was infatuated with Indian fabrics. The quality, the variety, the rock-bottom price. Papa, sensing a golden opportunity, took the company international. His timing was perfect, and as a result he became a wealthy man almost overnight.

"Oddly enough, in his youth Papa was quite the romantic. Shortly after he went to work, he met Ma-ji in a tailoring shop where she was being fitted for a *salwar-kameez*. Ready-made clothes were of poor quality then and not widely available, so tailor-made outfits were not unusual. In fact, they were the norm for the wealthy like Ma-ji's family. As Papa told me the story later, she had just put on a new tunic and pants set, lavender and pale green sequined at the border, and was standing before a mirror with her back to the door, when he walked in on a sales call. Their eyes met in the mirror. He lost his heart instantly. Maybe it was Ma-ji's proud head and her good posture, but whatever it was, Papa knew he had just seen his future wife. She wasn't just beautiful, but strong, solid, and protective. He told me, 'The front may put up a smile, but a person's back doesn't lie.' "

Raj laughs, a full, warm sound that mesmerizes me. I am beginning to understand where his power, confidence and vitality comes from.

"Papa was young and totally smitten. He came back later and bribed the tailor to get Ma-ji's name, address, and family background. He asked Nana to send a marriage broker to Ma-ji's family. "They'll never accept us," Nana warned. "We aren't rich." But in time he overcame his reluctance. Sure enough, Ma-ji's family wouldn't take a proposal from a middle-class, though well-respected, family seriously. So Papa threw himself into his work. And within a year he'd tripled his income, accumulated a substantial bank balance, and acquired a stylish wardrobe. He took to showing up at Ma-ji's college in the afternoon just as she was getting out of classes. At first she ignored him, then pretended to ignore him, but finally admitted to herself that she was as attracted to him as he was to her. Soon they were plotting together how to win her family over. Ma-ji worked on her mother, while Nana played chess with her father, and Papa took the whole family to a horse racing event. At an appropriate time Papa sent the family priest to present a certificate attesting to his fine character. By then Ma-ji's family had become fond of Papa. So in a little over two years' time, they were married. You might say they'd arranged their own marriage."

Raj continues, "Education was extremely important to my parents. Papa considered it essential to success in life. He was determined to see that I got into the best schools. Ma-ji made sure I did my homework every evening. By that time Papa had become a wealthy man and could afford a private tutor. Quite naturally I went to St. Stephen's College, considered the most prestigious in the country. Stephanians is what we were called. Papa encouraged me to participate in sports and arranged for me to have tennis lessons. I was never more than a mediocre tennis player. My true love was cricket. It was a happy childhood for the most part. I lacked for nothing, except that I didn't have a lot of close friends. A rich man's son is never really part of the crowd, but I did manage to make one good friend though, Prem."

The name causes a minor ripple of emotion in me, shaking my comfortable world with Raj. I draw closer to him in greater attention.

"We were teenagers when we met. I remember the first time I saw him—a shy boy, about my age, watching us practice cricket from a distance. He'd come to the park three or four times a week. I became used to seeing him. Then one afternoon following a game I had to catch a bus home. Normally Ma-ji sent the chauffeur to pick me up, but that day our car was at the mechanic. A bus pulled up and stopped right before me. It was jam-packed. A few people were standing on the steps, holding onto the handle. I should have waited for the next bus, but, cocky lad that I was, I tried to jump onto the bottom step and reach for the handle. It was a miscalculation, because just then the bus took off with a jerk. I'd have fallen off and been crushed under the wheels had not a hand snaked out and grabbed me by the belt. After I'd caught my breath, I looked at the face attached to that arm. It was Prem, his face scrunched in pain. I looked down and saw I was standing on his feet. His sandals were by then torn, almost unusable. I apologized, but he laughed it off and said it was far more important that I got on safely. I looked at him with new admiration. I saw a depth of character in that gentle face. As the bus bounced along, we began talking about cricket to pass the time. In a few minutes, when we came to a stop, he said good-bye and got off. On an impulse I got down too and followed him. I asked him if I could replace the sandals that I'd stepped on, but he wouldn't allow it. I invited him to at least have a cup of tea with me, and he accepted. We went to a *chai* shop and talked for an hour. I found Prem had a keen, disciplined intellect. Though he was attending a lesser-known college, he'd made the most of his opportunities there. He was the intellectual equal of my Stephanian friends. We could discuss most any subject.

"That was the beginning of our friendship. Over time as I came to know him well, I found out he was a Dalit, outside the caste, as some would say, but I didn't care. I'd confide in him whenever I had difficulty dealing with studies, relatives, or girls. Prem would do the same. There was very little about each other we didn't know. I invited him over to our house many times. Both Ma-ji and Neelu became quite fond of him.

"When I went to the States, we lost touch, but after I came back I looked him up again and it was as if I'd never been gone. We've remained close friends ever since. Some years later, when he was out of a job, Ma-ji asked him to be her chauffeur. He accepted. He believes all work has dignity. And he knew we would treat him with respect.

"Getting back to my story about Papa: When I left for the States, Papa was in his fifties and still showed no sign of slowing down. He drank, smoked, and was overweight. In spite of Ma-ji's scolding, he lived as if there was no tomorrow. And he was a big spender. Then one night in New York—I can remember it as if it was yesterday—I got a call from Ma-ji around midnight. Papa had suffered a massive heart attack and died. I caught the first plane back to Delhi. It was the biggest shock of my life. I'd have liked to have seen Papa one last time.

"I probably loved and respected Nana more, but Papa, by his example, had at least shown me it was possible to choose my own wife and choose well."

I glance at Raj at this reference to Roopa. Curiosity fills me and elicits a casual "How did you meet Roopa?"

"It's a long story."

"You don't have to talk about it if you don't want to."

"Oh, no, Sharmila, you're such a good listener and besides, I know I can be open with you. Though we were of the same caste, she came from a family of modest means that wasn't a part of our social set. Her mother was a seamstress and did a bit of work for my mother while I was in the States. The two women got on well together. Ma-ji met Roopa on several occasions and liked her, but I didn't know anything about them, since she never mentioned them in her letters. Then, just after I came back, Ma-ji began promoting a match with the daughter of one of her friends, whom I already knew casually. She was an accomplished sitar player, soft-spoken and pretty. I thought she might make a good partner, so I agreed to consider the proposal. Then one evening Ma-ji asked me to stop by her seamstress's house and pick up a tablecloth she needed for an elaborate lunch she was planning for my prospective bride's relatives the next day. Ordinarily she'd have sent our servant, but he was busy preparing dishes for the lunch.

"I had a party to go to and was naturally in a hurry, but the seamstress's house wasn't far out of the way. It was down a narrow cobblestone lane, I remember. It was a typical middle-class neighborhood. Children were playing badminton in the street. The smell of chili and fenugreek hung in the air. I heard the sound of some young beginner practicing on the harmonium and doing it badly. I took a turn and located the exact street address. A young woman was standing there, watering a flower bush with a bucket, her back toward me. I couldn't help but notice how she stood, all symmetry, balance, and strength. Then she turned around. Hers was a classic Bengali face—golden skin, bright eyes, high cheekbones, and a refined expression. Speechless, I stood there. It was Papa and Ma-ji all over again.

" 'Are you Mrs. Khosla's son, Raju?' she asked.

"I am Raj! I remember wanting to tell her. How dare you address me with a diminutive *u*? And do you know you're the first one ever to call me anything other than Raj? But as I said, I couldn't speak. I stood there with a silly schoolboy grin pasted on my face.

" 'I thought so,' she said. 'You look just like your picture. Your mother talks about you a great deal. Won't you please come in? I'm Roopa.'

"I followed her through the door.

" 'Ma will be back soon,' Roopa said. 'I don't know if she's finished with the tablecloths or not. You can wait for her if you want.'

"She spoke without inhibition, as though we were already beyond the stage of formality. I began to look around the room to hide my embarrassment. It was a small, spare flat. A cane mat on the floor, a few colorful cushions, an ivy plant on the window. That was it. Actually, there was no need for furnishings to fill the space. Roopa accomplished that admirably. Her presence was everywhere. She was slender and delicate, radiated a quiet energy, and moved about with graceful authority. I settled myself on the mat and leaned back against a bolster but, comfortable as I was, I couldn't relax. I was tingling with excitement in her presence. After a minute she went to the little kitchen to heat a kettle of water. Through the open door I watched her in fascination. I'd never seen a woman other than my mother make tea. Her bangles jingled like temple bells. The teacups clinked as she got them down from a doorless cupboard. Soon the kettle was whistling musically, and a few minutes later she came back with a tea tray. Her sari pleats rustled like tender leaves as she knelt in front of me and poured two cups. The tea smelled like a fruity Darjeeling. She took a seat herself and peppered me with questions about life in the States. It was marvelous.

"Soon I was telling her stories I'd never told anyone, incidents I thought I'd forgotten. She listened with wide, expressive eyes, leaning ever so slightly forward. I knew the look, but this time it was different. She was interested in what I'd experienced, not just who I was. I told her about my first skating experience in Central Park. How I spent more time on the seat of my pants instead of on the blades of my skates. How I got lost on the way home, being quite new in Manhattan at the time. I thought I'd cleverly reoriented myself by identifying the tops of some familiar buildings and charged confidently onward only to end up in Harlem. I had to take a taxi I couldn't afford home.

"Her laugh had a musical quality and came straight from her heart. She was neither a naive girl nor a sophisticated woman, but rather in that transitional stage: fresh, eager, glowing.

" 'You actually went to Columbia?' Roopa asked at one point. She had admiration in her voice. 'Didn't Amartya Sen give a talk there last year on the economic future of the ASEAN trade block?'

" 'You're familiar with Dr. Sen?'

" 'I'm completing a Ph.D. in economics."

"It was my turn to be impressed. Roopa confided that her parents had had to work hard to send her to the university. Her voice became soft and respectful whenever she mentioned her parents.

" 'I don't know why Ma is so late,' Roopa said.

"To be quite honest, I was more than happy to be alone with Roopa. Not until an hour and a half had passed did Roopa's mother walk in the door. She was a tiny, bird-like woman. As soon as she saw me, she drew a corner of her sari over her hair.

" 'Oh, I'm so sorry to keep you waiting, Raj.' She seemed beside herself with embarrassment. 'My bus got stuck behind a lorry which had hit a rickshaw. Please forgive me. Roopa, would you bring my sewing basket? And more tea for Raj, of course.'

"By then I'd already drunk three cups of tea. Still, I couldn't refuse. 'Please don't worry,' I told Roopa's mother. 'I wasn't busy tonight anyway. Oh, by the way, we have more sewing for you, if you have the time. I'll be needing a complete set of dress shirts for my new job.'

"Finally, when I got up to go, Roopa came to the door. I saw her face bathed in the silver moonlight and couldn't say good-bye. I walked off like I was in a dream and didn't want to wake up. By the time I got into my car, I'd reached a conclusion: Roopa was the woman I wanted.

"Roopa . . ." Raj repeats her name, emotion choking his voice.

Now I know how much he loved her. His pain must run deep, so deep I can find no words of comfort. All I can do is to sit beside him and, clasp his hand in silent support.

A clap of thunder and a flash of lightning propel me to my feet. The hissing wind brings with it leaves, stinging grains of dust, and occasional raindrops. In the murky darkness that descends, people nearby are reduced to shadowy figures. A man packs up his picnicware, shaking his head at the unexpected turn of the weather, and mutters a prayer. A woman wraps her veil across her face to protect herself from the dust. "Arun! Romesh!" she calls out to her children. "Where are you? What kind of children don't hear their mother's voice?"

Toys strewn on the ground, billows of dust rising behind them, the woman collects her offspring. The entire family runs for shelter.

In one sudden motion Raj surges to his feet. His eyes dart about, as though he has just awakened and is trying to regain his balance.

A gust of wind tangles my hair as I roll up the blanket. "Let's get going," I say.

I CURL up in a chair on the balcony, halfheartedly listening to the BBC world news coming from the radio in the living room—something about GATT tariff reduction affecting England's balance of payments. My attention drifts away. I recall the scene from last night as Raj and I returned home from Buddha Jayanti Park. Inside the gate, just as I was regretting the evening's end, Raj put his arm around me, tilted my chin up, and met my lips in a long, lingering kiss. The tingling warmth in my body remained as we ascended the steps together. At the landing he took my hand and held it for a moment. Then reluctantly we parted to retire to our respective rooms.

Only a few minutes ago, Raj left for the airport for "yet another business trip." Now I relive his parting words, the cushioning of his hand as it enfolded mine, the way his eyes seemed to encompass my entire being. Each new minute spent with him makes me miss him all the more when he is away.

I console myself by sketching the trails and meadow of the Buddha Jayanti Park in my sketchbook, complete with a flash of lightning. Underneath I record:

I left the trail for a sojourn through the rocks. Scrambling.

I notice the postman across the street, a cotton *jhola* hanging from his shoulder. He's coming toward our building. I hurry down the steps in anticipation, eager for news from home. Plucking the bundle from the mailbox, I climb up the steps and retreat to the living room to sort through it. Let's see: copies of *Femina* and *Filmfare* for Neelu. Several envelopes for Mrs. Khosla bearing stamps of different countries, reminding me oddly of a string of U.S. military bases. And then, an aerogramme for Raj from the States. I can't resist stealing a look at the return address. Helen Trillen. Helen of Troy? You, lurking just beyond the horizon, I want to ask, What do you want?

Ah, finally, here's a letter for me, a grayish blue envelope with a textured feel to the paper. It's from Liz in Chicago. I smile inwardly at the familiar, rounded lettering, gratified she has written so quickly.

Depositing the rest of the mail onto the coffee table, I settle into a chair with the letter. As I tear it open, I detect a faint, pleasantly musky fragrance. Liz has not given up on her idiosyncratic habit of putting a dab of perfume, a Guerlain, a Chanel, a Coty below her signature in a letter. Perfume is her passion, but though I've accompanied her on many a shopping excursion to Chicago's golden mile, I've never known her to actually wear the stuff.

> Dear Shari,
>
> By the time you get this letter, you will have been in India at least three weeks. So how do you like it so far? How are things working out with Raj? I'm just dying to know. I must say I admire your willingness to take such a big risk. I couldn't have done what you did.
>
> There are a few new things in my life, too. After neglecting my condo for many years, I've decided to redo the wallpaper in the bathroom and replace the living room furniture. I wish you were here to give me advice on color, shape, and texture. You have such a good eye.
>
> I'm also taking a creative writing class on poetry one night a week. It has turned out to be a lot of fun. Maybe I'll even send you some of the fruits of my labor—if I am brave enough!
>
> By the way, Mitch called yesterday out of the blue. Guess what? He broke up with the vegan blonde and dropped his

animal-free diet. Now he's complaining there aren't many places in Chicago that serve a decent ham-and-eggs breakfast. Oh, he asked me how he could contact you. When I told him you'd left for India to get married, he freaked out and actually blamed me for letting you go. He thinks you're making a big mistake getting into an arranged marriage and is eager to "talk some sense" into your head. He wanted your phone number, but I didn't give it to him. Just before he hung up, he asked me out for coffee and I agreed to meet him at the Bliss Café next Saturday. He seemed so frantic. I don't know if it's the failed relationship or the aftereffects of the vegan diet or finding out that you left for India to get married.

Last weekend I went to Lincoln Park Zoo by myself. The polar bear you used to adore has got his fur dirty and is noticeably fatter. I don't believe he's on a vegan diet. Somehow the zoo visit just wasn't the same without you.

Do write soon.

With all my love,

Liz

P.S. The fragrance is Fugitive. They should put a warning label: Wear at your own risk. So far I haven't.

I close the letter with a nostalgic sigh, slide it back into the envelope, set it down on the coffee table, then walk over to the window.

I don't believe Mitch would call me here. It has to be a bluff. Ten miles outside the Chicago metropolitan area is about the limit of his world. At best he'll try to influence Liz to talk me out of an arranged marriage. The usual Mitch. What does he know? He doesn't comprehend either me or the country I now inhabit.

14

My destination is the United Coffee House in Connaught Circus, where I'm to meet Mistoo, my mother's third cousin. As Prem drives me I feel a little edgy.

Though Mistoo is just three years older than I, my mother refers to her as a cousin-sister. Given that in India the family tree has a profusion of limbs, it's not unusual that she really treats this distant relative of a different generation like a sibling. Despite the age difference, they're close—age being less important in India in matters of heart. And so, in my mother's absence, it has fallen to Mistoo to handle our family's side of the wedding arrangements. Even so, my mother communicates almost daily with her by fax. These days fax machines are ubiquitous in India.

It's been over two decades since I last saw Mistoo. She was barely in her teens then. We may have plenty to talk about, but the first few minutes with a relative can be awkward.

She'll probably say, "Your eyes are just like your mother's, Sharmila."

Or, "Do you remember you broke my favorite bangle the last time you were here?"

Or, "I can't believe you're this tall."

Relatives reminisce about your cute baby self as if they refuse to believe you've grown up. Then too, modern Indian women tend to be warm, open, and voluble. I'm not sure I can match their spontaneity and exuberance.

Prem maneuvers through one winding side street after another, and I wonder why Mistoo wants to meet me at a place so far away from the Defence Colony. As I fidget in the backseat, I observe Prem surreptitiously. As he navigates through choking downtown traffic, he seems cheerful. His hair is neatly brushed to one side, except for a naughty curl that hangs down over one eyebrow. I'm sure if he was alone he'd be whistling.

Prem points to the right. "My sister's house is over that way."

"The newly married one?"

"Yes. Sapna. We visited her and her husband last night. It was very good, you know, sitting and talking, just like old times. We miss her very much. She even prepared a big *khana,* and to our surprise, it was delicious."

"Oh?"

"She wasn't ever much of a cook when she was at home. Her dahl used to be so watery, you had to fish in the bottom to find anything solid. What a change! Last night her dahl was thick, smooth, and creamy. How did she do it? I was about to ask when my mother reminded us of the old belief that the ritual wedding water changes a girl into a woman. Ma sounded so happy. She said it's true every time."

"I'd like to be a good cook, too. But in America everybody's so busy. When I was living with my parents in America, there was always some activity after school. I'd grab something on the way, usually fast food, because that's what everyone in my crowd ate. It's too bad because my mother is really a good cook and could have taught me a lot. Now it looks like I'll have to learn on the job, just like your sister. Do you come from a large family, Prem?"

"No. I still have one sister at home and a little brother. Our flat is always lively, though."

"Where do you live?"

"In Old Delhi."

He says the word "old" in a respectful way. I realize "old" to him means classic, having withstood the test of time, not discarded or decaying. "I haven't been there yet, but I'd really like to see it."

"It might be too crowded for you, madam."

He has laid down a challenge before me, and I respond without thinking. "No, I doubt that. Old Delhi is a must." I lean toward the back of the front seat and rest my chin on the soft leather. "New Delhi may have modern buildings, wide streets, and parks, but it's pretty much like a metropolis anywhere else in the world. My guess is if I'm to find the real India, it'll be in Old Delhi."

"My mother asks about you all the time, madam. 'Where did you take the lady today? What did you talk about? Does Sharmila like our country?' My sister pesters me constantly to bring her a picture of you. And my little brother is practicing 'Hello' and 'How are you?' in English in case you ever come to visit."

Surprised and pleased, I ask, "When do I get to meet them?"

"Are you sure you'd like to visit?"

"Prem, you're treating me like some smug foreigner who's come to India for the shopping and the monuments. I'm not like that. Even though I was born in the States, I was conceived here. I'm an Indian and I'm going to be here for the rest of my life. Or, do you actually have to be born here to qualify for membership?" I pull up short, embarrassed at my outburst. "I'm sorry, Prem. I didn't mean to—"

"Not at all, madam. I'll talk to my mother tonight." He turns his head for an instant, pleasure suffusing his face as though a great idea has seized him.

In the back of my mind a warning light blinks. Why did I accept his invitation so quickly? Though we're on friendly terms and at ease with each other, I don't really know the status of the relationship between him and Raj. Nor do I have the faintest idea how to broach the subject to Raj. Best to keep quiet about the whole matter until the invitation actually materializes.

"Has Raj-babu taken you to many places, madam?"

"Oh, yes." I sit back, relieved at the change of subject. "He's shown me quite a lot, especially considering his busy schedule. All in all, we've had a great time together so far. Things are working out even better than I'd expected. Just yesterday, while we were strolling in Buddha Jayanti Park, he told me all about how he grew up." I stop, realizing I've probably said too much.

"It's okay, madam, you can talk to me. I'm not a member of the Khosla family. Not only am I an outsider, I'm an excellent keeper of secrets. Even my younger sister confides in me all the time: which boy's hand she wants to hold, which one gave her a love note, which one is the best-looking."

"It's nice to have a friend like you, Prem, especially when I'm so new here."

"Friendship means more than money to me." Prem's laugh has a bittersweet quality. "Maybe that's why I'm only a chauffeur."

"Nothing wrong with that. Do you have other plans for the future?"

"Actually, yes. I'm saving up to buy a car so I can start my own travel agency. Also, I want my own home and to make a special woman happy. I want to be always there for my family. But two children only! My biggest joy will be to tell them bedtime stories every evening with my wife sitting beside me. Nothing very exciting, you see. No mansion or corporate jet or big business deals." Prem laughs. "I'm sorry if I'm boring you."

"Not at all." I catch myself sighing. "Those are goals well worth striving for, Prem."

15

I ARRIVE at the United Coffee House just after four o'clock. The
name is a bit of a misnomer as it's actually a full restaurant,
tiny yet gracious, with chandeliers, a mirrored partition dividing
the dining area, and an upstairs theater-style balcony where unescorted women can relax without drawing unwelcome attention. I don't see anyone on the main floor who could conceivably
be my mother's cousin, so I head upstairs, where I can watch the
entrance undisturbed. I slip into a seat at a pleasing oval table,
covered with a black-and-white-checked cloth and a single fresh
rose floating in a bowl as a centerpiece. An overhead fan runs at
full speed, its blades blurring into a shimmering disc as it whips
cool air down to where I sit.

Other than one Western tourist on the main floor, the customers are Indian, mostly executive types, taking a tea break
with family, friends, or business associates, all absorbed in their
own circles. No one has glanced in my direction since I arrived.
Finally I'm beginning to blend in. I'm wearing a comfortably
loose greenish blue brocaded *salwar-kameez*, carefully chosen to
contrast with the olive-brown tone of my skin, with a matching
green bindi on my forehead. My long hair is parted in the middle and pulled back into a thick braid that hangs down my back.
Stylish Kohlapuri sandals encase my feet in satiny comfort. Yet,

for no discernible reason, I feel a little apprehensive as I look at each new arrival.

"May I offer you a menu card, Madam?" the *sherwani*-clad waiter, bending from the waist, says in passable English.

Why isn't he speaking Hindi to me? I can manage restaurant Hindi. Is it that obvious I'm a foreigner? So much for blending in!

I flip curiously through the typewritten pages. All types of dishes are offered, from espresso coffee with whipped cream to *chole* to chow mein. I glance up from my menu just as a lone woman appears in the doorway. Her eyes scan first the dining area, then the balcony. As soon as they come to rest on me, they light up in recognition and she heads for the stairs.

Last time I saw Mistoo was on my first visit to Delhi as a shy ten-year-old. Mistoo was in her early teens then, only three years older, but already a world ahead of me. A bubbly, good-natured girl in a bright red skirt and a cardigan, she had copper-colored cheeks always dimpled with a broad smile. According to Mother, the intervening years haven't robbed her of her humor. When consulted about the Khosla proposal, she wrote that certainly she knew Raj and would have gone after him herself for all that she was worth, except her worth wasn't enough.

The woman coming toward me now is just a little older. Slender and thin-boned, she's elegantly attired in a georgette sari, but her smile is so dazzling I barely notice her outfit. It's Mistoo, all right.

"Hello, Sharmila." Mistoo slips into a chair opposite me. "Sorry I'm late. But I keep what is known as Indian time."

"Mistoo Auntie . . ." I half rise and fold my hands.

"I recognized you right away. You have your mother's eyes. But you're so tall, even taller than me. And please don't call me auntie. You make me feel old." Her voice, feigning annoyance, is full of warmth. "*Aare baa-baa,* I'm not that much older than you."

By the time the waiter appears, Mistoo is ready to order. That done, she proceeds to bring me up to date on the family news. Lots of comings and goings with some relatives leaving for Canada and Singapore for well-paying jobs, and of course the ones in Delhi are anxious to know all about me. When will I be coming to their house for a visit? I envy Mistoo for the ease with which she draws a semi-stranger into her confidence. The cozy atmosphere of the dimly lit restaurant adds to the intimacy, and slowly my inhibitions dissolve.

Mistoo pops a fish pakora into her mouth and closes her eyes blissfully with an "Aahhh!" I hear the crunchy sound and can tell she likes the sound as much as she likes the taste. She throws a glance at the next table, which is occupied by a family, and whispers that she knows them and that the woman is much abused by her husband. I'm shocked, but before I can ask any questions, Mistoo begins to fill me in on the wedding details. By the time I'm on my third pakora and Mistoo on her fifth or sixth, I know all about the *mehendi* artist she has reserved for painting my palms, her plans for the *sangeet*, music, and the six-door limousine she has rented for the wedding party.

"The *mehendi* artist will show you several designs to choose from," Mistoo says with a smirk. "And she will work in the initials R.K somewhere in your body. An ancient custom, but many brides nowadays want it."

"You mean . . . ?"

"It'll be a challenge for Raj to find them on your wedding night."

A pleasurable challenge, I vow to myself with a tremble of anticipation.

"You know, Mistoo, I find all these customs charming."

"Of course, you would. You grew up in America. This is your first time here as an adult, Sharmila. But it's different than when you were a child. I hope this experience isn't going to be too hard for you."

"I must admit even though I planned for months and read all I could, it hasn't been easy. I guess there's always a difference between theory and practice. But I think I'm adjusting well—"

"You'll go through three stages," Mistoo says, interrupting. "All my relatives from abroad say so. First, they can't stand the noise, the pollution, and the crowds. They complain about the bureaucracy. Neither men nor women like the restrictions. Then in the second stage, they become wild about India. Suddenly they've discovered a great culture with ancient roots. The men start to wear *kurta*-pajamas, the women spend a lot of time in the sari stores." Again the dazzling smile. "Finally, in the third stage, they become a bit more realistic."

"In the last few years I've been drawn to India more and

more." I speak dreamily. "Art, books, movies, music and dance, all pulled me to this country. I'm not sure I can put it in words."

"Oh, Mother India!" Mistoo cocks her head, giving me a sly look. The pearls dangling from her ears catch light from the chandelier above and shimmer like foam on the sea at night. "It's Raj, isn't it? Come on, the truth."

Ready for girl talk, I kick off my sandals and slide down into my chair. "Yes, yes, and yes." I burst out laughing.

"Raj is one of the few good men left in Delhi." Mistoo sighs. "I should know. Here I am in my mid-thirties, and I still haven't been able to find someone decent."

So it's true that Mistoo had a crush on Raj. To know your man is desired by other women can make you proud, but insecure, too. "When did you meet him?" I ask offhandedly.

"Not soon enough." Mistoo's laugh has a brittle quality to it. "Some other woman always seems to get there first. He couldn't marry the American woman he met in college—his mother wouldn't allow that. So when he came back, he scouted the prospects with a vengeance, you might say." Again the brittle laugh. "First there was Uma, then Sita, then Bela."

I experience a pinprick of jealousy. Who were these women? But then, do I really want to know?

"Finally, he met Roopa and . . ." Mistoo pauses. "I guess you know how that ended. So this time Raj decided to settle for a compromise that'd satisfy his mother. He decided the best choice would be an Indian-American woman, especially since he wants to move back to the States eventually. That'd be good for him. He needs to forget all that has happened here." She adjusts the border of her sari at the shoulder in a thoughtful manner.

"Actually, I don't know much about Roopa's death. Could you tell me about it?"

"Oh, well, she had an accident. She fell down a flight of stairs and broke her neck."

Just like that? In my mind's eye I envision a marble tumbling down the red sandstone steps at the Khoslas', bouncing from step to step, then striking the ground full force and shattering. It's the same staircase I climb daily.

My body sags against the chair. "What caused the fall?"

Mistoo raises her eyes. "No one knows for sure. She was home alone, and wasn't feeling well. The servants were off for the afternoon, and Mrs. Khosla had gone shopping. When she came back, Roopa's body was lying at the foot of the staircase."

I get the uneasy feeling that there's more to the story. The odds against a young woman falling down stairs and breaking her neck must be astronomical, but if Mistoo knows more, she's hiding it pretty well. "Was there an inquest?"

"Oh, yes. And they closed the case almost immediately."

I lean forward, my cheek against my hand. A sinister question is prowling in my mind, not for the first time. Its genesis is a story I read in the newspaper yesterday. A bride's family provided the groom with a refrigerator and some furniture, but failed to deliver a motorcycle that had been promised during the dowry negotiations. Shortly after the wedding the bride, living with her in-laws, died in a kitchen fire, which was conveniently blamed on a stove exploding. A woman's rights activist interviewed by the newspaper is highly skeptical, maintaining that too many newlywed brides perish in stove explosions for this one to be an accident. She thinks the groom's family was angry about the insufficient dowry. In this society, she says, a woman's life isn't valued much more than that of a sheep.

"I'm sure it must have been an accident, Mistoo."

"Of course it was!" The edge in Mistoo's voice is hard to miss. "What did you think? Another dowry death? Raj chose to marry Roopa even though her family wasn't rich. It was understood from the beginning there would be no dowry. In any case, the Khoslas were quite wealthy and didn't need it. Besides, women are working these days, and they've become more independent. So dowry is much less common among the educated people."

"Well, I'm certain my father isn't paying a dowry. I wouldn't marry Raj if that were the case." Then it occurs to me that only a few days ago Neelu spoke of family debts, and I feel a twitch of nausea in my stomach. "Is there anything to the rumor that Raj's father was deeply in debt when he died?"

"My very special niece." Mistoo pats my hand. "The Khoslas are an honorable family. Don't pay any attention to whispers."

That single cell of unease divides again, about to multiply into an embryo of suspicion. Has my father made a secret arrangement with Mrs. Khosla? Taking the exchange rate into consideration, American dollars convert to much bigger rupee numbers. Is my father paying a substantial dowry without my knowledge? Is that the primary reason Raj chose me over other candidates? I am going to pose some hard questions to my father when he arrives.

Yet there are millions of Indian women who face a situation far worse than mine. Unwelcome at birth because of their sex, growing up with sorrow, seeing their all too poor parents scrimp for their wedding, then, once married, facing beatings by in-laws, or even the prospect of having a fatal "accident." I feel a deep sympathy for those wretched souls. Truly we're sisters and our hearts cry as one.

"The Khoslas all liked Roopa." Mistoo crunches another pakora in her mouth. "Neelu cried for days when Roopa died. And I . . ."

"How well did you know Roopa?"

"I met her in college. Even though we grew up in the same neighborhood, we moved in different social circles and so we never met until then. She was quiet, and you know what I am. Being with her was like an evening walk through the park. Refreshing, relaxing, peaceful. And she was so talented. She was more than just an excellent student. She was quite keen on sports. She played badminton as well as Raj and made him work to win. Her singing voice was exceptional, and she played the harmonium. She even taught me embroidery. We were close." Mistoo lets out a sigh. "Even after her marriage she'd come over for a visit from time to time. We'd sit together and do embroidery just like in our school days. At the time of her death, she was lettering the corner of a bedspread in red: 'Raj and Roopa.' She was working on her last *a*."

Raj and Roopa. A bedspread embroidered with their names. A surge of jealousy boils up within me. I wait for the feeling to subside, then ask, "Was she happy?"

"She claimed to be, but at times I wondered." Mistoo's vivacious eyes cloud over.

I take a bite of a fish pakora, find the fritter to be tasteless, and put it back down on the plate.

With pain thickening her voice, Mistoo says, "Roopa came to visit her parents on the *baishakhi* holiday. Everyone was in the drawing room when I walked in—grandparents, uncles and aunts and children—all of them talking." She pauses, struggling with some powerful emotion. Stray hairs on her temple wave erratically in the breeze from the overhead fan. She leans forward with the effort of recalling a painful memory, one arm stiff as it rests on the table. "In the middle of all of that Roopa was standing alone by the window. When she sensed my presence, she turned. There was an expression in her eyes I couldn't fathom. With so many relatives around, I was unable to ask her what was wrong. Instead we talked about her embroidery project, my job, and my upcoming trip to Siliguri to visit an uncle. I told myself I'd ring her up when I got back and meet her here. She always liked this coffee house, especially their pakoras. On the day, just as I was getting ready to call her, the phone rang. . . ."

Mistoo's lips are taut with pain. The walls around us seem deathly gray, the air stagnant, the silence oppressive.

If truth is hard to bear, delayed truth is even more so. Such is my feeling about the Roopa story. I think I see why Raj travels, why he's opening up to me only a bit at a time. This tragedy has made him cautious. He wants to let me in, but pain pushes him back—it's easier to suffer alone. Strangely enough, I don't hate Roopa. Quite the contrary, I can picture her as though she were my previous incarnation.

Tears begin to seep from Mistoo's eyes, tiny diamonds trickling down over her cheeks. I cup her hand and offer her some tissues from my purse.

"I'm sorry to be so sentimental, Sharmila. It's time to bury old memories. After all, you're here and we've so many happy things to discuss."

"You had a great loss, Mistoo. I feel badly for you. But I am glad we had this chance to get acquainted. I know I'll never be able to take Roopa's place, but we can still be friends."

At that moment I notice Prem peeking in from the entrance. Satisfied that he's attracted my attention, he disappears. Just the sight of him helps drive out the darkness lurking inside me. I'll be glad to get out of here and go home in his company. With the possible exception of Neelu, he's the only one who doesn't look upon me as Roopa's replacement.

After a quick glance at my watch, I turn back to Mistoo. "Oh, I totally lost track of time. I have to get back."

Mistoo's eyes are riveted on the empty doorway. "Who's he?"

"Oh, my driver Prem. He's more than a driver. He's a most wonderful guide."

"What's his family name?"

"Last name? I know this sounds silly, Mistoo, but I don't know. I just never thought to ask."

"You can tell so much from people's family name here, Sharmila. Where they're from, their castes . . ."

I sense where she's going. "Prem is a Dalit."

"Oh?" Mistoo sharply withdraws her hand from the table. "But he's very handsome. Don't tell my mother I said so." Her voice is a little stiff. "She always asks about someone's caste and what kind of work they do."

I find myself getting irritated. "I suppose that's because Dalits are considered unclean, not fit to associate with."

"There's still a stigma attached to being an untouchable, Sharmila, but only when it comes to marriage."

"I can't believe what I'm hearing, Mistoo. I haven't met anyone here who's kinder, wiser, or gentler than Prem. When will people outgrow their narrow-minded prejudice and accept individuals like him for who they are?"

"My, my. You seem rather sensitive about him. Why should you care? After all, you have Raj."

Having Raj is starting to seem a lot more complicated than I'd expected. Though I don't agree with Mistoo's attitude toward Dalits, I don't want to spoil the afternoon or lose her goodwill. "I'm sorry, Mistoo. I didn't mean to blow up like that. I'm just tired."

"Not at all, Sharmila. And by the way, you're right. Believe it or not, India's changing, just not as fast as you might like. Most of her billion people can't read or write and are living as their ancestors did a century ago. To change a society like ours takes time. We have a saying here that a person's lifetime is but the blink of an eye in India's history."

I know what Mistoo says is true. Still, it sounds like a cop-out.

She seems to read my thoughts. "One time I asked my mother, 'Ma, why do you only ask: What's his caste? How much money does he make? How big is his flat?' My mother answered me with a story. It was about the partition of India in 1947, how Punjab was divided in two. One part joined India and the other, Pakistan. Her home happened to be on the Pakistan side. When riots broke out between Hindus and Muslims, and her family feared for their lives, they left their houses and most of their belongings and fled on foot toward the Indian border, hoping to reach Delhi.

"The trains had stopped running. Every one, even the children, carried something. It was a difficult journey that lasted for days. My mother was only fourteen. Many people didn't make it, including her ten-year-old brother, who collapsed from the heat. My mother tried to carry his body, but she kept falling farther and farther behind. She was forced to leave him by the side of the road. Once her family settled in Old Delhi, she, the daughter of a farmer who had formerly been rich, had to take a job as a maid. That day my mother said to me, 'I'm a survivor, Mistoo. I have lungs to breathe and legs to walk and I have my eyesight. But my heart has been cut out. Survivors like me only ask basic questions. Lower caste, lower pay. Lower pay, not enough food. Now do you understand, my child?' "

In the stillness that closes around us, I recall that my father's family was rich and long settled in New Delhi, but my mother's family had to flee from East Pakistan at about the same time. Does my mother have a similar reason for marrying me to a rich man? Whatever the answer is, history has never cut so close. But for a quirk of fate, I could have been walking that hot, dusty road to India. After so much suffering, I'd probably have reacted in a similar way.

Prem comes to mind. He's patiently waiting by the car outside. "I should probably go now, Mistoo. You've given me a lot to think about. Let's get together again soon."

"By all means, Sharmila. The next time you'll have to come to our flat and meet my mother, but I wanted to meet you here, to have a chance to talk to you in private first. And, of course, I'd like to introduce you to our other relatives as soon as possible."

Mistoo mentions the preparation our extended family is going through for my wedding. Uncle Akhil doing this, cousin-sister Bithika doing that, and our bedridden great Aunt Padma giving orders to everybody. At the prospect of getting acquainted with them all, once again I feel a warmth flowing between me and Mistoo. I gather up my purse.

"Please do call me if you need anything, Sharmila." Mistoo gives me her business number. "Promise?"

I squeeze her hand and walk with a straight back toward the

door, as if to deny the weight Mistoo's words have put on my heart.

An hour later, I sprawl on my bed staring at the ceiling fan, still trying to sort out the implications of Mistoo's revelations. Neelu appears at my door, her presence like sunshine chasing an afternoon shower. I sit up and invite her in, but she remains standing outside.

"The *daak* just came," she bursts out.

I get up and go to her. I notice that she has outlined her lower eyelids in blue. Her waist-length black hair is flowing down her back. She's wearing jeans, but they're only part of an ensemble that includes a white blouse woven with crystals and sequins, thick glass bangles, and long bell-shaped earrings. The overall effect is stunning. "Where are you going so dressed up?" I ask.

"To a party at a friend's house." She waves a blue envelope back and forth in front of me. "Can you believe it! A letter from Helen of Troy. Raj's old girl friend. This makes three times she's written this month. She must be working herself up for a visit."

"What for?"

"Raj mentioned she was doing research on Indian art. Writing some kind of paper. I doubt he wants to see her, but I'm dying of curiosity. Aren't you?"

I shake my head no. "What's past is past." And I hope it's true.

Except, old flames do have a way of burning your hand, just when you least expect it.

16

THE morning air outside is crisp. I sit by the window, listening to the whistle of tree-pies as they dart about in the intense light of a dazzling blue sky. I contemplate yesterday's encounter with Mistoo. What really happened with Roopa? She was bright, married into a good family, and was physically active. How could someone like that fall down the steps? And what about the family debts Neelu mentioned? Might there be a connection? I wonder again if Roopa's wasn't a dowry death in disguise.

Mistoo's sadness at the loss of Roopa somehow brings Liz to mind, and I experience a keen sense of loss myself. Liz is not just a friend. Rather, she's more like a sister without the usual sibling rivalry. Leaving her is one of my few regrets in coming to India.

We first met in kindergarten, though my only remembrance of that early period was that she snatched a toy train of mine and never returned it. Years passed before we encountered each other again, this time in a high school history class. Was this the same Liz Wojdala? At five foot four, she was shorter than I by several inches. Hair bobbed, her complexion pink-toned and smooth, she looked neat in a well-fitted dress. I'd gone the other way and worn baggy pants and a pullover that day.

We hit it off right from the beginning and were soon insepa-rable. Later when her family moved to Sheridan Road in north

Chicago, we became neighbors as well. Liz's parents were first-generation Polish. Her carpenter father, a big man with a Slavic accent, was the jovial type. I still vividly recall the first time I met him.

"Shari, sit down, sit down," he said. "I remember you from when you both were in kindergarten. You're Indian, Liz tells me. Curry-type Indian?"

Just as I started to laugh, Liz's mother appeared with a plate of cookies. She was sturdy, of medium height, a little wobbly like someone in high heels, though she wore only flat shoes.

"Try this, honey." She pronounced the word as "hauny," in a nasal tone, and handed me the plate. "I just baked them."

I took a bite from a cookie, found it tasted like sand, but swallowed it anyway so as not to embarrass Liz.

I learned that Liz's mother loved to cook, and in between her chores as the manager of the apartment building, she spent most of her time in the kitchen, making peasant-style soups and stews. That is, if her arm wasn't bothering her.

"I can barely raise my right arm," she said in her thick accent. Her consonants seemed to beat up her vowels. "It got stuck to my side the day I left Poland. I've hardly been able to use it since. I used to love dancing. Now it's out of the question." Then she abruptly switched gears. "You live only two blocks away, Liz said. Does your building have a foyer, Shari?"

In other words, how much money does your father make? I glanced over at Liz. She was squirming in her seat, a crimson blush coloring her cheeks. It wouldn't have done any good to explain to Mrs. Wojdala that my father had just started his private practice in dentistry, that we were content in our modest two-bedroom apartment, and that even if it wasn't the choicest address in Chicago, it was a hundred yards closer to Lake Michigan, a better neighborhood in Chicago real estate terms than hers.

I simply answered, "We have a small foyer. But it's going to look much bigger when they finish repainting our building in a lighter shade."

Saying that reminded me that our whole neighborhood needed a paint job. The buildings had such a dreary, grayish 1930s feel that regardless of the time of the day they seemed to be bathed in eternal twilight. As if in keeping with the general ambiance, the inhabitants had sallow complexions and puffy cheeks, nested atop stocky, squarish bodies. The most popular colors, if they could even be called that, were camel and brown.

We were the only Indian family in the neighborhood and initially drew a lot of stares wherever we went. The first time my mother wore a sari on the street, someone asked her if she was a gypsy dancer.

"I beg your pardon," my mother huffed.

As my friendship with Liz deepened, our families got to know each other. My mother invited Liz's parents to dinner. Liz's mother brought her usual cookies. Though there were differences in culture, educational level, and race, the two sets of parents, both recent immigrants trying to adjust to Chicago, talked plenty that night.

My father took to Liz's father right away. He said later, "Mr. Wojdala is a happy man. He has the best teeth in town. He'll live a hundred years."

But Mother didn't care for her new acquaintance or her complaints. "Mrs. Wojdala's jelly cookies stick to the roof of my mouth."

Liz was, however, the girl Mother wished I would be. She was quiet, opened her mouth only when she thought she'd be taken seriously, and obeyed her elders, or at least appeared to do so. I was outspoken, questioning, reluctant to follow orders.

Though Liz's background was Eastern European and mine Asian Indian, it turned out that our families held many values in common. In language, for instance. Both sets of parents spoke their native tongue at home to encourage fluency in their children. The results were decidedly mixed, though.

Oddly enough, I was more receptive than Liz. My mother spoke Bengali, some Hindi, and English. My father, who was raised in Delhi, spoke fluent Hindi and English and Bengali. At home I spoke mostly English, and occasionally Hindi and Bengali interspersed with English or, when in a frivolous mood, strings of sentences in Hindi or Bengali with the exaggerated hand gestures and head movements of a "Thousand Nights" type storyteller until I couldn't keep a straight face any longer.

Liz, however, refused to speak a word of Polish. To her parents' chagrin, she became proficient in Spanish and spent an inordinate amount of time in the high school language lab perfecting her accent.

"Why Spanish?" I once asked. "Do you really hate Polish that much?"

"Shhh," Liz answered. "The answer is yes. But don't tell Mom. I even dream in Spanish."

Liz and I ended up at different universities—Northwestern for me, Indiana for her—but we managed to stay in touch. I wasn't surprised when Liz announced she was going to major in Spanish. Her mother lamented that Liz had betrayed her family. For most of her stay at Indiana University, Mrs. Wojdala refused to see her, though she did attend her daughter's graduation. On holidays Liz often stayed with us.

Only after Liz got job offers to teach Spanish at several Chicago high schools did her mother finally relent. Her daughter had her own apartment and a respectable job. Mrs. Wojdala was proud of her. As a gesture of reconciliation, Liz took her mother on vacation to Mexico and asked me to come along, probably for moral support. Curiously enough, Mrs. Wojdala enjoyed herself. After a lifetime of bland middle European food, she was overwhelmed by the vibrant, spicy Mexican dishes. She came home bubbling with ideas of creating flavor combinations, such as spaetzle with mole sauce. That sauce, she insisted, had cured the stiffness in her arm. Finally she could polka again. And her beloved daughter knew just where to shop in Chicago for the necessary ingredients. To my mother Mrs. Wojdala finally confided, "I've raised a good daughter."

My first job as a graphic artist offered what seemed like plenty of money, so I fixed up my apartment, went to see plays with Liz, and began dating frequently. Liz, on the other hand, rarely went out with men. She didn't seem to undergo the chemical changes that take place when you meet an attractive person of the opposite sex. She remained her usual cool self. Men ended up being her friends. Then Mitch showed up. I didn't have an inkling when Liz introduced us that she and Mitch had gone out a couple of times. I was attracted to him, and since Liz showed no apparent interest, I accepted with a smile when he asked me to go to the Bliss Café with him.

The next morning Liz and I met at the Coffee Palace on Michigan Avenue. The spring day was already hot and humid, reminding us that another miserable Chicago summer was around the corner. We were sitting by the window.

"Oh, this heat," Liz said.

"My air conditioner has to be repaired. I have to get new shorts."

Liz murmured, "And I have to lose weight," then became silent and distant.

I tried to gauge her mood, quickly gave up and blamed it on the heat. I started to tell her about my date, but instead of bringing her out of her funk, it only made things worse.

"You could have told me," Liz said abruptly.

"Told you what?"

"That you were seeing Mitch."

"But why?" I asked, surprised. "You're not going out with him anymore."

Liz looked away. "It won't work."

My throat felt thick and constricted. I finally managed weakly, "What do you mean?"

"Just take my word for it."

"No, really. What do you mean, Liz?"

She clammed up, and I couldn't get another word out of her. In silence we finished our coffee and went our separate ways without even a good-bye. The rest of the day my stomach churned. I'd go to the phone to call her, then stop and retreat to the sofa.

Liz was wrong. Soon Mitch and I were seeing each other regularly. I was so happy that my estrangement from Liz faded from my mind.

Then one Saturday morning the phone rang. "So, where were you last night?" Liz demanded. "I tried you several times to see if you wanted to listen to some guitar music."

"Mitch and I were having dinner at The Bakery."

A long silence. Then Liz said in a low voice, "Mitch was mine." The hurt and anger at her next words were unmistakable. "You stole him."

"Liz, can we talk about it?"

A sharp click followed by a dial tone was my only answer.

I was standing there, paralyzed, barely breathing, when Mitch walked over, gently took the receiver from my hand, put it back on its cradle. "Don't mind her. She had a crush on me." He encircled me with his arms. "Don't let her get between us. She'll get over it."

In the months after Mitch moved in with me, I stashed all concern for Liz in a closet in the back of my mind. Only occasionally, when I heard spoken Spanish or guitar music, would I be reminded of her. A new love has a way of brushing aside unpleasant distractions, and soon I simply stopped thinking about her.

Fourteen months went by, and then it was my turn to call. "You'll be happy to know, Liz . . ." My voice choked up. "Mitch and I are through."

I heard a sigh at the other end of the line. I poured out my tale, and while Liz listened sympathetically, I detected a smug vindication in her attitude.

"There are changes in my life, too," she said much later, after I'd finished. "No man as yet. Just thought I'd try something new. I've changed my last name to Worthington."

Anticipating her mother's reaction, I asked, "Why, Liz?"

"Don't you think I look more like a Worthington, less like a Wojdala?"

I realized she needed to see herself in a new light. "Now that I think of it, the name does have a certain dignity. It suits you. Congratulations, Liz."

"Thanks. But you should have seen my mother when I broke the news to her last Sunday. She was bringing the main course in from the kitchen. She dropped it on the floor. Mole sauce all over the carpet! Naturally she wants me to pay for the carpet cleaning and the china."

Soon Liz and I were close friends again, which was not so surprising. We had so much past history, so much in common. We'd take the El to our old neighborhood even though driving would have been much faster. We were trying to relive the old times, though both of us were changing, especially Liz. Maybe it was her new name, or reaching thirty or perhaps a prolonged state of being without a man, the quiet, mousy girl known as Liz soon became a rabid environmental activist.

At her request, I attended a wildlife conservation meeting in which she addressed an audience of about two hundred. She delivered a passionate polemic against the encroachment of civilization on the habitat of the white-tail deer population. The speech dragged on for so long that an elderly man in the front row became violently dizzy and had to be escorted out.

Yet in many ways she remained the same Liz. She wore pearls

whether they were in fashion or not. Her skirts were always longer than those on the Michigan Avenue mannequins. Her red lipstick was a classic Eva Peron. She kept to tradition, even if it was one entirely of her own making.

A month ago on a sunless autumn Saturday we were at the Coffee Palace when I announced to Liz my upcoming arranged marriage in India. I extended her an invitation to attend my wedding in Delhi. I expected her to wink at me and say, "Can you find a match for me? Keep your eyes peeled."

Instead she said, "Are you sure you know what you're doing?"

"I do. It'll be almost like going home, Liz. I truly believe I can be happy in India in a way I'll never be happy here. And the success rate of those marriages seems good."

With a sigh Liz said, "That's your strong point. You jump into the fire even though you know you might get burned. Me, I just sit and rot."

Her cheeks looked puffy—she'd put on a little weight. I wondered sadly if she had given up on meeting men. "I'll miss you, Shari."

"I'll be back."

And so, on this cool December morning in Delhi, I pick up a rainbow stationery pad and Parker pen. Suppressing a feeling of uncertainty about my current situation, I begin:

Dear Liz:

Things are going great for me. Raj has turned out to be a fascinating man. I liked him right from the beginning, but as we spend more time together, I realize it's much more than that. I think I'm falling in love with him. I never dreamed that an arranged match could turn out this way

As for India, it's confusing and beautiful, jarring and provocative. One needs a receptiveness to a very different way of thinking and acting to live here. I had to check my Western preconceptions at the door after I arrived. Now I find myself changing. I'm less judgmental than usual, and I can let go of myself more easily. All my actions come from a center I didn't even know existed previously.

Hope you can make it to New Delhi one of these days. I'm sure you'll find it an eye opener. In the meantime, write whenever you can.

Always yours,
Shari

Underneath my signature I sketch the gray hornbill that is flitting about just outside the window, remembering that a flying bird is a symbol of hope in Indian tradition. I fold the sheet, slip it into an envelope, and seal it with my fondest hopes for Liz's well-being.

As Prem shows me around Jantar Mantar on a bright, sunny morning, it occurs to me that a month has passed since my arrival. On the vast grounds of the open-air observatory dotted with palm trees, Prem explains, medieval astronomers once gathered to observe the movement of heavenly bodies and calculated the passage of time with uncanny accuracy.

Every visitor seems to find a special point of interest, and I'm no exception. I become fascinated with a zodiac sign structure. Realizing that I may have interrupted Prem's presentation by lingering too long, I turn to him and ask, "Am I taking too much time?"

"Oh, no, madam. Not at all. I have all the time in the world."

"I thought you only worked for Mrs. Khosla part-time."

"Up until today that was the case. Now I'm working for her full-time temporarily. I don't think it was planned that way, but just this morning she asked me if I would take you out every day and show you new places."

Why the change? I wonder. Though I enjoy Prem's company, I'm perfectly capable of getting around on my own by taxi. "Why didn't she say something to me?"

"Mrs. Khosla never explains, madam. She just tells you what to do."

"And of course, everyone obeys," I reply sarcastically.

"You Americans want to know the reason for everything, don't you?"

"Is that a polite way of saying I'm nosy?"

"Oh, no, madam, please, I didn't mean to offend." Prem leans forward, his expressive eyes filled with remorse, his hand outstretched in a gesture of apology.

I start to reach out and pat his hand reassuringly, but just as quickly control the impulse. "For heaven's sake, Prem. I was just joking."

Relief registers in his eyes. We share a congenial laugh.

As we pause before a giant sundial casting a slanting shadow, Prem explains that it was used to calculate time before the invention of mechanical clocks, and was accurate to within half a second. "The reigning king then took to boasting that he was the master of time," he adds in a jovial tone.

Time and its fleeting nature is very much on my mind as I silently count the number of days till Raj returns. "I would rather say that time is the master and a harsh one at that."

"You miss Raj-babu, don't you? You have the ache, I can tell."

Why should I attempt to hide my feelings from this gentle soul? Though I smile faintly, a dull ache is indeed gripping my chest. "Well, it won't be long. Once we get married, he'll stop traveling."

Prem murmurs, "Perhaps," and continues walking.

It's obvious Prem doesn't believe this, confirming the warnings of an inner voice that my vision of a glorious future life may be nothing more than the product of a wishful thinking. I push the thought away as we arrive at a triangular pinkish-red stone tower, clearly another sundial. It is shimmering in the golden sunlight. Red is the color of passion, fertility, and abundance, Prem informs me, and a popular color indeed hereabouts. I am so captivated by the glowing structure that I ask impulsively, "Would you mind if I did a little sketching?"

"Not at all. Please take as much time as you need."

I sit myself cross-legged on the ground in front of the instrument and pull my sketchpad out of my purse. Just then I hear a sweet, clear female voice, "Hello, Prem."

A young Indian woman in a V-neck pullover and a knee-length skirt is gliding toward us in a sinuous, sexy gait from about thirty feet away. There's familiarity about her greeting to Prem, bordering on intimacy, conveying the impression that she's more than a casual acquaintance. Prem's face lights up at the sound of her voice, and the change in his demeanor is striking. No longer meek and deferential, he strides purposefully in her direction. Though I pretend to be absorbed in my sketching, I watch them out of the corner of my eye. While they smile at each other and converse in a patois of Hindi and English, my sketchpad remains blank. An art teacher taught me long ago that a drawing must have focus. Right now my focus is Prem. A few minutes later, the woman takes her leave after extracting a promise from Prem to meet soon for afternoon tea.

I close my sketchpad on the still blank page and rise in anticipation as Prem turns in my direction. We start toward the next point of interest. It takes Prem several seconds to recover. Finally he breaks the silence. "She's a friend."

What kind of a friend? How long has he known her? What does she mean to him? A stream of questions want to spill forth from my mind, but I force them back.

"We met as volunteers at a drug rehabilitation center," Prem says. "Her father was at one time our ambassador to France. She's rich, well educated, and has traveled in many countries. Still she's kindhearted."

I experience a twinge of discomfort. I feel not so much jealousy but rather a belated recognition that Prem is a sexy, attractive man. All along I've been suppressing a little tugging at my own heart.

We come to a flower bed, and I inhale the subtle scent of a clump of yellow lilies.

"The first time I came here I was a young boy," Prem says. "I spent the whole day here. My father brought me, then left me to wander about on my own and discover things. Eventually, when I got tired of walking, I sat by that bed and ate a packet of roasted *chana*. A day seemed to last forever then."

The scent of the flowers and the sight of tiny green shoots emerging refreshes me. I tell Prem as we keep walking, "I was the same. As a kid I used to think tomorrow would never come. If Dad told me he was going to buy me a toy the next day, I thought it would never come. Now I see time more as a distance between events quantified by the ticking of a clock."

My words so stun Prem that he recoils a step. "People in the West take time very seriously, don't they?"

"Oh, yes." I pause and reflect. "We attack time as though it were a beast that needs taming. To be kept track of, exploited, controlled. There's a beginning and an ending to everything—a day, for instance, or a vacation—and in between you cram in all you can, always with the ticking of the clock in the back of your mind. Sometimes I wonder who's the master."

"Time for us is much more elastic," Prem counters. "It's continuous rather than linear. Our stories never end. My mother has limited reading skills, but she still studies the Ramayana. That mythological epic goes way back, perhaps to five hundred B.C. But Ma says, 'Everything starts and ends there.' What happens or has ever happened doesn't have an end, not for us."

I throw a glance sideways at Prem's placid face, the relaxed yet supple body. His steps are graceful—he flows with time rather than racing against it. He has a keen, probing intellect, yet he's devoid of arrogance. What would have happened if I'd met him under different circumstances . . . ?

I catch myself. Back home we'd have become fast friends. But here? No. A friendship between us is not acceptable, especially since I'm engaged to Raj.

Prem laughs—an appealing blend of shyness and embarrassment. "But probably it's all an illusion on my part."

"Maybe not, Prem. We lack that sense of continuity in America. For the most part, our lives are an endless series of completed acts without links. There's no overall purpose. The pace is too fast, I guess. No time for reflection on the connectedness of things."

"Yes. Even here in Delhi, the pace is picking up as we look to the West. More and more you meet someone, have a nice conversation, then you each go your own way. It never used to be like that. We took time with each other. Still, once you form a friendship, it's forever." Prem seems to contemplate a purple-flowered shrub as we pass by it. "Events in our lives are perceived more in terms of the essence than their duration," he says. "For us the future holds less fear because it's just an extension of the present, which is just an extension of the past."

I sigh. "But the West still has much to offer."

"I don't doubt that. I've never traveled outside India, but I read a lot. And books about travel are my favorite subject, madam."

Madam? Still? It's way past time to dispense with formalities. I come to an abrupt halt and turn to Prem. "Please call me Sharmila."

"Sharmila." He pronounces my name with his whole mouth, then pauses for emphasis. As if the name alone is a story unto itself and further elaboration is unnecessary. Standing there under the brilliant light of the morning sun, I have become my name.

"I realize you Americans prefer to call each other by your names," Prem observes, "but I can't call you Sharmila. Oh, no. That would never do. That's not the custom here."

"Well, how about when nobody's around?"

Prem's lips curl in a hint of a smile. I'm sure he wants to call me Sharmila. From the way he's lowering his eyes, he's clearly enjoying this little secret between us. He walks slightly closer to me now. An expansive feeling fills my chest.

We resume our stroll. All of a sudden I realize I'm famished.

"I don't know about you, Prem, but my stomach seems to keep its own time. It's ready for lunch."

"Let me take you to the Bengali Market. It's not far from here." In Prem's voice is something new—he sounds more in control. "I know several restaurants there, and they all serve excellent food."

We get into the car and a few minutes later find a parking spot. After walking down a bustling lane, we come to a lively square lined with shops and restaurants.

"This market is famous in Delhi." Prem eyes the shops excitedly. "The shops are mostly run by Bengalis who originally came either from Bangladesh or the state of West Bengal."

I'm reminded that my mother is Bengali—and someone else, too. Here's a chance to learn a little bit more about her. I ask casually, "Wasn't Roopa Bengali?"

"As a matter of fact, she was."

"Did you bring her here often?"

"Yes, a few times for shopping."

"So you were working for Mrs. Khosla when Roopa died?"

Prem's eyes are shrouded by anguish and regret. "It was a few months after I'd left the travel agency and started working for the Khoslas. That very afternoon I'd taken Mrs. Khosla shopping here. She had lunch at Nathu's. Then she picked up some spices and sweets. Roopa was home sick. In the evening I dropped Mrs. Khosla off at her house and went home. Later that night I got the news. . . ."

"Do you remember what time you dropped Mrs. Khosla off?"

Prem turns to me. "Why do you want to know?"

"Just curious."

"As it happens, I do keep a little diary that notes my comings and goings."

I'm dying to ask Prem to go back through his diary for details about that fateful evening. But by now we've halted at a door that opens into an informal dining area with plastic tables and a huge showcase of sweetmeats in whites, oranges, and yellows. On one counter is set a juicer, flanked by a basket of oranges and a stack of brilliant red carrots. "Those carrots looks delicious," I observe. "I've never seen red carrots."

"Be sure to try the juice. It's especially sweet during winter. They mix *pudina*—you know, mint—to the juice. And don't leave without sampling the sweets. They're made fresh in the kitchen out back. The Bengalis are famous all over India for their cooking, and this place has the reputation of being the best in Delhi for Bengali food. I'll pick you up in an hour."

Why can't you keep me company? I'm about to suggest, but realize in a flash that it would be inappropriate. Instead I gaze wistfully after his receding figure. A tiny warning voice makes itself heard above my pounding heart: Careful. Prem's an employee of the Khosla family, and besides, he probably doesn't feel the same way about this friendship as you do.

A little numb, I take a seat facing the open door and place my order. Almost at once the waiter returns with a ruby red juice flecked with jade green bits of mint and a small plate of white, boat-shaped *cham-cham*. To my parched throat, the beverage tastes like nectar. I take bites of the intensely sweet, spongy confection and watch the passersby. Eating sweetmeats reminds me of my first visit to India at the age of ten.

We came in October, during Diwali, the festival of light. The monsoon season had ended, and every day the Delhi sky was a generous blue. We stayed with Padma Auntie. On our first evening, Mistoo, her parents, and grandparents dropped by. Three years older, Mistoo carried around a platter of colorful sweetmeats and served them with the confidence and poise of a much older woman. As I looked up expectantly at her, she inserted a flat white round, dripping gobbets of syrup into my mouth and asked, "Do you like this *rajbhog,* my dear? King's sweet in English. You'd better. Grandmother stayed up all night to make them."

The sweet taste was so overpowering that I could only nod mutely. Perhaps the wonder in my eyes was enough to elicit Padma Auntie's tender response. "We offer sweetmeats to those we welcome in our hearts. They communicate what we can't put in words."

Now, whom should I share this plate of *cham-cham* with? I toy with the thought for not more than an instant before a face insinuates itself into my consciousness. A pair of deep black eyes, a slender, wiry body, a smile so warm and inviting that my own lips part involuntarily in response. Feeling a bit flustered, I finish my meal, then rise abruptly in an attempt to banish the image of Prem.

For the next half hour I meander among the shops, unable to suppress an urge fighting its way to the surface. A new ache, Prem would have said.

A FTER a full day of sightseeing with Prem yesterday, I decide to spend today at home watching Mohan cook. It's early afternoon by the time I slip into the kitchen and ease into a chair by the refrigerator, notepad and pen in hand. Mohan is already hard at work at the black granite kitchen counter, the muscles of his upper arm rippling as he reduces a large red onion to a fine mince. He does this with a nonchalance born of years of practice. The *thwack-thwack-thwack* of his knife is accompanied by a growing pile of chopped bits on the cutting board.

Mohan turns his head in my direction as the chair creaks under my weight. His deep black hair is brushed back to one side, the stylish waves held in place by a light pomade. "Ah, Sharmila-memsahib, welcome to my kitchen. I'd have invited you here sooner, but—"

"Not everyone is allowed in the kitchen?"

Mohan's dark cheeks redden in embarrassment. "Traditionally the kitchen is the heart of the household, memsahib. It is usually tucked away out of sight of casual visitors. It's considered sacred. Only the mother and the cook are permitted. Just as you don't open your heart to everyone." A pause. "But please, forgive me. I don't mean to be impolite. And in any case, times are changing. To tell you the truth, I didn't know you'd want to visit the kitchen so soon."

"Quite the opposite, Mohan. I'm honored to be here. And please don't let me interrupt you."

He nods appreciatively and returns to his task. Though he's dressed much like an office worker—military green slacks and a cotton twill shirt—his concentration and efficient manner of arranging tools and ingredients reveal him to be a master of his craft. Whole spices and spice pastes in brown, yellow, and blue-black are neatly arranged in bowls in measured amounts. Pots and pans are within easy reach. My approach to cooking is less structured, more like painting a picture: A palette is present, but nothing else is predetermined. This man, however, seems to know exactly where he wants to end up and how he wants to get there.

Mohan's eyes begin to water from the stinging touch and scent of the chopped allium, and he steps away from the counter. He mumbles an apology as he wipes his eyes with his forearm. I take the opportunity to look around the capacious kitchen. It's modern by Indian standards, but not fancy. Only a stove, refrigerator, an Ultra brand mixer-grinder along with the usual assortment of cookware and utensils. Yet the meals prepared here bear eloquent testimony to Mohan's skills. I'm told he buys his produce fresh daily from the market.

From the adjacent maid's room come fragments of conversation and laughter. I strain to hear the words but can't.

"Champa's on a long break," Mohan says. Like many Delhiites, he speaks fluent English, delivered in a rapid-fire fashion. "She's supposed to grind the spices and chop the onions, but today her sister is visiting, so I'll have to do all her work as well as my own."

"Mrs. Khosla doesn't mind . . . ?"

Mohan shakes his head emphatically. "Not a bit. She's quite taken with Champa. Just the other day she gave Champa a new sari."

I saw her in an elegant new blue and yellow print the other day, and I remember wondering how she could afford it on a maid's salary. Curiosity turns to suspicion which nags at the edge of my consciousness. What is Mrs. Khosla's connection with the maid?

"Now I'm ready to make mutton kalia." Mohan's voice pulls me back to the present. He picks up a bowl containing glossy, purplish-red mutton cubes. "It's not a difficult dish to prepare," he says with an expert's shrug.

"My mother used to make it in Chicago." I recall the velvety taste of the deep brown sauce. "But I bet it's nothing like what you're making right now."

A shy smile registers on Mohan's lips at the compliment. "Thank you, Sharmila-memsahib. It's Raj-sahib's favorite. I hope you'll feel the same way. And I'll show you a trick or two to make it really special."

Now it's my turn to smile. "Oh, Mohan, I'm so happy you're willing to share your secrets with me."

"It's my pleasure, Sharmila-memsahib. I've liked you since the first day you walked into this house. Anything I can do to make your marriage happy, I'll do." Mohan's voice has lost its professorial tone. "You know, my older sister Deepti is about your age."

"Does she still live at home?"

"No, she got married and now lives with her husband's family. We used to fight all the time when we were children. She was more intelligent than I and went on to study mathematics in college. I took hotel management courses. Once when we were arguing about something, she called me a mule. I was very angry and told her I might be a mule, but at least I was a well-fed mule, because I cooked better than she did. My wish was for her to get married and leave. But the day she did, the house became dark and empty." A note of nostalgia enters Mohan's voice. "Oh, yes, I have other brothers and sisters. But still . . ."

Mohan seems to possess some secret about how to live with people. He and his siblings have an unusual capacity for loving each other and co-existing even in the presence of conflict. I have rarely found so in the West.

Mohan says, "If you and Raj-sahib ever move into that bungalow, perhaps you could take me along as your cook."

"You know about the bungalow?"

"Oh, yes." Mohan busies himself preheating a round-bottomed, wok-like *karai* on the stove. After a few seconds he continues, "Raj-sahib wanted a bungalow for Roopa-bahuji and himself, but then . . . the tragedy occurred. It is only natural that he'll want to buy one for you, too."

So, the bungalow idea isn't new—it's sort of a secondhand gift. I struggle to suppress the feeling of betrayal at this news.

Mohan takes a bottle of oil from the overhead cupboard and turns back to the stove. "And now . . ." He drizzles some oil into the *karai*. "Watch carefully. Next time you'll make this dish for Sahib. I'll be there to give you a hand if you need it."

Though the prospect of cooking dinner for Raj does not delight me at this moment, I come over next to Mohan where I can get a better view.

"The first lesson is heating the oil. If the oil's too hot, the food will burn and the flavor will be destroyed. But if the oil is cold, the spices will not release their essence. A good cook must first heat his oil to the proper temperature."

"Just like an aerobics teacher who must warm up her class before leading them into exercises."

"Oh, yes, young memsahib told me you teach aerobics."

I gather he's referring to Neelu.

"There's a health club in Maurya Sheraton Hotel," Mohan says. "They offer aerobics classes there. Raj sahib's cousin, who was a dancer, taught there until she became pregnant. Would you like to teach a class? I think they'd love to have an American teacher."

I'm mulling the idea over when Mohan adds, "Sahib works out there when he's in town."

That decides it. "What a great idea. I'd love to teach a class."

Mohan scoops up a handful of onion and scatters it into the bubbling oil. A pulse of heat, a brief spattering of oil drops, and a sizzling sound is followed by the fragrant aroma of frying onions.

"Next I show you how to stir the food." A large spatula has appeared in Mohan's hand as if by magic. "Slowly, slowly like this." He repeats the word to emphasize it, a characteristic I've noticed in my father's speech. Mohan flips the onions over lightly, almost automatically, as though the spatula were an extension of his arm. "Don't be jerky about it, Sharmila-memsahib. Bad energy will flow into the food and give someone stomach aches."

I detect a note of humor. "Has that ever happened to you?"

"Only once. Just after Roopa-bahuji's death." A shadow passes across Mohan's face. "I ruined every dish for two days in a row. Everyone complained of an upset stomach."

"Did you know Roopa very well?"

"No. I had only worked here for a few months then. But I noticed how she lit up the house. When she was around, Sahib never paid attention to any one else."

I don't want to hear any more of this. And yet I ask, "Where was Raj when it happened?"

"He had gone to oversee the remodeling work at the bungalow he was buying," Mohan says. "He'd kept the bungalow a secret from Roopa-bahuji. It was going to be a surprise for her. When he was told the news, he was like a madman. 'Don't bring me any food,' he told me. 'Bring her back to me.' I was sad, very sad for Sahib. You see, I respect him very much." Abruptly Mohan picks up a bowl and says, "Now it's time to add the mutton."

Steam is rising like a scented cloud from the pan. The rich smell of browning meat and onion makes me salivate. Yet my interest in the Roopa story is even stronger than learning how to cook mutton kalia. However, I sense I should not press too hard.

Mohan holds up a bowl of golden-orange powder. "What do you call this in English?"

"Turmeric."

"Without it, no taste, or color." Mohan sprinkles in several pinches. "But if you add too much or too late, it ruins the dish." He hands me two small bowls of freshly ground dark brown powders. "Cumin and coriander go next."

The combined aroma is pungent yet alluring.

"One is bitter, the other sweet," Mohan says. He adds, in a typically Indian sage fashion, "Balance is of the essence." He blends the spices into the oil with several clockwise stirring motions of his spoon. Satisfied, he adds a ladle of water and covers the pot with a lid. "Now we'll let this simmer. At the Maurya I used to cook huge pots of kalia that took several hours. But for this amount one hour will do."

I close my notebook, murmuring my appreciation for the lesson, wondering at the same time if I should give him a baksheesh. I don't even know what would be an appropriate amount. "Did foreign guests at the Maurya give the employees any baksheesh?"

"Oh, yes. But not all of them. Some foreigners didn't understand. They complained: why do you people always ask for a baksheesh? Well, it isn't just a tip. It's a way of life here. I do more than some service for you. I talk to you, I please you, I create a comfortable environment for you. So you pay me a little extra. What's wrong with that? The world runs a little more smoothly because of baksheesh. It's a fair exchange."

"Your sister was wrong, Mohan. You have a lot going on in your head."

Mohan mumbles, "I can read your heart, and you can read my mind." He busies himself putting the spice bowls back in the cabinet.

I know servants are like part of the woodwork, but over time they become such an integral part of the family life that they are privy to its innermost secrets. I take a chance and ask, "How did Roopa die?"

He doesn't answer for a long time. "I'm not the one to ask about that."

"Even for triple baksheesh?"

Mohan's smile is one of both sadness and understanding. "Triple baksheesh buys triple trouble," he says, then turns away and starts clearing the counter.

Now I know that the Khoslas don't want the details of Roopa's death to leak out. What are they trying to hide? I'll still give Mohan a baksheesh. He earned it. Besides, maybe he'll come around eventually.

"What time is it, Sharmila-memsahib?"

"It's four o'clock."

Arm extended, Mohan gestures toward the door. "Teatime. Mrs. Khosla and Neelu should be on the balcony by now. Today is the anniversary of Mr. Khosla's death. It's been ten years now. Mrs. Khosla never goes to visit the temple on this day. She prefers to spend the afternoon quietly with Neelu. Would you care to join them? You're family, after all. I'll bring some chai shortly."

There's a note of finality in his voice, telling me that my window of opportunity, if ever there was one, has passed. "Yes, I believe I will."

I make a note to myself to put some dollar bills in a red money envelope and leave it on the kitchen counter when Mohan's not around.

I walk toward the balcony, reflecting on the news I've learned about Roopa. The new information I've uncovered about her demise seems to be intertwined with the lives of the Khosla family members. So far my questioning has been met with either evasion or silence, which in turn has only made me even more determined to get to the bottom of this. But it's becoming clear that I'll have to exercise patience and subtlety if I am to get anywhere with my investigation.

In the meantime, Raj and I at least have a life ahead of us, regardless of how Roopa might have died.

19

THE air is hot and stifling as I step onto the balcony, even
though the afternoon sun has disappeared behind thick
clouds. Mrs. Khosla and Neelu are sitting across from each other,
poring over a faded street map of New Delhi. A lone dahlia
stands in a vase on a table between them. Mrs. Khosla's hair is
drawn back into the usual bun, but a few straggly curls hanging
loosely beside her ears bespeak a rare lack of attention to personal appearance. Absent too is the syrupy smile she wears as a
mask on more formal occasions. Alone with her daughter, she's
composed, even grave on the tenth anniversary of Mr. Khosla's
death. Though society no longer requires a widow to dress in
white, shun onion and garlic, and limit her public appearances,
still for an Indian woman of Mrs. Khosla's generation, the death
of a husband is a major loss.

She points at the bottom of the map and murmurs to Neelu,
"My father's house was right there."

Glancing up at the sound of sandals on the cement floor,
Neelu is the first to notice me. Her face brightens. "Oh, hello,
Sharmila. Come sit with us."

I suddenly realize I'm intruding on a private moment, but it's
too late. I pull up a cushionless cane chair that looks delicate but
not comfortable, and slide it next to Neelu. Perhaps I'll learn

more about Mr. Khosla this afternoon. Raj has spoken about his father in almost reverent tones, but I still don't have a real picture of the man, considered by all to be an outstanding individual.

Seemingly out of nowhere Neelu says, "Ma, would you tell us what it was like when you were a little girl?"

"You've heard it many times, Neelu." The tone is self-effacing yet indulgent. "And Sharmila would find it boring. After all, I'm not an airline pilot, cabinet minister or some such. I'm just a simple housewife."

"Oh, please, Mrs. Khosla, I'd love to hear your story," I tell her. "Even when I was growing up in Chicago, I used to be fascinated by my grandmother's tales when she came to visit us. Family was important to her. She wasn't concerned about herself at all. Never once did she say what she wanted in life, let alone whether she ever got it. I still wonder."

"In my generation and before, Sharmila, even in a rich family like mine, women suffered. No one cared about what we really wanted." Mrs. Khosla puts the map aside on a table. With a sigh she clasps her hands and rests them on her lap. "There's an old saying about Indian women. Our hearts may break, but our lips are sealed." Eyes unfocused, she glances away. For the first time I realize that despite her dignity, social skills, and overbearing haughty nature, Mrs. Khosla is a terribly lonely woman. She continues, "But this is a new world. And in any case, there's no harm getting a few things off my chest."

Mrs. Khosla must have drawn encouragement from the rapt expression on our faces, for as she continues talking, her voice takes on a girlish sparkle.

"I was my parents' youngest child. You know, 'the youngest, the dearest.' The servants called me *missibaba*, their dear little girl, or darling-ji. When I was barely six we moved to a twenty-six-room colonial house with archways and pale yellow stucco walls. I used to stand on the lawn, this tiny creature, and stare up at the tall Greek columns. The house was named after me: Manjari Bhavan. The house of Manjari. There was a flower garden in front, a tall mahogany tree off to one side of the entrance and a simul tree on the other. Even in the lightest breeze, cottony fluff from the simul would blow into my room through the window, and I'd make a game of snatching them from the air.

"We had servants for every purpose. One for shopping, another for grinding the spices, a day cook, and an evening cook. An *ayah* for me—a full-time nanny. The servants and the *ayah* ran the house. They'd ask me constantly, 'Would you care for a sandesh? The first mango of the season? A new doll?'

"If I was in the mood, I'd answer. Otherwise I'd be silent. At six I'd already learned that if you're rich, you don't have to answer anyone's question.

"Wherever I went, I'd hear people whispering behind me, 'There goes Vinay Sood's daughter.' His name gave me added status. I accepted being rich as normal.

"My father was rarely around. It was the custom for men to stay out of the house as much as possible. But I knew he cared about me. When he was home, he played with me or read to me, and sometimes on Sundays he'd take me places.

"You may find this hard to believe, Sharmila, but my family wasn't particularly religious. Oh, yes, we were Hindus and performed all the rituals expected of us during major festivals. But we didn't have a shrine at home. I didn't do *japa* or meditation. And to this day I don't. My parents, my older relatives, and later my husband were my gods.

"When I was eleven, my father taught me how to ride a bicycle. Every day as soon as I finished my homework, I'd go ride my bike. That was quite a daring thing for girls to do in those days. And no, Sharmila, I didn't wear a sari then. I wore frocks until I was twelve."

There's not a hint of condescension in Mrs. Khosla's voice, but from the way she explains these little details, it is obvious that she doesn't think of me as Indian.

Mohan appears with a tea tray, and I'm relieved at the interruption. He sets it on the table, pours three cups, hands one to each of us in silence. I accept my cup with a mumbled thank-you, Neelu hers with a hint of a smile, while Mrs. Khosla nods in acknowledgment. That barely perceptible movement, one she's probably been making since she was six, conveys her approval gracefully and at the same time notifies him he's dismissed. Mohan departs instantly.

Mrs. Khosla takes a sip, then sets her cup down with a steady hand.

"My college years were my best. I majored in English. Then

during my first year"—Mrs. Khosla gazes at Neelu, her eyes soft and loving—"I met Alok at a tailor shop."

I picture a younger Manjari, a stunning beauty posing before a mirror, an imperious arm extended. The tailor hastens to remove an errant thread from her sleeve. Just then the man of her dreams walks through the door.

"The attraction rolled over me like a tidal wave," Mrs. Khosla says. "I stood there in a daze until the tailor said, 'The fitting is done, memsahib. Should I call the driver?'

"From then on, Alok came every day at breaktime and waited just outside the college gate. He had bribed the tailor to get my name and whereabouts. We could speak for only a few minutes without attracting attention, but just seeing him was enough for me. The rest of the day I was capable of doing very little. We talked about every subject except love. But when you feel that strongly about someone, you don't have to put it into words. It seeps out in every little gesture. Of course, I couldn't mention any of it to my family, and that put me in turmoil because I was forced to hold it all inside. But in time things fell into place. Two years later my parents agreed to Alok's proposal, and we were married at the beginning of my fourth year in college.

"As was the custom in those days, I moved in with my husband's family. Right away I became pregnant and had to discontinue my studies." Mrs. Khosla picks up her cup and sips contemplatively. "The house we lived in was quite modest." She chuckles at the recollection. "No car, no air conditioning, and only *one* servant. Can you believe it? It was very difficult to get used to living so simply. Also, ours was a love match—the first in the Khosla family, and that made those early years difficult. Many of my husband's relatives were upset that we hadn't followed the tradition of arranged marriage, and because of that they were hostile to me. His oldest uncle, that awful Jahar, criticized me at every opportunity. If the radio battery went dead, he'd complain it was because I'd turned the news on. If I left so much as a grain of rice on my dinner plate, he asked in a tight voice if I knew the price of rice. If plums dropped before they were ripe, that was my fault because I shouldn't have leaned against the tree. I cursed that man silently countless times before he finally passed on to his next life."

"Maybe that's why I hate plums, Ma," Neelu says seriously, but we all laugh.

"Still, I got along with the relatives. I had no choice. I cried only in bed after your Daddy-ji was asleep because I didn't want anyone to know. Many mornings I woke up to a wet pillowcase.

" 'Manju, do you know why I chose you?' Alok would say. 'You're stronger than all of them. No matter what goes wrong, you carry on.'

"Just after our first wedding anniversary Raj was born." Mrs. Khosla smiles tenderly at Neelu. "A perfect child. Intelligent, good-looking, well mannered. He was adorable. That made up for all my trials. The relatives spoiled him. In spite of all the attention, he turned out fine. He was the most brilliant boy in the whole family. So naturally after he graduated from college, we sent him to America for higher studies. He could easily have stayed there after he got his degree. He could have had everything—a high post, a big house, an American wife. But instead he came back to be with his family. What more could a mother ask of her son?

"During the fifteen years before you were born, Neelu, your Daddy-ji's business prospered. Soon he was earning more money than my father ever did, and we were able to move to our own home. I had all the servants I ever needed and finally some free time and the peace of mind that comes from not having to deal with relatives. I was sure I'd be happy for the rest of my life." Mrs. Khosla's voice catches. "Then, gradually, my husband began to ignore and belittle me. He no longer took me to social functions. But then, I was a land he'd already conquered."

A crow flies overhead, its raucous cry splitting the air, startling Mrs. Khosla into momentary silence. Neelu twists the edge of her chantilly lace scarf around her right index finger and taps her feet on the floor, while I become suddenly aware that my spine is stiff, the back of my chair hard. Uneasiness steals over me at the prospect of hearing Mrs. Khosla's innermost secrets. I raise my arms above my head and stretch, hoping to indicate an intermission is needed.

"I'd suspected something all along." Mrs. Khosla rubs her forehead with her fingers. "But then one day I happened be on a street corner, waiting for the traffic police to give the signal to cross—"

"Ma, please," Neelu says. "Why are you bringing this up in front of Sharmila?"

Eyes hard as marbles, face in a how-dare-you expression, Mrs. Khosla cuts her off. "Who are you to question your mother, Neelu?"

Neelu leaps to her feet, overturning her chair, and runs in the direction of her room. She doesn't look back, but her sobs are audible through the thick silence she has left behind. Automatically, I twist myself out of my chair, intending to follow Neelu's lead.

"Please stay, Sharmila." With one hand Mrs. Khosla sets her daughter's chair upright, while with the other she grasps my arm and presses me back into my seat. "Neelu needs some time alone. She's at that age when she can get emotionally overwrought. I'd like you to hear the rest."

Bewildered, I drop limply into my chair. Mrs. Khosla resumes her monologue. The longer she continues, the more her voice becomes hoarse and throaty with emotion.

"A car pulled up right beside me next to the curb. A man and a woman, not young, but very much together. Lovers, I said to myself. How charming.

"Then something made me look again, and I recognized the man. It was Alok. He was so busy pleading with her, he didn't even notice me. I forced myself to look at the woman. She was pale, with a yellowish cast to her skin like spoiled milk, but handsome nonetheless. She had an air of class about her, from her silk sari and jewelry to the way she held her head.

"I could tell by the expression on Alok's face he was infatuated with her. And all this time I'd thought that loving look was reserved for me alone. As the traffic began to move and Alok's car pulled away, I burst out crying. I don't know how long I stood there before a traffic officer came over to me. 'You seem distressed, madam. Has anyone tried to harm you? Or perhaps you've lost your money?'

" 'More than money,' I said to him. 'I've lost everything.'

"You must understand, Sharmila, how tormenting it was. When you see infidelity with your own eyes, you no longer trust even the ground under your feet."

I'm outraged. How could Mr. Khosla treat his wife this way? What would I do if my husband was unfaithful? Where is the cutoff point for love? I'm not the long-suffering type like Mrs. Khosla. Yet no one wants to be left in middle age with only memories.

"By the time I got home, I was distraught," Mrs. Khosla resumes. "I yelled at the cook, broke my best teacup, tore up all of Alok's love letters. I asked myself over and over again where I had gone wrong, but there was no answer.

"But when Alok came home—it was almost dawn—I went to the drawing room and sat by him with a palm leaf fan in my hand just as I did every evening. That behavior was so ingrained in me that I couldn't be anything but a dutiful wife.

"He must have noticed something unusual. 'Are you feeling well, Manju?'

"I told him, 'Nothing to worry about. Life has its ups and downs, and, as you've often said, no matter what goes wrong, Manju carries on.'

"I thought he'd laugh as he usually did when I talked that way. But that morning he just sat there silently. I excused myself and left.

"Soon Alok was coming home late or not at all. He was often distracted and would upbraid me on the flimsiest pretext. As time went on, rumors began to spread: that he kept his mistress in a plush flat in Vasant Vihar; that the best jewelers in the city vied for her business; that he had secretly married her. Oh, yes, bigamy was against the law, but somehow I could never make myself bring a charge against Alok. After all, he was my *karta*—manager, husband, life itself."

Her cheeks flushed, her powdered forehead beaded with perspiration, Mrs. Khosla squints. It's as if she's attempting to lift a fifty-pound weight. "Not long after that I got a call from Alok's personal doctor. He had suffered a heart attack and died before he could be taken to the hospital. He was in her flat, of course, and I had to go there to claim his body. Can you imagine how humiliating that was, Sharmila? My college friend Parvin said later Alok should have had at least the decency to die at home."

My throat dry, I regard Mrs. Khosla with awe. This sturdy woman is alive and functioning and holding a family together. Still, her candor puzzles me. And why hasn't Raj mentioned this by now?

Mrs. Khosla pauses to wipe her eyes with a trembling hand,

then takes a deep breath. Her face clears and she throws off the strain. "I hope I haven't overburdened you. For better or for worse, you have a deeper understanding of our family now. My husband gave me two fine children, a good home, and a bitter lesson on what loving a man means. And oddly enough, Sharmila, even after ten years I still miss him every day. I spend his anniversary quietly—no *puja* or flower offering or burning incense for me. Alok's in my heart. Still, that affair left me scarred forever."

Seeming to read my mind, Mrs. Khosla adds, "Of course, I have regrets. Often I think of my friend Parvin. After graduating from college, she became a lecturer at a prestigious college, then moved up to the post of department head. Now she's retired and has started a computer study program for village girls. When I last saw her, she looked rushed and haggard, but somehow content in a way I'd never be. She had a life of her own beyond the demands of the family. I've often wondered what would have happened had I gone on to finish my studies, but that, of course, as you know, is like our proverb, 'praying to Goddess Laxmi after her honoring ceremony is over.' I've tried to make the best of each situation and go forward accordingly—" Mrs. Khosla stops as a wave of emotion chokes her voice.

In the silence that ensues I notice that even the lone dahlia in the vase has wilted in sympathy for her suffering. At the sound of footsteps we both look up.

"*Dhobi* is here," announces Mohan. He's standing deferentially just inside the living room door. Eyes downcast, he adds in an apologetic voice, "Should I ask him to come back tomorrow?"

"No, that's fine, Mohan. We were just finishing up. And I have instructions for the laundry. If you'd excuse me, Sharmila . . ."

The tycoon's daughter, mistress of servants, wife who has been wronged, rises in one smooth motion and takes a step. She stumbles as her legs get tangled in the front pleats of the sari, but she recovers her balance quickly and walks away composed and erect.

Fuzzy-headed and drained, I slowly rise and shuffle off to my room. After a long, hot shower, a few stretches and lunges to release tension, I lie down on my bed and doze off. A half hour later, my eyes open to the revolving fan on the ceiling. It produces a low, wailing moan, and the rapid clacking of the three black blades fills me with a sense of foreboding. Uneasily I get up, pull my sketchpad from the desk drawer, and sketch the fan, hoping to be able to figure out its mystery later. For now I'm content to jot down the day's questions underneath:

Why did Mrs. Khosla tell me all this in spite of her daughter's disapproval? Why now, just before my marriage? Is there a lesson, a warning?

MRS. Khosla has been aloof the past three days. At nine this morning, with a perfunctory good-bye she left for Agra. I suspect she is embarrassed for revealing her secrets. Not surprisingly, I haven't seen much of Neelu either lately. My guess is, she was mortified. She seems remote. Feeling very much alone in my room this morning, I take up the sketchpad and draw a kite rising outside the living room window, determined that my day will be just as carefree and light.

I close the book, set it aside on my desk, pick up my novel, and begin to read where I left off yesterday. The young queen is cloistered in a red sandstone fortress in Old Delhi of the seventeenth century. Intricate latticed windows have been carved in the deep thickness of the walls especially for her and the women of the royal court. The outside world isn't allowed to cast eyes on her beauty or intrude on her serenity. Only through these windows can the queen gaze out at a courtyard and the market beyond.

The queen has been left alone for a hundred days by her lord, who has marched off to do battle with an invader. On that day, growing restless from the endless confinement, she rises up from her gilded chair and peers through the window. Just beyond the inner courtyard is a teeming bazaar reserved for the women of the city, a place where they come to shop, safe from the eyes of men. This morning they are moving about, patches of pinks, blues, and yellows seen from this distance, many with infants in their arms, their perspiring faces glistening in the mid-morning sun. As the queen watches the vivid tapestry, suddenly a thunderstorm appears. A torrential downpour sends them all scurrying for cover under soggy, soot-covered awnings. Only splashes of color are visible through the curtain of rain. As the queen leans into the window, she hears the peasant women laughing and talking, then voices rising in an impromptu song welcoming the rain, though it causes a delay in their daily schedule. Minutes later, before the queen's eyes, the sun comes out as suddenly as it disappeared. The women traipse out into the market again and resume their pedestrian tasks.

Hearing footsteps at the door, the queen hurries back to her chair. Her maid walks in, as she does every morning, carrying a perfect rose bud in a vase. She's about to place it on a table when her mistress asks, "Why do you always bring me a rose?"

The maid bows before replying. "The flower blushes like your cheeks, mistress. It has a velvety touch like your skin. Each of its petals is perfect like your life."

The queen snatches the bud from the maid's hand, crushes it beneath her feet, and orders the maid out. The terrified girl quails before the queen's indignation, then flees the room in tears, whereupon the queen collapses in a corner, buries her head in her lap, and sobs.

I close the book in a pensive mood. I am just looking around the room when there's a knock at the door. It's Prem.

"Are you ready for another round of sightseeing?" he asks.

I promptly reply, "Let's go to Old Delhi," then add, "I have the whole day."

"Excellent, madam, that will give us time to see both Red Fort and Jama Masjid."

"We can do monuments some other time. Today I'd just like to wander the back streets." And I think of the frustrated queen.

Within an hour, we're walking down a narrow lane somewhere in the labyrinthine streets and alleys that make up Old Delhi. It's hotter in the lane, walled on both sides by houses. I am in the midst of a throng of people, yet I don't feel threatened. The smell of sweat and urine seems normal. As I look curiously at cow dung patties plastered on the wall of a house, Prem explains they're used not only for fuel, but also as insect repellent. How resourceful, I think. A blanket of flies buzz around a pile of rotten vegetable peels in the middle of our path. My nose crinkling from the overpowering stench, I jump over it, nearly twisting my ankle as I land on a sharp rock. Thank God I'm wearing jeans and cross-trainer shoes. To avoid a reeking open gutter and a water pump with a puddle around it, I head toward the center and collide with an old man, knocking his walking stick from his hand. I grab the cane, retrieve it from the chaos of feet milling past me, and hand it back to him with an apology. Frightened from having lost his balance, he mutters a curse, shaking the plastic toy snakes on his arm.

As if sensing my unease, Prem rushes up from behind and appears by my side. Chastened, I pay close attention to how he navigates through this dense mass of people and animals streaming in both directions. His face displays no irritation. He dips his shoulders from side to side and slides by whoever is in his path, weaving like a fish. I emulate his technique and soon find myself moving along with a minimum of hassle.

The winter sun is high in the sky and beating down into the passageway. The heat combined with the effort of navigating the maze leaves me disoriented and short of breath. To borrow an Indian phrase, I'm seeing "mustard flowers before my eyes." The thought occurs to me that I have no idea where we are.

"Don't worry," Prem says, as if reading my mind. "You can't get lost here. No matter which direction you take, you'll come to Jama Masjid—Friday Mosque, in English."

At the next turn I find we're at the edge of a gigantic red sandstone mosque at least a block long. My attention then is drawn to the bustling shops lining the narrow street: Pedestrians in turbans, dhotis, *ghaghras,* and the usual assortment of cars, buses, cycle rickshaws, and handcarts. Stalls—some little more than makeshift awnings—are squeezed next to each other, with businesses overflowing into the street, filled with silver craft and candles, flowers and books, dried fruit and spices. I breathe in the carefree mood. Shoppers jostle one another as they wend their way through a chaotic tangle of cows, feral dogs, ox carts, and other pedestrians. A serene woman in a sari riding a motorcycle bullies her way through. The aroma of incense, spices, and dust blends together in the air. Drying laundry from the balconies above casts ripples of colors: rich reds, iridescent blues, and frosty greens. Voices rise and fall as bargains are hammered out and pleasantries exchanged. In my mind's eye, I see the bazaar in the story of the frustrated queen. When I mention this to Prem, he informs me that there is no longer a market for women only.

So dense is the crowd that it's hard to tell where the sidewalk ends and the street begins and whether I'm being swept along by the mob or walking on my own two feet. At the first opportunity we escape into a less congested alleyway. Prem comes to a stop before a shop wall where copies of today's newspapers in Hindi and English are posted.

"They're put there for people who can't afford to buy a newspaper," he says. "When I was a boy, my father used to put me on his shoulders so I could read the headlines to him out loud. You see, my father didn't know how to read and write, and I wasn't tall enough yet to see over people in front of us. He didn't trust the man who came to our neighborhood every day to read the newspaper, suspecting that he was paid by one of the political parties. That man read only certain news items and glossed over the rest. So my father would ask me, 'Why does the prime minister spend so much money entertaining? Why are the Chinese trying to take land from us in the Himalayas? Nothing grows there, you know, not even weeds.' "

"Sharing a newspaper is a good idea," I tell Prem, as I consider the benefits. Fewer trees being cut down, less pollution, bringing the community together. Just as we turn to leave, a man comes toward us. He heads for a rope hanging from a lamp post and touches his cigarette to a glowing coal smoldering at the rope's lower end. He draws in several times until his cigarette is lit and then, with a scent of tobacco rising in the air, strolls off into the crowd.

"A communal cigarette lighter," I murmur. "Another good idea."

"You'd be surprised. We have corruption, power shortages, and bad roads, all of which holds us back, but we also have some good minds. Given half a chance, our brothers and sisters can be very resourceful indeed."

How very Prem-like to refer to all of India as family. Perhaps that's what enables him to live here with pride, and not bitterness at his casteless fate.

"Maybe I am explaining too much," Prem says. "It's an Indian weakness, you know. We have twenty official languages and hundreds of dialects. You can never be sure who understands what and how much. So we go overboard, trying to make sure we're understood. At least that's the way I like to think about it. On the other hand," he says, flashing a smile, "maybe we just like to talk. We have a word for it. *Adda,* an 'idea exchange' party. One of our English magazines has even created a new verb, 'to ideate.' "

"It's helpful, Prem, because I don't always understand what's going on, what's said, how to react."

"That doesn't surprise me, Sharmila. At the travel agency where I worked, most of my clients were foreigners. They came from all over. Our country affected each one differently, but there was one thing in common. If they stayed here for a while, they saw beneath the chaotic surface. While they made peace with India, they made their peace with themselves."

"The reality hits you hard here, Prem. You're either forced to see things as they are or leave."

At the moment I have an overwhelming urge to leave due to the heat. I dab the perspiration on my temples with a tissue. "Funny thing is, back in Chicago I taught advanced aerobics three times a week and felt refreshed at the end of each session. But here, an hour's walk, and I'm beat. . . ."

"Would you like to stop somewhere and rest?" Prem inquires solicitously. "Perhaps you want a glass of lime juice? Perhaps you want some food?"

"Sounds good. Let's find a place."

We're on a wider street, walking past a food vendor who's perched on a stool behind his mobile cart. Mounds of plump yellow chickpeas, slender red chilis, sliced tomatoes, and green coriander leaves are arranged around a huge pan set atop a portable stove. We stop to watch. The man stirs a rich brown stew in a circular motion, sprinkling in spices from small tins, then serves small platefuls to his customers. There's an orderliness and rhythm to his work, and though he probably does this every day, the focused attention and the grin on his face suggest he enjoys it. The aroma of frying onions, cloves, cinnamon, and cardamom wafting out in swirls draws in shoppers more effectively than a billboard. They gather around the cart, three or four deep, waving rupee notes, shouting orders. I find I can decipher much of the conversation.

"Please, I've been waiting here longer than the fellow you just served."

"No, me. My son says he won't go home until he has another plate."

"Oh, come now, don't be so skimpy with chili."

All at once I become aware that hunger is pounding in my stomach. But the place is so crowded that I don't consider waiting. As we continue down the street, I see a sign proclaiming KARIM'S over an archway leading into a cul-de-sac, and a long line waiting to get in. I've read about this venerable Old Delhi institution in guide books. "I think I'm ready for lunch, Prem." Then an idea strikes me: we're anonymous in this section of town. I add impulsively, "But only if you join me. After all, we're friends now, aren't we?"

"Karim's would be impossible to get in at this time of the day. May I propose an alternative?" Prem clears his throat. "I live only five minutes from here. Would you like to come to my house for lunch?"

"Your house?" In theory, Prem had issued his invitation days earlier, but now, faced with reality, I find myself beset with doubts. What would be Mrs. Khosla's reaction? How would I explain it to Raj or my mother? She left India long ago, when untouchability was still taboo. I slow down my pace to buy time as I consider my options.

"It's not going to be anything fancy," Prem says as we cross a street. "You'll have to try what we eat every day."

Let me think this invitation over, I tell myself as I reply, "That's not a problem at all. I'm not hard to please."

"You have an Indian soul, Sharmila. My guess is you'll find our simple food quite pleasing."

"You're one of the few people who sees me that way, Prem."

"Frankly, that's the easiest side of you for me to appreciate." Prem's eyes twinkle in mischief, then in an instant turn serious. "You are a sort of cultural intermediary, one might say."

His earnest demeanor makes me feel elated. The blazing sun is suddenly milder, the crowding less oppressive, the noise muted.

"I haven't traveled much," Prem continues, "but I, too, am an intermediary. I look for what's common rather than what keeps us separate. I wish there weren't so many barriers between people. My family is open and friendly."

I feel both a sense of anticipation and one of reticence at the prospect of meeting his family. "Has Mrs. Khosla met them?"

"Oh, don't worry about her. This morning she was preoccupied with her trip to Agra. Tomorrow is a special day. She and her relatives will honor an older aunt of hers who has seen a thousand moons. We consider living that long a special privilege. There will be a big ceremony."

My resolve crumbling, I murmur softly, "You and Raj have been good friends for a long time."

"Yes, and he came to my house once. These days he calls me often." I detect a hint of irritation in Prem's reply. "I'm sure he'll call at least once while you're there."

If Raj calls while I'm having lunch at Prem's house, what will I say to him? Does he even have to know that I'm there?

"He's very interested in where we go together," Prem continues. " 'Where did you take her? Why Jantar Mantar? Where did she have lunch?' I tell him, 'Raj-babu, I'm only doing what you and your mother have asked me to do.' " Prem shrugs. "Perhaps he's pressured at his job."

Another caution flag goes up. Should I risk upsetting the man I'm going to marry? Then again, I know if I refuse Prem's offer, I will never again have a chance to meet his family. The Khoslas are rich and westernized, and my introduction to life in India has been easy because of that, but I'm unlikely to have many opportunities to discover "the other" India through them. In the end, the chance to experience real India proves difficult to resist.

As I swelter in heavy denim jeans under the midday sun, I begin to understand why Indian women wear flimsy cotton saris or *salwar* suits. Voluminous in appearance, they allow air to circulate freely and keep a woman cool. And that brings my last reservation to mind: I'm not wearing a sari. I understand pants are not considered offensive in New Delhi, but here in Old Delhi none of the women I've come across have been wearing them. How would Prem's mother react to an outfit of jeans, sweat shirt, and no scarf? "Am I dressed properly?" I ask Prem.

"My mother would be delighted to lend you a sari." Prem laughs. "You know how mothers are."

"There must be a universal mother from which mothers all over the world are descended."

Just past a sweet shop we round a corner, enter an unpaved passageway, and walk between rundown houses. The buildings are streaked with black mold; their paint is peeling. But life beats within them, heard in the calls, laughter, and movements of people dwelling there. Prem points ahead at a boy, about eight, in a fresh white shirt and white shorts, standing at the entrance to a building. "That's my brother," he says happily.

"Could we go back to that little shop at the corner for a minute?" I ask in a trembling voice, still not quite prepared to meet his family and also remembering guests are supposed to bring sweets, fruit, or flowers. "I'd like to buy a box of sweets."

"That's not necessary."

The boy rushes up, a younger version of Prem, looks at me with big eyes, then scurries behind Prem. As his eyes shyly peek out, I smile. It's clear he's struggling to contain his excitement.

"This is Sharmila-didi," Prem says to him. Then with mock sternness, "What are you going to say to her?"

The boy comes forward, stands stiffly like a student who's been called upon. "Hello, how are you? My name is Jay. How do you like Delhi?"

"You don't ask all those questions at once, Jay," Prem says.

"*Bhai-saab*," a woman's voice sings out from inside the doorway. "There was a call for you from Raj Khosla just now."

Cellular phone in hand, a young woman approaches Prem. She gives me a shy glance and speaks to Prem in a mixture of Hindi and English. "The sahib was in a hurry, as usual. He said he'll ring you again in fifteen minutes."

Raj is about to find out I'm having lunch with Prem's family. My mind races frantically, seeking a graceful way out. Prem introduces me to his sister, Ratna, and I realize the time for backing out has long since passed. "We've heard so much about you," Ratna says brightly. Dressed in a loose-fitting *salwarkameez*, she has a round face and almond eyes set off by long dark eyelashes. "You look just like *bhai-saab* described you—"

At that moment an older woman, dark as a summer night, emerges from the flat. Her lively eyes glow against the simple background of a plain white sari. Her chiseled face reflects a lifetime of hard work, dignity, and character.

"This is my mother," Prem says.

He turns and speaks to her respectfully in Hindi. Immediately the woman draws near, and with a friendly expression and a delicate gesture of her hand she beckons me inside. The last remnants of my reluctance vanish. Kicking my shoes off at the door, I follow her inside and find myself in a tiny yet spotless apartment. The old, faded walls seem to expand to accommodate family, sunlight, and laughter. Save for a low cot and cane mats on the floor, the front room is bare. Prem's mother invites me to sit on the cot. As they arrange themselves around me on the mats, I experience a deep feeling of comfort at their welcoming closeness.

Prem stands a short distance away, very much in charge now that he's the man of the house. Gone is the subservient manner he affects in the presence of the Khoslas. His shoulders seem broader than usual, and he looks quite virile. I'm beginning to understand the undercurrent of tension between him and Raj, which is at once pleasing and disquieting.

In a deep voice Prem translates what his mother has just said. "She's asking why it took you so long to come visit her."

I'm about to explain when I notice her gazing at me curiously. She starts speaking with urgency and excitement. I can't keep up with her rapid-fire Hindi and look to Prem for another translation.

"My mother says she has seen you in a dream," Prem says. "You were a pretty little girl holding a cup, standing on her doorstep. You walked up and just stared at her, saying nothing. But she knew what you wanted. She was about to pour you some water when she woke up. She has been wondering for a long time now who that girl was."

I want to respond, but a tear tightens my throat. Prem's mother accepts me, she has been waiting for me, I was expected to come. Elation swells in my chest. As our eyes meet, I am awed and humbled by the wisdom and compassion in her eyes. They convey a depth of understanding far beyond my experience in life.

"I wish I could dream like my mother." Ratna tugs on her mother's sari train to get her attention. "I want to be a writer, you know, Sharmila-behen, but I can never come up with stories like she does. And I barely remember my dreams in the morning."

"I only remember whether they're good or bad, Ratna."

"She taught us that good dreams make us wake up with a smile, but the bad ones are more important," Prem says. "They tell us to make changes."

He repeats those words in Hindi for his mother's benefit. She chuckles softly—more like a throaty laugh—and excuses herself to finish preparing lunch. She enters the kitchen, and soon I hear the clank of pots and savor the aroma of frying spices.

"Hello, how are you?" Jay says from a far corner.

"You're only supposed to ask that once," Prem says to him. "Now, can you get Sharmila-didi a glass of water?"

Jay gives an "oh, not again," look as he scurries out of the room. Through the open door to the kitchen, I see the boy pouring from a narrow-necked earthenware jug. With a full glass in either hand, his feet steady, he returns with exaggerated care lest he spill a drop. Just one cooling swallow of the sweet, earthy-tasting water gives me a pleasant, settled-in feeling. In slow, appreciative sips, Prem and I finish our water.

Several times now I've noticed Ratna eycing my jeans, trying her best to conceal her envy. I am about to say something about it when the cell phone in her hand beeps shrilly. I jump, startled by the discordant sound.

"Let's not answer it," Prem says to Ratna firmly. "Put the cell phone aside until after we've eaten." He rises and walks over to stand in the kitchen doorway, his face hidden from me. The phone keeps ringing.

"But, *bhai-saab*," Ratna says to Prem with a plea in her eyes, "it could be my friend Charu."

"Very well, then," Prem assents in a flat voice. I sit, heart in my throat, cognizant of the turmoil inside him. An uneasy silence settles over us.

Ratna presses a button as she strolls out the door. I hear, "Hello? Charu? I've been expecting your call." And I exhale in quiet relief. I roll my shoulders, but still can't relax completely. It feels as though I've been taken hostage by an invisible Raj.

While I watch Prem pushing a window open, his mother calls to me. Her kitchen is a bare-bones operation—a shelf for storing provisions, a rickety table which serves as a work area, a charcoal-filled clay stove on which she fluffs chapatis. In no time at all she has set out several appetizing-looking dishes on woven mats on the floor. When an ant crawls up her arm, she simply flicks her wrist so it lands on the worn cement floor alive. As she goes about her tasks, she carries on a running conversation with me in Hindi. To my surprise, not only can I understand her, but I manage an occasional response.

In a lull in the conversation, I overhear Ratna whispering to Prem in the front room. "Go ahead, *bhai-saab*, take your lunch. If Raj-babu calls again, I'll tell him you're not back yet."

"Aren't you going to eat?" Prem asks her.

"I'm not hungry. I'll be just outside."

It dawns on me that I'm going to be served Ratna's share of the lunch. I am at once touched and discomfited by this selfless gesture, so gracefully executed that refusal is out of the question.

Within minutes, Prem, Jay, and I sit down on bamboo mats to a meal of chapati, spiced mustard greens, and a savory dahl soup with several fresh chilies served on the side as a condiment. I notice that as the guest of honor I've been served the biggest portions. How I wish I could find a diplomatic way to share this with Ratna. I peer through the open door looking for her.

Prem hands me a wedge of fragrant lemon, a special variety, he explains, and directs me to squeeze it over the soup. I do so and pass it to Jay. This simple act of sharing is fun and imparts a wondrous taste to the food. At my first bite into a hot chili, my mouth reverberates with searing heat, and I twitch with the fiery sensation, spilling a few drops of dahl on my jeans. Oh, great! I say to myself. First pain and now embarrassment. Prem's mother immediately wipes off the spots with a wet towel, as though it were a common occurrence, though I'm aware that the turmeric in dahl will leave a stain. Soon everyone is speaking to me at once in an effort to put me at ease. But even as I finish one delicious bite after another, a part of me wonders if Raj has called again and how Ratna will answer him.

Prem's mother hovers over us, making sure all goes smoothly. She beams with pleasure every time I look up. Though we don't communicate directly, I understand her perfectly. There's an austere beauty about her and an air of pride that comes from living fully with the barest of essentials.

When we finish the meal, we retire to the front room. At the insistence of Prem's mother, I change into one of her simple cotton saris. It has been worn numerous times, and the natural coarseness of cotton has been softened from countless washings. Somehow putting on her garment draws me closer to her and her family. She gazes up at me, dark eyes conveying goodwill and perhaps an excitement at meeting someone from a distant land. She says to Prem, "See how the red border frames her face." Then to me, "It makes you glow."

Ratna comes back inside and says, "How lovely you look, Sharmila. Did you know there was a different person inside you?"

I shake my head giddily, elated with my new self. On an impulse I ask her if she'd like to try on my jeans. Desire wins out over shyness, and after hesitating initially, she agrees. She disappears into the bedroom with her booty. A few minutes later she emerges looking like a twentysomething Western woman. She strokes the jeans as if to reassure herself that she's really wearing them and beams with delight when I compliment her on looking chic.

"Very costly here, you know," Ratna says. "I've always dreamed of owning a pair, but it's only a dream."

"No longer. They're yours now."

After a moment of dumbfounded silence, Ratna says, "Sharmila-behen, you're so very kind and generous. I don't know how to thank you, but I'll think about you every time I wear them."

Jay skips up to me, plops down on the cot beside me, and explains that his name means "to salute." I snap my hand sharply to my brow in a mock military salute, and the endearing little imp dissolves in laughter.

"All our names have meanings," Ratna says. "My mother's name is Vijaya, which means 'victory.' Victory over our mind. Mine means 'precious stones,' and I love them all—rubies, emeralds, lapis lazuli." With a sideways glance at her older brother, she says teasingly, "Prem means 'love.' You know how to love, don't you, *bhai-saab*?"

Come to think of it, I've always known what 'Prem' meant— it's a common Hindi word. I've stored the meaning quietly inside me, for giving it expression would have been disturbing.

In feigned anger Prem tries to snatch the cellular phone from Ratna's hand, while stealing a glance at me. The moment is like a crystal—transparent, fragile, a thing of sharp, clear beauty. It evokes a delightful trembling inside me, followed by a jolt of fear. Am I betraying Raj? How can I think of Prem and love? It's impossible. I should go back home now.

But in this sari? Fortunately, Mrs. Khosla is away and Neelu has been coming home late. Perhaps I can manage to slip in before she returns. Anxiously, I consult my watch. "Oh, my," I say with a sigh. "It's time for me to get back. I've been gone far too long."

"Must you leave so soon, Sharmila-behen?" Ratna asks with obvious regret. "We've never had a visit like this."

Much taken with her sincerity, I say, "I'll be back."

I rise reluctantly, and Prem and I take our leave with many wistful eyes looking after us. We walk toward the car in silence. I contemplate on the various facets of the afternoon: the food, the conversation, the joy, the wisdom. This time I glide through the surging foot traffic, not even aware of the reeking piles of garbage. When a man brushes against me, I sidestep smoothly with no trace of my previous annoyance.

Unwilling to let the afternoon's fantasy end quite so soon, I slide in next to Prem in the front seat of the car for the first time, half expecting him to protest. But he merely starts the car and pulls into the traffic. We drive home in comfortable silence, aware of each other's presence. In less than an hour we've reached the Defence Colony. It's dusk, and in the muted light the familiar outlines of the neighborhood blur. Even the majestic pink aura of the Khosla building seems faded.

I ask Prem to drop me around the corner. As he stops the automobile, I turn. "Prem . . ." I start with a vain attempt to thank him. As soon as my gaze falls on his face—I've never seen it this close—my body begins to throb in hidden expectation. Our eyes meet and hold, my lips are drawn toward his. Words we cannot utter, sentiments we dare not express, desire that should remain secret, metamorphose into a kiss—brief and passionate, yet filled with gentleness and meaning.

I tear myself away, open the door with a trembling hand, step out, dash down the street and in through the gate of my fortress as though its walls can somehow shut out the previous moments. I don't look back, afraid of the current of temptation that could engulf me. My sari flapping behind, I tiptoe up the stairs, hoping to slip quietly to the privacy of my room and change into a pair of pants before anyone can see me.

I'm barely at the top of the staircase when a familiar voice stops me. "Hello, Sharmila."

Neelu stands in the hallway, watching me. Her ever present smile is absent, her eyes lusterless, her gaze fixed. "Where did you get *that*?"

My guess is this sari is not fine enough for a member of the Khosla family. "Oh, I was visiting some relatives." I hate that the lie slips out of my lips so easily. To recover from the slithery, black feeling, I close my eyes for an instant. "I dropped some sauce on my jeans and got yellow spots all over from turmeric. My aunt gave me this sari."

"Ma called from Agra a little while ago. Her usual checkup. She wanted to make sure we both were all right."

"Of course I'm all right. Why shouldn't I be? I had a great day. How was yours?"

A shadow crosses Neelu's face. Eyes downcast, she fingers her gold necklace.

"Is anything the matter, Neelu?"

"Oh, Sharmila, can we talk?"

"Of course."

I steer her to the living room, thankful that her focus has shifted. For once I'm glad she has a problem. I'd much rather worry about hers.

The maid has drawn the blinds, turned on the lights, and put a Hindi movie soundtrack on the stereo. A singer is crying out, "Oh, oh, oh . . ."

The muted red upholstered sofa done in a soft Indian fabric looks plush and inviting. Yet there is a definite sense of unease as Neelu and I take our seats.

21

I SINK back on the sofa, put my feet on a stool, and turn to an un-characteristically serious Neelu. The soft white light of the lamp beside her lends her young face a platinum sheen. She twists a section of her long, flowing hair into a corkscrew, straightens it, then twists it again. Growing aware of my attention, she abruptly points to her necklace.

"Dinesh gave it to me a month ago. This is my first chance to show it to you, Sharmila."

As I look at her necklace, a weave of gold and emerald with a geometric pendant, it occurs to me how little I know about Neelu. Heretofore she has been flighty and frivolous as a grasshopper around me, but now it seems she leads a double life. "Who's Dinesh?" I inquire casually.

Sucking in a breath, as if preparing for a great expenditure of energy, Neelu says obliquely, "It is easier to talk when Ma isn't around."

I nod in agreement. Most people would find it difficult to dis-cuss their love life in the presence of such a formidable person as Mrs. Khosla, and for someone as young as Neelu, the mere prospect could induce a state of paralysis.

I ask, "Is this a boy you met in college?"

More silence, then evidently having made up her mind to

trust me, Neelu blurts out, "I'm in love!" The flushed face and fervent tone leaves little doubt as to the depth of her feeling.

I suppress unbidden images of Prem that pop up uninvited in my mind. Other than my friend Liz, I can't think of a single person to whom I'd confide my feelings about him. Perhaps not even Liz, and certainly not about that unexpected kiss. I hope I'm not blushing.

"He's someone I've known since I was seven."

"How did you meet him?" I ask politely.

"One day Daddy-ji and Ma had a fight. As he left the house, he took me with him. I was glad to get out. We drove around for a while. Then Daddy-ji asked, 'How would you like to meet Kaveri Auntie?' He said she was a widow and had a son two years older than I. We went to a well-furnished flat, and he introduced me to the lady of the house. Contrary to what Ma believes, Kaveri Auntie was gentle and soft-spoken, not at all a shrew.

"I knew we had escaped a storm at home. I knew Kaveri Auntie was Daddy-ji's ally. I knew that. She served my favorite sweetmeat—sohanpapri—on a lovely glass plate with a petal-shaped border. It became my plate from that day on. She stroked my hair as I munched on the sweet, and when I was barely finished, she called out to her son. 'Dinesh-beta, why don't you take Neelu down to the courtyard and show her the bird's nest?'

"A cute boy rushed into the room with a toy airplane in his hand. He had big eyes, hair combed to one side ending in a wave, and the widest smile. When he saw me, he slowed, raised one eyebrow, and gawked. Almost like we could read each other's mind, we headed for the staircase together. The door closed behind us. I had only gone a little way down the stairs, my hand on the rail and Dinesh leading when, feeling terribly alone and missing my daddy, I burst into tears. Dinesh seemed to understand my mood. He put his arm around my shoulder and comforted me until I began to smile. An hour later, when Daddy-ji called me to take me home, I was sad. We got into his car and drove away. Dinesh stood at the door and waved and waved." Spoken in a voice that is soft and clear, Neelu's words flutter and hang in the air, like little birds released.

"On the way home, I told Daddy-ji how much I enjoyed my time with Dinesh. Daddyji smiled. After that, whenever he took me out, he picked up Dinesh as well. We'd visit Kaveri Auntie for hours on Sunday. Daddy-ji and Kaveri Auntie would be in one room. Dinesh and I would play ludo and carom in another, then go to the garden to chase butterflies.

"Ma couldn't have known where we were. If she found out, I'd never have seen Dinesh again. She wouldn't have approved of his mother or Daddy-ji's visit to their flat."

I wonder if Neelu's referring to Mr. Khosla's mistress. I begin to fidget, yet I know Neelu will clam up at the slightest hint of dismay on my part. I do my best to look neutral.

"Did I know who Kaveri Auntie was? Of course not. I was too young." Neelu touches her necklace as if to seek solace there.

I ask myself, How could a father take his child to the home of his mistress? Both fascinated and revolted, I am not sure I want to listen. I stare out the window for a moment, looking for a momentary distraction, but find only slate gray darkness. The glow I've carried inside me since the visit to Prem's house this afternoon has faded. Neelu's voice starts again:

"Dinesh and I became fast friends. I took to calling him Deen, which means 'day' in Hindi. In time he became the light of my day."

I marvel at her sweet innocence in the face of such a strange and complicated childhood. Empathy for Neelu mingles with disgust for the grown-ups involved.

Neelu hums a line from a current pop tune, "*Yeh, deen hamara hai.*" This day is mine. After a moment she goes on, "Ma was very distracted and unhappy, but she never asked questions. I guess she felt it was better not to know to preserve her dignity. She managed to wish a whole situation away to avoid unbearable humiliation. Yet if she knew who I was playing with, I think she'd have gone after Kaveri Auntie with a kitchen knife."

I shudder.

"Just joking." There's not a trace of humor in Neelu's voice. "I don't really think Ma could have done anything like that. I know it's difficult for you to listen to all this, Sharmila, so I'll get to the point."

Ah, yes. So this is not just a venting session. I'm going to be asked for a favor.

"After Daddy-ji's death," Neelu resumes, speaking carefully, "I lost all contact with Deen. I was only ten then. There was no longer any reason or place for us to meet. At first I missed him terribly, then I forgot all about him. Then two years ago, as I walked in to a party, I noticed a man mingling with other guests. There was something familiar about the way he stood. He turned and looked at me, and the instant I saw those eyes, the smile, that way of raising one eyebrow, I knew who he was. For a minute I couldn't remember his name, but then it came to me. I broke into a sweat even though the flat was air-conditioned." Again, Neelu looks down at her necklace. "My first impulse was to flee. But by then the hostess had come up. She introduced me to Deen. After a little chitchat he asked, 'Would you like to step to the balcony?'

"Deen! Neelu! That was all either of us could say when we were alone. Then slowly we began to fill each other in about our present lives. I felt the same closeness we'd shared so long ago. Much later, we separated to circulate among other guests. But for the rest of the evening our eyes kept meeting wherever we were. It was as if each of us had a special radar that kept us aware of the other's location. Of course, no one at the party had a clue we had known each other before, let alone the circumstances.

"We exchanged phone numbers before I left the party. That night I didn't sleep a wink, and as soon as it was light I called him. We arranged to meet in a park, where we talked for hours. I found out we still had much in common." Neelu leans forward in excitement. "Deen had taken a 'beauty' course, learned all about makeup, and gotten a job as a makeup artist."

"And that's your ambition, too, Neelu, as you told me."

"Yes, Sharmila. In the last two years Deen has become one of the best in Delhi. Some of the richest women in the city patronize him. He has asked me to join his company as an apprentice as soon as I graduate from college. And . . ." Neelu's voice drops to a murmur. "He wants to marry me."

The tension in her face magnifies the intensity of her feelings. This is not the standard schoolgirl crush, I realize. Neelu is very much in love. In spite of my best intentions, the obvious question slips out of my mouth. "But what about your mother?"

"Precisely!" Neelu's eyes glow with passion. "You see, I'm so very much in love with Deen that I could never marry anyone else, no matter what Ma wants."

Ah, young love, the voice of my own sad experience says, perched high on a fragile twig of impossible hope. She's infatuated, just as I was with Mitch, and we broke up. Confidently, assuming the role of older sister, I begin, "Neelu, you're quite young. You haven't met all that many men. How do you know he's really the one?"

She has anticipated my question. "Sharmila, this is India. Romance runs through our veins. Women sacrifice their lives for love. Our commitment is to one person for the rest of our lives. We don't go from one to the next like you do in the States."

Caught off guard, I retort, "In the States we find out if a relationship is going to work or not. If there are major problems, we end it before any lasting damage is done. But do you think that means we have no feelings? No depth—"

I break off in mid-sentence. Champa is passing through the room, and I detect a hint of a smile. I've never seen the maid smile before. Does she understand English that well? Uneasily I remind myself that although everyone here tends to treat the servants as if they have no eyes or ears, in fact, they know everything that goes on.

Neelu must have assumed I'm more upset than I actually am. She bursts into tears. "I'm so sorry, Sharmila. I shouldn't be burdening you with my troubles. You have enough problems of your own. It's just that I'm very upset. Forgive me for being so selfish—".

"It's okay, Neelu." I reach out and squeeze her hand reassuringly for a second. "I understand."

She wipes her eyes, but new tears well up behind her thick lashes. "Life is never easy, is it? I grew up wanting for nothing. Ma literally fed me my first rice with a silver spoon. Still, I was always in Raj-bhai's shadow. The firstborn son, a brilliant student. Our family, especially Ma, was doubly proud. I'm sure by now you've noticed what Indians talk about most of the time."

"Degrees and jobs—"

"Yes, Sharmila. Every mother prays to educate her sons, and I'm sure Ma did, too." She bites hard on her lip, drops her hand to her lap. "I'm only average. And I'm a girl."

"But, Neelu, you have other talents. They may not be in formal academic—"

"If Daddy-ji were still alive, he wouldn't have cared. Those things weren't as important to him in his last years. He called me Neela, 'blue gem.' He told me I was more precious than his eyes. You're the only other person in the family who thinks I'm special."

"If there's any way I can help, Neelu—"

"Maybe you can. You're so resourceful and independent." Neelu is suddenly ice calm. "Let me tell you about a phone call I got. My cousin Preeti confided that Ma has already found a husband for me. It's her best friend's son. He's twenty-five, an electrical engineer, another genius. Preeti warned me Ma has arranged for us to meet soon. She wants to make it seem casual, so I'll not suspect anything. And she has taken Preeti's mother into her confidence."

"Mrs. Khosla has said nothing to me about this."

"Ma will wait until after your wedding. I didn't tell Deen about this. He thinks I'm working on Ma, trying to get her approval for our marriage, but I've never once mentioned him to either Ma or Raj-bhai. Especially Raj-bhai. He knows how much Ma has suffered, and he'll be on her side completely. You're the only one in the family I can turn to." Neelu chokes back a sob.

Though her body is still, I sense turbulent emotions are churning inside her. In the past few weeks she's become like a sister to me, and I have an earnest desire to help her. Perhaps, after my wedding, I can persuade Raj to intercede on Neelu's behalf. If I can talk him into it, I'm sure we can find a satisfactory solution to Neelu's problem. Suddenly I notice I'm still wearing Prem's mother's sari. I awaken to the reality that Raj and I are due to be married and I'm not at all sure how I feel about it.

Neelu asks innocently, "Would you like to meet Deen?"

I stammer, "Well, yes, sometime—"

"You can see for yourself what kind of a man he is. Then you can convince Ma."

Meeting Deen clandestinely means having to risk incurring Mrs. Khosla's enmity. "Why would she listen to me?" I ask, playing for the time to think.

"Ma likes you."

I doubt it. "How's that?"

"You're what she wanted to be," Neelu says. "An independent woman. But she'd never let you know that. It's hard for her to show her feelings."

It is true that the imperious woman has treated me as an equal by confiding in me. If Neelu is right, perhaps I'm in a position to help her get what she wants. Still, doubt assails me. "I would like to wait—" I manage to get only a few words out before Neelu interrupts.

"What if Deen gave you a facial?" Though her eyes are crimson from crying, they gleam with an eagerness born of desperation. "Of course, it'd be a coincidence. His salon is the best in the city, so nobody will blame you for wanting to go there."

"Oh?"

"You'd love it, Sharmila. You lie down on a comfortable bed in a private room with your head raised, covered up to your neck with a satin blanket. Deen will clean your face and massage it. You'll feel so rested that you'll fall asleep. Then Deen will apply a clay mask all over your face to tighten your pores and increase blood circulation. After that he'll leave you alone to take a nap. He'll ask you to 'surrender.' That's the name of his shop, by the way. An hour later he'll come back, wash it all off, and hand you a mirror. You'll look at yourself and say, 'I can't believe my skin.' I bet you're wondering how I know all this. I've never been there myself. That's much too dangerous. There are no secrets in Delhi." Neelu laughs. "I send spies—my friends."

I would never have expected that much self-control in someone so young, and I wonder if her dream might not come true, after all.

"Finally Deen will make you up. Just a few dabs of color. The way he puts it—he'll find 'your true face and enhance it.' " Gently Neelu adds, "You know, Sharmila, you could use a facial. You look kind of exhausted."

She's got me. To be truthful, I have pleasant memories of my first facial years ago—Liz gave it to me as a birthday gift after Mitch and I broke up. I came out of the beauty salon with a "life is a flamenco dance" type feeling. Yet a little voice keeps whispering: this is madness. As Neelu said, there are no secrets in Delhi. If the secret ever leaks out, I'll have to face Mrs. Khosla's animosity. Glancing pointedly at my watch, I say, "I don't think Mrs. Khosla would approve of my meddling in her marriage plans for you, Neelu, to put it mildly."

She collapses against the cushions, imploring me with her eyes. The silence that hovers about us is tense, prickly.

Abruptly she straightens and asks, "So you had a pleasant afternoon?"

The question mark is almost nonexistent. Behind the casual remark is an unspoken insinuation that Prem and I have developed more than a friendship and that everyone in the house—the servants, Mrs. Khosla, and Neelu herself—have noticed. Blackmail is in the air. With what I hope is a tone of finality, "As a matter of fact, I did."

Yet Neelu keeps staring at me, and that throws me off balance. I catch the *pallu* of my sari, which is about to fall off my shoulder. In my frazzled state of mind, I envision a stray rock bouncing down a mountain slope, going faster and faster, ready to ricochet off a boulder and shatter into pieces unless I grab it right this instant. With a sigh of resignation I say, "I suppose I could use a facial."

"Wonderful."

"What do I have to do?"

"Nothing." In victory Neelu is breezy. "Your appointment is at ten next Monday. My spy was supposed to have a facial, but her time is now yours. I'll arrange for a taxi to pick you up."

My only hope is Deen will turn out to be a jerk. Then I'll be able to express my disapproval with a clear conscience and extricate myself from this ill-advised matchmaking venture.

Neelu springs to her feet. "Excuse me, I should telephone Ma and let her know you're back, so she doesn't worry. Thank you, Sharmila. I know I can count on you." At the door, she turns and adds, "Oh, yes, Raj-bhai will be back in two days. He wanted to surprise you, but I thought it best to let you know." She pauses poignantly. "In case you had other plans . . ."

Raj is coming back! I walk to my room on wooden legs, wondering who has seen me with Prem and where. Were spies involved? The thought troubles me more than the threat of discovery.

Emotionally drained by fear and guilt, I slump exhausted into a chair. After a moment I unsteadily jot down the Monday appointment with Deen in my calendar. As I do so, I picture Raj, his face a shade of mauve and swollen with anger, questioning me about Prem, and a knife-wielding Mrs. Khosla at my back, ready for revenge.

22

P LEASE don't forget you're teaching aerobics this morning, Sharmila-behen." Mohan leans forward as he serves me a steaming cup of tea and rich brown toast slathered with butter.

I look up into the dark eyes that convey eagerness to please and an almost motherly concern for my well-being. "I appreciate that you came to work early just to fix breakfast for me and to see me off. And no, I haven't forgotten."

In fact, I rose an hour early to choreograph my routine, discovering in the process how stiff and out of shape my body had become in a short time. I have lost a lot of flexibility and range of motion. Mohan slips away to the kitchen, and I roll my neck to calm myself down, realizing I'm keyed up at the prospect of teaching in a new location, especially after a month layoff.

Mohan's timing is perfect, I gloat with wicked delight. He has arranged this class at the Maurya Sheraton's health club to coincide with Mrs. Khosla's absence. Of course, she'd never directly interfere with my teaching aerobics. But if she's at all like my mother, a piercing glance or frigid silence and a subtle undercurrent of disapproval would communicate her feelings far more eloquently than words.

Mohan, who returns with a pot of steaming tea, confides without disapproval that his sisters don't exercise at all. That's

normal. As far back as I can remember, none of the women relatives who visited us even so much as bent over to stretch. They
were content to sit around and gossip, regal in their flowing
saris, oblivious to the steady increase in their hip measurements.
Though the lake shore was only minutes away from our home,
it never occurred to them or to my mother to go for a stroll.

They belonged to a generation, a culture where women were
sequestered at home—the world outside belonged to men. Their
clothing conspired against them. Even a moderately fast walk in
a sari is nearly impossible. And formal exercise was considered
indecorous.

"You'll have many rich women in your class." Mohan refills
my cup carefully. "They all go to the Maurya Sheraton health
club, you see. In the last few years exercising has become very
fashionable here. Our former prime minister Rajiv Gandhi
jogged, and many others were encouraged by his example. Still,
very few women run, because they are likely to be harassed. The
majority of them feel safer taking indoor exercise classes."

My God, I'm going to show Delhi society matrons how to
raise their knees, roll their wrists, and pump their arms? What if
a movement strikes them as improper, suggestive, or obscene?
Setting my cup down, I rise from my chair. I better practice my
routine some more. "I'll be in my room, Mohan."

I put some music on, turn the volume low, and start to stretch.
Nothing strenuous, just raising and lowering my arms, bending
forward, and shaking out my palms. Almost the way I started a
decade ago. I recall the day when, on a whim I decided to enroll
in a gym. My mother was incredulous. "Sure, you have had
dancing lessons as a child. But will you be able to exercise now
that you are much older?" she asked. "You don't have it in your
genes." And a moment later, "What if you gain all those muscles?"

Just out of college, I was bursting with plans for new activities, one of which was getting fit and staying that way. I didn't
know my gym catered to weight lifters when I joined. On my
first day I saw a female bodybuilder with grotesque muscles, a
veritable caricature of my mother's worst fears, strutting about.
She viewed the aerobic dancers with disdain, even though they
looked trim and determined.

For me, however, from the beginning aerobics was far more

appealing than weights. As a result, my muscles didn't bulge, and a great burden was lifted from my mother's shoulders. I looked forward to my class in the evening. Standing with my spine straight, raising my hands, and doing a spin, I would enter a new space, light and lively. My pleasant mood would linger long after the session was over. Soon I became the best and most consistent aerobicist in my class. And so, one night when the regular teacher failed to show up, it seemed quite natural when the club manager drew me aside and asked if I'd mind filling in for her.

It was a big order, but I decided to give it a try. There I stood in front of my peers with a thumping heart, without a prepared routine. Just then I noticed the bodybuilder sneaking in—the weight room was being remodeled that day—and a wave of energy washed over me. I led the class for the following hour in a frenzied series of movements, twirling, jumping, ad-libbing new moves, as though I'd been given permission to ignore all conventions. At the end I felt like an empty potato sack, but with my last ounce of energy managed a final twirl ending in a bow. The students applauded deliriously and clustered around me as they gasped for breath.

The bodybuilder stood at the edge of the circle, bathed in sweat, complaining to anyone who'd listen that she was so wasted that she'd probably have to miss her weight-lifting session the next day. I suspected her outburst had nothing to do with her missing a workout. She looked around for support, but received only derisive looks in return. With a final expression of disgust she limped off, vowing she wouldn't return until the regular teacher came back.

I snap out of my daydream and realize I'm in the Khosla apartment with only two hours before my class. I turn up the music and start to do more twists and turns. I notice Mohan sitting on the floor just outside the door, watching me with a mixture of approval and curiosity. My guess is he wants to make sure I'm well prepared.

I've been teaching aerobics for a number of years now and have found it to be a perfect complement to my work as a graphic artist. Soon after I became an aerobics teacher, I noticed I was beginning to sketch with my whole being. The lines I drew were cleaner and more precise and had a life about them. There

were other benefits as well. My boss noticed that I was more focused and took less time to finish my projects. I received a series
of promotions.

My mother was half embarrassed, half proud of me, the way
she had always been about everything I did. To her Lycra tights
had a shameful connotation, and so did female legs in any position other than straight with knees together, preferably beneath
a sari. Yet she liked the fact that her daughter was not only more
pleasant and attentive, but had acquired a more positive attitude. As if to justify the new me to my father, she recounted a
story of a Hindu goddess. She was dancing with other maidens
in her garden when one of the gods stole up to watch from behind a tree, and was so smitten by her carefree abandon that he
fell in love with her. That was in 1000 B.C., Dad pointed out, and
besides, he hadn't noticed me bringing any gods over to meet
the family lately. Nevertheless, I was glad my mother had come
to appreciate aerobics.

As I finish my moves this morning in the privacy of my room,
I hear applause. Mohan now standing at the threshold.

"Very nice, Sharmila-memsahib. You dance well."

"You can come in, Mohan."

Mohan stays outside the door. Despite his encouragement, I
worry about how Indian women, who dismiss exercise for the
most part, will handle this eclectic, American-style workout delivered by a perfect stranger.

I check my watch. "Could you get me a taxi, Mohan?"

I've decided not to use Prem's services for getting around. In
the last three days, I've thought about the matter and decided to
limit my exposure to him. It was a mistake for us to have gotten
so close. But today I feel secure, knowing Raj is coming back.
Everything will return to normal between us. I'm determined
that it will.

Within a half hour, I arrive at the Maurya Sheraton. The acres
of greenery all around showcase a magnificent, ultra-modern
hotel that seems out of place in a city where poverty and squalor
reign. I walk through the high-ceilinged lobby with floor-length
windows that opens onto an L-shaped swimming pool. The bodies reclining on the chairs on the poolside would not seem out of
place at a luxury hotel anywhere in the Western world. I take the
steps down to Kaya Kalpa health club. An attendant directs me

past the indoor Optigolf to the women's weight room. The club looks the same as any in the States, with varnished wood floors, free weights, the astringent smell of cleaning liquid, the squeals and thumps of exercise machines. Women in their forties and fifties intermingle with taut young tigresses with insolent eyes and bored expressions. The aerobics room is rectangular, without mirrors. Sunlight floods in through a row of open windows. My twelve students, all women, are chatting idly in small groups, some wearing bulky sweat pants even though the temperature is in the seventies. A Lycra-clad, gray-haired granny is already stretching, while a matron in a heavy choker necklace is lounging in a canvas chair. A slender woman with the carriage of a *bharatnatyam* dancer glides across the floor, all grace and agility. Does she even need this class?

After I meet the attendant, she begins an introduction. "Today we have a teacher from the States. Sharmila Sen, artist and aerobic dancer who . . ." and she switches to Hindi.

Soon I'm only half listening, and my gaze wanders to the back of the room just as a latecomer sneaks in the door. She looks familiar. Oh, it's Mistoo. She seems self-conscious in her thin pajama-type outfit. She is probably feeling half naked without her multilayered sari. She flashes a warm smile at me.

At last the club attendant gives me the go-ahead and shuts the door behind her. The students take their place in neat rows. I stand in silence a moment to collect myself and distribute my weight evenly between the legs, then begin a low-key warm-up.

We lift our arms, stretch our hamstrings, and bend forward. Just as our bodies are yielding to the commands, the door opens and a man tiptoes in. Several women turn and stare. Is it because he's late? The only man in the class? Or does it have to do with his handsome features? Oh, well. Another look through the bright sunlight and I recognize the unmistakable shape of the head. I meet the intense gaze that I have come to feel should be mine alone. "Raj!" I exclaim to myself.

His eyes say, "Surprise, surprise." Gorgeous in white shorts and a fitted T-shirt that display his muscular body to advantage, Raj smiles impishly. He slides in next to Mistoo without recognizing who she is, exchanges a glance with her, then with annoyance steps back from her. I have a fleeting impression that they've been intimate in the past. I pull my gaze away to focus on the rest of the class.

Yet something has been triggered in me, perhaps the result of too much adrenaline at seeing Raj. I discard the routine I've prepared so carefully. The warm-up now over, I lead the class into a much bolder workout. For the next half hour, hands shoot out, legs kick, midriffs twist—each movement blending into the next—then stopping momentarily for balance before starting over again. Raj is a little out of breath, though he tries his best to copy me. The dancer follows my cues perfectly, performing even better than I, and Granny throws herself enthusiastically into what certainly is a daring experiment for her. The woman with the heavy necklace takes her ornament off and shoves it into her sweat pants pocket.

An hour later, I finish the class with a cool-down, all the while praying no one faints. There is momentary silence. Then my students come forward, wiping the sweat from their foreheads, and gather silently around me, showing they've recovered from their shyness. Perhaps they've come to think I'm one of them.

"Indian women can meet any challenge," Granny declaims. "And you have given us a chance to prove that."

The heavily jeweled woman pushes herself through the crowd. "You must come over for lunch soon, Sharmila. I'll send my chauffeur."

Everyone smiles at me, and I take that as a sign of acceptance. Ever since I arrived in India, I've felt cowed by social situations. Today for the first time I come away with a sense of self-confidence.

"I must get back to work now," Mistoo says by way of a good-bye. Her face is drawn from the exertion, but somehow I don't feel guilty. "Let's get together soon, Sharmila."

"I'll call you," I reply with one eye on Raj. Drenched in perspiration, he's waiting in the back for me.

The students depart, depositing more smiles and good wishes in my direction. A towel around his neck, Raj strides toward me. The moment he's within touching distance, he slows down and his manner becomes tentative, almost as if he's asking permission to approach me.

Forgetting that my body is still wet with perspiration, I reach out to embrace him. I squeal in glee as a warm, sensuous rush surges through me. As we separate, I say, "Mohan gave me no inkling that you'd be coming here, Raj."

"I wanted to surprise you"—the voice is high and breath-less—"so I took a taxi straight from the airport. The workout was wonderful."

And now I suspect Mohan of setting up more than a class. "We can take a taxi home together, then."

"Why go home now?" Raj murmurs suggestively. "I can get a day room here, Sharmila."

I associate hotels with clandestine activity, even one as fancy and intimidating as this. My head whirling, I reply, "But, Raj—"

"Wait till you see the rooms here. They're the ultimate in lux-ury. We've hardly been alone together, Sharmila. You're precious to me. I'd like to be able to talk to you in private. Just as we did when we took a stroll in the park."

His voice encircles me. I ask myself: So what's wrong with a hotel room? I'm about to marry this man. And my mother isn't around. She'd have said, Make him wait, dear, until after the wedding.

"Stay here a minute," Raj says rapidly. "The hotel manager knows me. He'll get a room for me right away." Eyes riveted on me, he takes one step back, then in a smooth motion turns and strides down the hallway.

I stand there, bound in a swing that slides me to a yes one mo-ment and a no the next. To clear my head, I step to the water fountain and take a big swallow of chilled water, all the while brooding about this fast move by Raj. Have I known a man like this before? Yes, Mitch.

Ten minutes later, Raj is fumbling with the electronic lock at the door of an upper-floor room. I notice the familiarity with which he turns on the lights. I hesitate for a moment, then decide to leave my concerns outside. The cool room is pretty in a generic way, complete with a view of a waterfall and acres of a luxuriant garden. An abundance of natural light reflects on the textured white walls. There's a bed, so large that it seems to be the room's sole purpose for existing, without a single wrinkle on its satiny cover. By now my muscles are screaming for rest, and I eye the sturdy bed with its fluffy pillows, smooth white sheets, and springy mattress.

Raj takes off his wet T-shirt and throws it toward the marble floor of the bathroom but misses. "I must admit you've worn me out."

We laugh in chorus, and it eases the tension that has built up since he closed the door. I plop down on a chair. While Raj jumps into the shower, I study the details of this plush room some more—a huge bowl filled with fresh fruit, fine monogrammed stationery, an invitation card to the happy hour.

Humming a tune, Raj wanders back minutes later. Now it's my turn. I don't take too long bathing, either.

Stepping back into the bedroom, I find Raj seated by the window. "You know, Sharmila," he says in an urgent voice, "I haven't been able to stop thinking about you. I must have driven Prem crazy these last several days."

The mere utterance of Prem's name jars my relaxed body, but Raj seems not to notice. "Finally, my boss said, 'Raj, you're useless. Go home. I'm giving you time off until after you're married and gotten back from your honeymoon.' "

The good news staggers me. At last, an end to my concerns about Prem. I'll be able to push all thoughts of him out of mind for good. "What could be better," I exclaim with relief, "than to spend time together? In such beautiful surroundings and at an unexpected hour like this."

"Do you know what else my boss said? You must be quite a person to make the kind of change in me that you have."

"I guess I'll have to forgive him."

"And me." Raj stands up and confidently draws me closer with both arms.

All my sensations are concentrated on my lips as they meet his in a fierce kiss. In a mist of desire I find myself being lowered onto the bed. Boldly we explore each other's bodies. The pleasure accumulates until I can contain it no longer. Much later, I drift off into a dreamy sleep. My last remembrance is of Raj's lips brushing my eyebrow, his fingers entwined in my hair. When I awaken, he is still molded to me, sound asleep, his half-parted lips pressed to my cheek, his special smell enveloping me. The images of our lovemaking are so vivid that I'm not sure it ever ended.

Outside, the brilliant day has gone on without us, and in the deepening twilight the garden beyond has taken on a placid, indistinct quality. Mohan, that friendly cook, I think warmly. He planned it all. I sense the cook has taken a liking to me and is trying to be of help. I'll be sure to reward him with another baksheesh later. I'm far more grateful this time. These intimate hours shared with Raj have helped settle my confusion about Prem.

Then rises a nagging suspicion. This whole aerobics class setup was so smooth, as though orchestrated by a master manipulator. Apprehension about Raj's motives, his character, washes over me, and I'm no longer bathed in the glow of lovemaking. Am I naive to assume I have an ally in the Khosla household? Could Mohan have been told by Raj to arrange this tryst?

Raj stirs, snakes his arm around me and, in between a few kisses and nuzzles, mentions something about dinner at home with Ma-ji. We get up leisurely and dress with far less urgency than when we entered, me buttoning Raj's shirt and he fastening my brassiere.

"Room 331 will be our temporary nest," Raj murmurs.

We hold hands until the elevator door slides open. A bellboy is standing there. He says, "Mr. Khosla, how nice to see you again."

I want to ask Raj what brings him to this hotel so often. As we stroll through the lobby, I avoid the eyes of the other hotel clerks and am relieved that a free taxi is waiting at the curb. As it weaves through traffic toward the Defence Colony, I settle back in the seat. Raj draws closer to me, and though one part of me responds, another part is trying suppress a question:

Why did our first lovemaking have to take place in a hotel room and not in the sanctity of our own home?

23

I AWAKEN from a deep, dream-filled sleep and contemplate the day ahead. After breakfast I'll begin preparations for the surprise dinner for Raj I've been planning for days. This afternoon I'm booked for that dreaded facial with Deen, Neelu's secret boyfriend. Finally, there will be a cozy family meal in the evening, prepared mostly by me.

Mrs. Khosla is coming back from Agra today. Though I doubt I could impress her with my culinary skills, I'm sure Raj will be ecstatic just because of my effort. His eyes will glow as Mohan brings his favorite dishes to the table. Right now he is out running errands and hasn't a clue of what I'm up to; neither does Neelu. She's rarely been home during her mother's absence.

In the kitchen, an array of fresh vegetables and spices dazzle me with their vibrant tints and scents. My hands are strong as I grind the dark mustard seeds into a bright yellow paste, cut the smooth, round potatoes in quarters, and slice the fragrant green coriander leaves to thin ornamental slivers. Mohan, my co-conspirator and mentor, hovers at my shoulder to wash a bowl, hand me a spoon, or offer an occasional word of advice.

"Your masala has just the right color, Sharmila-memsahib," he says, eyeing the spice mixture I'm preparing. "The oil is nearly ready," he observes minutes later, checking the shimmering heat waves rising above the *karai* on the stove.

I am truly grateful for his help. A meal at the Khoslas so far has been nothing if not elaborate: rice, three vegetable dishes, dahl and a meat preparation accompanied by several chutneys and, of course, chapatis. Such variety might appear extravagant by Western standards, but the portions are moderate and the end result is well balanced, not excessive. I was raised on a similar diet, though by the time I reached my teens, my mother had already begun to cut down on the number of dishes.

"Three things and I'll quit," she'd say, growing more like her American counterparts than she'd ever have been willing to admit as she bustled about the kitchen. But in the end, true to her Indian soul, she always made at least one more dish for good measure.

Now that the oil is about to smoke, I throw in several dried red chilies. They curl up, turn black, and exude a pungent, nutty aroma. I turn to Mohan and exclaim, "What a joy to cook a meal like this!"

"When Raj-babu is at home, everything is different, isn't it?" In a whisper he adds, "I've noticed how you look at him. Your eyes talk, Sharmila-memsahib. I can tell, Raj-babu makes you happy."

Cheeks burning in embarrassment, I give a weak smile. I try to change the subject. "Been seeing a lot of films lately, haven't you?"

"I'm happy, too," Mohan continues, undeterred, "for both of you." He shakes his head to move a glossy strand of hair back in place. "Only three more weeks to go before the wedding. Soon Mrs. Khosla will buy new clothes for Champa and me. That's the custom."

The wedding music rings in my head: the *shehnai*, the flutes, the bells. I remember my Wednesday appointment with Raj to shop for some last-minute items. I hurry to finish the saag, then begin working on the mutton. When that starts simmering, I wipe my hands on a towel that Mohan is holding for me.

"I'll take care of the rest, Sharmila-memsahib."

"Oh, thank you, Mohan. Cooking is hard work."

Neelu sweeps into the room, her face flush. "Oh, Sharmila, you're here," she says in surprise. Her eyes take in the stove and the countertop covered with vessels, and she sniffs. "You're cooking today?"

"Shhh," I reply. "Raj doesn't know."

"Oh, no! I've ruined your plans."

"What do you mean?"

"I've invited a dinner guest." A pause. "Helen Trillen."

Damn! Raj's old American girlfriend. Not a question of jealousy, I reassure myself. It's simply that a stranger will detract from the private atmosphere I've planned. Without realizing it, I let the towel drop from my hand. Mohan catches it unobtrusively, almost before it leaves my hand.

"Helen will only be here for a few days." There is a faint smile on Neelu's lips. "She's staying at Hotel Chanakya. Her last letter to Raj-bhai had all the details, but he apparently didn't receive it. She came anyway, waited a couple of days, then decided to call. I heard the phone as I came in a half hour ago. Helen's so friendly. We talked for quite a while. She said she really wanted to meet me, so I invited her to dinner."

I can't blame Neelu. Indians extend dinner invitations all too easily. Touch their heart and they'll want to share what they have. My father, for example, wouldn't think twice before calling home at the end of a workday and saying to my mother, "I'm bringing an out-of-town colleague home for dinner, dear."

My mother would get all wound up, concocting one dish after another on the fly, an anguished expression on her face. But when the guest arrived, she'd glow, fluttering like a moth, monitoring every detail to ensure the visit was perfect.

Neelu couldn't have known of my plan. Or could she?

"Is it okay with you, Sharmila?" Neelu inquires, slightly breathy, perhaps aware of my reaction.

I put on my most complacent face. "Of course."

"Oh, good! She'll be here at six. Ma will be back by then, too." Neelu flounces out of the kitchen.

"True love is tested again and again," Mohan observes sagely. "If you saw the Hindi film *Pyara*, you know what I mean."

I laugh in spite of myself, then glance at my watch. It's already time to get ready for my facial.

At exactly two o'clock, I walk through the door of Surrender, a glass-and-chrome beauty salon that would not be out of place in the States. Inside, the color scheme is sea-foam green. The check-in counter is staffed by chic young women attired in smart designer dresses made of lush Indian fabrics. Thoroughly preoccupied with the burden of Neelu's secret, I ask for Deen, the facialist. The next moment I remember that Neelu, young, vulnerable Neelu, wants to marry him. I'm definitely not in the restful state of mind I should be in for a facial.

An assistant guides me to a tiny room with a massage table made up like a daybed, exactly as Neelu had described it. She pulls up a chair for me and asks, "Could I offer you something to drink? Tea, coffee, Limca, Bislery . . . ?"

I check the time, wishing they'd get on with it. I'd much rather be home finishing the cooking. "I don't care for anything" is my reply. "Thanks just the same."

"But you must have something." A man's voice enters my ear. Not a command, it simply reflects an earnestness born of goodwill.

I look up to see a young man in his twenties, lithe, tall, his full head of hair gelled and brushed back. Though not handsome in the fashion of Hindi movie stars, there's an aura of quiet dignity about him and a calm maturity that makes him quite attractive. Once again I'm forgetting all the social rules. Indians automatically offer food or drink to a guest, or to a customer, even insist on it. My ingrained American resistance to such niceties collapses in the face of his charm. "Actually, I'd love some water," I murmur.

Palms together, he bows slightly. "I'm Deen."

We exchange a conspiratorial smile. We both know I'm here for more than a facial. Our secret has already become the foundation of a special relationship. In a low voice Deen orders an assistant to fetch me bottled water.

A tray soon arrives. I lift the tall glass to my lips, savor the chill, and sip. The lime slice reminds me of another lunch not so long ago. Reluctantly I push the event and Prem out of my mind.

Almost before I know it, I'm lying on the massage table, clad in a loose housecoat, under the cover of a gray Kashmiri stole and with cold pads over my eyes. Just as I'm becoming accustomed to the black silence, Deen spreads a thick creamy lotion over my face and throat. My skin revels in the unctuous sensation.

"This cream is excellent for your face," Deen tells me. "It's called Tropical Paradise. There are herbs in it that'll make your skin smooth as marble."

Deen's fingertips move slowly in tight circles all over my face, then once the cream is worked in, slightly more urgently in a kneading motion. The strokes dissolve my cares and leave in its place a vibrant energy. Neelu's absolutely right about his skills. I sink deeper and deeper into a trance-like state.

Deen asks me about my impressions of India. It's hard to talk with cream on the face and especially in this relaxed condition, but I do my best, speaking in sentence fragments. From his responses I can tell he's not only listening but considering my opinions seriously. I realize for the first time, lying down with my eyes closed, somehow vulnerable, that sometimes it's easier to talk to a stranger than to confide in my closest friend. Within minutes, Deen is describing his recent visit to England for his aunt's wedding.

"I did the makeup, you know." The voice is bold, proud. "And the bride looked like an *apsara*. The groom was completely flabbergasted. He just stood there, totally rigid. His eyes bulged out. Though he'd known her for two years and loved her deeply, he'd never seen her quite that beautiful. His sister had to sprinkle cold water on his forehead, but he finally came alive." In an instant the voice changes. "Personally, I'm against arranged marriage, Miss Sharmila, but I'd be honored to do your wedding makeup."

No doubt he'd do a fine job. But I'm not quite sure how I can slip out on my wedding day to have my makeup done by someone who doesn't meet with Mrs. Khosla's approval. I attempt to shift the subject. "You're against arranged marriage? Most Indians still marry that way."

"True. But our generation is beginning to question that practice. In my opinion, an arranged marriage is basically letting someone else make a serious mistake for you."

A cold shiver creeps down my spine. "I happen to look at it differently," I manage after a moment. "It's quite a sensible way of finding a spouse. Especially when you can't meet the right person in your limited circle of friends. Why are you against it?"

"An arranged marriage creates an illusion of romance. That wears off."

"What do you mean 'an illusion'?"

"By keeping the bride and the groom separate until the wedding day, the two families manipulate an artificial attraction between them. But it has to be all downhill from there. I believe that's the expression you use in America."

"You're telling me arranged marriages don't work? Love can't develop between the two? Your parents with their contacts, experience, and concern for you are all wrong?"

Deen's fingers hesitate as he applies a cooling paste with an earthy aroma on my skin. "You see, my mother was married off early," he says. "Pretty soon she had me. Oh, yes, my father was quite well off, but he was a scoundrel." Bitterness creeps into his tone. "He abused her. Many times I heard my mother crying. As a child I thought all mothers were unhappy. But after his death my mother decided to have her own life. She didn't go to the temple or wear white as widows were supposed to do. Instead she rented her own flat. I still remember how happy she was the day we moved in. As though she were afraid that her laughter would dry up if she didn't let it out all at once."

Deen's hand trembles. "Then she met Mr. Khosla and fell in love with him. He liked her spirit, her beauty, her way of comforting him when he needed it. He paid for anything she wanted. She liked the way he treated her. And he became a second father to me. I called him Khosla-ji. Oh, yes, people gossiped, but my mother didn't care what anybody thought. I guess I'm a lot like her. I feel strongly about . . ." Deen's voice catches and he falls silent.

I feel capricious as I ask, "Neelu?"

Again his fingers begin to tremble, then become limp, and finally cease their strokes. "I can't do without her," he cries. "Mrs. Khosla must agree to our marriage."

What a wonder it is to hear a man so openly express his feelings to a woman. And yet I have to say, "That might not be possible."

"I'll move to England with her. Even if she doesn't want to go, I'll convince her. We can disappear in London. Let Mrs. Khosla try to find us there."

Flicking the cold pads off my eyes with one hand and throwing the shawl off to the floor with the other, I bolt upright into a sitting position. My voice is harsher than I mean it to be. "You mean you'll kidnap Neelu?"

Deen shrinks away, as if I've physically struck him, and bumps into the wall. But his face betrays his struggle to maintain a professional demeanor. With his voice full of apology for having offended me, an esteemed client, he says, "Please, Miss Sharmila, lie back down. I didn't mean to upset you. It's just that I can't bear the thought of a life without her."

I catch a reflection of myself in the mirror on the opposite wall and gasp—a charcoal black clay paste hides my entire face except the area around the eyes. My anger dissipates at the hilariousness of the image. "Deen, promise me you won't do anything rash."

Relief spreads over his face. Bowing slightly, he says, "I promise. But would you be willing to help find us a way? Please, Miss Sharmila."

I sink back down onto the bed, though not as relaxed as before. My mind is already in high gear seeking a way out of this mess.

"Please take your rest for about forty-five minutes, Miss Sharmila. The biggest compliment you can pay me is to fall asleep. I'll be back then to wash your face and add a touch of makeup."

The tension broken, I reply playfully, "Will you make me look like an *apsara*?"

"Your face will tell your story." I hear him flick the light switch off as he leaves.

24

MOHAN has set the dining table just the way I had in-
structed. Arrayed are white china place settings against a
background of chartreuse linen; gleaming silver cutlery with intricate designs etched by a master craftsman; and a subdued,
aesthetic centerpiece of scented white flowers.

The faces around the table—the Khoslas and Helen Trillen—
glow in the rich light of the tall candles in the background. Raj
made the introductions earlier, and now general pleasantries are
being exchanged. Mohan arrives bearing a huge tray containing
a platter mounded high with fragrant steaming rice, a bowl of
leafy green puree called saag, and a tureen of thick yellow dahl
flecked with brown mustard seeds. And that's just the beginning. As the aromas permeate the room, the conversation slowly
dwindles. Everyone looks up at Mohan—eager faces dazzled by
the colors, sniffing, suddenly aware of a ravenous hunger. Satisfaction suffuses me; I haven't made a fool of myself, after all. My
mind finally at ease, I turn my attention to the guest of honor.

Helen Trillen is a big woman, even by American standards.
Right now she's laughing at a cryptic remark by Raj, obviously
a private joke between them. Her voice is commanding but not
harsh, with just the right amount of New York in it. I notice she's
about his height, though considerably heavier. Large blue eyes

dominate her pale oval face. The woman still shows traces of the beauty and energy that'd have drawn Raj to her a decade ago. She's dressed in a deep purple sari with a flashing gold border and blouse to match. I recognize the fabric as a lush *banarasi*, one meant for weddings, too dressy for an intimate social gathering.

At the same time, Helen has a spirited personality. It is evident that she has had a privileged upbringing and education. She clearly has a wide range of interests. Under different circumstances I'd enjoy her presence.

But not now. As the wedding date approaches, and Raj and I begin to get to know each other, I hunger for more time together. Helen is an unwelcome intrusion.

In his eagerness to serve her properly, Mohan nearly trips. He steals a glance at her, as if a word of praise will cover his embarrassment.

"What do you call him?" Helen asks, the question addressed to no one in particular. "Boy?"

I'm ready to blow up but bite down on my lower lip. No one responds, and the question hovers in the air. Finally I reply above the clattering noise of serving spoons, "His name is Mohan."

Either Helen doesn't hear or chooses to ignore me as she says, looking in Mohan's direction, "I'd like some iced tea."

Iced tea is a foreign concept. I long to inform Helen that Indians serve plain, chilled water without ice at meals and that Mohan will have enormous difficulty meeting her request at this point. Angry words are almost ready to burst on my tongue.

"So sorry, memsahib," Mohan says sweetly to Helen. "The refrigerator is broken."

I catch Mohan's gaze and hope the twinkle in my eye tells him that I relish his cleverness. Helen falls silent, and Mohan smoothly proceeds to serve the rest of us uninterrupted. Seated at the head of the table, Mrs. Khosla averts her eyes, pretending not to notice any of this. Her face shows new lines, what I'm sure is the fatigue of travel, yet she laughs and nods at Helen's every utterance. All this from the mother who vehemently opposed her son's proposed marriage to this woman.

On my other side, Neelu, food-loving Neelu, seems to have misplaced her fork. Engaged in small talk, she frequently picks up her tumbler and sips. Her one chipped nail indicates an appointment with a manicurist is imminent. As if reading my thoughts, she flashes me a faint knowing smile. We haven't had a chance to talk since my facial with Deen, and I'm sure she's dying to know what transpired. Meanwhile Raj, sitting next to me, is busy passing all the chutneys to Helen, one after another.

"This dark one is made with dates," he says. "It's sweet. You had a sweet tooth, I remember. Do you still? Oh, and the green chutney's on the hot side, so try only a drop at first, just in case . . ."

Has he noticed the luscious kalia on his plate that I've prepared so painstakingly?

Perhaps the family feels guilty about Raj's former girlfriend being alone in Delhi for the past two days. Or is it just innate Indian hospitality? Then too, I conclude from Helen's speech and manners that she is what Indians would call a *pukka* American, an East Coast blue blood with an eminent family name, whose summer vacation to any island twenty years ago would have made the social page in the local newspaper. Though the clippings have yellowed and the money's all gone—these again are my guesses—this descendant of a once powerful family titillates the fancy of the Khoslas. It is I who am unimpressed and who feel like an onlooker.

Helen excuses herself from the table and wriggles out of her chair for a trip to the powder room.

As soon as she's out of sight, Raj whispers, "She always was a big girl. Now she's terribly overweight. But that's the least of her problems." With a mixture of affection and compassion, he informs us, "She's legally blind, or so she told me. Quite brave to be traveling alone, don't you think?"

Legally blind? Helen didn't have any trouble finding her silverware, getting up from her chair, or finding the bathroom. But to Raj I say, with a sweet smile, "Oh, yes, I don't know how she manages, poor girl."

Murmurs of sympathy flows back and forth across the table.

"Helen must be taken every place," says Mrs. Khosla.

"Maybe that's why she wears such a loud-colored *banarasi*," Neelu says. "Do you suppose we should give her a plain sari for a present?"

"Better to send the tailor to her hotel to get her measurements," Mrs. Khosla counters. "Someone of her proportions would look better in a *salwar-kameez.*"

As if suddenly discovering his appetite, Raj pays attention to his plate and digs in with gusto. Eyes shining, he turns to me, "Sharmila, this is great—" then breaks off and looks up as Helen comes through the door.

"New Delhi is absolutely fascinating," she announces as she takes her place. "I've been here two days and already seen Raj Ghat, the National Museum, and Qutb Minar." She pauses to take a bite of kalia. "Oh, and the National Gallery of Modern Art, too." She starts a monologue about the parallelism between modern Indian art and that of New York. Food forgotten, Raj leans forward with apparent interest.

A recent visitor myself, I put in, "I saw a nineteenth-century lithograph collection at that gallery recently—"

Mrs. Khosla interrupts. "Are you an artist, Helen?"

"No, I'm a fund-raiser for a nonprofit organization. We support public art projects."

"How nice." Mrs. Khosla motions to Mohan to bring more rice for Helen.

Noble-sounding job, but poor pay, I conjecture. But there must still be enough in the trust fund for Helen to live comfortably. Soon she reveals that her research trip here is for a freelance piece on modern Indian art for which she's yet to find a buyer.

An art review to be done by a blind person? My skepticism turns to incredulity.

Mrs. Khosla puts her fork down and asks eagerly, "What about the Red Fort in Old Delhi? It's a stunning example of Mughal art."

"Old Delhi?" Helen asks. "Ah, of course, the famous old city, originally called Shahjahanabad. I've heard it's so crowded that it's difficult to get around there."

Raj turns to me. "You had quite a time up there, didn't you, Sharmila?"

"Yes—" I mumble. Helen doesn't let me finish.

"In that case, why don't *you* show me Red Fort, and whatever else you find interesting there, Sharmila?" She looks up toward the ceiling as if her appointment calendar is hung there. "Tomorrow would work for me."

I've never visited the Red Fort, having only glimpsed its exterior in passing on the way to Prem's. "Tomorrow may not be best." Keeping my voice low, I say, "Raj and I have planned a shopping expedition for wedding things."

Helen doesn't seem to hear. Is she deaf as well as blind, or just plain rude? "And you might like to join us, Raj," she commands. She pronounces Raj to sound like "rage."

"You do remember tomorrow, don't you?" I whisper to my fiancé. His hand searches out mine under the table and squeezes it reassuringly. He asks his mother, "Do you suppose we can get Prem to show Helen Old Delhi tomorrow?"

Poor Prem. Instantly I feel sorry for him.

"I called Prem tonight," Mrs. Khosla replies. "He told me he won't be available the next few days."

Is it because of me? I return to the conversation to hear Raj saying, "Wait till you see the sword collection in Red Fort, Helen. It's exceptional. Weren't you studying fencing the year I met you?"

I almost hear the click, click, click sounds. An invisible sword of neglect wounds me.

Helen and Raj begin reminiscing about their college days. Face suffused with warmth, eyes holding nostalgia, Raj calls up old New York memories one after the other, reassembling the pieces of their once shared life. Getting caught in a blizzard and buying a beer to keep warm. Raj's first beer. The bet they had on a stern-looking professor, Dr. Chatterjee—Indian he was—to make him smile. The falafel joint where they were such regulars that the waiter brought their orders automatically. Raj cups his chin in his palm and bends forward on his elbows as he speaks. As if seeing through his eyes, I picture him then. An inexperienced young man in New York, trying to make up for what he has missed in life thus far. She, older by one year and more experienced, is nearly irresistible. Chemistry. Adventure. Fulfillment of fantasies. He revels in their first sexual experience. He's a kite on her string.

Out of nowhere a vision of Prem flashes in my mind, and I wonder if I'll ever see him again. Is it for the best that we're apart?

I pick up another thread of conversation at the table. Mrs. Khosla is telling her daughter about the relatives she's just visited. Who's graduating this year, who just got married, who bought a flat, who's pregnant. Oh, it's the same person doing all four things.

I look at a plate of food gone cold, the steam and aroma having vaporized along with my expectations of a fun evening. A family fragmented at the dinner table is not what I had in mind. Suddenly I realize it's not Helen Trillen I dislike, but rather how she affects Raj. He hasn't grown out of the cocoon she built for him long ago. She'll be gone in a matter of days, but her shadow will be on Raj's face forever.

Two hours later, Mohan calls a taxi. As it arrives at the front gate, Neelu hugs Helen and Mrs. Khosla extends her good wishes. In between her thanks, Helen flicks her "sightless" eyes over Raj and me. I notice a hint of unresolved pain on that alabaster face and am on the verge of feeling sorry for her when she says, "By the way, Sharmila, the biriyani was excellent."

Biriyani? It wasn't even part of the menu. Is her comment an honest mistake or a put-down? I manage to say, "I hope you enjoy the rest of your stay, Helen."

Eyes ahead, her steps light and sure, Helen descends the steep staircase. Raj follows closely behind, watching her every move, leaving me standing alone. I watch as Helen makes her way to the gate, opens it, and approaches a waiting taxi beneath a dim streetlight.

That woman can't be blind, I want to scream to Raj. Don't you see? Her supposed blindness is a crutch, a bid for sympathy, a cover-up for her uneasiness in a new situation. My thoughts are followed by a wave of recrimination and self-doubt.

Should I be so judgmental? Am I just indulging in petty jealousy? After all, I'm the one who's marrying Raj.

Then again, maybe it's Raj who's blind.

R AJ is showing Helen around Old Delhi, so my time is my own. I could have joined them but decided not to. Yet as the morning passes, an oppressive mood engulfs me, like a fever coming on. Oh, I could have stopped him from going. God knows, I wanted to, but when he got up from the table after a hurried breakfast, the morning was so fresh, clear, and full of promise that such an act would have seemed petty and inappropriate. So I kept my mouth shut, and now I feel left out.

Sitting at my desk, my mind wandering all over the place, I open my sketchpad and halfheartedly begin to draw an impression of a boat—a stationary one with algae-coated sides. It is anchored at a dock with waves rolling around it, as if beckoning it to come out and play, to no avail.

Trying to regain my motion

That's how I sign off. Flipping my sketchbook closed, I stand up. Out loud I say, "Whatever happened to Sharmila the explorer?" From out of nowhere, a beam of hope pierces my somber mood and brightens my spirit. Helen will be leaving tomorrow, at which time I'll be able to be with Raj. We have much to say to each other.

I know I've been putting off my talk with Mrs. Khosla about Neelu and Deen. I can't let the future topple onto her without warning. Still, the idea of confronting Mrs. Khosla about Neelu's future petrifies me. A visit with her is what Indians call a *darshan*, an audience. My plan is to be honest and direct, though she may be unhappy that I'm meddling in her daughter's affairs.

It's nearly noon when I tiptoe into the living room and find Mrs. Khosla perusing the *Hindustan Times* as usual. Her deep focus is manifested by the stillness of her body and a face line-less in its repose. Clearly, this is a private time, not to be violated without a good cause. I sink as unobtrusively as possible into a chair across from her.

Needing a diversion, I pick up an English-language women's magazine from a basket and bide my time. As I flip the magazine open to a page at random, I come across an advertisement for Sherlock Holmes mystery novels and another for jewelry: All that glitters *is* gold. An article about how sex is good for your skin is sandwiched between pages and pages of saris purported to make a woman "ethereal as a twinkling star." Finally I come to the cover story: Ten tips on what to do if your next-door neighbor is extremely attractive. How ludicrous, as if this were the major dilemma facing Indian women. But soon, in spite of myself, I become absorbed in my reading, and the trembling inside gradually subsides.

I'm on tip number six, which is to find a suitable excuse to go visit him, when Mrs Khosla's voice interrupts my concentration. "Oh, Sharmila. Sorry. Didn't hear you come in."

I close the magazine, drop it on my lap and, despite tight jaws, put on a smile. Then in my best conversational voice I toss off, "I saw you sitting here alone and thought I might join you."

"I'm glad you did." Mrs. Khosla folds the newspaper care-fully so the edges align, and sets it down on the coffee table. As she shifts into a more comfortable position, the heavy gold ban-gles on her arms make an ominous clinking sound. Her orna-ments are a part of her body language, which at this moment seems to indicate she's in the mood for a talk.

"You know, when I went to Agra for a few days, Sharmila, I missed you. I realized you've become a part of our family." Mrs. Khosla's voice trails off.

Despite my ambivalence toward my future mother-in-law I

experience an unexpected constriction in my throat. So I've made a connection, after all. "I guess I had many concerns when I came from the States, Mrs. Khosla. I might as well be honest. I didn't know what I was getting into, and India is so hard to take in. All I had to go on was what my parents told me. The first week was very difficult, but I got so much caring from your family, and now I'm surprised how close to people I've become. Neelu's like a sister. Mohan I feel I can trust—"

"It's Raj, isn't it?" Mrs. Khosla cuts in. "You must be concerned about Helen, her past history and all."

I shift my position. Mrs. Khosla fiddles with the hem of her sari. The creases tell me she, too, is distressed about the matter.

"You see, Sharmila, Raj has always been popular with women. But he wants to settle down. He'll make a good husband."

"We're getting closer. And the moment you begin to care about someone, you start worrying about losing them." I sit up straighter. "I guess I should look at the bright side of things. We'll be married soon, and I'll make him a good wife—that'll keep him home."

"I find it surprising that although you've been brought up in a very modern country, Sharmila, you're willing to make the same adjustments Indian women do."

"I'm not exactly from the West, Mrs. Khosla. Though I was born and raised in the States, I adopted the values of my parents. I suppose, though, that I have a different set of expectations, especially about men." Sensing an opportunity to honor my agreement with Neelu, I slip in, "But then, Neelu's in somewhat the same situation, even though she has learned her values from you. She's growing up in a more modern time than you did. Her attitudes are a lot different than those you had as a teenager. Neelu and I both face similar problems."

"My darling daughter is pretty and bright, wouldn't you say? Still, there are times when I wish she was the innocent baby I used to hold to my breast. I worry about her."

That picture of Neelu as a child on her mother's lap—hopeful, secure, giggly—fades into my image of her as an adult who's grown strong and confident from being in love. "You've started to think about seeing Neelu married, haven't you?"

Mrs. Khosla shrugs and smiles. "I've been thinking about that since she was a toddler. In a Punjabi family like ours, we start looking for a husband early on. Someone who will treat our daughter well. Someone who will satisfy her material needs and keep her nearby. So she won't be 'left on the shelf,' as we say about unmarried women. But now our children are growing up in a television culture. They go to dance parties, picnics, and get-togethers unchaperoned. They must have their freedom. Just like teenagers in America."

She pronounces the word "freedom" as though it's synonymous with forbidden pleasures. What she's referring to, I know, is the new practice of dating in India. In the pause that follows, I hear the ice cream vendor through the open window. "Kulfi! Mango! Vanilla!" The words run together as if he were hawking one flavor.

Taking a deep breath, I brace myself for what promises to be a grim conversation. I ask, "Would it surprise you to know there's a man in Neelu's life?"

Mrs. Khosla looks away. "Really!"

"Someone she has known since childhood," I hurry on. "She sees him often, especially when you're not around. They have many common interests, and . . . they want to get married."

I expect a glass-shattering outburst and am ready to cup my ears with my palms when I hear an intense voice, saying almost in a whisper, "I know everything that goes on in this house. The walls, the floors, and especially the servants are my eyes and ears. There are no secrets here, Sharmila. I know all about Deen. I've known about him for a long time."

"You do?" I manage to croak. Relieved, I take a deep breath and force myself to go on, "Well. That makes my job easier. You see, I've met Deen."

Mrs. Khosla's eyes widen with shock and despair at the news. She obviously wasn't aware of this. So much for knowing all the secrets in the house.

"I've gotten to know Deen a bit. And if I may say so, Mrs. Khosla, he seems like a good match for Neelu." Then before she can regain her composure, I race on. "Don't you think a marriage between them might be possible if both sides agreed?"

Moving forward in her chair, Mrs. Khosla points a quivering index finger. "Marriage!" she exclaims. "How can you suggest that? Don't you know who Deen's mother is?"

Too late I realize I've misjudged how strongly Mrs. Khosla feels. Sparks of indignation flash in her dark eyes. Her dusky skin takes on the purplish coat of storm clouds. I bow my head in remorse at having caused her such anguish. "Please, please forgive me for upsetting you. I didn't mean to—"

Mrs. Khosla nods dismissively, indicating I needn't apologize.

But since I was the one to bring up the sensitive subject, I feel compelled to see it through to the end, hopefully a happy one. The woman shouldn't go on torturing herself over wrongs committed long ago. "I know you've been mistreated, Mrs. Khosla, but you must consider another way of looking at this. It's been ten years now. Perhaps the fault lies not so much with Deen's mother but with the nature of our society. Here a man can have many licenses, a woman few, if any."

"No!" Mrs. Khosla's answer shakes the walls. "I blame her for everything."

"Her only mistake was to love a man. A man of high caliber. A man considered worthy by your parents to be your husband. A man you loved yourself. From all I've heard, he was larger than life. And so, in a way, really, you and Kaveri have much in common. One in particular is the happiness of your children."

"A woman like her steals your very life." Mrs. Khosla's voice trembles, but she keeps on speaking. "You are left without breath, light, or hope. You don't hear music anymore. The *ghunghurus* on your ankles no longer make you want to dance. Your world is like a desert." She closes her eyes. "Don't ever mention that name here again, Sharmila. Do you understand?"

"Perfectly. But you must understand in return. My only concern is Neelu and our family. She and Deen are quite serious." With hesitation I utter the ultimate threat. "What if he were to take her away to someplace far from Delhi?"

I have just told Mrs. Khosla she's beaten, and she knows I'm right. The newspaper falls from her lap and flutters noisily to the floor. I'm about to bend down to pick up the pages when she hisses, "I will kill him with my own hands."

I look up to see those sturdy hands shaking before me. They certainly look capable of killing. Dowry death headlines seen in the newspaper flash one after another before my eyes. Was this how Roopa, who was poor and unable to afford a dowry, met her end? What about me? My father is a successful dentist, but

I'm not bringing any dowry, either. Do I really fit in this household? Do I really meet Mrs. Khosla's standard to be Raj's wife?
Is she having second thoughts about this marriage? Trembling, I
turn.

Mohan appears in the doorway with a tray of fruit juice. The
intensity of Mrs. Khosla's voice causes him to gravitate in my direction, as if to shield me from her ire. "Kulfi, kulfi," I hear the
vendor resuming his cry.

"Is the ice cream wallah disturbing your peace, memsahib?"
Mohan asks Mrs. Khosla. "Should I send him away?"

"It's okay, Mohan." I manage to infuse a gentleness into my
voice. "And we don't want any juice right now."

Head down, Mohan hurries away, the tumblers on his tray
shaking, clinking. His stooped posture indicates that now he,
too, is burdened with a family secret. Lips pursed, eyes brim-
ming, Mrs. Khosla sinks back on the sofa. Little tremors ripple
through the length of her white chiffon sari like the aftershock of
an earthquake.

My voice low and calm, I continue. "Perhaps by being so strict
about this matter, you're making Deen all the more attractive to
Neelu. Suppose you didn't pressure her to marry anyone right
now. If you gave her the freedom to choose on her own for a
while, she may meet someone else. Or . . . you may find Deen acceptable, after all."

Mrs. Khosla steeples her fingers, rests her chin on them, and
stares off into space. "You've been raised by Indian parents in
the West, Sharmila." The voice is hoarse but authoritarian. "You
weren't burdened by the ghosts of your ancestors, or thousands
of rituals and taboos. You see things differently. You respond to
each situation based on its merits. Those traits are good. I was
brought up in a society where we have more past than present
and where the future is in the hands of gods. How can I change
so quickly, Sharmila?"

Mrs. Khosla rises in a tentative manner, as though still considering what I've suggested. The keys tied to the *pallu* of her
sari make a tinkling sound, a reminder she's still mistress of the
house.

"Please let me know if I can be of help," I murmur respectfully after her.

My words are swallowed by the silence that descends on us. I watch as Mrs. Khosla walks out of the room. While I wish happiness for Neelu and Deen, I can't help but wonder what turn of events would bring a satisfactory solution. Can I really do anything more to help them?

26

SHOPPING is one of my mother's favorite pastimes. From the moment she enters a store, she can spot the promise of a bargain at twenty paces. She touches the merchandise, scrutinizes it from every angle, and finally stands back from it in blissful triumph if she has decided to buy. Frequent trips with her in my adolescent years, when I'd much rather have been with my friends, gave me an implacable aversion to shopping. To this day, a mall gives me claustrophobia.

Perhaps because of that my steps are reluctant this morning on my way to shop for the wedding with Raj. Originally scheduled for yesterday, our errands had to be postponed because of Helen's visit.

Raj is driving. As I slide into the seat next to him, my mind is preoccupied with a variety of other matters, foremost being Raj's playing tour guide with Helen yesterday—an excursion that lasted well into today. True, she's an old friend of his and they had much catching up to do, but when his footsteps on the staircase woke me and my clock showed two a.m., my mind raced. The rest of the night I was tormented by the darkest suspicions. By morning I managed to calm down again and promised myself not to mention my feelings until such a time that we both were under less pressure.

Raj takes me to Connaught Circus. Perhaps he has a sixth sense or he's made a lucky choice of a place guaranteed to delight me. We come to a pavement stall displaying a haphazard collection—computer manuals next to Vedanta—laid on a piece of cloth. Clearly this market is not on the list of places to go for last-minute wedding items, but just as clearly Raj has recognized that my mood needs lifting.

We enter a small English-language bookstore whose shelves are so crammed with books that they nearly pop out. I lose myself in the enormous selection, scarcely conscious of Raj's broad-shouldered presence. Usually voluble, he stands quietly by me, letting me take my time. He hands me a hard-to-reach volume, explains a title, talks about India's thriving publishing industry, then steps away, though not too far. Before long, my shopping bag is piled with recent *New York Times* best-sellers I've been meaning to read and many titles published in India. Raj says he'll borrow these books, too. On impulse I throw in a copy of *Let's Learn Hindi* by Mohini Rao. Though I have spoken a few words and phrases at home, I'm still too embarrassed to speak the language in public.

As we leave, I turn a bright face toward Raj and am rewarded with a happy, knowing smile. But the pleasant moment is clouded by thoughts of the matters we have yet to discuss. It takes a conscious effort, an oar pushing away seaweed, to force them out of my mind.

We wander down to a stall a few doors down, where a food vendor mixes a handful of this and a dash of that on a table.

"I can't do without *vel puri*," Raj says in a low voice, as though sharing a deep secret. "I can go to the best restaurants, but every so often I get a craving for street food."

Within seconds, a look of total contentment suffusing his face, Raj is chewing a savory mixture of puffed rice, onion, and potato topped with chili bits, coriander slivers, and a red chutney. I can tell he has surrendered completely to one of life's little pleasures. I sample a bite and understand why he likes it so much. The hot, sweet, sour, and salty tastes form an exuberant chorus in my mouth. What's even better, I enjoy learning about his little weakness. I want to get closer to the space inside him where he's not the powerful and commanding Raj, but just a simple man with simple tastes.

My belly full, palate sated, senses heightened, I announce, "I'm ready for more shopping."

"Let's go to Hauz Khas," Raj says. "There are lots of fine shops there."

We drive on through the broad avenues of Delhi toward the affluent southern section, our carefree spirits merging in laughter and an intimate remark or two. At upscale Hauz Khas we enter a shop that specializes in bedding and bath linen. Inside the door hangs a bold sign, FIXED PRICE, to warn away those who might be inclined to haggle. Out of a band of salesmen lounging in the back, one bustles up to greet us. The middle-aged man looks us over. His eyes seem able to measure the thickness of a shopper's billfold from halfway across the room. He fetches two stools for us. As we take our seats, Raj explains to him what we're looking for in long, careful sentences. I want to assert myself, but I let him do the talking.

The salesman replies yes, yes, but the moment he hears the word "wedding," his face lights up with an anticipation of a big sale. A tray of tea arrives. A lull in the conversation follows, and I start to fidget. My old distaste for shopping is magnified by a busy Chicago native's sense of time going by: We're here, let's get the job done, and move on to the next errand. My impatience must be evident, for the salesman sets his unfinished tea aside and with quick, eager hands begins to spread a high-quality selection of bed linens on the counter.

Raj asks, "What do you think, Sharmila?"

So he wants me to make the decision. I begin to review the selection of bedsheets, pillowcases, and comforters. The color and the design must not be so loud that they lash out at us. I also feel the density of the fabrics against my skin, notice how they lie on a surface and how the overhead light plays on them.

Pleased at my interest, the salesman asks me, "What language do you prefer I speak to you, madam? Tamil? Malayalam? Or are you from Spain?"

The old uneasiness returns. Though it is a pleasant, mild day, a prickly, damp sensation settles over me. I say, "English, please."

"Film star Mithun Chakroborty uses this particular brand," the salesman says. "Super excellent!" Then seeing the blank look on my face, he responds with dismay, "You haven't seen his films? Take my word for it, then. Price? I'll sell this one to you for fifty rupees less."

"What about the fixed-price sign over there?" I ask, pointing.

"In India, every rule can be broken, madam." The salesman smiles. "You just have to find the man in charge. I'm the owner."

Raj shoots me a glance that indicates we're getting quality items at a bargain price. He sips from his cup, looking away absentmindedly, while I search through the assortment spread before me with the same intensity as my mother used to display in Carson, Pirie, Scott and Company. Finally, consulting my list and having selected towels and lamp shades, I turn to Raj. He nods with a benevolent expression on his face, giving me his agreement. We pay for our purchase.

The package is so huge that the proprietor orders his young son to carry it to the car for us. Raj hands the boy a generous baksheesh of several rupees. With a shriek of joy, the boy touches the money to his forehead and scampers away.

"Thanks to you, Raj, not only did we find what we wanted and at a good price, but it was pleasant."

Raj's eyes radiate mischief and affection. Looking around quickly and seeing no one nearby, he bends down and gives me a short, warm kiss. My lips are inflamed. I almost lose my balance as I slide into the front seat.

Raj steers confidently down an avenue dappled with sunlight. Trees on either side reach for each other in the middle, birds peek through the leaves, sprawling whitewashed bungalows flash by. There's hardly anyone on the sidewalk, creating an impression of dreamy leisure.

After we turn back onto an arterial, Raj breaks the contented silence. "This morning when we left the house, you looked piqued and I could tell shopping is no fun for you. So I've been taking you to places where you'll have the least hassle."

His sensitivity and eagerness to please, combined with the memory of his kiss, soothe me and return me to my former thralldom with this charismatic man. The rest of the day passes easily with purchases of useful and frivolous things.

Back at the Khosla apartment, we stash our packages in Raj's closet. He switches on the overhead fan, and a gentle current of cooling air washes over me. I kick off my shoes and flop down on his ample bed draped with a red and white patchwork bedspread, murmuring something about how good it feels to be back home.

This room, easily twice the size of mine, is going to be our bedroom—that is, until we can move to the bungalow Raj promised. I allow myself to own the place, visualizing the day when every corner, every object, every bit of space will be subject to my touch. Like that blank spot on the south wall, where light doesn't fall directly. I see a painting there, nothing too large, with a yellow or orange burst of color, something intense but blurred, like Joan Mitchell's *Two Sunflowers.*

Raj slips a disc into the CD player, taps his foot on the floor, and hums along with the pop vocalist, flipping his wrist every now and then. As the accompanying sitar takes over, Raj explains that the lyric is about peacocks dancing in the first rain of spring. He makes for the door.

Warning bells go off. I must not let him close the door. Against all the coziness, I blurt out, "There are some things we need to talk about."

I must have sounded grave. Raj turns down the volume on the CD player and moves to a chair by the bed. A patch of pale afternoon sunlight falls at his feet like a maid. "Let's discuss them, then." He looks at me, his soft eyes smiling. "It must be Helen."

I sit up and lean against the headboard. "Yes and no."

"I should make it clear that Helen's the first woman I dated in the States. To a man raised in India, that meant a big discovery." Breaking eye contact, he gazes at the floor. "You've been here long enough to understand how restricted our social life can be. For me Helen represented abandon, discovery, the opportunity to become a man. And for that she'll always have a special place in my heart. But, Sharmila," he says, lifting his eyes, "she's gone—along with a part of my past. I doubt I'll ever see her again."

Part of me is satisfied with his statement; another part is frightened by it. Helen was loved once, now she's discarded. "Raj, it's not about another woman." I speak slowly, thinking of Mistoo and her possible past intimacy with Raj. "I'm asking about what our marriage is going to mean."

His eyes darkening, Raj reaches to pick up my hand from my lap. "What do you mean, Sharmila?"

"I don't want to get married just for the sake of being married."

He lets my hand drop. My words echo on the walls of the room. I hear the uncertainty in them and am reminded of the trouble my parents went through to arrange this wedding. I feel guilty. One side of me toys with the idea of marrying Raj without making a fuss. Yet I hear myself say, "You must understand, I want a real relationship. A commitment. I'm not sure you have that in mind." I see him swallow. "Since I arrived, you've been mostly unavailable, Raj. It's like mailing in an absentee ballot instead of going to vote."

"I too want a relationship." The voice is affectionate and earnest. "I guess I simply assumed we'd build ours over time." Raj leans back against the chair in a kind of managerial posture. "We seem to get along great. We sense each other's needs." Looking deeply into my eyes, he adds, "We're physically attracted to each other, aren't we?"

No doubt about that. "True, Raj. But I'm beginning to wonder if this is going to be a typical Indian marriage. One where the wife is a package delivered to the door, expected to be there, always flexible, understanding, and selfless. The husband goes when and where he pleases and does whatever his heart desires. The wife is a support system first, a lover second, or maybe, a second lover." I draw in a breath and continue before he can interrupt, "If this marriage wasn't arranged, I believe you'd be eager to nurture our love. You'd be here more."

"I agree that we have different expectations, Sharmila." Raj's voice caresses my name, entraps it. "What makes you think we can't grow to love each other just as much as if we'd met on our own? Our love may be even deeper, because it'll have a chance to develop. We'll learn to love slowly, in a more realistic way."

"Will we? Does arranged marriage always work that way? Or only in certain cases? The other day when I met Mistoo at a restaurant, a family was seated next to us. I couldn't help but notice how kind the woman was to her children. It was just as clear she was unhappy. All the light had gone out of her eyes. Her husband kept lecturing her on one thing or other. She sat there, withered and resigned, like her insides have been stolen away. Love given time and time again but never reciprocated, until she realized she had been drained. Maybe I'm imagining things, but

I swear to you that woman was alive on the surface, dead inside." I pause, overcome by powerful emotions I had been repressing. Now they tumble out. "That's not how I want to end up. Maybe it's my Western expectations, but I want to feel loved and respected as an equal. I want you beside me, not two steps out in front, or not there at all. I want our lives intertwined. Tell me, Raj, is that unrealistic?"

His hand grips the side of the chair. He opens his eyes wide, as though trying to see through darkness. "My darling, ever since you came, I've been so much happier. I'm opening up like I haven't been able to for the last couple of years." The hand relaxes. "I'm flattered to know that you want to get to know me, to merge your life with mine."

Closing my eyes for a second, I summon up my last bit of courage and decide to be totally honest. "I'm not agreeing to our marriage until you agree to a life in which I can be an equal partner."

Raj swallows, and I'm not sure whether love or anger is his dominant emotion at the moment. "You're tough," he says, smiling. "You're tender, too." He nods. "That's what I like about you. You're a fire and a flower at the same time. I've never felt so fully desired. Or as scared of it."

Soft light pouring in through a gap in the window curtain lends a halo to Raj's face. His eyes flicker with intensity, and I feel myself weaken, a tender bud in his hand. But no—I get hold of myself. "Raj, you have this ability to charm—it's easy to get carried away. But I must be certain my feet are on solid ground."

"Sharmila, I need you—I can't tell you how much. Everyone thinks of me as a highly eligible bachelor who has everything going for him. In some ways that may be true. But I don't want that anymore. I don't want to be on the go. I want a solid base, a woman who will anchor my life. It would never have worked with Helen, or with the typical Indian woman, but you're just right. You understand my culture, but you're not carrying its baggage. You're free and so I can be free. Let's enjoy our freedom together."

My doubts are all but swept away by his sincerity. The sitar pulsing from the CD player evokes sentiment. "And I can show you a new way of life, Raj."

His voice becomes soft and throaty. "That's the life I want. The two of us. In the mountains, in the woods, in our home. I even have a new name for you. Please, will you let me call you Mila?"

That's an endearing diminutive I haven't heard before. I feel like his queen. I lower my head, partly in assent, partly to conceal the tears.

"Mila, Mila, Mila." Raj whispers my new name as though stringing together spring blossoms. In my imagination I wear it like a garland. He draws me close, his fingers wiping away my tear with satin-smooth strokes. "I love you, Mila."

The rustle of a sari, delicate but intrusive, shatters the moment. Pulling apart, we turn toward the door.

Mrs. Khosla, dressed in delicate white, stiffens and almost shrinks away as she says, "Oh, you're back." Then her face smooths with a nonchalance that she seems to be able to draw on at a moment's notice.

I blink to clear my eyes and look toward her with what I hope is a bride's radiant face.

"I have some good news for you, Sharmila. Your friend Liz called just after you left. The number's by the phone."

"Liz? From Chicago?"

"No, she's here, at a hotel in Karol Bagh. I had a hard time hearing her because the area is so noisy. She's just arrived. I said you'll call this evening and she said she'd wait for your call. She has a pleasant voice."

Liz in Delhi? And already charming the Khoslas? But then both Liz and I can charm other people's mothers better than our own. I can't wait to see her. It's been six weeks. "Excuse me, Raj, I must call Liz."

As I go to the phone, Mrs. Khosla says from behind, "Your friend should move out of that wretched place at once. Our guest rooms are free for the next few days. She can stay with us quite comfortably. Relatives won't arrive for another week. And some more good news. Prem will be available tomorrow. Since you'll be busy getting ready for the wedding, he can escort your friend."

Prem? Just the sound of his name makes me feel I'm coveting something forbidden. I'm trying not to mind that he'll be giving Liz a guided tour. Thinking about him I'm suddenly cognizant of how far I've come from that day when he drove me from the airport.

I rush to the phone in the living room, dial the hotel number, and after being switched to Liz's room, I am thrilled by the sound of my friend's voice. I picture the round face, the pale coloring, the pecan-colored hair always worn straight.

"Shari, I'm here, I'm here." It's the most excited I've ever heard Liz. Her Midwestern accent sounds as fresh as shaved ice. "You invited me so many times to your wedding. And since you're my best friend, I took you up on it."

"I'm dying to talk with you, Liz."

"What's the matter? There's something in your voice. Last-minute jitters?"

I'm wondering if, like Raj, I don't have things to put behind me. "I'll tell you all about myself when you get here, Liz. Mrs. Khosla is offering you a guest room. Just pack up, check out, and take a taxi here. It'll be easier for us to catch up, and you'll be able to meet all the Khoslas."

"Oh, to spend my days in a palace," Liz gushes in a mock falsetto voice, "with you and prince charming and the queen mother . . ."

We both break out laughing, a good clean laugh that chases out the sighs I have been holding inside. "Let me give you the directions." I tell her the route her taxi should take, using expressions as a Delhi-ite would: opposite this cinema or that, past a petrol pump, five hundred meters from such-and-such temple. . . . I'm quite pleased with myself as I hang up the phone.

Waiting for Liz at the front steps, I begin to feel more upbeat. At last I'll have someone to talk to about Raj and the Khoslas. I open my sketchpad and draw the open gate, the sun striking it at an angle, the forecourt and the driveway, ending with the line:

A chariot is coming. Its passenger my hope

A TYPICAL Khosla breakfast is in progress with Neelu consuming a lioness's share of the food. A straight-backed Mrs. Khosla, enthroned at the head of the table, is ordering Mohan to bring this or that in a firm voice. As he bustles about, he bobs his head up and down and utters a servile "Yes memsahib" every few seconds.

Raj is present, too, but unusually subdued, as though absorbed in his own universe. The occasional comment he makes to me seems considered rather than spontaneous. I wonder if it's the result of our talk yesterday. I realize I drove a hard bargain and am not surprised at his remoteness. Still, I'm not certain I really got through to him.

I keep an eye on the door for any sign of Liz. It still seems unbelievable that my friend from Chicago is actually here in Delhi. The hours flew by yesterday as I filled her on my stay here, leaving out only the most intimate details. She, in turn, brought me up to date on her life in Chicago. Nothing much has changed and I'm glad, desperately wanting someone or something familiar to cling to in the midst of the turmoil surrounding me.

Liz glides in, dressed as usual in a longish skirt that hangs halfway between her knees and ankles. However, the fabric isn't the gray wool seemingly coordinated to match the grim Chicago sky. This new skirt is made of a flowing rayon fabric in fuchsia teamed with a lavender blouse decorated with a myriad tiny reflective glass discs. In a breathy voice Liz recounts her first day in Delhi. Yesterday she watched a camel go by, an artist painting a huge cinema billboard, and a wedding procession in which the groom arrived on a horse.

I listen with amusement. She's still in that first stage of infatuation with this exotic new bond. The bloom in her cheeks confirms this.

"I also watched some cricket players practicing in a park," Liz says.

"Get Raj to tell you about cricket, Liz," I venture. "It's an Indian obsession. I'm told you'll never understand India unless you understand cricket."

At the mention of the game, Raj comes alive. Face lit by a sudden burst of pride, voice filling the room, he proclaims, "We used to call it the 'cricket fever.' "

He begins to talk about his days of running between the wickets. My eyes lose focus. I visualize him in the batting cage, dressed in an immaculate white uniform, a white cap on his head. He swings the bat under a brilliant sun, and the crowd surges to its feet, cheering wildly as the ball soars into the distance. I'm a spectator approaching the field, first attracted to Raj's long shadow on the ground, then his tall form. Coming even nearer, I try to make out his face but find I can't. A great chasm yawns between us.

I reach out to touch Raj. The warmth of his skin is sufficient proof it was an odd daydream. He senses my need, and in a gesture of gentle reassurance he cradles my hand in his. The soothing touch restores me for the moment.

As the breakfast hour winds down, Mohan begins to clear the table and one by one the Khoslas depart, Raj being the last. Liz and I are finally alone.

She steals a glance at Raj's disappearing back and whispers, "Dashing, isn't he?"

Breaking into a smile, I accept the compliment with a tentative "Oh, yes," leaving an unsaid *but* hanging in the air.

"I haven't seen you glow like this since the time with Mitch."

I find her comment annoying. Why does she have to remind me of an old boyfriend? "They're as different as they can be. How could Raj remind you of Mitch?"

"I didn't say they were alike."

So Liz thinks I'm reacting to Raj the same way I did to Mitch when I first met him. That's so Chicago. There you look for what's common among people and situations. Still, her perceptiveness disturbs me. My unspoken rebuttal is that the circumstances in which I met the two men are different. Besides, in many ways I've changed as well. Just as I'm ready to voice my objection, Champa, wearing a stunning teal blue sari, enters the room bearing a jug. I haven't seen that sari before. How could she afford it? Is it a hand-me-down from Mrs. Khosla? But Mrs. Khosla dons only white.

Champa acknowledges me with a glance, then asks Liz, "Water, memsahib?" She's tiptoeing in her eagerness to serve.

Champa didn't speak to me like this on my first day, as I recall. Why does she treat Liz differently?

"*Nehi.*" Liz's accented refusal comes across as a warm and spirited attempt at a foreign language.

Champa asks in barely understandable English, "Speak Hindi, no?"

"*Chaar baajey.*" Liz's reply means it's four o'clock. I bet she meant to use the word, *thora, thora,* "a little," but got it confused.

"Memsahib . . ." Champa is unable to finish the rest of her sentence in English and gives up with a giggle.

Mildly flustered, Liz retrieves a Hindi phrase book from her purse and, with Champa looking over her shoulder, flips through the pages looking for the correct response. When she finds it, she practices more of her Hindi on Champa, who answers in English. They laugh at each other's mistakes as well as their own. The two are having such a great time that I excuse myself and return to my room.

My denim pants are rather plain, so I select a pale print blouse with a daring neckline edged in red to spruce up my outfit. I slip a stack of silver bangles on my arm in the fashion of young Indian women. As I step out of my room, the bangles give off a flirtatious jingling sound.

Prem is standing at the far end of the hallway, talking animatedly to Liz, Neelu, and Mrs. Khosla. I notice the hair curling at the nape of his neck, the muscular arms beneath the sleeves of a pure white shirt, the inclined head that conveys humility without appearing servile.

My pulse thudding, I take a step back. From the snatches of conversation I'm picking up, the planning for a city tour appears to be well under way. I stand rooted there, wondering what to think, where to flee.

Prem is the first to notice me. We hold each other's gaze until I break the eye contact. I begin to shake, tremble, and burn. In the silence hangs an unspoken question. What did that kiss really mean?

Mrs. Khosla, Neelu, and Liz look my way. I force myself to come closer and join them with what, I'm sure, is a crimson face.

Mrs. Khosla addresses me in a breezy manner. "Prem has worked out a great itinerary for Liz. It'll take most of the day."

"Would you come with us, Shari?" Liz asks. "At least for part of it?"

Even with wedding preparations and all, a part of me wants to go. But another part warns me about Liz. She has always been able to read my mind and, given the situation, I wonder if I should risk her guessing my feelings for Prem.

Mrs. Khosla decides for me. Waving a sheaf of pages in her hand, she says, "I'd like to go over some details of your honeymoon with you, Sharmila. The travel agent called with some alternative hotel suggestions. And two of Neelu's aunts are coming over for lunch. They want to meet you. But if you'd rather keep Liz company . . ."

"We can wait awhile," Prem says to Mrs. Khosla. "It's still a little early. Most places won't open till ten." He pulls a map out from his pocket and unfolds it. "In the meantime, Liz, I can give you a general layout of the city."

Prem's extending me a hidden invitation. I find it impossible to refuse and so tell Mrs. Khosla that I'd like to keep Liz company for a couple of hours. "I'll take a taxi back before lunch. Liz, you can continue your tour without me, if that's okay with you."

"I don't mind," Liz says amiably. "I can get lost in the museums here."

Prem puts in, "While she's doing that, I'd be glad to bring you back home."

Does he want to spend time with me alone? The very anticipation balances me precariously on the border between pleasure and pain.

Mrs. Khosla mumbles a grudging "All right, all right," and I follow her to the living room. Prem guides Liz to the garden below. Yet a part of me remains with them, wondering what they're up to.

An hour later, we're cruising down one of Delhi's broad avenues. Liz and I are comfortably ensconced in the backseat as Prem weaves in and out of the thickening traffic. Prem makes small talk with her while I, distracted by his presence, can only stare at his neatly trimmed hair. We arrive at the Connaught Circus area, and Prem points out one office tower after another. With an eye to the red sandstone structure of the Jeevan Bharati insurance building, Liz mumbles a comment about how imposing it looks.

"Don't be too impressed," Prem deftly replies. "The local joke is that new buildings make good ruins and that's about all."

His cheerfulness is like bubbles fizzing in a glass of champagne. Is it due to Liz? I wonder, a knot of jealousy twisting my stomach.

The arched stone India Gate comes into view. "It's a war memorial, Liz," Prem says, "built for the brave sons who gave their lives for Mother India."

I notice they're already on a first-name basis. They obviously like each other. And why shouldn't they? After all, they're two of my favorite people, with similar calm dispositions despite their vastly different upbringings. I'd be even more uncomfortable if they hated each other, wouldn't I? So why am I so miserable?

"Elizabeth Worthington." Waiting for traffic to clear at an intersection, Prem utters with respect, "Ah, surely a poet's name."

"Oh, no, not really, although I try to write a line or two every night," Liz says modestly, though I suspect the subject is a turn-on for her. "By no means am I an artist like Shari."

"We have an ancient tradition of poetry in this country, Liz," Prem answers. "Especially in Delhi."

I try to include myself in the conversation by saying, "Indian languages are well-suited for that form—the rhythm of the consonants, the expressive vowels, the nuances of the words."

"Very much so," Prem replies dreamily. We drive past a shallow ornamental pond with water lilies floating on its surface. "Last night before going to bed I read an Urdu poem."

"So you understand Urdu, too?" I'm both surprised and irritated. Prem hasn't shared this side of him with me, but he casually flicks off this information to Liz. With its rich, flowing sounds, that language emblemizes for me uplifting ideas, undercurrents of passion.

"One particular line from that poem stuck in my mind," Prem says. " 'After love's chatter dies, then only you listen to your heartbeat.' In Urdu it sounded so musical. Later in my dream I heard a voice singing that line again."

"It's a beautiful sentiment," Liz comments. "How about reciting the Urdu version?"

Prem responds, augmenting the guttural cadences of the language with his entire being. The exact meaning of the words escape me, but the rich sound caresses me like a beam of morning sunlight. Despite that I can't stop thinking that this isn't the diffident chauffeur I met on *my* first day. He was reserved then, all "please," and "madam," and "if you so desire." He didn't call me by my first name or recite a love poem.

"Liz, now I'd like to hear you read one of your poems," Prem says, "if that wouldn't be an imposition."

I expect Liz to shyly refuse, but instead she responds, "I carry a notebook with me all the time. Just in case." She rummages through her purse for a small reminder pad, and flips it open to a mostly blank page. "I'm struggling with a line, actually. Oh, well, maybe when we take a break I'll read it to you."

"This is Purana Qila." Prem slows as the old fort comes to view. "There's an archeological museum inside." While he explains the structural form of the building, a fascinating blend of Hindu pillars with Muslim arches and domes, I consult my watch. Much as I like poetry and architecture, my time's up. Mrs. Khosla and her lunch guests will be waiting.

"I'd like to spend some time here. That way Prem can take you back, Shari." Giving me a quick hug, Liz hops out of the car. I watch her head toward the fort with quick, bouncy steps, a whirl of fuchsia and lavender.

I slide into the front seat with Prem. A gloomy silence fills the car. The Delhi zoo with its vast grounds looms before us. Shoveling words desperately into the void, I attempt, "I've never been there."

"I meant to take you there, Sharmila, to show you my favorite elephant. I guess we ran out of time."

I detect a dull sadness in his reply. I struggle to stifle the alarm ringing within me. "What do you mean?"

"I'm not working for Mrs. Khosla as of tomorrow."

"You're not?"

"Didn't she tell you?" Prem turns and looks me in the eye. "This is my last day. I'm buying a car and starting my own travel business."

"I'm so glad for you." I manage to speak around a lump in my throat. "I'll miss your company, though, Prem."

Of course I can't tell him, however much my heart is crying out, that I think I'm in love with him. That I want to spend time with him. That I trust him in a way I don't trust Raj. We're separated by social position and caste, and yet, as in my art, when it comes to choosing a man I draw no boundaries. If the situation were different, if I wasn't going to marry Raj—a shiver of excitement runs through my body—I'd go straight to Prem. But I am going to marry Raj, and so, I submerge my feelings beneath a veneer of politeness and gratitude, and thank Prem for sharing so much with me in such a short time.

"I want to tell you something before I go, Sharmila. You asked me what time I dropped Mrs. Khosla off on the evening of Roopa's death. It seemed important to you, so I went back over my old diary. I dropped her off on Lajpat Marg about four blocks from her house around five minutes to six."

I seem to hear only the last sentence clearly. "Did she ask you to drop her there?"

"Oh, no. She'd never walk if she didn't have to, but the street was blocked by a big crowd. Some sort of a demonstration by a striking trade union was in progress, and I couldn't get through. I remember feeling a little concerned about leaving her there, but she didn't seem to mind. It was her neighborhood."

"How long would it have taken Mrs. Khosla to walk those four blocks?"

Prem thinks for a second. "If you want to be absolutely sure, you would have to retrace her route."

Just then Prem pulls in at the gate of the Khosla apartment. The sun has disappeared from the sky, and the air is dusty and gray. I hear Prem saying, "I hope you and Raj will be very happy."

No more respectful *babu* he previously attached to Raj's name, and that delights me. He's Raj's equal, has always been in my mind. I slide across the seat toward the door, preparing to leave.

"Sharmila," Prem calls out from behind, "just one moment, please. I have a gift for you from my mother." He offers a small locket of tarnished silver with a stylized mango etched on it. "She has kept only three pieces of jewelry from her childhood. Two she has given to my sisters. This is the third."

"But . . ." I protest weakly, ambivalent about accepting a family heirloom.

"Please, it's not much. She wore it on a chain around her neck for years. She says she'd be honored if you'd put it on once in a while and remember her. It's not as beautiful as your wedding jewelry will be, but this one holds her special blessing. If you touch it, you'll feel she's there wishing you well."

Prem places the locket in my palm, then covers it with his hand. As we hold the locket together, the warm beauty of the moment transforms me. I find a certain strength in my pain. Looking at Prem's face I find it softer and rounder with unspoken sentiment. With a choked word of thanks and trembling legs, I jump out, carrying this last image of him, and rush up the stairs to the Khosla home.

After making it through lunch without falling apart, I retreat to my room. For the next hour I'm weepy, distraught, and forgetful. I look all over for my sketchpad before finally discovering it in my closet. I sit down at my desk, open the book to a blank page, and proceed to draw the pond with floating leaves I'd seen earlier, an outline of Prem standing by it, ending with the notation:

You gave me a new loaf

I can't seem to relax. Even sketching doesn't soothe me. Suddenly, an image of Deen pops into my mind and I hurry to the phone in the living room.

"Miss Sharmila, I'm so glad you called." The excitement in Deen's voice is genuine. "You see, I've been wanting to get in touch with you, but I can't really call you there." In a whisper, "Is anybody around?"

"No one I can see."

"Well, your talk with Mrs. Khosla seems to have done some

good. She obviously trusts your judgment and is rethinking Neelu's marriage. Last night Neelu brought her a box of pistachios, since Mrs. Khosla loves to munch on them. Then Neelu sweetly put in a request to invite me to your wedding. At first Mrs. Khosla said, 'Oh, my dear God,' but Neelu kept pleading, and after an hour she said, 'Oh, very well.' So I'm now invited."

"I'm delighted, Deen. In the short time I've known you, I've become fond of you."

"We still have a long battle ahead, Miss Sharmila. But thanks to you, at least we've gained some ground. I'm very grateful. As a wedding present, you'll get a complete treatment at my shop— hairdo, manicure, pedicure, and a full-body message. I have the appointment book in front of me. When would you like to come in?"

"How about tomorrow at ten?" When I hang up the phone, my spirits are much improved.

My watch says five o'clock when I hear footsteps on the staircase. It must be Liz. As she looks up at me from the entry foyer, her face beams. Arms out, skirt billowing out about her, she does a pirouette. All that buoyancy only serves to irritate me. "Would you like to go for a twilight walk before dinner, Liz? It's pleasant outside."

Soon we're ambling down a sedate street lined with posh houses. The sidewalks are bordered with slender *ashok* trees and red gravel. In less than fifteen minutes we reach the neighborhood's business area. I become conscious once again of the bubbling, passionate, and relentless energy of the city. A noisy urgency in both the foot and vehicular traffic makes conversation a battle until we happen onto a small park, all shrubs and grass, with only a few people strolling about. We find an empty bench shaded by a spreading *gulmohar* tree and take our seats with grateful sighs.

"I had a great day," Liz begins. "Your chauffeur is really a neat guy."

"He's a Dalit—an untouchable."

"I think he's quite touchable." Liz giggles. "You don't think so? Well, I'll take him back to the States with me, then."

"Oh, sure." Suddenly my voice sounds as if it has been through a knife sharpener.

Liz holds my eye. "I know your problem. It's not what you think. Come on, Shari, you can't hide anything from me."

"Really?"

"Shari, you've always been more direct than I. It takes me longer to make the point, but I'll try to shortcut to what I've to say. I'm going to tell you something you probably already know, but don't want to face. Or perhaps you want to hear it, but you won't agree with me. Maybe it'll embarrass you, or make you angry. Maybe you'll never speak to me again—"

"Spit it out, Liz."

"I've noticed that you're very aware of Raj when he's around. You're a little too alert, like you don't want to miss the sound of his footsteps. And the moment he opens his mouth, you look up at him with your big eyes. But those eyes are full of doubts. My guess is you're impressed with the man but not in love with him." Liz pauses and shrugs, as if doubting whether to continue. Then taking a deep breath, she plunges on. "On the other hand, when you're with Prem—your face softens, your eyes glow, your whole body radiates energy like there's a dance inside you. You're so happy when he's around that you're not conscious of how time passes, or if you impress him. I think Prem is the one you're attracted to. And you know, Prem's in the same boat. He can barely keep his eyes off you."

"How can you say that?" I blurt out, fighting to keep my voice from rising. "It's totally ridiculous. You obviously haven't seen Raj and me together that much, or you'd know we're attracted to each other and love being together. Sure, there are a few wrinkles; we don't have a long history of dating, but even so, we can talk about any problem. You don't know how intimate we've become—"

Liz laughs as though what I just said is funny. "Shari, you should see your face now. You're angry because what I said is true."

"You totally misunderstand me."

"Listen, Shari, we've talked a lot the last two days. One thing I've noticed is you don't mention Mitch at all. You've finally gotten over him."

"I don't know what I saw in him in the first place. Even though I always had doubts about him in the back of my mind, I put blinders on, I guess."

"The last time I met Mitch at the Bliss Café, we talked about you for a long time—we're both your friends, you know. Mitch is totally against an arranged marriage. Later, after I got home, I made the decision to come and visit you." Liz pauses. "I remember your years with Mitch. You tried hard to forget that period. The same fate is waiting for glamour boy Raj. I'm afraid he's not going to be *the man* in your life; he's just another phase."

"You're wrong, Liz. I *am* committed to Raj and it's a serious commitment." With a sigh I add, "Today I pretty much said good-bye to Prem. I saw him flirting with you, by the way."

"I was just trying to get a reaction from you, Shari. He caught on right away and played along. You know the Urdu poem he recited? 'Listen to your heartbeat.' Do you think for a minute that message was meant for me? Get real, kid. It was for you."

"You two tried to manipulate me." I throw a sharp glance at Liz. "That's unfair."

"Maybe so, Sharmila, but with the best of intentions."

"Your intentions didn't work out."

"I think you should break your engagement with Raj."

"It's too late, Liz. The festivities start next week. You know, it's finally beginning to sink in."

Her voice is shaded by doubt as she says, "You're actually going to go through with this wedding?"

"I am." I say it a bit too cheerily, even as I realize that the weight of this lavish affair is already crushing me.

Liz asks, "Do you know Raj winked at me?"

A jolt, a burning sensation of anger and embarrassment, rises from within me. I realize this behavior is not at all out of character for Raj. Nevertheless, I smile sweetly. "Might you just be envious?"

"Of course," Liz says. "Why, you'll have an exciting life. A fancy house, parties with the right people, jetting around the world. I think though that some afternoon when Raj is out of town, you'll be sitting on your patio with your cat and your children and all of a sudden, out of nowhere a tear will trickle down from your eye. It'll wet your cheek, drop onto your expensive sari, and leave a wet spot. You'll ask yourself: Where did this tear come from? Isn't Mrs. Khosla happy and fulfilled? Days will go by before you'll admit to yourself that the tear was in memory of your true love."

I feel as though Liz just passed a rapier through me.

Liz adds, "And one more thing. Your mother-in-law is so

domineering. Last night in my dream I saw her dressed as a traffic cop directing cars at a busy intersection. That's her role in real life as well. Those huge arms, those ponderous steps, and gimlet eyes that can see all that goes on around her. She seems to have a master plan for everyone in the family. And she's ruthless. Quite frankly, Shari, she scares me."

I hide my already nagging dread of her and reply with a grin. "Now, *there's* something we agree on." With that I stand to go. "I'm so glad you're here, Liz."

"Only until tomorrow." She falls into step beside me. "While you're busy with the wedding stuff, I'll be taking a side trip. But don't worry, I'll be back in time to snap pictures of you in your wedding sari. And how many pieces of jewelry did Mrs. Khosla say you'll have on? Twenty-four?"

I'm disappointed. I'd hoped Liz would be here to support me through the days leading up to the wedding. "Where are you off to?"

"I'll be bumming around on the golden beaches of Goa. Who knows? Maybe I'll meet a handsome French tourist under a palm tree. I'll call him Jacques. That's my favorite French name. Will you be okay? I kind of feel like I'm deserting you."

"I'll be fine. Don't worry about me, Liz. Go enjoy yourself. Dad's coming the day after tomorrow, and Mom will be arriving a few days later."

"Sometimes I wish I had your problems, Shari."

We share a laugh, then start walking toward home quietly, matching steps at first, then separated by a stream of pedestrians, losing each other, yet each sensing where the other one is, the way it has been since high school.

My best friend thinks I'm making a big mistake. I could be angry with her for leaving me, but in a way, I can't say I blame her. Liz never did like unhappy endings.

My eyes are on the silver jet that has just materialized from the inky black sky, reflecting a wan moonlight. From the well-lit visitors balcony at Indira Gandhi International Airport, I watch it approach, touch down, then taxi to a halt on the runway. A portable staircase is trundled to its side, and passengers begin to disembark. I hold my breath, searching for Dad.

And sure enough, there he is, his tanned face illuminated by flashing runway lights. As he strides confidently toward the gate, I notice that he's tall by Indian standards. I wave my white handkerchief to attract his attention. Smiling, he waves back with a wide gesture.

Can this excited, energetic man really be my father? At home he has always been the opposite of my mother, mild-mannered and taciturn, not given to open displays of emotion. He always hovers a few steps behind my mother, seemingly content to live in her shadow. But now it's as if he's come to life.

It'll take Dad at least an hour to get through immigration. I go to the busy passenger lounge, sink down in an empty chair, flip open a paperback novel to do some reading. My mind begins to wander, and an image of an evening in my childhood comes to mind. I was five years old at that time. Holding Dad's hand, I was crossing a busy intersection in Chicago, lights flashing all about us. Cars whizzed by, roaring, honking, the noise filling my head, swelling in my chest, until I felt I might pop. I clutched Dad's hand tightly and gazed up at him. He looked away, lost in thought, as if he didn't even remember I was there. Frightened, I began to cry silently. "What are you crying for?" Dad asked, wiping my eyes with a Kleenex. "We'll be home in a few minutes."

He continued to drag me along, oblivious to my distress. When we arrived home, I was still crying. I remember the sticky eyelashes, the salty taste in my lips, the burning sensation on my cheeks. His remoteness scared me more than the traffic.

Ever since that time my relationship with him has been hard to define. I've never been quite sure how I fit into his life. Did he really want a female child? Was I the right kind of daughter? Does he care about me at all? These questions first came into my mind long before I reached my teens, and they remain there to this day.

I close the novel and direct my thinking to Raj. Since I've arrived, he, too, has been absent most of the time. The prospect of living my life under such circumstances is as terrifying as that street crossing with Dad at the age of five. I yearn for a far closer relationship, more meaningful than what either has permitted so far.

Suddenly Dad is coming toward me, clad in a checkered sports jacket, a carry-on bag slung on his shoulder. My eyes catch the marigold garland that hangs around his neck and the dab of beige sandalwood paste smeared on his forehead. Though his hair has thinned in recent years, the dark curls on the sides are still thick and dance with every step. The fatigue of travel notwithstanding, his carriage is erect, his strides long and vigorous.

"Sharmila!" Dad sets his luggage down to hug me tightly, causing a strand of hair to fall over my eye. Taking his garland off, he stands back and examines my face minutely, as though to ensure his little girl is still intact.

Satisfied, he announces, "I'm in India, finally!"

I laugh. "Dad, I'm so glad you're here—" Then I see that he hasn't arrived alone. The man who has stopped at his side must be his old college chum, a hotelier who has offered him a suite gratis for the next two weeks. They maintain an ongoing correspondence via e-mail.

The stout man in *kurta* and trousers is grinning good-naturedly. And now Dad turns to him. "Sharmila, this is Amit Khanna. He pulled some strings. I was allowed to pass through customs and immigration with a minimum of delay. I'm getting VIP treatment."

"Gods make rules, we mortals break them." Mr. Khanna greets me with hands pressed together. His plump cheekbones, highlighted by the fluorescent light above, give off a metallic sheen. "I've arranged everything," he tells me breathlessly. "I e-mailed my personal Brahmin priest, who was in Haryana for the wedding of his cousin. He hopped on his motorcycle and drove back here to bless your father on his arrival with *maalaa,* sandalwood, and holy water. He broke a coconut on the runway. Auspicious. Most auspicious, wouldn't you say?"

A saffron-robed *sadhu* who's cyber savvy and rides a motorcycle? I'm still digesting this latest evidence of India's gleeful mixing of worlds old and new when Mr. Khanna announces, "I have a car waiting. I'll take you both to my hotel. After you have had breakfast with your father, Sharmila, the hotel car will take you back home."

I mumble a word of thanks to Mr. Khanna for going to all this trouble. A warm smile spreads across his cherubic features. "Please don't mention it. What do time and money mean? In the end, people are everything."

Within the hour, Dad and I are lounging in plush chairs in Dad's suite on the top floor of Hotel Ajanta. In the companionable silence I hear the early morning sounds of the world outside—a car, a cricket, a gentle breeze rustling the leaves. Last night in the Khosla house when I couldn't sleep, I was calmed by the same sounds. It seems each day has a different vocabulary, but the language of darkness is identical.

Collecting myself for the conversation to come, I take in a sip of water. Dad, the dentist who normally shuns all things sucrose, takes a healthy pull from a large glass of Fanta. Jokingly I point out its sugar content.

"Lovely," Dad says, his chest expanding. "You don't know what it's like for me to come back home."

It's difficult to imagine that Dad could look this dreamy or express such heartfelt emotion, and I'd never have believed the Fanta. This is a different man sitting across from me.

Stretching his arms languorously, Dad continues, "I didn't get much sleep on the plane, but I have tons of energy. And I'm going to eat and drink all I want for a change." As if to emphasize his point, he takes another long, appreciative swallow of his orange soda. "So how is it going, Sharmila?"

"Just fine." I'm reluctant to bring up what's bothering me. "Things are moving along quite nicely, I'd say."

"Are you sure?" Dad's eyebrows bunch together. "I have this sense you're not telling me everything. You have dark circles under your eyes, a sure sign you're worried. And you're sitting here with your hands clenched. When you were a child, that was a dead giveaway that something wasn't right."

His keen powers of observation both please and confound me. Perhaps he has more fatherly concern than he shows. "Oh, well." I laugh again, and my words become musical and light. "I guess there's not much point in trying to hide things. My experiences here so far—as the critics say about books and movies—rate a mixed review."

"I had no idea until I saw you. I've phoned Mrs. Khosla several times since you got here, and your mother has talked to you a couple of times. After we compared notes, we got the impression that everything was going extremely well." Dad leans forward from his waist, almost falling off the chair. "What seems to be the problem?"

"Dad, I don't want you or Mom to start worrying."

"Really? Since when . . . ?"

"You just arrived. I should go home now and let you rest."

"Please stay, Sharmila. I won't be able to sleep in any case."

"We can continue this conversation later, you know."

"Do you realize how much your mother and I care? Since you left, there hasn't been a single hour when I didn't think about you. Now, I want you to tell me what's wrong."

"It's not any one thing in particular. I'm just bothered by some things. Like certain aspects of Raj's character."

"What? What are you talking about? He has outstanding credentials and references. That's one reason we chose him over other candidates."

"Raj has had a lot of women. Maybe that's all in the past," I say, my throat tightening, "but when Helen, an old flame of his friend from Columbia University, came to visit, they spent a good bit of time alone. One night he came home at two."

Dad clears his throat. "And are you above reproach?"

I look him squarely in the eye. "What do you mean?"

"Mrs. Khosla hinted you were very friendly with their chauffeur."

"She purposely put us together, hoping, I guess, to embarrass me."

"Sharmila, you probably don't understand India as well as you think you do."

"Prem and I are just friends. We were. He's no longer chauffeuring me as of yesterday or any of the Khoslas, for that matter."

"I'm glad to hear he's not the reason you're having second thoughts about this marriage." Dad sets his glass down and nods to himself, concern furrowing his forehead.

The Khoslas all have their secrets. Apparently they wish to turn me and Prem into a dirty little secret, too. I'm outraged at being caught in an entangling web. As I lean back, the cushioned chair, so soft and supportive minutes ago, tortures my spine. I ask, "Did you know Raj's first wife died under mysterious circumstances?"

"I checked that out," Dad says firmly. "Raj is not to be blamed for it. When it happened, he was with the workmen at the bungalow he was buying."

I'm astounded. My father really has been looking out for me.

Dad shrugs and flashes a smile with his perfect white teeth. "What family doesn't have an accidental death, insanity, illegitimate child, or some such skeleton rattling in the closet?"

Suddenly I'm smiling myself, and for a moment Dad and I have a secret understanding between us.

"You met my friend Khanna," he resumes. "His youngest daughter just turned twenty-five. Not only she's a knockout, she has an M.A. in zoology. If the girl was not a little too young for Raj, Khanna would have jumped at the chance to get her married into that family." Dad sighs, and his eyes cloud over with worry. "But you've grown up in America. For you everything must be perfect, just like on television. Real life, my daughter, is more like a succession of potholes on a winding road."

"Dad," I tell him, "I won't be forced into a marriage if it's not right for me."

"It wouldn't be right for me, either," he says. "A lost opportunity is just that. Call it a father's intuition, but my feeling is you're better off with an Indian man. And if so, who better than Raj? I can tell you're attracted to him."

I study Dad's face in the soft yellow light emanating from the lamp on the side table. Gone is the remoteness I've come to expect. Away from his office, wife, and household, he seems younger, carefree, and impetuous. He has risked telling me what I am feeling. "You're sure of that, Dad?"

"One moment you are very sure, Sharmila, and you have your bright face peeking out. The next moment you hide behind your doubts and you're invisible. I remember hide-and-seek was your favorite game as a child."

"I am not a little girl now."

"Exactly. My dear, you can't play hide-and-seek with love. Nor can you impose conditions. A woman can regret the conditions she puts on love. You know, I fell in love soon after I finished college." Dad leans back, as though he's going to tell me a story. "Rekha was beautiful and intelligent, but very emotional. A rosebud with a drop of dew glistening on it could bring tears of joy to her." Dad's voice softens. "I know because I gave her one once."

By all the gods, this man, my father, is telling me of his first love.

"After we met at my aunt's house, I couldn't think of anything else but her. We took to meeting in a park to stroll. One afternoon we were walking back to her home when I blurted out my feelings for her. 'Rekha, I love you—' Just then a button popped off my shirt, and immediately I forgot what I was going to say."

"That's so wonderful, so normal, Dad."

"She picked up the button, handed it to me, and ran away. Can you imagine my embarrassment? The next time I wore a sweater on top of my shirt even though it was hot."

I begin to laugh. Dad cuts me off.

"I asked her to marry me. She refused. I didn't have a good enough job yet. How would I support her? And when was I going to learn how to dress? I saw my whole world crash before me. She was my sky, my light, the very air to breathe." Dad gulps some soda, then continues, "After a couple of terrible months, I agreed when my parents arranged a marriage. The wedding date was set and invitations were sent out. But when Rekha found out, she started showing up wherever I went. For me, it was too late. I ignored her. She wrote me a long letter urging me to come back. I didn't answer. By then, you see, I was quite taken with your mother. I knew she'd make a fine wife. It was a more cerebral decision and a safer one perhaps. On our wedding night your mother and I were just getting ready to go to bed when—" Dad pauses, a sigh of desolation giving added emphasis to his words. "I heard a noise at the window. I got up to check. Rekha was in the courtyard below, calling out, 'You're mine, you'll always be mine. Please don't do this to me.'

"Your mother burst into tears," Dad goes on. "I yelled at Rekha to go away, and she started to scream. The whole household came running. They had to force Rekha to leave."

I can imagine her shame. In this rigid society, family, friends, and neighbors would never forget. "What happened to her?" I ask.

"She left for England to visit a brother and never came back. I heard she married after some years, but wasn't happy. Meanwhile, your mother and I had a good marriage. We had you."

A dense silence falls between us, and I replay the final scene with Rekha in my mind. Impulses were at work in that woman. Her happiness at peril, she galvanized all her strength and acted, even if it was all in vain. And for Dad too. Despite what he said, he still loved her. Am I being driven by such impulses, too? Dad is forcing me to reexamine my course of action. Will I regret my decision not to marry a suitable match?

In my twenties, I ignored the advice of my elders, ready to make my own mistakes, but having acquired a scar or two over the past ten years, I'm willing to listen. And yet I must be true to myself.

A band of light streams into the room through the window, as though the sky is hoisting its flag to announce a new day. Dad walks over to the window and stands there, mesmerized by the golden arc of sun. "My first sunrise in India!" he says. Then suddenly he turns. "Strike the iron when it's hot, Sharmila. Cold, it's solid as stone."

His meaning couldn't be clearer. Marry an eligible man while you're still young and in love with him. This is as intimate a conversation as I've ever had with him. And while "the iron is still hot," I decide to take advantage of Dad's newfound frankness. If he's open enough to tell about a former love just now, perhaps he will tell me about any secret arrangement with the Khoslas.

"Dad, as long as we're discussing family secrets, can I ask you if you're paying the Khoslas any dowry?"

Dad's strained laugh tells me all I need to know. "My modern girl," he says, "that's a no-no, isn't it? But my generation looks at it quite differently. Ever since you were born, your mother has been putting money in an account for your wedding. It's a duty she learned from her own mother. A few dollars here, a few dollars there, even when we didn't have much."

I wonder what makes family members keep secrets from one another. And why does one learn about them so late in the game?

"You see, your mother always wanted a big wedding for you. It was more important than her own needs. I remember once, when you were only six, she came across a set of towels at Carson's she really liked. She kept going back to the store, but just couldn't bring herself to buy them. 'Better to put the money in Sharmila's wedding fund,' she said. 'The old towels will just have to last another year.' "

My eyes are stinging, but Dad laughs. "That fund has grown considerably," he tells me. "Even after we deduct all the wedding expenses, the account will have over fifty thousand dollars. And my practice has gone so well in the last ten years, we don't need that money."

How could my parents pay a dowry knowing how I feel about that custom? It's as though I've been lashed three times: this story of the early sacrifices of my parents, the substantial amount they have saved, the very fact that there is a dowry. Even after living in the States for all these years, they can't let go of the old customs. They'd like to mold my needs and wants to the expectations of what to me is an antiquated, unfamiliar culture. Really, how much they love me! But I can't live a life based on a system that is unacceptable to me. Sadness and bitterness creep into my voice. "So my price is fifty thousand dollars?"

"Sharmila, dear." Dad shakes his head in quiet frustration. "Good things aren't handed to us on a silver platter. Always there's a price. Think seriously. You can have a wonderful life with Raj, or an uncertain, possibly miserable one alone if you refuse this opportunity."

This is intolerable. Love and marriage reduced to a business deal. I, a human being, diminished to an object, my worth calculated in dollars. How foolish I was to talk to Raj about having a partnership of equals when my parents were paying him to take me.

I will not accept this. My very core is being violated. I don't care if I'm a stranger here, innocent of the traditional ways. I don't care if my parents insist on those customs. The whole idea of dowry outrages me.

The doorbell rings. On leaden legs I rise from my chair. It's the bellboy, who informs me that the car is ready.

Dad says, "I'll come over a little later to pay my respects to Mrs. Khosla."

Dowries are paid in advance, so Dad must be planning to pay more than his respects to Mrs. Khosla. I have to act fast.

Seized by an inspiration, I kneel humbly before Dad, my hands folded, palm inward at my chest, head slightly bowed, eyes at his brown loafers in the ancient posture of submission. It's an old trick my mother uses to soften him up when she wants to change his mind about a matter.

"Daddy, would you promise me one thing?" I murmur softly. "Would you hold off paying the dowry until I've had a chance to think and we can talk again?"

Dad puts his hand on my head in a Hindu gesture of blessing. With a smile in his voice he agrees. "Of course, Sharmila. Now go home and get some sleep."

Eyes still downcast lest I betray my relief, I rise and pick up my purse. Dad, now in control, walks me to the elevator, saying, "Glad we could have this little talk." Then with surprising sentiment he tells me, "I've never admitted this, Sharmila, but I'm proud to have you as my daughter. You're strong like your mother. I'm sure everything will work out. Believe me, I'm on your side and always will be."

His praise has a momentary feel-good effect, but I still experience resentment at his duplicity. He's not the god in a chariot I thought he was if he still believed he had to pay fifty thousand dollars to buy me a husband. And I hurt because he's my dad and I love him so.

My plan of action becomes clearer in my head during the elevator ride to the first floor. A little later this morning I'll step into Raj's room, pull up two chairs, and lay my concerns before him: his fidelity or lack thereof, my place in his life, and the importance of knowing the true circumstances behind Roopa's death. If satisfied with his answers, I'll ask him point-blank if he loves me enough to marry me without a dowry and watch his reaction. If he throws his arms around me, holds me tight, and whispers in my ear that he loves me, that he doesn't care about what I bring with me, then I'll return his embrace, body and soul. I will say, yes, yes, yes!

Otherwise, there'll be no wedding. This course of action will devastate my father and I'll risk the displeasure of Mrs. Khosla, but I have no choice.

A creeping sadness steals over me as I slip into the hotel car. I stare blankly out the window, oblivious to the passing scenery. Out of nowhere an image of the princess in the Mughal painting comes into my mind. The face has changed. She's no longer the happy, excited bride I saw the first time, but a broken woman with an anguished, desolate expression, reduced to the status of a bejeweled chattel, accepted only by the equally miserable women of her court . . . and me.

29

THE burnished iron of the Khosla gate glimmers dully in the morning light I check my watch as I enter. It's only six-thirty. I fight to keep my sleep-deprived eyes from closing of their own will on the long climb up the staircase, and a delicious thought pops into my mind. What if I slipped into Raj's bedroom, the one we're going to share anyway, and snuggled up next to him in bed, soaking up the warmth of his body and feeling his heartbeat against my breast? What better way to soften him up for a frank discussion of a sensitive subject?

At the threshold of his room, my foot bumps into a tray with a cup, a teapot, and a fresh dahlia. It has obviously not been touched. That's curious. Raj likes his bed tea early and is usually up around six. I'm about to continue on in when I hear a low throaty moan coming from inside the room. I freeze in shock at the unmistakable sound of a woman in the throes of ecstasy. Heart hammering, I nudge the door open and tiptoe in, coming to an abrupt halt about three feet from the bed.

In the dim hallway light filtering in through the door, I can barely make out indistinct, writhing shadows on the huge bed. As my eyes adjust, I see two bodies undulating in sinuous harmony, oblivious to my presence barely an arm's length away. As I stand rooted to the floor in shocked disbelief at the sordid scene, a wave of emotion edged with pain sweeps over me. Who's that woman? I can't tell. And the man? Oh, my God, it's Raj. I can't breathe. A part of me deep within wants to scream in rage, but my vocal cords are numb. Unbidden, my body begins to move of its own accord. I turn to leave. Raj must have sensed my presence, for he lurches into a sitting position. The bed squeaks, protesting noisily as if in embarrassment.

"Sharmila," Raj rasps, his breath coming in ragged gasps.

The sound of my name, coming from his mouth, here, now, makes me cringe in revulsion. I take in his bulging eyes, slack jaw, hair pasted to his head as if he's just risen from a swamp. It's a face I don't know, never knew, one that repels me. In slow motion my eyes shift to the cowering woman, half hidden behind Raj on the bed. I gasp in shock as my eyes widen in recognition.

A naked Champa scoots past me, a trapped animal, clutching a blanket to her chest, toward the door. I raise a hand as she rushes by, wanting to strike her, but she's out the door before I can act.

Raj, on his knees in bed, leans over, drawing closer and reaching for my hand.

I step back in disgust, saying, "Don't," and turn on my heel.

Now Raj gets off the bed. The naked body reaches for my arm, grasps it roughly, and tries to pull me onto the bed. As I struggle to free myself, my thoughts turn wild. If he forces himself on me, there'll be no one to intervene. A trick learned in a self-defense class flashes in my mind. Drawing energy from my belly, I raise my knee and kick him in the groin.

Grunting in pain, Raj slumps to the floor, where he curls up into a fetal position. I spin away and hurry out the door with a barely suppressed scream welling up in my throat. As I run down the hall I'm vaguely aware of a pair of sharp eyes peeking out from behind a half-open room across from Raj's.

Legs wobbly, black spots wavering in front of my eyes, I grope my way through the living room. My purse brushes the south wall, striking a wooden frame. The painting—the one of the Mughal princess—falls and hits the end table, shattering its protective glass pane and tearing the priceless heirloom in half. I skid to a halt. I am staring at the damage I've caused when Mrs. Khosla rushes into the room, her flabby arms outstretched, her face set in a grim mask of anger and determination.

It dawns on me in a flash that she'll do anything to stop me—
to protect the family name, to keep this story from getting out. I
bolt past her, along the hallway and on down the steep staircase,
taking two steps at a time. My aerobics training begins to pay
off. Mrs. Khosla, some thirty years older, overweight, and bun-
dled in a cumbersome sari, is no match for my youth, jeans, and
gym shoes. The sound of her wheezing and gasping fades as I
lope through the gate with easy strides. Once out on the street, I
pause to look back, but there's no one there. Mrs. Khosla won't
follow me out of the house, I realize. It'd cause a scandal the
family could ill afford if she was to be seen chasing her future
daughter-in-law down the street.

Memories stir within me as I glance back at the familiar pink
and red building that has almost become home to me. The large
window on the side with lace curtains that invited the sky into
my room; the green courtyard that soothed my eyes; the grilled
iron gate that played hide-and-seek with sunlight as it let me in
and out. Once I had hopes for a happy life there, but now they've
disintegrated into powdery dust.

As if in a feverish dream, I jog up the road. Raj may well be
looking for me. I have no desire to see him or speak with him.
That man has violated me in spirit, if not physically. It is as
though he has snatched a diamond and left a glass bauble in its
place, a cruel joke.

The streets are deserted and businesses still shuttered. It's
cool and, in contrast to the turbulence I feel inside, strangely
peaceful. As I continue on down the street, hair billowing, my
purse swinging back and forth, a Defence Colony dandy, standing on a second-floor balcony and brushing his teeth, leers at me
over his toothbrush. Inside I hurt so badly that I'm beyond embarrassment. I keep running without any thought, without recognizing the buildings. A huge movie billboard says:

Never seen before. Rape under water.

As I tear my eyes away from it, I almost bump into a vendor
pushing a cart of tomatoes to market. By now I must have covered a couple of miles, though I have no idea where I am. Ready
to collapse, my breath coming in gasps, I come to a halt just before a Pepsi poster and am suddenly aware of a burning thirst.

A middle-aged man appearing out of nowhere approaches me. "Is anything wrong, madam? Do you need help?"

Right behind him is the door to a barber shop. I guess he's the owner. He's wearing a Gandhi cap and an all-white outfit that is pressed and starched. His thinning hair visible under the cap is well combed. There's a dignified nineteenth-century quality about him. I wipe my eyes and nod.

He gestures to the room inside. "I have a telephone if you'd like to use it."

The shop isn't open yet, so it'll be a good place to collect myself in private. With a word of thanks I step inside and seat myself in a high chair by the telephone. I smell shampoo, hair oil, and cheap cologne. I force my hand to relax and let go of the purse that has been dangling from it so I can pick up the receiver. Who should I call? I wonder dejectedly.

Not Prem. There's nothing I need more than his calmness, but I don't have his phone number or address. The tattered telephone directory is five years old. And in any case, the name Prem Das is too common for the phone book to be of any use.

Definitely not my father. All this would be too much of a shock for him so soon after his arrival. Certainly not cousin Mistoo. I know what she'd say. "So what if Raj has a fling with the maid? You're going to be his wife, Sharmila. She's nothing to him. You'll have all the benefits and security."

Neelu? She's off to Agra to visit relatives for a few days. Liz? She'll be impossible to reach in Goa. Mother? I can't make an international long-distance call from this local phone.

Deen! Of course! Why didn't I think of him before? And my manicure appointment just happens to be at ten this morning. Rummaging through my purse, I retrieve his card. His home number is also listed for emergency cancellations. With trembling fingers I dial the number.

A groggy male voice answers, "Dinesh here—who's calling so early?"

"This is Sharmila." I hesitate, frantically searching for an explanation as to why I am calling my manicurist at this hour. "Sorry to call so early, Deen. But I thought I should let you know before your day started that I want to cancel my appointment."

"What time is it, Miss Sharmila?"

I check my watch. "Almost seven."

"Where are you calling from? I hear traffic noise."

"I'm in a barber shop."

"What are you doing in a barber shop at seven in the morning, Miss Sharmila, if I may ask? Are you okay?"

"I just walked out of the Khosla apartment." My voice thickens. I sigh as I add, "Other than that, everything is just great."

"You did what?"

In spite of myself, a sob escapes me, though I know at once I'm not crying for Raj. I'm crying for me, for the humiliation I suffered at the Khosla house.

"Let me come and get you right away," Deen says. "I live with my mother. I have a car. We can come back here and talk."

"Deen, I'm sorry for getting you up from bed and imposing on you like this—"

"Not at all, Miss Sharmila. I am always interested in what goes on in the Khosla house. Just give me the address where you are. I'll be right over."

The shopkeeper must have been eavesdropping from outside the open door, for he pops his head in and asks, "The address you want?"

After hanging up, I give him some rupees, probably five times as much as a phone call would cost, for his kindness.

"Thankyouverymuch." He says it as one word, beaming with delight at my unexpected generosity. "You can wait here, madam. And anytime you want to use the phone, just come back. I'm always here to serve you. Yes, anytime, madam."

"Thank you, I'll wait outside," I tell him, thinking to myself, I won't need to use his phone again. I'll never be back this way.

Twenty minutes pass before Deen shows up. He drives me to the fashionable Vasant Vihar neighborhood. His eyes dance with curiosity, making him look younger than his twenty-two years. With a sideways glance at me he says, "You're shivering, Miss Sharmila." The tone is worried, protective. "Do you feel cold?"

He has enough sense not to press for information. I nod. I feel as if I'm coming down with the flu.

At the next intersection, Deen takes off his black leather jacket and hands it to me. "Put this on, Miss Sharmila, please."

Thankfully, I accept the garment and slide it around my shoulders. Relaxed by the warmth, I find myself describing this morning's incident at the Khoslas'. Every sentence I relate brings back renewed pain. I am forced to admit to myself that the Raj-Champa affair wasn't a total surprise. Back in the recesses of my mind, I'd suspected it all along. What upsets me is that I still trusted Raj with my dreams and set myself up for disaster.

Deen's lower lip curls. "Like father, like son."

"I was really beginning to care about Raj. Now I feel utterly betrayed."

"What are you going to do?"

"I'll look for a hotel a little later in the day."

"Oh, no, Miss Sharmila, that's not necessary. You can stay with us."

"Deen, that's very sweet of you. But you hardly know me."

"I'm sure the Khoslas are looking for you. If you try to register in any hotel, you'll have to show your passport. The hotels are required to report all passport numbers to the police." My eyes follow Deen's to the uniformed policeman on the sidewalk. "That's a police gypsy."

Though amused by the quaint local terminology for a beat cop, I am concerned about my safety.

"The Khoslas will easily find out where you are. You can be sure they'll show up at your room with the police in short order. They'll make up a lie as to why you left. But Mrs. Khosla wouldn't come looking for you at our flat." Deen lets out a full, throaty laugh. "Oh, yes, indeed. That would be the last place. My mother and I live quietly. We don't have many visitors."

"What about Neelu?"

"I'll be sure not to tell her if she calls from Agra," Deen says. "We don't like to keep secrets from each other, but I think she'll understand later. After you've rested for a few days, you can decide if you want to go back to Raj or not."

"No, I never will." The words are so firm I'm surprised. "I had doubts about Raj from the beginning, but this was the last straw."

"I'm so sorry, Miss Sharmila, even though I confess I don't much care for the Khoslas, except for Neelu. She's different. Perhaps now you can see why I want to take her away."

Deen pulls into the driveway of a modern apartment complex on a wide boulevard. A swimming pool and a tennis court come into view in the landscaped grounds beyond the apartment house. This is even more posh than the Khosla residence and very private.

We roll down a flagstone driveway past a garden filled mostly with greenery, enlivened by the occasional patch of brightly colored cold-hardy flowers.

"That's *raat-ki-raani.*" Deen points at a flowering bush. "Queen of the night. The little white flowers smell only after dark." He eases to a stop in front of the entrance and pulls next to a Jaguar XK, adding, "It was Neelu's favorite flower when we played together in that garden as a child."

That reminds me of the Khoslas. I hesitate before climbing out. "Are you absolutely sure this is the best thing to do?"

"I'm positive, Miss Sharmila. You've had a most difficult morning. You look like you're not feeling well. My mother will take good care of you."

At any other time I'd have been amused by the irony of having to meet Raj's father's mistress under these circumstances. I probably would have politely declined such a meeting. But right now, vulnerable and a bit unwell to boot, I follow Deen quietly up the steps.

"Do you know what Mr. Khosla said about my mother?" Deen continues cheerfully as we climb the smooth marble stairs side by side. " 'She can turn a sunset into a sunrise.' "

A woman of my height, trim in an ivory high-necked satin chemise and pants, opens the door to the apartment. As Deen makes the introductions, her face melts into a smile. Kaveri gestures to a reclining leather chair with a gracious wave of her hand. She's straight as a bamboo rod, with a pearly sheen to her complexion. A gossamer scarf partially covers her shiny black hair and swaddles her throat. "Please sit down, Sharmila."

Deen explains the situation to his mother in a few short sentences. Out of respect for her, I suspect, he omits most of the sordid details about Raj and Champa.

Kaveri's voice is a mixture of humor and irony without a trace of bitterness. She remarks, "As if it wasn't enough to get rid of one wife." Then turning to me, she says, "You will be fine here. No one comes here except a maid three times a week."

It's obvious English is not Kaveri's preferred language. She often searches for a word in mid-sentence. But the softness in her voice and its gentle lilt more than make up for any linguistic deficiency. I conclude I'll be cared for here, and allow myself to stretch out on the recliner. In spite of the exhaustion sweeping over me, the newness of the surroundings keeps me a little bit on guard. Kaveri excuses herself to go fix some beverage, and Deen follows her.

In their absence, I survey my surroundings. The sitting room holds a few well-chosen pieces of furniture: An ornately carved coffee table of polished mahogany, two upholstered chairs, a beautifully worked brass floor lamp. The light flooding through the open window is bright without being harsh. Kaveri fetches a glass of coconut water and a shawl of blue-gray wool, which she spreads over my lap. Its fleece-like softness acts like a healing balm. As I finish the beverage and set the glass down, she touches my forehead lightly with her palm.

"*Bimar.*" Her face shows concern as she addresses her son urgently. "She has a fever. Please call Dr. Bedi right away."

A surge of worry jolts me upright on the recliner. What if the doctor checks my identity? And if he happens to know the Khoslas, will he tip them off? In the upper strata of Delhi society, gossip flows freely. "Please," I tell Kaveri, "it's nothing serious. I don't need a doctor. I'm just tired. I think sleep will be the best medicine."

"Then close your eyes. I'll be right here beside you in case you need anything." Kaveri pulls the venetian blinds on the window, then starts to fan my forehead with a palm-leaf fan.

The generosity of this total stranger brings my mother to mind. Tears start to seep from my eyes. Kaveri moves her chair slightly closer and hovers over me as though to listen to my breathing. After a moment she speaks to Deen in Hindi.

"My mother says each person cries differently. You must listen carefully to understand what someone's crying about."

The gentle sound of the fan and the warm hospitality offered by my new friends conspire with my monumental fatigue, and soon I drift off into a deep sleep.

Many, many hours later, I awake to the faint sound of vocal music floating in from another room. It's dusk. Darkness is descending on the room. Fully alert and feeling energetic, I realize it's Kaveri playing the sitar. She's pouring her heart into a song. Like all Indian classical music, hers has a devotional undertone and a poignant edge of lament.

The music stops in mid-stanza. Moments later, Kaveri enters with light steps and a knowing look that says she sensed I was awake. She turns on the floor lamp and comes over to my side.

"I was enjoying listening to you," I tell her.

"Oh, I have no talent really." Kaveri checks my forehead with her palm. "When I feel sad, instead of crying I sing. I write my own lyrics, too." Then with a note of cheer, she observes, "Your fever has disappeared."

The door opens, and Deen comes into the room. "Miss Sharmila, how are you! I called many times during the day. And every time Ma said you were sound asleep. I was worried."

"She's feeling better," Kaveri tells him. "She'll be even better after she eats something. Come, Sharmila, it's dinnertime."

We gather around the dining room table. The aromas wafting from the kitchen exhilarate me. Kaveri serves me a light vegetable soup and sliced bread. In my weakened condition, I can barely swallow any food. The solicitous remarks of mother and son are a marked contrast to the formality at the Khoslas'.

"Ma, you must take more rice."

"My son, what about some yogurt? It cools the stomach."

"More soup, Sharmila? *Sabji* is easy to digest."

"This is very tasty. And the amount is just right."

"My mother taught me all styles of cooking," Kaveri replies. "You see, I was born into a rich family and . . . married into one with even more status. But in spite of that I'd always cooked for my family. It wasn't unusual for us to have fifteen or twenty people over for dinner several nights a week, mostly my husband's relatives. Unfortunately, I was widowed young."

The shadow of anguish in Kaveri's face, makes it clear that she has never gotten over the tragedy of her husband's untimely death. I look away, not wanting to cause her any more discomfort, but she continues speaking. "I fought successfully to keep my husband's property, even though it is customary for the in-laws to control the money. A widow is socially dead. The best she can hope for is an allowance and a room in the back for her and her children. In return she's expected to do all the housework and spend her free time worshiping in the temple. So you see, I'm quite fortunate. I moved out and rented my own flat. My in-laws have never forgiven me for that. They've kept me at a distance ever since. But I didn't care. I had my freedom and lived a luxurious, if lonely, life. Then I met Alok Khosla, a successful businessman, and fell in love with him even though he was married. That was also taboo, and as a result my family—my parents, my five brothers, and my two sisters—disowned me. I've not been invited to their homes since. Even now relatives, when we meet on the street, look right past me as if I were invisible. Only strangers will accept me as a friend."

Will my parents forgive me for not marrying Raj? I wonder. Will I, too, end up as an invisible woman?

Kaveri senses my unease and begins to gently draw me out about my family. Soon I'm spilling out the entire story of how I grew up in Chicago and ended up here living with the Khoslas. I find myself speaking about Prem, too, a subject I have been unable to discuss freely with anyone until now.

After we finish the meal, Deen and I retire to the sitting area while Kaveri clears the table. I offer to help, but she refuses, explaining that it's not the custom in India for guests to help clean up.

"Guess what?" Deen announces theatrically. "Neelu called me at the office from Agra. 'Sharmila's missing,' she said. She told me to keep it a secret."

"How did Neelu find out?"

"Mrs. Khosla called her this afternoon. She told her that you and Raj had had a disagreement and you walked out on him. She wants Neelu to come home immediately. Neelu's taking the first train tomorrow."

I'm struck by a horrible premonition that no one will believe my version of what actually happened at the Khosla residence. "Oh?"

"Raj is apparently in terrible shape. He hasn't touched any food since you left. He drove around all morning looking for you. He's blaming himself. But Mrs. Khosla blames you. She calls you the hotheaded American girl. She hasn't contacted the police yet. It'd draw too much attention. You see, even with all the stories of corruption, people here think of calling the police first when something goes wrong. She has phoned all your relatives, with instructions to contact her as soon as they hear from you. Poor Neelu's caught in the middle. She likes you, and my guess is she doesn't believe her mother's story entirely, but then the Khoslas all stick together in the end. Oh, by the way, the wedding is still on, according to Mrs. Khosla."

In the past few hours I've pushed Raj out of my heart. But his mother and I are still locked in a test of wills. Undeterred by the

Khoslas' show of force, I'm resolved to get hold of Dad tomorrow and cancel the wedding. I sigh deeply. What an abject failure this whole endeavor has turned out to be.

"Mrs. Khosla's cook is extremely upset," Deen adds. "He burned both the rice and the vegetables at lunch. The whole flat smelled. Mrs. Khosla had to send out for food."

Good old Mohan, my friend.

Deen continues, "Neelu seems to think Mrs. Khosla will find you somehow and put pressure on you and your parents to go through with the marriage."

"Isn't this supposed to be a free country?" I ask bitterly.

"A woman is never free," interjects Kaveri, who has just rejoined us, taking a seat next to Deen. "If we were, we'd be singing a different song."

I have had enough of the Khoslas, the idea of arranged marriage, and women being powerless here in general. A desire to return to the States grows inside me as I fall back into a dark mood again.

"But, Miss Sharmila, let me advise you there's also a bright side to this," Deen says excitedly. "Of course, I'll wait for all this to die down, but here's a perfect opportunity to *persuade* Mrs. Khosla to consent to my marriage to Neelu. Otherwise, the Raj-Champa affair could regrettably become public knowledge."

I burst out laughing. "Now, Deen, you must not do that, as much as I'd like to see you and Neelu together."

Kaveri interrupts gently, "And I'd like to see you marry Raj."

"How could you say that, Kaveri, after all I've told you?"

"It is quite simple, my dear. You see, I could have asked Alok to cut his ties with his family completely and move in with me. But I didn't. I was content to love him from a distance. We were even married secretly. But he stayed with his first wife for Raj's and Neelu's sake. I could have forced him to leave. But I didn't have it in my heart to do that. I know what it's like to share a man. Sometimes that's the only way."

Though I can't accept her suggestion, I decide against arguing. Encouraged by my silence, Kaveri continues, "Don't let Raj go, Sharmila. He's Alok's son, and Alok was a great man." She touches my hand softly yet urgently. "The maidservant is just that, nothing more. My first husband had two maids, and he was an old man. Even when Alok and I were together, I suspected he was visiting another woman. Not that much has changed. You'll be the wife. You'll have the children, the name, the respect, the money."

Until now I've felt so welcome in this household, but I'm appalled that Kaveri believes I should marry Raj and accept the compromises that come with a marriage to a philanderer. And this from a woman who has been so grievously wronged by the Khoslas. She wants to pass the same fate on to me. I'm beginning to see how women perpetuate their deplorable condition in this society. Now that I'm in disagreement with Kaveri, I must move out of here first thing tomorrow morning.

For that I'll need my passport. Prem! Only Prem could enter the Khosla residence and fetch it for me without attracting suspicion. How do I find Prem in chaotic Old Delhi? Even more important, why do I keep thinking about him? My wedding to Raj is—actually, was—only a week away. I wonder if Prem really has such strong feelings toward me, or I am just imagining things. He certainly never articulated them. Could his behavior have been merely a fleeting fascination with a woman from another country, one with looser standards and a freer spirit? It's not difficult to imagine how attractive that would be for one living such a restricted life. But fascination and love aren't the same.

Kaveri gives me a nightgown, then with a think-it-over look, she walks out of the room to retire for the evening.

I sit forlornly in the living room, feeling drained and numb. Deen returns, pulls up a chair, grabs a notepaper from his pocket, and inscribes the name "Prem" in flowery, flowing Hindi script. I see loops and curved lines done in India ink, black as a crow's back. Once he finishes, he waves the paper in the air a few times to dry the ink and hands it to me with a flourish.

"You mean, you approve?" Then seeing him bob his head, I add, "I'd very much like to locate him, but he lives in Old Delhi and I don't have his address."

"We can explore Old Delhi together tomorrow," Deen whispers. "I might be able to help you find your 'Prem,' your love."

"You'll be going against your mother's wish, you know."

"She's wrong in this case."

"What about work?"

"My assistant can cover for me. She's a Dalit herself, by the way. I'd never have known that except she confided in me once.

To tell you the truth, I'm more than a little curious about Prem. A man who can upstage Raj Khosla is certainly worth meeting."

An odd mixture of pleasure and apprehension fills me as Deen and I pore over a city map and come up with a plan. Later, after Deen goes to bed, I slip into the nightgown and lounge by the window. As traumatic as this day has been, it has ended on a promising note. I'm fatigued to the bone, but instead of collapsing on the bed, I get my sketchpad out and attempt a drawing based on a song Kaveri played earlier in the evening. After a few futile efforts to give the music a shape, I content myself in scribbling the name "Prem" in my version of stylized Hindi script copied from Deen's impromptu gift. Each pencil stroke contains the slender but steady hope that tomorrow will be brighter and that it'll compose a song of its own.

30

A RE you okay, Miss Sharmila?"

Deen's formal manner of addressing strikes me as incongruous in the ninety-degree heat of a narrow Old Delhi lane reeking of urine and cow dung patties. We're weaving in and out of a steady stream of humanity clothed in saris, dhotis, turbans, and *burkhas*. Our destination is Prem's home. We've wandered for an hour in this maze, and I have no idea whether Prem or even his mother will be home at this time should we locate it. I ask Deen, "Would you just call me Sharmila?"

"But, Miss Sharmila, in my family a person's name is considered sacred. We don't call anyone by their first name alone if they're older. That's disrespectful." Then with a thin, shy smile he adds, "But I'll give it a try."

The winter sun is high in the sky, and my forehead beads with perspiration. Other pedestrians have gauzy white handkerchief triangles protruding out of pockets or trailing from their hands, whereas the tissue in my tightly clenched hand is soggy and tattered. The cuffs of my jeans are stained with mud. My blouse is grimy and sweaty. The rest of my belongings, including the passport I need desperately, were left behind at the Khoslas' during my hurried departure. I still have the thin gold necklace I always wear around my neck. Earlier this morning I remembered that Prem's mother's locket was still in my purse. I slid the locket on my gold necklace, and now I run my fingers over the cool silver design for good luck.

Though my mood has improved since yesterday, I escaped unharmed. As I search for the landmarks that'll lead me to Prem, I find myself worrying, Does he still feel the same way about me? Am I rushing into one more amorous misadventure?

Taking note of the by now useless tissue in my hand, Deen proffers a delicate white handkerchief. Such gentlemanly manners have all but disappeared from North America. I blot my forehead with the piece of cotton, delicate as a spring leaf.

Deen asks, "How much farther, do you think, Sharmila?"

Immediately ahead of us the lane splits in two directions. Again I wonder which branch to take.

Fatigue shows in Deen's narrowed eyes. "Nothing looks familiar?" he tries again.

The water pump on the left does, sort of, with the huge puddle beneath its dripping spout. I jump to avoid getting wet, thereby colliding with a sprightly old man, a door-to-door peddlar. He looks up at me with a grimace that says clearly, oh, no, not you again, and bursts into a stream of invectives. It's the same old codger I bumped into the last time—same frown, same cane, same curses, only this time he waves the cane even higher and curses me twice as long and at least twice as fervently. I am seized with an inspiration. "We'll go in the opposite direction he does," I whisper to Deen. "That's what I remember doing the last time."

Suddenly a row of shops topped with a Bombay Dyeing billboard looms before us. "We're getting warmer," I tell Deen. "I recognize that billboard and the sweet shop just below it. Let's stop there if you don't mind."

Deen's relief is evident as we step inside. Shoppers are crowded into this bustling establishment, little more than a cubbyhole tucked in between larger stores. Most of its space is occupied by a glass showcase shielding an array of multihued confections from a cloud of flies. Deen's eyes become as wide as a ten-year-old's. While we wait our turn, my attention is drawn inexorably to the kala jaam. I've previously tried them, reddish black sponge cakes that ooze with a fragrant rose water–scented syrup, and found them delicious. The shopowner notices my interest.

"Very good, very good, madam. Please try one and you'll be happy. Buy more. Make your friends happy, too!"

I purchase a boxful for Prem's family, hoping this will please them. We leave the shop and go left into a side lane. As we round the corner, I see a young boy skipping up the path toward us. Even at this distance I see the resemblance to Prem. "Jay!" I cry out.

The boy races toward me with a shout of joy. "Hello! Sharmila-didi, how are you?"

His "how" sounds like "cow." He comes to a halt, having forgotten the rest of the English phrases he'd previously memorized.

It doesn't matter, I think. His cheery face is welcome enough. "I'm fine, Jay. I came to visit you."

He giggles, grabs my hand, and leads me on through a maze of alleyways that seem familiar, Deen trailing along in our wake. A scrawny dog follows at a respectful distance.

Jay shows me his tiny marigold plant by the front entrance, then ushers me into the house. His sister Ratna, clad in jeans I gave her, emerges from a room. Absent is the cellular phone that was glued to her palm during my last visit.

"Oh, Sharmila-behen." She rushes up to me and touches my hand affectionately. "I can't believe it's you. Ma isn't home." She yells, "Prem-bhai, where are you?" Then to me, "Mrs. Khosla has called many, many times."

"I have to explain a few things—"

"Oh, that horrible woman," Ratna says. "She has harassed me so often that I'm not answering the phone anymore."

"Mrs. Khosla," a very familiar voice says, "is overreacting to the situation."

I turn to see Prem standing in the doorway. It's as though I'm seeing him for the first time, this strikingly handsome man in a checked shirt and brushed cotton trousers which, I guess, are his new work uniform. His eyes seem to read my face.

"I've been very worried, too."

Prem notices Deen, who's been standing quietly behind me. Now Deen steps forward and introduces himself. The two men exchange pleasantries, and I sense in each an instant liking for the other. After a few moments Deen excuses himself and turns to leave. "I'll go wait in that sweet shop, Sharmila. Take your time. I have much sampling to do."

Jay has just opened the box of sweets. His eyes are as big and as dark as any kala jaam. He tries to hide the sweets from his sister, and she chases him playfully around the small but uncluttered room, the two laughing wildly in what I conjecture is a favorite game of Jay's.

Smiling faintly, Prem says to me in a quiet voice, "Let's go for a walk." Then to Ratna, "I'll be back in a little while." His siblings barely notice our departure, intent as they are on the sweets.

Alone with Prem, my heart beats faster, and I try to find the right words to say to him. He's calm and quiet, and I'm thankful to him for a few moments of silence.

We pass a triangular structure about three feet tall, sheltering an image of Shiva, a lamp, a bell, an incense holder, and an offering bowl. Worshipers kneel on the sidewalk before the image, shake the bell, then move on in peace.

"Many people stop here on their way to and from their jobs," Prem says.

"How's your new job?" I ask.

"It's going well," Prem says warmly. "Just this morning I took a group of French industrialists sightseeing. Though they're here looking for new business opportunities, they're also very keen about Indian culture. One Frenchman told me he wouldn't mind settling down here. He could rent a nice bungalow with servants and live like a king—much better than he ever could in France on his salary. An Indian wife wouldn't be bad, either. *Très belle,* he kept saying every time he passed a young woman on the street."

Our steps matching, I reply, "My dad's reacting like a tourist himself. He's enjoying his return to Delhi after many years. And my mother is arriving tomorrow evening."

"Where are they staying?"

"At the Hotel Ajanta. I'm going to move into the same hotel if I can. I don't feel right imposing on Deen and Kaveri for more than one night. Unfortunately, all my luggage is still at the Khoslas'. The only clothes I have are the ones I'm wearing. But my biggest concern is my passport."

Prem is silent for an instant. "I have to go see Mrs. Khosla tomorrow to collect my wages. As long as I'm there—"

"The passport is in my room. But Mrs. Khosla—"

"Mohan might be of help."

"Oh, Prem, you'd do that for me?"

"That and much more, Sharmila." Prem's liquid eyes examine my face. "Will you stay in touch with me?"

"Oh, yes, if you'd give me your phone number."

Prem jots down the number for me on a business card. The sunlight illuminates his forehead, the crown of his hair. Our fingers brush against each other, and I wish I could catch and hold them.

"You don't know how much I appreciate your help, Prem. Right from the beginning I've felt more at ease with you than with the Khoslas."

"What really happened at the Khoslas?"

I tell him, pausing often to compose myself. Prem listens, staring down at the ground. He reacts to my discovery of Raj and Champa making love with a shocked expression, as if he'd witnessed the scene himself. Taking a deep breath, he attempts to console me. "I'm so very sorry, Sharmila. I can only imagine how painful that must have been. It's such a shame. Raj—how could he? But then again, I've known him for long time. And I must admit that doesn't come as a complete surprise."

"Has he always been like this?"

"We've been close friends for many years," Prem says with a sigh. "Raj is a good man, but he's incapable of being faithful, I think. Oh, yes, he loved Roopa. He once told me he'd never loved anyone as much. But that didn't stop him from seducing as many women as he could."

"Did Roopa know?"

"I'd be surprised if she didn't."

"How did it affect her?"

"Over the course of several months she became more and more withdrawn. I would drive her around, but instead of talking as she used to, she just sat quietly."

"So maybe she didn't care if she lived or died."

"I don't know what was said between them, but Raj was devastated when she died and he suffered terribly. He eventually recovered, though he still feels very guilty. He goes to the temple several times a week for peace of mind, and perhaps forgiveness. Then you came and I said to myself, Raj Khosla has finally found the one. After his grief over Roopa, I hoped he'd behave differently this time. But no, Raj can't change who he is."

"A tragedy . . . for himself and for others."

"You know what my mother said when she first met Raj? 'He's such a big man . . . and yet he is so small.' "

"It's too bad. You know, he was buying a bungalow for us."

Prem's eyes widen and he hesitates. "No, Sharmila, that's not true. When I drove by the bungalow yesterday, I noticed another family was living in it."

My face burns at this duplicity. "Raj has made a fool of me two times over. I'm so lucky to be free of him."

"He must have been ashamed to tell you that the sale fell through. A vintage Khosla performance, a *jalsha,* as we call it." Then he laughs. "But I have no secrets, Sharmila. No dark past, no ugly shadows. What you see is what you get, as they say in American films."

Our shared laughter breaks the embarrassment and the gloom. "I'm glad this happened before we got married. I had many doubts before but I'd put them aside. Oh, Prem, I'm so glad."

We've been walking for some time now. Prem stops, turning toward me. Outwardly I am calm, but desire surges up beneath the surface of my skin. An insistent desire.

"Do you remember our first meeting at the airport, Sharmila?"

"I sure do," I tell him as we resume our stroll. "My mother's astrologer had calculated the most auspicious time for Raj and me to meet. Raj the Great was late, but you showed up at the precise moment." I hate feeling so vulnerable and laugh to hide it. "That made a believer out of me—well, at least a little."

Prem pauses, then says in a soft voice, "I've been waiting for you, Sharmila. It's been so very hard to keep my feelings inside. Since I'm not of the same social class as you, I couldn't take the first step. Even more important, Raj is my friend. It'd have been like stealing from a friend. I could only wait and hope someday you'd come to me."

"And here I am, Prem," I say happily. "It's not just because I broke up with Raj. I've wanted you all along. It took me a little while to figure it out. You've given me something very precious." A tear wells in my eye. "Something no one else ever could."

"And you've changed my life, Sharmila. Just the fact that you wanted to talk about larger things, about life with me, meant you had respect for me. I could tell you were thinking, 'Why does he have this job?' That gave me the push I needed to break away from the Khoslas. There was no future for me there. Now I have begun to work for myself. You taught me how to fly." Prem looks into my eyes. "You see, I grew up poor and casteless, always standing at the end of the queue. In school the other kids would call me *chamar*, a nasty word that means low-class and uncultured. I learned to be stronger. When I came home crying, my mother would say, 'My son, so what if you don't have money or caste? You have a thousand hearts.' Sharmila, I want to give you every single one of them."

"Like thousand *diyas* on Diwali night. I'll keep them burning forever."

"That first day, during our walk I noticed when you stepped on a dried leaf. Even though it made just a tiny crunchy sound, you paused in mid-stride and took note. That told me you're in tune with everything around you. When I'm with you, I feel I'm connected to a wider world. I'm bigger than myself."

Just talking with Prem exhilarates me. As we round a bend in the lane, the familiar sweet shop comes in view. Deen will be waiting there. From underneath my collar I dig out my gold chain with the dangling silver locket. Prem's face lights up at the sight of it. We wrap our hands together around the locket in our own private rite. I raise my face to Prem's expectantly. He bends to meet my lips, and suddenly, just short of contact, he stops and pulls away as Deen emerges from the sweet shop. Prem's withdrawal is a disappointing reminder of the Indian taboo against showing affection in public. Any moment now, Deen will see us. Once again Prem and I look into each other's eyes. Our love is written there. Then I turn to go and meet Deen, casting a last soulful look over my shoulder. Prem waves, smiles wistfully, and turns away. A dot of bright light is swallowed in the crowd.

As I continue on toward Deen, I review the events of the last two days in my mind. To an outsider, my situation might appear to be a mix of tragedy and farce. But to me, the embarrassment of canceling a large wedding, trying to placate angry, disappointed parents, and making the final break with the Khoslas no longer seem daunting. I can brave anything the future holds, bold and secure in the knowledge that Prem loves me.

THREE days have passed since I fled the Khosla apartment. Now I am in residence at the Hotel Ajanta. It is a mid-range establishment catering to Indian businessmen and budget-minded tourists. For sure, my room on the third floor isn't up to the Maurya Sheraton standards. The furniture is a no-frills combination of bed, dresser, and writing table on a thin gray carpet, and the television doesn't work. The window opens onto a narrow one-lane street, which is an anarchy of pedestrians and vehicular traffic as well as the occasional flock of goat, or meandering cow, even guinea fowl. This is the Paharganj area bordering the old section of town. The sidewalks have been taken over by street vendors hawking everything from shoelaces to fresh fruit juice. Even a wedding ceremony was conducted there last night on a makeshift pavilion.

It's reassuring to know that my father is staying only two floors above me. His friend Mr. Khanna has graciously provided me with this entirely adequate accommodation at a bargain price and even thrown in a few extras. Two nights ago, shortly after I checked in, the bellboy brought me tea, cookies, and a soft drink, "compliments of the hotel manager," then returned with a deck of cards. He must have thought I was bored.

I haven't seen much of my father lately. He's been spending

most of his time convincing the Khoslas that the wedding is off, as well as visiting close relatives and breaking the news to them. Though he hasn't said much, I sense he is embarrassed and ashamed. I wonder if he'll pay the Khoslas some money to cover their costs. At this time, he's acting as my intermediary. Being older and a man, he's far more effective in this role in this society. The result is, I'm feeling much less threatened by the Khoslas and have began to move about more freely. Yesterday I spent two hours working out at a downtown health club equipped with the latest exercise machines. After a long session on a stair climber, I returned to my hotel room with sore muscles but an improved mood. As I walked in the door, I was surprised to discover my luggage stacked neatly in one corner. All of my belongings were packed inside along with a red envelope from Mohan, containing the three ten-dollar bills I'd given him as baksheesh several weeks ago and a note:

> Dear Sharmila-memsahib,
> After you left, the Khosla flat became dark and gloomy for me. I ruined every dish I prepared, and Mrs. Khosla yelled at me constantly. I liked you very much and regret that I couldn't help you.
> My new job at the Ambassador Hotel will start soon. Will you please come for dinner sometime? I'll prepare all your favorite dishes, even those not on the menu card.
> Enclosed please find the money you gave me as baksheesh. I'm returning it. How can a man take baksheesh from his sister?
> I wish you much happiness.
> Your friend,
> Mohan

As I held the note, I visualized Mohan's clear eyes and eager hands. I made a mental note to call him later. Rummaging through my luggage, I found my money and passport. So Prem managed to spirit them out of the Khosla house, after all. A small slip of paper stuck inside the passport said:

> See you tomorrow morning.
> Prem.

I traced the lines of his precise handwriting with my finger and found myself wishing the message was longer.

This morning I wake up leisurely, fragments of a happy dream about Prem still floating in my head. The sparse surroundings bring back fond memories of my cabin in the foothills of the Sierra Nevada range. With my face half buried in a pillow, I envision granite peaks, pine trees, and golden eagles, and sigh contentedly.

After luxuriating in a hot shower, I slip into my nubby white bathrobe. My wet hair wrapped in a towel, I stand in front of the mirror over the dresser, pick up a bottle of gardenia-scented hand lotion, and am on the verge of squeezing some into my palm when the phone trills. Who might be calling? Prem? The hotel desk? I pick up the receiver.

"Mila . . ." Raj's sultry voice oozes out of the line, the voice that thrilled me less than a week ago. My jaw tenses at the unwanted tone of intimacy, and I grip the receiver more tightly. Mila, the name he gave me during one blissful interlude in his room. "Mila . . ." he utters again, lingering on the last *a*. "Baby."

In a sharp, businesslike manner I answer, "The name is Sharmila." Even I am surprised at the curtness of my response.

The ensuing silence squeezes like a too-tight belt. Raj goes on. "Your father came here to tell us the wedding is off. I could tell he's extremely disappointed after he flew all the way from the States for our wedding. But he loves you, Sharmila. How can he deny you anything? You're his only child."

Again a pause. I wait it out. "After much persuasion he gave me your number. I meant to come over and talk to you face to face, but—"

With ice in my voice, I cut him off. "You decided to send another absentee ballot instead, Raj?"

"You really don't believe I care about you, do you?"

"Honestly?" I sit down on the bed and eye a watercolor of Kanchengungha mountain range on the wall. "Would you have married me without a dowry, Raj?"

"Sure, I would have," Raj answered quickly. "I never wanted a dowry. It's my mother. Her dream is to have an elaborate wedding for Neelu, and she needs money for it. No, Sharmila, I wanted to marry you because I saw something very special in you. You're a free spirit, totally your own person." With a faint sigh Raj adds, "You touched my very soul."

The dread has changed into a stirring in my chest, a familiar one from the past, brought on by the rich voice, the poetry of the words, the silences that add weight to them. But I believed him in those days. Not anymore. Did I love him? I think so, though not in the same way I love Prem.

"I am still waiting for you, Sharmila."

Raj has mistaken my silence for indecision. His words cascade out. "I know I'm flawed. I haven't done right by you. Suppose we have a fresh start and move to the bungalow right after our marriage. Our own little nest."

"How nice, Raj. Except I happen to know that 'our own little nest' is occupied by other lovebirds."

"It was that son of a pig, wasn't it?" Raj hisses. "That swine was lucky I didn't break his neck when he came sneaking in here yesterday to pick up your things. The next time I run into him—"

"You're a real class act, Raj—"

"Class, Sharmila? Who are you to talk about class? You who chase after a filthy Dalit—"

"He may be a Dalit, but he has a thousand times more class than you, a *khatriya* in name only. He's everything you can never be. Never!"

By verbalizing it, I realize how true it all is, and suddenly further conversation with Raj becomes pointless.

"You didn't really get to know me, Sharmila."

"How long do you think it'd have taken me to know you for what you are . . . and aren't?" My vocal cords straining, I add, "Screwing the housemaid with your mother's acquiescence, and that would have been just the beginning. No, Raj, I have no intention of being the meek wife while you do what you want and maybe end up like Roopa."

That brings on a deadly a silence. Then in a small voice he says, "So you know." Again a pause. "Roopa was oversensitive. She always overreacted."

"I'm sure you had a lot more to do with her death than you've admitted. By the way, who killed her, Raj?"

The line seems to go dead. I suspect we've lost the connection, perhaps in more ways than one. Then I hear Raj's voice, so low that I am sure it's finally coming from within his heart. "No one, Sharmila. She killed herself."

"Suicide? Why would she commit suicide? Tell me the truth, Raj."

Silence. "Was there a suicide note?" I ask.

"She came home unexpectedly," Raj whispers. I'm positive his face is wet with tears. "She committed suicide because of me."

Oh, my God. I visualize the poor woman, coming home just like me, peeking into the bedroom. She retreats in pain and horror, rushes out of the house unnoticed, returns hours later, but doesn't say a word about this to anyone, least of all to her husband. What she'd suspected for a long time has been brutally confirmed. She burns, burns, burns inside, then one day crumbles into ashes.

"How could you have taken advantage of her great love, her innocence? And for all the pain her death might have caused, you apparently haven't learned a thing. You pulled the same trick on me."

"Only that one time, Sharmila, out of habit." Raj is quiet for a moment. Then, in a thin, despairing tone he pleads with me. "After Roopa was gone I thought I had nothing left to give to a woman. Then you came. Your presence was like sunlight warming the morning grass. I was so refreshed. I told myself: Don't mess up this time. You see, I have no intention of ending up like my father. He was a drunk who couldn't keep track of which wife to go home to at night, but I've ruined it."

I've finally stripped away the veneer, the worst disaster Raj Khosla could endure. My guess is this is the first time he's fully admitted to anyone of his part in the suicide, an admission that'll force him to face the truth about himself.

"You did the right thing running away from me. But please don't hate me the rest of your life. I'm not perfect. No one is. We're all light and shadow, Sharmila."

There's a knock at the door. I leap from the chair, startled. My voice is heavy with a sigh as I say, "I'm going to put it all behind me, and I hope you can, too. Good-bye, Raj."

The click on the other end bears mute testimony that I've truly bidden Raj farewell.

SECOND, more insistent knock on the door follows. Warily I
open the door a crack and peer out. A sweeper in gray
clothes is swishing a hand mop back and forth as he duck-walks
down the hall. On his left is Prem, fresh and vital in well-pressed
clothes, leaning forward in eager anticipation. His composed expression dissolves in a broad smile as our eyes meet.

"I'm a little early, Sharmila. Did I wake you?" He glances at
my bathrobe. "I'll come back—"

His presence dissipates the sour, tangy aftertaste in my
mouth. "Oh, no, please come in." My voice is cracked. "It'll only
take me a few minutes to get ready."

Prem tiptoes in, holding his body tight. Clearly he doesn't
want to invade my private space, and I am both appreciative and
impressed by his sensitivity. I lean against a chair and draw a
deep breath.

"Are you okay, Sharmila? You look upset, and your hands are
trembling."

"I just got off the phone—it was Raj."

"He's still pressing you to go through with the marriage?"
Prem says, half joking, half serious. "He has found out about us,
you know." He shakes his head, then lowers it in a vain attempt
to conceal his anguished expression from me. "He called me vile

names. It still hurts. That's why I didn't come to see you last night, Sharmila."

"He opened up to me quite a bit just now." I take Prem's hands in an attempt to reassure him. "I finally managed to get the truth about Roopa."

As I recount the conversation to Prem, expressions of horror and disgust contort his face. "Raj never told me. And I thought we had no secrets between us. Knowing the truth helps. I've always had a little pain in my heart about Roopa. Now I can let go."

We sit on the edge of the bed and gaze at each other. I find the lustrous glow in Prem's eyes quite appealing. The morning sunlight stealing through the window showers us in a soft yellow light, adding to the already intimate feeling in the air.

Prem strokes my face with a light touch. "I told my mother— actually, my whole family—about us last night. Everyone likes you very much, you know."

I nod. Prem withdraws his hand.

"True to form, the first thing my mother said was, When are you getting married?" Prem looks at me questioningly

I stammer, "You mean—we're—"

"Yes, Sharmila." Then as if sensing my hesitation, he hurries on, "I know things are moving very fast. We Indians are generally a patient lot. But there's a Sanskrit saying, *shubhosyo shighram.* If it's good and auspicious, don't delay it." He sucks in a deep breath to calm himself. "I don't have the right words—but . . ."

Sitting here in a bathrobe, wet tendrils of hair clinging to my shoulders, tears running down my face, yet somehow sensing all this is right, I cry out, "Yes, Prem, I will . . ."

He enfolds me in a tender embrace, saying, "Sharmila, darling." Lips merging, closed eyes shutting out distractions, we kiss. Passion mingles with gentleness and caring. As I open my eyes, I see the sun-drenched bed, and we ease ourselves down onto it. My body softens at his touch, my voice becomes a song inside, and together our flesh creates its own heaven. Then comes a moment when my whole life seems to become one joyful, concentrated point. If there's another knock at the door, I don't hear it.

Much later, we lie contentedly side by side, body heat our only blanket. As his fingers stroke my hair idly, Prem inquires, "What kind of a wedding would you like?"

"No caterers, no guest list, no marriage limousine." With a laugh I add, "A simple ceremony will do. Just our families attending."

"My mother said we can have a small traditional wedding in the style back home in our village. She'll hang a garland of colorful paper triangles between the trees in the courtyard. On the day of the wedding, she'll draw designs on the ground—of flowers, stars, and heaven—with white rice flour. She told me that sparrows twittering on the branches above her head will offer their advice. Later, in the afternoon, the neighborhood women will come and join her in singing. The place will be so filled with melodies that the wind will die down in respect. I'll be waiting for you. You'll walk in, gorgeous in a transparent red *banarasi* sari with the *pallu* and border woven in gold. Your bare feet will be outlined in red *aalta*. Little girls dressed in red will start dancing in your honor." Prem pauses, studying my face, as if embarrassed by the rush of his imagination. "Here I'm telling you all this when I should be asking you what you want."

The vivid scene has so overwhelmed me that I can only agree. "I want exactly that, just what you described." Truly, I couldn't imagine a more beautiful wedding.

Lying side by side, our eyes caressing each other, we talk softly, full of anticipation about our future. No details, plans, or decisions. Right now we're content just to share this interlude. There's a calmness, a feeling of being rooted, I never experienced when I was with Raj.

An hour later, we take the elevator up to Dad's floor. A happy, goofy smile is spread across my face. Dad opens the door.

"Come in, Sharmila."

His voice is clouded, his posture stooped, and deep lines are creasing his usually smooth forehead. All these are no doubt the aftereffects of my breakup with Raj. Two bottles of Fanta stand untouched on the side table.

Prem steps forward and offers his hand. There must be something about his easygoing demeanor, because Dad extends his immediately. "And you must be Prem." After a firm handshake he motions for us to have a seat. "I've heard so much about you, Prem. Once Sharmila started talking about you, she couldn't stop." Then perhaps to put him at ease he says, "I hear you're a historian."

Prem settles more comfortably into the sofa. "History interests you, too?"

"Oh, yes. Even though I went to dental school, I've always
read history in my spare time. Especially about Delhi. This is
where I grew up, you know. There's something in the air I feel
even more after being away so long. It's laden with the weight
of the past."

"History and mystery, as we say," Prem replies.

I'd expected the conversation to gravitate to more personal
matters, but instead my two men start sharing insights about
past rulers and invaders. I guess this is their way of getting acquainted with each other. Before long they've launched into a
discussion about the influence of local weather and traffic conditions on the temperament of the Delhi-ites.

I excuse myself and return to my room to call Mistoo at her office.

"Tea tomorrow?" Mistoo says. "Sure."

She doesn't even mention the wedding. Whether she's angry
with me or not it's hard to tell. She has gone through a lot of
trouble to arrange a lavish wedding with a guest list of hundreds. Typical Indian politeness, I gather, a desire not to offend.
With a "cheerio" she hangs up.

Sitting at the writing table, I try to gather my impressions of
this singular day. Then, inspired by the bed Prem and I shared so
pleasantly, a new window, and a fresh view, I retrieve my sketchpad. I do a pencil-pen study of the bed, flooded by an incoming
stream of light. With a flourish I sign in the margin:

Oh, the joy of soaring high

I pick up the phone and call Mohan. At the sound of my voice
he cheers up. We chat for a while about his new job as a cook at
the Ambassador Hotel, about discos he's visited recently, and finally about my leaving the Khosla house.

Mohan says, "I was just as sorry when you left as when
Roopa-bahuji died."

"I've found out what happened to her."

There's a pause. "I couldn't tell you this earlier, Sharmila-
memsahib. It was I who found Roopa-bahuji's body."

"Where?"

A thick, black silence now. I picture Mohan swallowing, trying his best to control his anguish. "I found her in that room," he says.

"What room?"

"The one you had, memsahib."

"Oh?"

"They used it as a guest room at the time. It was late afternoon, and I'd just come back from the market. I noticed the door was shut and for some reason I went inside. Later, I came to realize it was because Roopa-bahuji's spirit was calling me. I found her hanging by a pink silk scarf from the ceiling fan. There was a chair tipped on its side beneath her. Though I was shaking, I got a knife from the kitchen, cut the scarf, and lowered her to the floor. When I was certain that she was dead, I was so horrified that I screamed and ran out of the house to look for help. As I went down the stairs, I slipped and fell. Just as I was trying to pick myself up, Mrs. Khosla came in through the gate. I still remember her words: 'Oh, you clumsy oaf.' She laughed. 'Did you slip on a banana peel, Mohan?'

"All I could do was cry out. 'Oh, please, madam, Roopa bahuji is dead.' We called the police. Neelu came home as we hung up. She broke down crying. 'My sister, my dear sister . . .' Mrs. Khosla comforted her. Just as they were taking the body away, Raj sahib came up the staircase with flowers. He went mad. 'Roopa darling . . .' he screamed. I had to hold him. Mrs. Khosla is the only one who didn't cry. She shut the guest room. It stayed empty for two years. Nobody would ever go in there." A pause. "I once asked Mrs. Khosla to do a *puju* there to get Roopa-bahuji's ghost to leave. But she just laughed at me and said I was superstitious. So many times I wanted to tell you this story, but I knew Mrs. Khosla would find out and it would go very badly for me."

"Now I know why I had such a spooky feeling in that room. No wonder none of you would ever go there. And that black fan was so ominous. Every time I saw it, I got uneasy. How dare Mrs. Khosla put me in there. Mohan, did Roopa ever confide in you?"

"Oh, Sharmila-memsahib. The day before her death I found her crying when I brought her tea. '*Bahuji*, why are you crying?' I asked. 'You have everything.' She said, 'No, Mohan, someone has taken away my *prana*. I can't breathe anymore.' I knew then it had to do with Raj-sahib. She had given him all her heart. I decided to talk to her the next day, though it was not my place and I was new in the house. I waited until it was too late."

"Mohan, I'm glad we had this conversation. Though I am sad, the puzzle is finally solved for me."

"I have to go now, Sharmila-memsahib. Would you do the honor of sending me one of your drawings, so I will always be reminded of you." I'm touched by his request and instantly agree. He says good-bye hurriedly.

I hang up the phone in a bleak state of mind, momentarily unable to move. Then I think of Neelu and our conspiracy with Deen. That young man put me up overnight, helped me when I needed it, and I'm eternally grateful. I decide to buzz her—after all, she was a friend—ready to hang up instantly if anyone else answers.

On the first ring Neelu picks up the phone. "Oh, it's you, Sharmila."

Must be Khosla solidarity. Her terse response tells me she's maintaining a certain distance. "I just called to see how everything is going for you, Neelu."

I hear a long drawn-out yawn. How quickly I've been cut out from her heart. It seems all of the Khoslas will eliminate me from their memory of the last two months.

Neelu says, "Sorry, I was up late last night reading *Stardust*."

"It's hard for me, Neelu, to think I won't be seeing much of you from now on. I truly enjoyed our time together."

Neelu thaws a little. "That's nice."

"I really like Deen. You're right, he does give a great facial. And I think he may have a way of changing your mother's mind about the two of you."

"Ma is going through a lot. But thank you, Sharmila. It might all work out over time."

Will it? I wonder if Mrs. Khosla will continue to hate Kaveri and therefore never accept Deen completely. And Mrs. Khosla will exert control over Neelu invisibly. The girl will suffer. The only hopeful aspect of the situation is Neelu's career. I ask, "So you'll be a makeup artist, after all?"

"Yes. I'm going into both makeup and fashion design. Ma has even given me your room for extra space. I'm going to have it repainted and redecorated first."

So every trace of me will be erased from the Khosla house.

Though the room is blurred in my mind, I'll carry a fond image of the desk, the window, and the birds outside.

Last I tell Neelu, "Just make sure those gray hornbills don't go away."

We finish our conversation with a short farewell. As I hang up, I suffer a twinge of melancholy. Then slowly, with great effort, I get up and return to Dad's room.

"You've given me a much better picture of what's going on in Delhi, Prem," I hear Dad saying. "Even my friend Khanna doesn't keep up with politics or social issues as much as you do. Money, money, money is his mantra."

The two Fanta bottles by Dad's side are now empty, a sure indication of his improved state of mind. Seeing me return, Prem drinks the last of his orangeade, rises, and prepares to take his leave. He says in parting, "Don't forget, sir, the boat tour is at ten on Sunday."

"I'll be there," Dad replies brightly. "Sharmila's mother will have arrived by then. She likes to sleep late on Sundays, so she probably won't join us. Sharmila, maybe you could take her out shopping."

Prem and I walk down the hallway to the elevator, so close we're touching, flashing each other a loving glance from time to time. Leaning toward me, Prem says, "I wish I could spend the rest of the day with you, Sharmila."

The thought of impending separation is painful. But remembering my mother's imminent arrival, I reply, "You've already made this a wonderful day, Prem. And you've won Dad over. Now there's only my mother to worry about."

"I really like your father, Sharmila."

His words delight me. Waiting for the elevator, we clasp each other's hands for a brief second. The same sweeper has now transferred himself to this floor and is busily scrubbing this section of the hallway. He stares at us. Has he no sense of propriety?

Prem half turns to avoid the man's impudent stare. Just then the elevator doors squeak open. Prem lingers and squeezes my hand tightly for a moment, gives me a brief kiss—with the sweeper still staring up at us—then steps into the cage of the elevator. The door closes. I carry Prem's last warm look within me as I mentally fortify myself for my mother's arrival tomorrow.

THE entire day has been overcast and dreary, and peering out the window, I watch even grayer shadows of evening blanket the earth. Dad picked Mom up from the airport and brought her to the hotel just a few minutes earlier. The three of us are now sitting in Dad's suite in absolute silence, something I'd not have previously believed possible with Mom in the room. The atmosphere is tense. Sensing that she is about to erupt, I don't so much as tap my foot on the floor.

Mom huffs, "No wedding?" She turns to Dad. "A new boyfriend I haven't even heard of? Why haven't I been told?"

I'm about to comment when Mom bursts out, "What if we get rid of the maid?"

"Mom, it's not that simple. The maid's just one in a long line. When Raj gets tired of her, he'll find someone else. He lacks character. Women are nothing but a sport for him."

"She's right, Aruna," Dad interjects calmly. "After hearing of Sharmila's experiences and talking with Mrs. Khosla in person several times, my opinion of the Khosla family has changed. When I confronted Mrs. Khosla about her son's dalliance with the maid, she said, 'Men are like that. And Raj will be Raj, after all.' I couldn't get through to her that all men aren't like that. Besides, Sharmila was raised in the States, where this behavior is less tolerated. I just don't think it'd be right for our daughter to marry into a family like the Khoslas."

I watch Mom for her reaction. Her hair is freshly combed, and her sari of fine calico print shows only a few creases even after her long journey from Chicago. But the red dot on her forehead, a cherry-like imprint, is smudged. That never happens unless she's sick or terribly upset. It has to be the latter in this case. She left Chicago the same day I walked out of the Khoslas' but the poor thing has been traveling for nearly four days due to a lay-over in Tokyo. She only got the news about Raj and me from Dad on the long ride in from the airport. Her reaction can be put down to a combination of travel weariness and an anger at a cherished plan gone awry—she always did like predictability—with a severe caste complex thrown in for good measure.

"For all of Mrs. Khosla's gentility on the phone," Dad says, keeping his voice in control, "in person she struck me as ruthless and conniving. She wouldn't be above going through with the marriage just to preserve the family's name, without any regard for Sharmila's welfare."

I nod slightly. Inside I'm filled with admiration for Dad's stance. Mom wipes her eyes, pressing with the tissue as if it's a kitchen sponge, the way I do. I find a strange comfort in our sharing of small gestures.

"Our mistake was not getting to know the family better first," Dad says. "After all, the family's the thing in an arranged marriage. Maybe we shouldn't have relied on Mistoo and other relatives so much. I should have come over first and followed up. They're looking at this from their perspective, not Sharmila's. Raj is a good catch to them." Dad gazes at the small table lamp and the white light around it. With a brighter face he goes on, "From what you told me, Sharmila, Prem has a warm, close-knit family. And though he may be a Dalit, he's well educated and cool-headed. He'll balance your tendency to jump into things."

"Dalit?" Mom grumbles. "What does that mean? We used to call them Harijans."

"Dalit means downtrodden, and indeed that has been the case," Dad replies good-naturedly. "Yet Prem has a fine education! Aruna, he graduated with honors from Delhi University. All on scholarship to boot. He knows more, thinks more about important topics, than I do. And obviously he's a person of the highest integrity. He kept his feelings for Sharmila a secret out of friendship for Raj."

Mom's shoulders sag under the weight of Dad's arguments. Finally, in a petulant voice she says, "But how am I going to explain the canceled wedding to my friends in Chicago?"

"Just tell them the horoscopes didn't match," Dad says glibly. I always knew he possessed a streak of brilliance.

"Do you know why I like Prem, Sharmila?" Dad's warming to his subject. "I see a bit of myself in him. The me before I left India. In the last few days I've tried to go back to those days and be who I was, but I can't. I've let money, the getting of it, crowd out all other interests. A part of me whispers that in spite of all my success, I've paid a heavy price. I've lost some valuable qualities forever. But Prem still has them." He pauses. "It pains me to admit that things have turned out this way—"

"What has come over you?" Mom pipes up. "You hardly speak back home. Only 'Yes, yes, whatever you say, dear.' Now suddenly you're a professor of philosophy."

"You've surpassed me, Sharmila." Dad carries on as if Mom hadn't said a word. "When I asked you to go to premed school, you argued about staying with your art program. At the time I thought you were ungrateful, not to mention impertinent. But not only did you do well, you cultivated interests outside your profession. You've obviously figured out there's more to life than professional success, that there are more important things than a fat wallet."

From Mom's scowl I can tell she doesn't understand much of our conversation and what she does, she doesn't like. But I'm both surprised and impressed by Dad's candor and gaze at him with newfound admiration.

"If I had it all to do over again, Sharmila, I wouldn't be a dentist. I've become as predictable as a metronome and as dull, I fear. But you, you have had the courage to seek a new life in a strange country. And to reject the conventions when they conflicted with your principles. You've run into difficulties because of your decisions. And yet you've had the presence of mind to recognize the right man when he came along. I saw this morning how happy you are when you're with Prem. I wouldn't trade that for any amount of prestige or security."

Mom's face is mottled with anger. A black vein on her temple pulses rapidly. I realize she feels she has lost control over her husband. She asks Dad, "Have you taken up writing novels now, Kishore?"

"I wish I had a few pages in me at that." Dad sighs. "But all I have to look forward to are some new sets of teeth."

Abruptly Mom stands up and heads for the bedroom, mumbling something about a long, hot shower. Her march is that of a warrior in retreat, but her erect posture indicates her pride is intact.

"Maybe I'll survive life with the two of you, Sharmila." Dad massages his forehead as he stares out the window into the gloom. "Maybe I'll recapture what it means to be young and full of optimism."

He rises and wanders out to the balcony while I sit and ponder my parents' situation. Dad has his career and he seems to be more or less at peace with himself, but Mom hasn't been so fortunate. She went to the States because of Dad and never established a new base of emotional support to replace the one she left behind. Her home and her family have always been *the* domain where she exercises control, and now that fragile edifice has crumbled around her. Let it be, Mom, I'd like to tell her. Quit trying to control everything. Even as I do so, I realize she loves me deeply and that, no matter how much I disappoint her, her resentment will one day be submerged in a limitless reservoir of love.

When I met my cousin Mistoo in United Coffee House several weeks ago, I was taken by the luxury and quiet efficiency of this quaint establishment. This afternoon the restaurant seems crowded beyond its capacity. The ceiling fan barely moves the unseasonably hot New Delhi air, and I have to signal the waiter three times before he finally fetches me a bottle of water.

Late as usual, Mistoo sails in. Her smile is tight-lipped as she greets me with a perfunctory "How're you, Sharmila?" Then without waiting for an answer she says, "So your mother arrived yesterday, I heard."

The coolness, I'm sure, stems from the elaborate preparations she undertook for an aborted wedding. "I want to apologize, Mistoo, for all the inconvenience and embarrassment I've caused you."

"Not at all." A tone like that of polished glass. Then more

sharpness creeps in. "To be honest, our relatives *are* concerned. This has never happened before in our family—a wedding canceled at the last minute, one with such a prominent family."

"Better than a divorce later, wouldn't you say?"

"My divorced cousin would probably agree with you, Sharmila. We went to the cinema the other day. Sri Devi and Rajesh Kumar got married. So lovey-dovey, so very romantic in film, not at all like real life." She pauses. "I think my cousin was laughing and crying at the same time. Maybe only Roopa had a marriage like that."

I press my lips together to erase a painful image. "Roopa committed suicide."

"*Kee balchish?*" Bengali for "What?" Shoulders rounded, hands clasped tightly on the table, Mistoo hunches forward, in apparent shock. Just then the harried waiter arrives, bearing masala tea and fish pakoras, which he plunks down with a thud. She doesn't even look up. Then moments later, she exhales, uttering "*O ma,*" a Bengali expression of futility, followed by, "The Khoslas have hidden it well—but I should have known."

She picks up a pakora with her fingers and examines it without nibbling on it. "Raj is discreet, but Roopa must have found out about his other women. Poor Roopa. She loved Raj so much. She must have been devastated, though she kept it to herself. It wasn't her nature to make a big scene."

"Mistoo." I take a deep breath. I have to know. "How about you? Were you one of Raj's women?"

Mistoo sets down the pakora on the plate and rubs her greasy fingers together. "Why do you ask?" Her voice is like a hammer hitting a porcelain saucer.

I look down at my cup and stir it idly, finally saying, "I guessed as much when I saw how you two reacted to each other in my aerobics class. But mind you, I'm out of the Khosla house now, and it no longer matters to me who Raj sleeps with."

Mistoo looks away unwilling to meet my eye. "As I remember, on that day Raj didn't seem too happy to see me."

"Tell me, Mistoo, did you keep meeting him at the Maurya Sheraton even after he and Roopa were married?"

Lips parting in astonishment, Mistoo pulls away from the table. "Did he tell you?"

So it's true. Struggling to control my contempt, I continue. "And did you two keep seeing each other even after I got here?"

The *jhumkas* on Mistoo's ears sway back and forth as she shakes her head vigorously, as if to emphasize her reply, "No, he didn't call even once after you arrived." With pouty lips she adds, "He still hasn't called."

"But you saw him while he was still married to Roopa?" No longer trying to conceal my disgust, I ask, "How could you do that and still call yourself Roopa's friend? Can you tell me?"

"I don't understand you, Sharmila. Why are you so bothered about Roopa? You never even met her."

"Because it could have been me. It would have been me, had I not called the whole thing off."

"But you did." There's much anger in Mistoo's voice. "Come down from your high horse, Sharmila. This is the new way: Grab what you can for yourself, and if you have to step on someone's foot in the process, well, that's life. Your famous Me generation values have finally arrived in India, even if it is twenty-five years late." She catches a breath. "My chances of getting married are slimmer than having a dry monsoon season. So, if I spend time with an attractive married man from time to time, what's wrong with that?"

"Do you ever think for a minute how your actions affect other people, especially your friends? Do you, Mistoo? Funny, when I first got here, I thought we'd be friends. But now that I know you, I don't want to have anything to do with you." I get up, pull out some rupees from my purse, fling them on the table contemptuously, and head for the exit.

Outside, in the early darkness of a January afternoon, I take several deep breaths to calm my stomach. The fetid odor of rotten vegetables coming from an alley in the back puts my insides in even greater revolt. Did I really need to hurt Mistoo that badly? What has gotten into me? I walk unsteadily down the block and cross the street even though I don't need to. I'm just beginning to get hold of myself when I hear, "Taxi?"

A teenager is standing on the curb by a parked taxi with a cream-colored top. His T-shirt, proclaiming, JE T'AIME, is obviously a tourist hand-me-down. His smart-alecky expression repels me. I wave no and quicken my pace.

"You're better off in a taxi, madam," he calls from close behind—just a couple of feet behind. "Tourists don't know how to walk our busy streets."

Tourist? After how hard I've tried to assimilate here? I should be made an honorary citizen. "*Nikalo.*" I tell him to bug off in firm, clear Hindi. The boy jerks to a halt, turns on his heel, and stalks off without another word.

At my hotel, I make a beeline for the elevator, past the bellboy and two clerks behind the registration desk, who stare at me curiously. I need some privacy to restore my composure.

Back in my room, I'm about to collapse into a chair when I hear a hesitant knock at the door. Who's there? The bellboy with another freebie? I must tell him not to bother me the rest of the evening. Cautiously I open the door.

It's Prem. Head bowed, his usually gentle face wooden, he's staring blankly at the floor.

"Oh, Prem, come in." I beckon him eagerly inside and pull out a chair for him, but he remains standing. I notice the stiffness in his posture. The creases in the corners of his eyes are deeper than usual. I've never seen Prem this disconsolate. An extra current of affection surges through me, and I have to fight to keep from taking him in my arms. Then my mind begins to function. "You took Mom and Dad out this morning?"

"Yes."

It's clear the tour has been a disaster. How to make amends? I wonder. "Like a cup of tea, or a soda?

"No, thank you, Sharmila."

I search his face. "Was it Mom?"

"Yes. She doesn't approve of our marriage plans. It may be necessary to wait."

I gaze into Prem's eyes, dim stars bereft of their usual shine. "Where was Dad? How could she talk to you like that?"

"We had a private conversation when your father left us to buy some souvenirs. She told me I was a nice man and a good guide, but she didn't want her Sharmila to marry a Dalit."

"What did she say to make you change your mind?"

Prem's face shivers in pain. "She offered me fifty thousand dollars. The money she's saved for your wedding. She asked me—no, begged me—to take the money. Not to say a word to you, just disappear for good."

"That's crazy."

I look at the man I love, a man in distress. Damn my mother, her money, and her ideas about what's good for me. I reach out to console Prem, to embrace him, to bring him so close that our differences would disappear. His arms remain glued to his sides.

"I refused, of course."

His face reddens in what must be the memory of the insult. "Prem, my mother's still in a state of shock over my breakup with Raj. She's pinned a lot of hope on that marriage. You must understand she's traditional and still has those old ideas about caste. Look, we'll get married as we planned. Let her accept both of us or lose me entirely."

"No, Sharmila, we can't. Your mother must bless our marriage."

I gaze imploringly into his eyes. "That might never happen."

Prem won't return my look. He presses his lips together, as though determined not to let any more words of gloom escape. I conclude he's reacting the same way he would to his mother's negative response about an issue. The values and traditions that he's been taught run deeper than I'd ever imagined. Under other circumstances, I might have admired him for his integrity, but our happiness, the dearest thing in the world to me, is at risk. "You mean you'll sacrifice our life together for the sake of some arbitrary cultural standard that puts a mother over everything?"

"That's who I am, Sharmila. I know you're extremely upset. Perhaps you think I'm leaving you. No, my love, I'm not."

"If your mother and I clash on some issues—if she wants me to wear a sari all the time and I don't, for example—tell me, Prem, who would you rather make unhappy? Whose side would you take?"

Prem grimaces. Clearly, his honest nature won't let him lie or dissimulate.

"Then it's not going to work, Prem. These differences would not allow us to be together for very long."

The note of dead finality in my voice reverberates off the walls. Prem stiffens as though he's been slapped. He turns and gropes blindly for the doorknob. Finally locating it, he jerks the door open and walks out. I glimpse his glistening wavy hair, the well-chiseled profile, the curve of the strong shoulders under the shirt collar. At that moment I realize with terrible certainty that I've lost. For all I've just said, for all rational arguments, for all the talk about principles, I love the man. I'm willing to suffer, sacrifice, and reinvent myself simply to be by his side.

Too late I reach out with an arm to stop him, but my knees lock and my voice is a mute scream. And then he's gone. The only trace of his presence is a lingering hint of his body aroma. All too soon that vanishes as well, leaving me so alone and distraught that I want to bang my head against the wall.

It's seven in the morning when I knock at Dad's door. He opens the door to his suite. "Sharmila, come in. I wasn't expecting you so early."

I stand in the hall, too upset for small talk. "Is Mom up?"

"She left for Jaipore in a hurry this morning. Her uncle had a massive heart attack. She was going to buzz both you and Mrs. Khosla before she left, but she wasn't sure if you'd be up."

I've spent a sleepless night, prowling around my room, working out what I was going to say to Mom. And now Dad tells me she's gone? I step inside and lean against a wall.

A bottle of Fanta, two glasses, and a newspaper with a WAR ON CORRUPTION headline are set on the side table. Soft vocal music is playing on the radio. It sounds like a woman's playful nagging. Dad's obviously been relaxing. His face reflects a serenity that I can only envy. "I need to talk to her badly. Is there a phone number where I could reach her?"

The beginnings of a frown knit Dad's eyebrows together. He returns to his seat. Then with a look of fatherly concern he asks, "What's the matter, *beti*? Are you coming down with a cold?"

Taking a deep breath, I plop down onto a couch opposite him. "I didn't sleep at all last night. I'm not feeling very well, but it's not a cold. . . . Prem has left me."

"What?" Dad hiccups the word as he leans toward me, shock tattooed on his face. "Tell me what happened."

"It has to do with mothers—both mine and his," I begin. Dad listens in silence, his eyes never leaving my face.

"My mistake," he says sadly. "I was supposed to have spent the day alone with Prem, but your mom insisted on joining us. I suspect her offer has to do with Mrs. Khosla."

"You've mentioned her twice now. What does she have to do with it?"

"She's worried sick about her son. Raj can't live with himself.

Mrs. Khosla will do anything to get you back. I found out only yesterday that she's secretly been in touch with your mother almost from the minute she arrived. Your mom knew in minute detail all that had happened. They've apparently joined forces to try to change your mind."

I sag backward on the couch. Dad pours from a Fanta bottle with steady hands, the burbling fizzy noise of the orange liquid being the only noise in the room. He offers me the glass. I straighten up a little and refuse with a shake of my head.

Dad shrugs and takes a sip. "The two women have somewhat the same position." A long sigh. "It seems your mom is having a bout of 'Raj fever' herself. Raj can do no wrong."

"Fortunately, a fever doesn't last forever, Dad. So Mom's not only objecting to Prem's being a Dalit, but even if he wasn't, she'd object to his not having money and flash like Raj has. Right?"

"Right!" Dad's enthusiastic agreement puzzles me. His eyes light up with sudden inspiration. "Listen, *beti*, I've lived with your mother for almost thirty-five years. Though we disagree on some issues, for the most part we've a good marriage. It's my fault that I've let her make all the family decisions in the past. It just seemed easier than endless arguments, and most of the time things worked out acceptably. But this is different—your happiness is too important to be left in her hands. It's time for me to get involved. I know just how to influence her in this particular case."

I experience a feeling of elation at having an ally. However, I'm not going to leave it all to Dad, either. I'll visit Mrs. Khosla one last time on my own, and that soon.

"Sharmila," Dad is saying, "do try to be patient, just this once. I know you want things to change instantly, but this time that won't happen. Your mother will come around—eventually. And my friend Khanna is dying to help for reasons of his own. You see, he's wanted to marry off his daughter to Raj for a long time, and now he senses a golden opportunity. He plans to have a proposal for Mrs. Khosla soon." Another poor woman, I sigh when I think of her fate. Dad gives me a searching look. "As for Prem, no doubt he's suffering badly. He's like me in that respect. I'll give him a couple of days, then call him. We have much to talk about."

I'm not ready to believe any of this will work, but what more do I have to lose? Appreciative of Dad's effort, I spring up from the couch and give him a big hug. "I'm so glad you're my daddy."

Calling him Daddy takes me back many years, to when I was a little girl, and I feel warm and secure. My expression of love must have touched him. His eyes seem misty. I pull back and point at the Fanta bottle with a jovial flick of the wrist. "By the way, what's a dentist doing drinking this stuff, Daddy?"

"Only for three more weeks, with your permission, of course, Sharmila. Then it's back to Chicago and my usual routine. But I must say, Fanta and all, this trip has done me a world of good. I just have to get back here more often. By the way," Dad adds as I reach the door, "Khanna says he'll help you find a flat. He also mentioned that one of his business associates is looking for a graphic artist to do advertising work. The pay is supposed to be good."

An apartment? A job in an advertising department? I should be overjoyed, but without Prem I can't see myself making any kind of life in Delhi.

I UNLOCK the door to the Khosla apartment and walk down the hallway, hearing the rattle of pots and pans ahead in the kitchen. A thick, spicy smell assaults my nostrils, and I find Mrs. Khosla stirring a *karai* on the stove, her fingertips stained yellow with turmeric. She looks up, adjusts her sari on her shoulder. "Sharmila! I was hoping you'd visit me."

The voice is as commanding as on the day of my arrival two months ago. How intimidated I was then, how unsure of myself. Today I'm here to extract a confession from her regarding Roopa's death, to make her realize that my breakup with Raj is truly final. I dispense with the usual pleasantries that normally precede any serious discussion in India. Looking her straight in the eye, I state flatly, "I want to discuss a few things with you, Mrs. Khosla."

She wipes her fingers on a towel and lowers the heat on the stove. Acting as though I had dropped by for a friendly visit, she says cheerily, "Let's go to the balcony." She glances at the stove. "I was just making mutton korma. Now that Mohan's taken another job and the maid's on holiday, I'm the one who has to cook. But I don't mind. Actually, I quite enjoy it. Will you stay for dinner, Sharmila?"

Without waiting for an answer, Mrs. Khosla waves me toward

the hallway. I follow her—acting the obedient daughter-in-law as a way of being polite.

As I pass through the lavish living room, my eyes are drawn to a newly blank south wall. The painting of the Mughal princess is missing, gone along with my one-time dream of being a part of this household, Raj's very own Mughal princess. How utterly ludicrous the idea of an arranged marriage now seems.

I pull up a cane chair and notice by the tracks it leaves that the balcony floor is dusty. Mrs. Khosla seats herself across from me, picks up an envelope, retrieves some photos from inside, and holds them up one by one for me to see. "Your father's friend Khanna has sent these pictures of his daughter. Pretty, isn't she?" Her bracelets tinkling, she slides the photos back into the envelope and places it neatly on the table so that its edge is parallel to that of the table. "But I told Khanna I wouldn't even show them to Raj. My children can arrange their own marriages."

"Neelu must be delighted. Where is she?"

"She and Deen are doing the makeup for a fashion show in Mumbai. She was terribly excited when I gave her permission to go. Of course, she can't get married for another two years."

"That's very . . . progressive of you, Mrs. Khosla."

"The times are changing," Mrs. Khosla says, wearing a look of self-satisfaction. "Your father has helped me understand that. You see, Sharmila, as a parent I felt it was my responsibility to make all the major decisions concerning my children's lives. And I truly did the best I could."

"But I'm not your child."

"True, but you are your mother's child. She'd have talked to you, except she had to catch an early morning train to go to Jaipore. You see, Raj is moving to Mumbai. He decided he'll work from that office temporarily. I'll miss him so. Of course, he will call me every day. He wants to get away from here for a while, and he also feels that would give you a chance to think about what you want in life."

The mention of Raj's name activates the build-up of frustration and anger inside me. Leaning forward, I say, "I know what I want. And I'll get it in spite of your and my mother's interference."

"Your mother was shocked when she heard you've taken up with Prem. She came to me for advice."

"And what did you tell her?"

"That I like Prem. He has been like a son to me. He is Raj's equal, except when it comes to jobs and social status."

"And character."

"Don't you ever bad-mouth my Raj."

"Never mind your scoundrel son." I startle myself by being so brash. "You thought you could buy Prem off with money, didn't you?"

"He was foolish not to take the money." There's an edge of contempt in Mrs. Khosla's voice. "Can you imagine what fifty thousand dollars would have done for his family?"

"You who only worship money and status will never be able to understand a man like Prem. But I didn't come here to talk about him. I came here to settle another issue: the reason behind Roopa's death. I hold both you and Raj indirectly responsible."

"How can you say that? It's insane. Roopa committed suicide. I was very sorry when it happened. I liked her."

"You liked her until your son fell in love with her, and you were terribly displeased when he married her. Because you had great hopes that his wife would bring a huge dowry, money you were going to use to pay off your husband's debts and to marry Neelu to a rich family. Your plans fell through because Roopa was poor and didn't bring any dowry with her. So you resented your new daughter-in-law. You were cold to her."

"That girl was weak. Not like you—you have the temperament of a hot chili."

"Poor Roopa knew you hated her. You made her feel she wasn't good enough to be Raj's wife. She was miserable in this household. When Raj finally realized that, he made plans to buy a bungalow for the two of them. They'd have moved in a matter of months. But oh, no, you couldn't have that, could you?"

"Nonsense, nonsense."

"You knew what was going on between Raj and Champa, but you didn't try to stop it. You even supported it silently."

"No!"

"Of course you did. How else could a maid afford to wear expensive saris?" The downward pull on Mrs. Khosla's face tells me I hit the mark. I begin with new vigor. "Roopa came home one day and caught Raj and Champa in the act. She was devastated and lost her will to live. That's why she hung herself from the ceiling fan. And I'm sure it came as no surprise to you, knowing how sensitive she was. Why didn't you just have a kitchen fire? Oh, yes, Mrs. Khosla, the blame rests squarely on your shoulders. You did it to her, and you tried to do it to me."

Her pupils bulging in horror, Mrs. Khosla stands up. She throws the scarf end of her sari in the air like it's a whip. She fixes me with an angry, hateful glance. "Who are you to say all this? I came from an honorable family, the Soods of Delhi. All my married life I worked and sacrificed, for my husband, for my children, for our family name. And what did I get in return? Twenty-six years of living with a liar and a cheat. An ungrateful daughter who defies me at every turn. And when she sneaks around, who does she choose but the son of my husband's mistress? Only Raj appreciates the sacrifice I've made. He was too good for Roopa, and he was too good for you!"

"No, he wasn't too good for either of us. That's not the real reason and you know it. The real reason is—perhaps you don't even realize it yourself—you just can't stand to see any other woman happily in love after what had happened to you. So you destroyed Roopa and you tried to destroy me. Who's next? Poor Neelu? Rest assured, Deen will not allow that to happen. And know this. Even your precious Raj will not be spared. For a long time now he has craved a lasting relationship more than anything else in life, but thanks to you, he couldn't have one. So his life has been a series of empty affairs. It'll break him eventually. And," I say this with sadness, "when he finds out, you'll be left alone with your hatred."

Totally spent, I lapse into silence. Still trembling, I turn to peer down at the oddly quiet scene in the sunny garden below. The gardener is sprinkling the bushes with a water bucket as usual, to the melodic accompaniment of a golden oriole perched on a tree branch above. Droplets of water on the winter-dull leaves catch sunlight and shine momentarily like golden beads.

I turn to Mrs. Khosla. Standing stooped, hands gripping the back of a chair, she rambles on, something to do with the corrupting influence of television on the younger generation. I see a woman old beyond her years, no longer the formidable demigoddess. In defeat she seems to have shriveled. The glare of truth falling on her illuminates her haggard features. Once she commanded my respect, even fear, but now I feel contempt and pity. This crumbling image of her is what I'll carry from now on.

A mellow calm settles over me. Doubtless the Khosla family saga will continue, but I'm no longer a part of it. Instead of being shattered, I've gained strength from this misadventure. I will always know that I'm stronger than Roopa and Mrs. Khosla.

My legs light, I get up, take the Khosla house keys from my purse, and drop them on the table. They make a discordant metallic sound. Then I walk out the door without a backward glance.

Back in my hotel room, I half expect Prem to call, but the telephone just sits there in silent mockery. After a long, agonizing wait, I give up and take out my sketchpad. With a blank page before me and a pencil gripped between wooden fingers, I wait expectantly, but no mental picture, no inspiration, no mood emerges.

Am I still alive? I take my pulse. It's a jittery seventy—an alarming fluctuation from my usual even beat in the low fifties. I'm shaken. Not only my art, but my health and sanity are in imminent danger. In a panic, I snatch my purse from the bed and rush out the door, headed for the international travel agent down the block.

IN the ten days since I've spent unwinding in my cabin in the southern Sierras, I've existed only in the present. Delhi is memory, mostly of frozen pain, some of joy. I've immersed myself in the tranquil beauty of my surroundings, and that has restored me.

This morning I park myself in a chair by the fireplace, my body wrapped in a gray Kashmiri shawl, a pair of wool slippers on my feet. I look out the window at a view of the snow-layered peaks and lose myself for a time in the grandeur. The February wind, crisp and cold, blows against the window pane, the delicate snowflakes ethereal and pure. The luminous pattern of sunlit frost on the glass appears as intricate as the weave in a piece of organza. I shove an extra log in the fireplace and luxuriate in the heat creeping up my legs, while listening to the sound of occasional foraging nutcrackers and bluejays and the sighing of the wind in the pines.

There's mail today. As I sort perfunctorily through the sleek oversized junk letters, I come across an aerogramme of soft sky blue paper. I recognize Prem's neat handwriting and return address and smile to myself, almost as though I was expecting this. Dad must have tipped him off as to where I was. Elated, I delicately open the letter along the dotted lines.

Dear Sharmila,

I can't forgive myself for leaving you so abruptly that day. It was my pride, not your mother's rejection or her offer of money, that really was the cause. Being a Dalit, I've always held on to my pride, oftentimes being in possession of little else.

And yet my behavior was foolish. For days your face has been before me constantly, and I am beside myself with grief at my stupidity. I heard your voice on the grounds of Jantar Mantar and looked for you, but you were nowhere to be found. I saw you in jeans and a red T-shirt in the Bengali Market and started after you, but you disappeared into the crowd.

I knew I'd made a terrible mistake. My love for you was so strong that it bulldozed my pride into dust. I was ready to sacrifice everything, including my precious pride, so that I could return to you and offer you my humble self.

Then I heard you were gone and knew why I couldn't find you. Still I saw you in the street, in the park, just outside my house, and in my dreams. At first I took your decision to leave as final. The days became punishingly long, and in the interminable nights it seemed as though all of Delhi's lights had been switched off. My hours were a black void. I couldn't sleep.

My wise mother saw my misery, which I thought I'd concealed from the world. She insisted your last trip to India was for Raj. That was why it was so difficult, and to complete your circle of destiny, you had to return to the States. She believes you'll be back, though only you know when, but this time you will come for my sake. My mind tells me this is a fond superstition. My heart tells me this is my only hope.

And with this hope, I live my days.

As I write this letter, I'm watching little Jay water his marigold plant. It's growing fast. He believes his Sharmila-didi will be here soon to see it bloom.

I will always love you.

Tumhara,
Prem

I clutch the aerogramme to my chest, as if to cup a sheltering hand around the nascent flames of a thousand tiny *diyas.*

Carefully folding the letter, I slide it under a paperweight on the table and stare out the window rapturously. Now that the snow is tapering off and the wind has dropped, the trees are festooned with glittering trinkets of ice. A pair of cobalt blue California jays chattering outside startle me. The moment my eyes fall on them, they launch themselves in unison from their perch outside the window and soar into a brilliant morning sky.

Ready to compose a reply to Prem, I open my sketchpad. With swift, sure strokes I draw a tree, two birds flying side by side in an immense sky, and a path below that stretches to the far horizon. Underneath I sign:

And this road we travel together
Love, Sharmila.